some stories about some guys doing the best they can in the Nowhere City

C. Bradford Eastland

iUniverse, Inc.
Bloomington

L.A. Journal
some stories about some guys doing the best they can in the Nowhere City

Copyright © 2012 by C. Bradford Eastland

All rights reserved. No part of this book may be used or reproduced by any means, graphic, electronic, or mechanical, including photocopying, recording, taping or by any information storage retrieval system without the written permission of the publisher except in the case of brief quotations embodied in critical articles and reviews.

This is a work of fiction. All of the characters, names, incidents, organizations, and dialogue in this novel are either the products of the author's imagination or are used fictitiously.

iUniverse books may be ordered through booksellers or by contacting:

iUniverse
1663 Liberty Drive
Bloomington, IN 47403
www.iuniverse.com
1-800-Authors (1-800-288-4677)

Because of the dynamic nature of the Internet, any web addresses or links contained in this book may have changed since publication and may no longer be valid. The views expressed in this work are solely those of the author and do not necessarily reflect the views of the publisher, and the publisher hereby disclaims any responsibility for them.

Any people depicted in stock imagery provided by Thinkstock are models, and such images are being used for illustrative purposes only.

Certain stock imagery © Thinkstock.

ISBN: 978-1-4759-6121-8 (sc)
ISBN: 978-1-4759-6133-1 (hc)
ISBN: 978-1-4759-6132-4 (e)

Library of Congress Control Number: 2012921347

Printed in the United States of America

iUniverse rev. date: 12/27/2012

also by C. Bradford Eastland

WHERE GODS GAMBLE,
a tale of American mythology

U.K. JOURNAL
*(The tales and travails...
of five Americans...
lost in the British Isles.)*

THE BASKETBALL EXPATRIATE

A VERY L.A. EASTER STORY

MILLENNIUM MINUS FIFTY

Boy Into Man

THE BLACK BEE	3
A HAND OF POKER	9
OH-FOR-FOUR	21
ROLAND BARNES	39
LAND OF THE FREE	75
KING CHARLES	111
STRAITS OF MESSINA	127
SEASICK	163
THE SHORT STRANGE STORY OF HAL HAPPIWELL	185
THE IMP OF BERKELEY	221
THE GOOD OLD DAYS	229
THEATER-IN-THE-ROUND	243
WELCOME TO MISS IDA PARROT'S BED & BREAKFAST	257
A YANK IN WINSDOR	293
A COMMUNITY OF HOLINESS	303

Some Misfits Misplacing Some Golden Dreams

REFLECTIONS OF A CAR WINDOW	319
CLOSE FINISH	341
THE BEGGAR DRIVES A METAL HORSE	349
THE GRUMP AND THE GROUND SQUIRREL	359
THE SOAP OPERA THEORY OF EXISTENCE	375
TWO THOUSAND FIVE	391
homeless man	405

Author's Foreword

Although I've written four novels, I've always considered myself first and foremost—in my heart of hearts—a short-story writer.

And it's not because I have a short attention span.

Nor is it because I don't consider myself any good at novel writing, or that my four novels aren't any good. Quite the contrary.

Yet it is true that even though both are children of Fiction, I do consider the novel and the short-story to be two genetically separate and decidedly dissimilar Art species, and it is equally true, as both an artist and a reader, that I do decidedly prefer the latter. Stories are more fun than novels. When I read a really good short-story, I always feel like I did when I was a little kid and I unwrapped a really cool present I didn't expect. Accordingly, the twenty-two stories comprising this collection about Los Angeles are my unexpected gifts to you.

Ever read a novel and come away feeling gypped? There are reasons. Too often in the world of literature, or should I say in the world of letters (I hesitate to employ the word "literature" all-inclusively, lest it threaten to legitimize the entirety of what passes for good writing nowadays), the novel becomes a safe haven for the undisciplined, egomaniacal hack. Hack as in pimp, cheat, grifter. Hack as in a snake-oil saleman who uses a gift of gab to peddle his pulp, preferring to pander to the petty frailties and base appetites of his audience, at great length, rather than favoring that audience with the genuine work of Art a good story writer can bring to bear upon the printed page *in a hurry*. The short-story writer (who I call a "storyist") must work quickly, efficiently, and well. He must command the attention of his audience long enough to ultimately produce that elusive "sudden shock of enlightenment" in the mind of that audience, his oft-skeptical reader, in order to justify both his qualifications for writing the story and the reader's wise decision to invest a few minutes exploring it. It's quite ironic, really. A reader usually trusts a novelist simply because it *is* a novel. He expects the novelist to take his time, and will usually forgive him if he starts slow. Whereas the same reader will often hold the writer of a much shorter work, a short-story, to a much higher standard....

....Not surprisingly, held to a lower standard, a guy might get away with churning out a novel for reasons other than a desire to actually churn out something good. Fame, money, exposure, ego, paying for bad investments or paying off crafty ex-wives, whatever. Perhaps even guilt. Therefore there are a lot of bad novels out there; and not just the pulp, romance, and genre-type novels which, by definition, are doomed to mediocrity from the moment of their conception....

....But it has been my experience that you almost never read a truly bad short-story. Why? Because writers who write stories are carpenters. Storyists care about their craft. Every word is a nail, every well-turned phrase a necessary coat of varnish, then every cerebral slope, slant, and surface is planed and sanded and buffed to a high mirror spit-shine. For a *real* writer, a good short-story is never a means to an end, it *is* the end. And it's no accident that down through the ages many of the truly great writers whose names we all know—Hemingway, Fitzgerald, Crane, Capote, Chekhov, Salinger and Joyce—cut their teeth on the short-story. Because they cared about their craft. Even if many of them did stray from the story later in life, seduced, like their readers, by the irresistible charms of the novel.

To take it one giant step further, I have always considered the short-story to be the ultimate artistic medium. You heard me right. I place the story on a higher plane than music, than film, or painting or sculpture, and yes, it is a thing I consider greater than even the novel, its own seductive—yet all-too-often disappointingly shallow—big sister. (Come to think of it I actually defend this minority opinion with a somewhat swashbuckling vigor, in one of the better stories contained herein....)

Maybe it is my high opinion of the short-story's ability to introduce and transport history, philosophy, wisdom, truth, and beauty into the mind of Man, into any mind willing and eager to absorb those wonderful things, which explains why I chose the short-story as the foundation of my life's work. And this book, for all intents and purposes, is surely the quintessential encyclopedia of my life's work. My legacy. For richer or for no doubt poorer. For better or for probably worse.

In other words, I realize that "L.A. JOURNAL" is not likely to make me rich or famous. I realize that we live in the age of Reality TV and

Facebook, that we are spoon-fed our entertainment and burped to sleep by electronic gizmos designed to make the old-fashioned and oh-so-tiring act of thinking easier. I've been fighting this fight, and losing, for decades. But I refuse to go to my grave believing there are no silent legions of thinking readers still out there, folks who still crave a good short-story before bed.

And who knows? Maybe a few of you folks out there will put aside your prejudices and skepticisms, and work your way with incredulous glee through all twenty-two stories in this volume. And maybe most of them, or at least a handful of them, or maybe even only one or two of them might stick to your ribs sufficiently enough that soon you'll be at a restaurant, or a party, or any good gathering of people and you'll say, to any and all within earshot, *"Hey, 'you hear about that book of short-stories by that Eastland guy? I just read it. He's pretty good!"*

Well, then. That wouldn't be the same as great wealth or international fame, but at least it would be something. At least it would be some semblance of compensation for all the thousands of thankless hours that went into hammering these stories out. Not to mention the countless endless hours of self-regulated solitary—ah, the sweet, satisfying agony of rewrites!—spent on poring over each successive draft of each story. And then finally the joyous, necessarily painstaking hours mortgaged in editing and meticulously cobbling this collection together. Yes, that would indeed be some measure of compensation. But would it be enough?

Yes. Oh god, yes. A kind word or two is all I was ever after. That would be payment enough.

C. Bradford Eastland

…this book is for Rob, whose mere existence makes everything else make sense.

Boy Into Man

THE BLACK BEE

Author's Notes

Not the first story I ever wrote (I think I sketched out the rough draft in the early 80s), but certainly the first chronologically in Part One of this collection, which I call "Boy Into Man", but which just as easily could be called "The Charlie Barnes Chronicles"; i.e. a series of 15 stories told, in chronological order, about a boy growing into a young man and then into a not-so-young man in Los Angeles, California, U.S.A. In *The Black Bee*, Charlie is only about three or four years old. Therefore, absent any stories about his conception or infancy (of which there are none, thank God) it is obviously story #1.

In a collection of so-called short-stories, this is truly a 'short' story. As in the shortest I have ever written. Exactly 1,647 words, 93 words shorter than *homelsss man*.

There is also a little bit of literary license at work here. The story actually takes place in Iowa, not in L.A., and I confess that the narrative itself has really nothing whatsoever to do with our beloved 'City of the Angels'. But for both perspective purposes and character development, I definitely needed it in the "L.A. JOURNAL" collection. (My convenient loophole for including an Iowa story in a book about L.A. is that at least it is mentioned, in the final paragraph, that the lad's family is moving to "a strange new land", and soon. That strange new land being, presumably, Los Angeles. More literary license.)

My mission with the Barnes stories was never for them to be either individual personal histories or collectively part of some sort of serial autobiography (they aren't and it isn't), but rather to lay down some stories about a character created from the residue of my own personal experiences and beliefs, who shares my questions and confusions, and frailties, in other words it's a serial fictionalization of my struggle to interpret this world of ours and at the same time lay down a history of the times in which I lived. So that the events of the day might be better understood. And if not better understood, at least more easily (and hopefully more entertainingly) digested.

For me, the main thing that distinguishes the average writer from the artist-writer, the *literary artiste* as it were, is that the artiste is also an Historian. Is in fact primarily an Historian. With a capital H.

Call it my personal artistic credo, for whatever it's worth.

THE BLACK BEE

A small boy (though admittedly *"corn-fed big for his age"*, per the quaint local expression) sat bellybutton deep in a pile of loud leaves and watched the wind blow between his toes.

Some of the just-flattened leaves were green, but most were red or yellow by this time, and it wouldn't be long before all the leaves had turned a brittle brown; only to be buried by the December snows. The best time of the year around these parts. Iowa. A place not exactly famous for good times or fun things to do. It was the time of year that has always afforded the people of this flat uncompromising state a brief, happy respite, a temperate truce to mediate between the sweltering humidity of summer and the prohibitive cold of winter. Yes, that was the best part of being an Iowa child, all right….along with the fireflies….which everyone called "lightning bugs". The leaves. It was the leaves. And the small boy was particularly fond of these rejected, discolored leaves. They were his friends. Soon he was happily reshaping them into a gigantic pile. He clutched the leaves gently in his soft chubby hands, crinkling an occasional brown one until it sounded like aluminum foil, and then threw them on the pile until the pile had grown above his head. Finally he was ready for his next leap. They hadn't told him yet, but it would be the last time he would ever see the leaves fall….

"Chaar*lieee*! If I catch you without your *shoes* on, it'll be all day and *half the night* with you!"

It was obvious that the woman's voice had issued forth from somewhere within the two-story white house, the square white house which she ruled, but it might just as well have rained down from the strange invisible kingdom in the sky they had recently begun to tell him about; such was the cold power and absolute authority it carried. The small boy's first impulse was one of fear, fear of that power (fear of Consequence herself?), but that fear quickly gave way to the more natural inclination to resist absolute authority absolutely. Nobody was going to tell *him* what to do, not if *he* could help it. *Nobody*! Especially if unquestioning submission to authority meant limiting the unchequered happiness he chose to afford *his own two feet*! Interestingly, there was nothing at all perilous about the rest of his November costume. His brother's baggy hand-me-down corduroys protected his legs, a matching blue coat with a white fur-lined collar hid an old flannel shirt, and a bright red stocking cap fit snugly and contentedly over most of his unruly blond curls. There was even a matching bright red scarf to keep the wind off of his plump, pink-white face. He was warm and safe, ankle to crown. But the small boy simply didn't go in for wearing shoes, even when it was frostbite-cold outside. Because when it came to his delightfully free feet a little chilly air was flat-out insignificant, was virtually unnoticeable, and therefore an unnecessary thing to fear or worry over in any way. *Nothing* was going to get in the way of the wealth of good feelings he experienced, year round, simply by going barefoot. Nothing.

The woman now stood on the porch and looked in all directions. Her son looked down at the top of her head. He had climbed the ladder, one giant step at a time, and was now crouching quietly on the porch roof. From there he could survey the entire southeastern Iowa town of Washington, which wasn't difficult, because every town in Iowa is a small town. He could see the old soybean factory to the south, and the shiny-round Methodist Church dome (which looked just like his neat new silvery-smooth fireman's hat) and the flat greenness of the baseball field (long ago christened, in a perfectly brazen display of Midwestern simplicity, "Green Field"), and all the houses of everyone in the world he now chose to consider important. The view gave him a feeling of great power. And the view also warmed his heart, and filled him top to bottom with affection for all the segments, castes, and humble representatives of Humanity dwelling within his vast visual reach....including affection even for those humans he did not actually know.

The woman called out again, but the small boy made himself keep quiet. He continued to peer straight down at the top of her head, at the blue and white checks of the bandanna hiding most of the shaggy auburn hair he knew she never had time to wash to make pretty for his dad until just before dinnertime, and he wanted to aim a drool at her head because he knew that because of the bandanna she wouldn't be too mad but he didn't because he knew it wasn't nice and because it would give him away.

Unable to find him the woman finally went back inside the square white house, back to her housework, and the wood-on-wood slam of the screen door made the small boy giggle. He had won. He had already been taught that this formless, confusing thing called "winning" was important. And of course he took great pleasure in deceiving his mother, maybe because, like all good mothers, she was always telling him what to do. But this small boy didn't like being told what to do, or wearing shoes, and so, shrouded in victory, he returned to the business at hand, which was jumping off the porch roof and into the pile of leaves. The jumps involved a drop of some seven or eight feet, but he wasn't afraid. As a matter of fact, he liked jumping into a pile of leaves better than just about anything. After all, he might have said were he older, what else is there to do in Iowa....

He jumped. The leaves reluctantly made room for the little body, voicing their protest with a gentle crunching sound. After all, Nature had decreed only that they should change color and fall, not that they should then be pulverized again and again by the hind end of this happy little boy. But the little boy didn't yet think seriously about such things. He wasn't nearly old enough for thinking seriously. For this was way *way* back when. Back when Ike was king and cares were few. And so, as he stretched out in the leaves, looking up at the puffy white clouds, his thoughts were the essence of pure, uncluttered joy. The world was his, and anything in it—including the leaves, the clouds, his house, and even his mother—was only valuable to the degree that it might supply him with pleasure.

There was a low buzzing sound. bzzzzzzzzz The little boy immediately shut his eyes. It couldn't be an airplane, he thought....or even what he once overheard his grandmother nervously refer to as a "damn spudlick spaceship"; it was too close without being loud. He already knew airplanes and spaceships were loud....and it wasn't the next-door neighbors' newfangled *lectrik* saw....finally he sat up, opened his eyes, and instantly spied an unusually large black flying bug, which just this last summer he overheard his father refer to as a "bee". The bee was playing upon a rare green leaf, buzzing even as he sat, and the little boy couldn't understand why the bee was there. Shouldn't he have left with his friends a long time ago? Well, whatever the reason for the delay the little boy was glad for it. The old people were always telling terrible tales about these large black bugs, these flying buzzers, these bees, but *he* had no reason to fear them, no reason in *his* world, and he was proud to consider this particular black bee his friend. "Hi, bee!" he chortled, and the bee responded by lighting on the little boy's left big toe. The bee was larger than the toe, and wobbled to and fro trying to keep its balance. The little boy smiled and playfully wiggled his toes.

Then it happened. The bee's hind end rose up for an instant, and in a quick blur of motion it came down, driving something sharp, like a sewing needle, deep into the soft pink flesh. Then it was gone.

Legend has it that the scream which followed actually interrupted work down at the old soybean factory, ruined the timing of a perfectly plausible double play over at Green Field, floated all the way to Ainsworth and halfway to Kalona, and some of the old-timers that still live in Washington County maintain that it was heard even as far away as Columbus Junction. So magnificent, in fact, was this scream that it is still a conversation piece at PTA meetings and YMCA bean feeds, and in between rounds of bingo at Methodist Church socials, and its origin and cause are still hotly debated among the gossip-crazy housewives of the town. It was an epic scream if ever there was one, and the boy's good mother rushed alertly to the door to see what was the matter. The smile on her face said that she instantly understood....

The boy limped bravely to the house, dragging his swollen foot behind him. Both feet were strangely cold now. The look on his face cried out "*Why?*", but even his good mother lacked the tools to construct an answer. The boy would leave Iowa soon, and grow up in a strange new land, and lost, incredibly, somewhere within the relatively crisis-free chapters of his adolescence, would be any memory of the black bee. But as he huddled in his mother's arms, fighting back the tears, he couldn't possibly have known what a difference it might have made to his adult edition if he could only have remembered. Oh, if only he could have remembered.

A HAND OF POKER

Author's Notes

Another in a bushel basket of stories produced between 1977 and 1982, when fiction was flowing out of me like blood from a hemophiliac. I had so much life, angst, thought, and theory rattling around inside of me back then, I needed a vehicle to help me get it all out, and literature was apparently that vehicle. I couldn't have stopped the flow even if I had wanted to. So I wrote several stories in rapid succession during that beginning period of my career, as any 'new' writer would. Most of them were Barnes stories. This is one of them.

One of my brothers and I played a lot of poker growing up, and we would often invite our friends over to our house in Altadena for an all-night game. It was always small stakes and big bellylaughs. My mother would often vacuum the floors during our games, even if it was two or three o'clock in the morning. She'd roll that old prehistoric vacuum cleaner into whatever room we were playing in, just to give her some sort of an excuse to be involved and thus observe whatever godlessness was going on. But she didn't really mind us gambling all that much, as long as we didn't drink anything stronger than beer. Sometimes we'd even let her sit in and play a few hands. Those are great memories….

The Rick Barnes character is actually derived from a mixture of *both* my brothers. My oldest brother Jeff was a true 'older brother' growing up, as in more of a mentor and a surrogate parent than a buddy. Being the oldest, he always seemed so serious and preoccupied. He loved baseball but never gambled. Conversely, my other brother Chris was much more fun and much less responsible. He wasn't crazy about baseball like Jeff, but he sure loved to gamble. And smoke and swear. And he was always threatening to pound on me. Put those two guys together and you get Rick Barnes.

A Hand Of Poker is pretty short and yet it contains a kitchen sink of topics and sub-topics, including (but not limited to) peer-pressure, non-conformity, American political history and allegory, National League baseball, Willie Mays, religion, sibling rivalry, honesty, and temptation.

One more thing. All writers steal, or at least they 'borrow' unashamedly. At least the good ones do. The name of the character Scrub White in this story was borrowed from a character in one of my favorite old movies, the 1939 John Ford classic "*Young Mr. Lincoln*". Until you've read the story, I think that's all I had better say on the subject.

A HAND OF POKER

"Go ahead and take it, if ya want....but I know you cheated."
"Did not."
"Sure. That's what all you cheating scum-bags say."
"What makes y'think I'd cheat you, you crudhead."
"Everybody cheats. I saw you palm that dead card, Scrub, you *know* I saw you!"
"Y'want a fuckin' refund, man? We can split up the pot right now and deal over if y'want, y'know."
"Nah, it doesn't matter. Small pot, small potatoes. Just watch yer mouth in front of the whelp. I promised the folks."
"You sure?"
"Sure. Take the pot."

{ ....*The boy pulling in the chips is Harold "Scrubby" White, a family friend. His bored accuser is Ricky Barnes, fifteen years old, in charge of the house while his parents are away for the weekend. Tall, blessed with far less acne than his fellows, and finally beginning to grow some serious muscles, Ricky is well qualified for his unofficial role as Group Leader. Leaning over his shoulder is his younger brother Charlie, six years younger to be exact, and very anxious to get in the game: "Can I play?" he now queries boldly...* }

"No."
"Oh please, Ricky, *pleeze* let me play!"
"I said no. Poker is a man's game, it's not for annoying little punks."
"*Who's* a punk!" shrieked the younger brother, all arms and legs poking out of baggy plaid shorts and one of Ricky's old white T-shirts which was still too big for him, the kind with the pen pocket stitched to the left breast only. (The younger's curly blond head was constantly bobbing and

pivoting this way and that, as if a great challenge for the scrawny frame supporting it.)

"*Yer* a punk, and if you'd like me to prove it I'll be more than happy to pound you," Ricky Barnes calmly suggested. "Remember. I'm in charge."

"Oh let'm play, Rick. Does he got any money?"

Charlie's huge head bobbed excitedly.

"Let'm *play*," Scrubby repeated with urgency. "At least we'll get his money."

"Okay, twerp, I guess you can play," Ricky decreed. "But no cryin' in yer beer once yer busted, okay?" Charlie nodded and took the seat at the kitchen table to Ricky's right, but scooted it back and over a few inches, in deference to his frail left arm, to avoid getting it pounded too badly if he ever won a hand.

"Hey Rick, isn't Lonny supposta show?"

As if in reply the kitchen door swung open with a creak and a groan and in shuffled another boy of fifteen, Lonny Atkinson. He was the tallest of them all. The spurt of growth had obviously occurred quite recently, his clothes clearly a couple of inches too small. A series of perfunctory grunts for greetings later he was sitting in the chair to Charlie's right, opposite Ricky. As Ricky counted out chips to the two new players, Charlie considered his brother's friend Lonny. He wasn't much like Ricky's other stupid friends, Charlie decided. For one thing, he wasn't much for talking. He never talked just to talk, but only when he actually had something important to say. That was something. And he carried these wire-rimmed glasses around in a glasses case, wherever he went....and he was sort of funny-looking, 'speshly for a kid, almost ugly even....and he had the blackest hair of all time. But the *mostest* thing that was different (no one had taught him yet, or rather convinced him, that mostest is not a real word) was that Lonny already had whiskers. *Whiskers*! Black whiskers too, as if to match his black hair, faded black jeans, and frayed black T-shirt. Gosh....a real beard, the boy marveled, which is to say the near-authentic suggestion of a beard.... more like a stiff shaving brush of chin stubble, with black, smudgelike streaks of sideburn decorating each thoroughly pockmarked cheek. Even Ricky didn't have face hair. It would probably be forever until he had his own beard, Charlie correctly surmised....

"Okay here we go, gents, five card draw comin' atcha, guts fer openers, got a hunch bet a bunch," Ricky rattled off in purely professional poker-speak. His right hand was a blur. Indeed, the clockwise speed and spray of his older brother's dealing style reminded Charlie of their father's new pinwheel hose sprinkler. Charlie was always impressed by the way Ricky handled himself at the poker table, all those groovy terms and bitchin' slang phrases....not to mention how easily his big teenage hands managed the deck. The boy was not yet ten, but he was smart, and he knew enough to know that Ricky was cool. And Charlie loved to gamble. Even as he sat—warm, content, and utterly aware of everything—within the soft, fraternal flame of his brother's select inner circle, he knew he loved to gamble, and that he would always love to gamble....

"Hey Rick, since we're playin' winner's choice ain't it my deal?"

"Yer not trustworthy enough to deal."

"Oh."

"Can *I* deal?"

The youngest player's request was ignored by all, and a rare breath of silence prevailed as all four players collected and sorted their cards. Charlie and Lonny glanced at each other, and Charlie smiled. But Lonny's face remained a wooden, humorless thing. It was something....*he* was something....

"Hey dudes, y'know the Dodgers are back home this weekend, my dad's gonna take me to the game on Sunday," Scrubby said suddenly, and with great animation, as he tossed a red chip—valued at five cents—into the pot. It was a friendly game, so there was no ante: "Koufax is pitchin', we'll win easy."

Lonny carefully slipped on the wire-rimmed spectacles.

"I dunno, man, I heard on the radio that Koufax probably won't pitch," Ricky revealed with genuine portent and despair. "They say his crummy elbow is acting up again."

"Ah, that's a lotta bull," Scrubby insisted. "In fact, that's pure bullshit!" he added, no doubt sensing that the utility of a more adult expression might elevate him in the eyes of his superior: "It's not a Saturday game. You know the deal with Koufax, they'd only try t'pull something like that if it was on a Saturday and it was before sundown....or after sundown, or whatever the rule is. I tell ya, Koufax *will* pitch, and that means the Dodgers'll *def'nitly* win."

"Lookit, stop sayin' shit and fuck in front of my fuckin' little *brother*," Ricky said earnestly.

Lonny took a quick look at his cards and dropped them to the table. He removed the glasses and carefully put them back in their case. Charlie, after careful consideration of all of his options, called.

"*Attention, ladies and gentlemen....Long Lon....from the planet Conservatron....folds again*!" Scrubby said, in his public address announcer's voice, then, more quietly and respectfully, "Yer bet, chief. Sorry about the swearin'."

"I like swearing," Charlie said.

"A nickel, huh? Well, I'll call just to see my cards."

"The Dodgers are your favorite team too, ain't they Rick? Or do y'like the Angels better."

"Nah. The Angels are okay, but they're not the Dodgers. The Dodgers are the greatest. Besides, the Angels are just American League."

"You like the Dodgers, right Lon?"

Lonny half-smiled and shrugged his shoulders, like a man who either hadn't quite made up his mind or had grasped the simple genius of neutrality.

"How 'bout you, kid? *Yer* a Dodger fan, yeah?"

"Nah, he likes the Giants, if you can believe that."

"The *Giants*?" Scrubby wailed. "Y'kiddin'? How can y'like the cruddy Giants and live in L.A.? God, it's like bein' a *traitor* or somethin'! One."

"Three."

Ricky dealt one card to Scrubby, three to Charlie, and gave himself two.

"C'mon, kid, how in hell can y'like the scuzzy Giants?"

"Oh, he says it's because everybody else likes the Dodgers, or some dumb thing."

Charlie hated it when Ricky answered questions for him. "I like Mays," he said crisply.

"Oh, Mays....yeah, he's all right," Scrubby somewhat grudgingly acknowledged. "Did'ja know the old nigger's hittin' over four hunnerd in September? I read it in the paper. That's up-tight and outasite, man! Best player in baseball. But there's not enough time, we got too bigga lead. Anyway, one lousy jig with a sweet stick is no good reason t'be a *Giant* fan," he declared, capping the airtight logic of his position with a twenty-cent bet. The four red chips were delivered into the pot with a toss of unnecessary enthusiasm, and the crash of plastic coin sounded like dishes breaking. Ricky laughed, Lonny lowered his eyes. Charlie was holding a pair of Queens. One pair. He was excited about it. He'd never liked Scrubby very much. He called.

"Well, I missed my lousy flush again," said Ricky. He slapped his worthless cards face down in the center of the table. A couple of white, one-cent chips fell on the floor, but nobody bothered to pick them up.

"You called, didn't you...." Scrubby said, a streak of shame running weak and hollow through his voice. Charlie's toothy smile and spring-action head nods confirmed that he had indeed called, and, out of turn, he unnecessarily laid down his pair. Avoiding any eye contact with his peers, Scrubby sheepishly mixed his cards face down with the discarded ones in the center.

"Ha! He called yer bluff!" Ricky Barnes crowed. "Ya can't even bluff out a punk kid."

"But if one neither knows nor cares if he's being bluffed, can it even be done?"

Charlie looked at Lonny and realized that this was the first thing the whiskered face had said. He was right, too. Charlie wouldn't have known a bluff if it had dropped from the sky to his lap. And he *didn't* care. His decision to call was pursuant only to the dangerous yet sound philosophy which states: *"if you don't call, you can't win"*. And so he called.

"Here, twerp, you won so now you gotta deal," Ricky said, pushing the cards and chips angrily, or so it seemed, over to his little brother.

"Boy it's a hot one today. Y'got anything t'drink around here?"

"You know where the refrigerator is."

"No, I mean *drink* drink," said Scrubby. He bounced nervously about the kitchen like a loose ping-pong ball. Practically all of his chips were gone.

"Are you kidding? My folks'd kill me if they found out I was even playin' cards! But they don't drink anyway, so you won't find anything."

"So how 'bout some cigarettes."

"Now that we can do. Smokes are in the drawer," Ricky said, motioning to a cabinet next to the sink. "Bring one for me, too."

Charlie Barnes shuffled the cards as best he could with his nine-year-old fingers. He was getting in a lot of practice, having won three of the last five hands. (He had taken particular joy in acquiring most of Scrubby's stake, seeing as how Scrubby's grudging endorsement of the boy's hero, Mr. Mays, had been delivered in such grotesque, left-handed fashion.) Scrubby returned with a pack of cigarettes and he and Ricky lit up. Soon the table blurred under a cloud of wispy gray smoke, prompting Lonny to draw the Venetian blinds and open the lone window. The open window did little to render the table smokeless, but it did allow the light of day to cut a golden angle through the cloud, bringing the action of the table into sharper focus. Evidently Lonny didn't smoke....Charlie dealt five cards to each player, slowly, taking great care not to suffer the colossal embarrassment of a mis-deal.

"Here, punk, want summa my cigarette?" asked Ricky. "C'mon, take a puff. You'll feel cool." But Charlie made it clear he didn't want any and picked up his cards. He was pretty sure Mays didn't smoke, and if Mays didn't smoke that was good enough for him....and he had a feeling that he'd be embarrassed smoking in front of Lonny, though he didn't exactly know why.

"Okay, geek-face, if that's the way you want it," Ricky said, pushing a precious, 25-cent blue chip into the pot. "But you can bet'cher crummy geek life yer winning streak is over. I'll see to it personally."

Charlie felt the hot, familiar flush of red invade his face and neck.

"A quarter! My God, man, whaddaya tryin' t'do, break the bank? I fold," Scrubby moaned. He hadn't bothered to sit down.

Lonny carefully slipped on the wire-rimmed spectacles. He took a quick look at his cards and dropped them to the table. He then carefully removed the glasses, folded them up, and quietly slipped them into their case.

"I raise," Charlie said. He coolly, coolly for his age at least, dropped five blue chips into the pot.

"A dollar? You raise me a dollar? Ha! That's a good one! Look, Scrub, my little brother's raisin' me a dollar!"

"They're growin' a rich crop of Giant fans this year," Scrubby ad-libbed. There was light laughter from all except Charlie. No young boy likes to have his favorite team made fun of. He wanted to win this hand badly, as badly as a nine-year-old boy can want to win a hand of poker. The red in his face was stubborn. He could still feel it. It made him wish he had some muscles. In the blink of an eye a friendly game had suddenly become the most serious sort of business imaginable. He looked again at his cards. His hand read four hearts and a spade. All he needed was another heart. He knew a flush was a good hand. If only he could draw another heart....

"Listen to me, little man—are you sure you wanna—you know, raise that much?" Ricky inquired. His voice sounded funny. "It takes you a mighty long time to scrounge that kind of money. Look, I'm just tryin' to help you out, outa the goodness of my notoriously big heart."

But Charlie assured him that he very much did wish to raise, with a slow, gravely serious nod of his head. Besides, he reasoned privately, so far he was only risking funds that had been liberated from Scrubby. Ricky, after first throwing up his hands in half-serious exasperation, and after an extended study of his own cards, called the bet: "Okay then gimme three, queerbait, and they better be good or I'll beat the snot outa you," he said.

Charlie flicked three cards, one by one, out toward his brother, while Scrubby leaned over the latter's shoulder to investigate. "Only one for me," declared the dealer, discarding the worthless spade and smuggling the top card of the deck into the void he had so created.

Scrubby was having the usual gambler's difficulty not playing the hand: "God, it's hot out—smoggy too," he said, both hands fidgeting with his cigarette. He took a tentative drag and coughed. "Yeah, *real* smoggy. It even makes these cigarettes taste bad."

"You said it," said Ricky, inhaling deeply as he picked up his new cards. He exhaled upwards, and the smoke swirled above his baseball-capped head. There was a curious look on his face.

Scrubby wasn't yet through with Charlie: "Now c'mon, kid, it's not right you not likin' the Dodgers."

"Why not?"

Ricky rapped his knuckles once on the tabletop and said, "Check."

"It's just not right, that's all. They're y'home team and you should like 'em just because a'that, if nuthin' else. Don'tcha wanna be bitchin'-ass dudes like us big fuckin' tenth-graders? We're *all* Dodger fans! Anybody who's *any*body is a Dodger fan! And y'know why the *chicks* dig the Dodgers, son? It's just because they're the home team, try'n feature that! Believe me, kid, it's great t'be a Dodger fan in Dodgertown, 'specially when we're in the lead."

"I told you to watch yer yap, man."

"Oh yeah. Sorry."

Charlie felt the hot redness in his neck again, which explains why he bet a quarter without even looking at his cards. Scrubby was always needling him, bugging him, trying to convert him over to their way of thinking. He hated it. And he knew then—as if touched from beyond, somehow, by the mischievous messenger of a far less popular team—that he would never be a Dodger fan as long as he lived....

"A blind bet! First he raises me a dollar, then he bets without even looking to see if he made his hand!" Ricky yelped. He shook his head and fired a look of angry supplication into the ceiling. Then, eyes panning quickly down to his little brother, he declared, ever-so-portentously, "Well, I'm just the man to make you pay—*raise* a quarter!"

It was one of those pivotal moments in this hallowed game, in any worthwhile field of endeavor, when the spectators lean forward in their seats and the players sharpen their wits, clear their lungs, ready all their resources, and steel themselves for the last leg of battle:

Charlie looked at his cards....heart, heart....spade! Another worthless spade! He'd missed his lousy flush....darn it, he swore in silence. If only it could have been another heart, gosh, why *couldn't* it have been....just this one time....but the hand was not over (he knew the rules), and so, all but beaten, he did the only thing he could do. He raised the bet a dollar.

"My God, what the hell are you *doing*!" cried Ricky Barnes. He sounded like a young man suddenly and unjustly put at the point of a gun. Charlie didn't reply, but instead did his best to intimidate his brother with his steely-eyed stare. Ricky made doubly sure his cards were the same ones he'd looked at a few seconds before, then smiled: "So you wanna bark with the big dogs, huh? You couldn't just leave it alone, huh? Well, stupid, you asked for it," he said, whereupon he reached into his shirt pocket, producing instantly, as if readied in advance, a five-dollar bill, which (after much fondling and public display) he placed atop the wealth of colored chips in the center of the table. "It's brother against brother, and only the cool shall survive. Let's see you call four bucks," was his emboldened challenge. He was puffing wildly on his cigarette.

And now Scrubby White wailed and Lonny Atkinson smiled, and Ricky Barnes accepted the plaudits of a would-be crowd with a wave of his hand and several rapid nods of the head. Charlie was in a pickle. He wanted desperately to win this hand, but four dollars was practically all the money he had in the world....

"Y'better fold, kid," Scrubby advised the youngest player. "I'm tellin' you, he's got you dead-ass beat—"

"Shut up, Scrub," Ricky said.

Scrubby did as he was told and lit up another cigarette.

"Take all the time you want before you quit, twerpo," Ricky said, looking the other way, adding, sarcastically, "all the time you need. I've got all day!" Then he and Scrubby commenced an in-depth discussion revolving around the merits of that most glorious of all their blessings, Mr. Koufax's remarkable left arm.

Charlie remained in a quandary. His mind told him that he should drop out, but something inside him told him that if he sat there long enough he'd figure out some way to win. And then, possibly in half-conscious response to that illogical feeling, he discovered along the tortuous, serpentine path of his thinking that he was staring directly at the deck of cards in front of him. Suddenly the possibility that the top card might be a heart intrigued him. It all felt so....so *natural*! Could anything so natural, so deliciously tempting, possibly be *wrong*? He glanced at Ricky and Scrubby, still praising Koufax, still not paying attention. Then back to the top card....suddenly he knew he had to have it, at least see it. It wouldn't be that tough, he thought; he could just slide it off and along the table top and into his hand while they were still talking. It would all be over in a couple of seconds, who would know? Slowly his fingers snaked their way across the table top to the deck of cards. His thumb deftly pried the top card from the deck....a heart! The six of hearts! What a break....ah, but now for the tricky part, the transference of card from deck to hand....make sure they're not watching....stupid Dodger fans....that's it, slowly, slowly....

"This is ridiculous!" Scrubby said suddenly. Charlie's fingers quickly pounded out a musical rhythm on the table top. "Yer gonna feel like a sap when the Dodgers are in the World Series and the Giants are pushin' up daisies! C'mon, kid. Even Mays can't help you now. He's just one guy. C'mon. When the whole town's out celebrating, y'don't wanna be *left behind*, do you?"

Charlie forced himself to smile and shrugged his insubstantial shoulders. "Sheesh!" Scrubby exclaimed in defeat, whereupon he and Ricky went back to railing on the Giants and extolling the various fringe benefits of Dodgerdom.

Now was the time. He brought his left hand—the hand palming his cards—down on the deck, and smuggled the six of hearts into the other four. He had done it. He'd made his flush. Stupid Dodger fans....

But somewhere within the glowing penumbra of his victory he could sense the darkness in the center, and soon felt cold, sad eyes on the right side of his face. He looked to his right and there was Lonny. In all the excitement, he had totally forgotten about Lonny.

"C'mon Charlie, I'm a busy man. I can't wait all day for you to give up," Ricky said, impatience infecting his voice, but he was still looking the other way. Charlie didn't respond. Or move. He just looked at Lonny's face. That whiskered, unusual face. Other than the whiskers he had a face like a wooden board. It was drawn and flat, and tired and worn, and *old*; seemingly far too old a face for its owner. The glasses were back on. The two dark knotholes behind them which served as eyes looked bigger through glass, and they seemed to cut clean through the frightened nine-year-old. He had never experienced that feeling before....And yet, despite their guilt-producing power, there was also a softer, far-away, unmistakably plaintive quality to these eyes, Charlie thought, as if they had already been forced to witness Mankind commit its most heinous crimes against itself (though, naturally, it would be a long time before he would be able to plug words like "plaintive" and "heinous" into his recollections). Years later, a far more seasoned and worldly Charlie Barnes than this one would often think about that sad, tired face….a face that had earned its whiskers.... and now he looked at Lonny long and hard. Then he looked at the pot, at all the chips, and at the five-dollar bill that glared back at him. And then he knew, knew at that unprecedented, watershed moment, that he had committed a most cardinal and contemptible error.

All eyes were on him now....

"Well, what's it gonna be?" said Ricky.

"Yeah, what's it gonna be?" said Scrubby.

"I fold," said Charlie, as he quickly mixed his dead hand into the discards. "I fold," he repeated, as if intuitively sensing the need to reaffirm the irrevocability of such a splendid reformation.

Ricky Barnes took a deep breath. He quickly mixed his winning hand with the discards. "It's about time," he exhaled.

"Yeah," exhaled Scrubby. "It's about time."

OH-FOR-FOUR

Author's Notes

I was not quite ten years old when the Watts Riots broke out in Los Angeles in August of 1965. I didn't know anything about riots, but, as one can tell from this story and *A Hand Of Poker*, I did know an awful lot about the 1965 National League pennant race, and even at only nine years of age was fairly consumed with it.

On August 22nd of that year I was watching a Dodger/Giant game on TV, and stared in horror as my favorite pitcher, San Francisco's Juan Marichal, slammed his bat down on the head of Dodgers catcher John Roseboro. Sandy Koufax ran off the mound to come to Roseboro's aid, while simultaneously trying to keep Roseboro from killing Marichal. The photograph in the paper the next day of Roseboro, a black man, Marichal, an Hispanic man, and Koufax, a white guy and a Jew all rolled into one, all grappling wildly on the Candlestick Park infield, well, suffice to say that picture was burned into my brain forever. Their disagreement wasn't racial, yet for some reason it felt that way. And it was the first time in my life when I realized there was something wrong with the way adult people treated each other and regarded each other. I was pretty confused about it at the time. Hopefully less confused now.

Oh-For-Four was one of my first attempts at taking on an important issue or two—racism, race riots, class divisions etc.—and using the more mild, comparatively mundane events of the day (in this case a fight in a pro baseball game and one of Charlie's Little League games) as effective prisms through which to view those issues in a different light and, hopefully, achieve a better understanding of them. While also, most importantly, laying down an historical perspective. Remember, the 'artist-writer'—the *literary artiste*—is primarily an Historian. At least according to the writer in question....

The name of the maid in the story, 'Tillie', by way of tribute, is borrowed from the maid in that fine Stanley Kramer movie "*Guess Who's Coming To Dinner?*", which also deals with racial issues.

(*final note: In 2010, 45 years after-the-fact, I was walking down Colorado Boulevard in Pasadena with my girlfriend at the time, doing a little window shopping, whereupon I spied, hanging in a clothing store window for all to see, a T-shirt depicting the photograph of the Marichal/Roseboro/Koufax incident. I was stunned. That's all you need to know about the hold that particular baseball game still has on our collective consciousness here in L.A. Anyway, I had to have it. But I doubt if I'll ever pay $35 dollars for a T-shirt again.)

OH-FOR-FOUR

What he remembered years later was thinking how she didn't look guilty or scared or self-conscious or ashamed or anything.

Especially for a maid. After all, wasn't she rifling through the cupboards like a common criminal? Sure looked that way....And then there was the distinctly un-guilty way she buttered the two stolen squares of toast; toast which naturally should have popped up golden, but had just been burned black by mistake. Such errors were so typical of her. Furthermore, he observed, she clearly had no qualms whatsoever about relieving the refrigerator of a pitcher, *our* pitcher, the thick-white contents of which she poured sweet as you please into one of *our glasses*, geez....Of course more than a few drops were spilled, which at the time made the whole thing seem worse somehow, but to be fair it must be stated again that, by then, such consistent unsteadiness of hand was expected. But what the boy did not expect was a smile....she was smiling....darned if she wasn't smiling....

This boy, Charlie Barnes, then a lad of ten (well, almost ten), was this fateful day observing these deliciously questionable goings-on as best he could, from the front yard, where he was practicing his baseball swing. He could see everything perfectly clearly, he was sure, right through the convenient slits in the kitchen window. Venetian blinds were always good for spying. You could squint right in and snoop on anybody you wanted and nobody ever noticed....and he really had somebody now! He would have hoped it would have been somebody more deserving of his deceit, like his little sister for instance, but Tillie would have to do. After all, she was *almost* like family....why should *she* get away with anything? Oh sure, it was just a couple pieces of bread and some milk, but the whole thing just didn't set well with him. It just didn't. And wasn't his father always saying something wise and portentous like "food costs money"? Sure. Always was. But Charlie's little sister saw nothing at all unusual in a bite of lunch (it was, after all, lunch time) and went back to doing whatever it is little sisters do. What does *she* know, he thought....

He took a few more healthy cuts with his brand-new bat—a genuine two-tone, 28-inch, "Hillerich & Bradsby" special—to help him decide what to do. The issues had to be weighed. It was a case of to tell or not to tell, and the boy didn't feel totally comfortable with either course of action. He wasn't a tattle-tale, or at least he didn't consider himself one, but heck, with grown-ups it's *different* he reminded himself. With grown-ups there's really no such thing as telling. And besides, there was no getting around what he saw....no sir, there was nothing to cover up Tillie's obvious criminal tendencies *this* time. She'll probably just get yelled at....and certain things simply have to be dealt with "in the prescribed manner", he had once overheard his father say. Yeah. In the prescribed manner....

But all that was only the case for the prosecution. Speaking for the defense was his own conscience, needling him and whispering to him, hey, just forget the whole thing....this is a *pal*....be a pal and let it go, c'mon. The friendship defense. Yes it's true he did like Tillie. But with an unprecedented swirl of confusion currently in charge of his young head, he found himself incapable of vesting his personal feelings for the defendant with any real significance. Irrelevant and immaterial. Besides, he reminded the conscience, it's no fun turning somebody in unless you like them....

And so, with a mighty swish of his new bat to provide some much-needed self assurance, he resolved to report what he saw to the proper authority.

He approached his parents' bedroom with all the stealth and professionalism of a true informer; waiting till his little sister wasn't paying attention, then crawling up the side yard, finally tiptoeing through the back door. It was important that Tillie not suspect anything. Charlie's mother was asleep, as was usual for this hour of the afternoon on her day off. Open-mouthed and all-but-motionless, a drop of drool on the pillow, it was a sleep of utter exhaustion. Naturally he was afraid to wake her. The easy thing to do would have been to just forget the whole thing, as his conscience had advised him, and by this time that's pretty much what he wanted to do, but the youngster was fairly consumed with the drug-like euphoria that comes with an opportunity to turn somebody in, and so, the compulsion bubbling up and over and out of him now, hurtling himself past the cut-off point, he gently drum-tapped her shoulder with the flared knob at the end of his brand-new 28-inch piece of wood.

"Mom, wake up!"

"Hmm."

"Mom, the maid's eatin' all our toast and drinkin' all our milk. She's not supposta eat *our* food....is she?"

"Ungh....wudja say?" said a semi-conscious Betty Barnes, and then, only seconds later, "*What* did you say?" She sat up amazingly quickly.

"It's Tillie. She's eating all our food."

Betty Barnes's eyes widened and narrowed, like a cat aching for a kill. She flung off the covers and grabbed her robe in the same urgent whirl of motion, and, so much faster than her son had thought possible, was suddenly wide awake and marching thunderously down the hall to a confrontation with the hired help. Charlie followed her plump rear carriage at a safe distance.

When they reached the kitchen the maid was casually cleaning up the messy evidence of her crime. She was almost through. She smiled, but only as long as it took to get a good look at her employer's face.

"Alright, Tillie, what's this I hear about you helping yourself to my food!"

"But Missus Betty, it was jes—"

"Never mind!" Betty Barnes cut back in, obviously in complete control and just as obviously enjoying it: "I don't wanna hear about your *reasons* for doing it, the point is you *did* it—you're fired!"

"But Missus Betty—"

"I said, I do not want to *hear* it! Just get your things and leave, there'll be a check for you in the mail."

"Yes'm."

Charlie Barnes stood statue-still, suffering through the shock of his young life. He was instantly sick and tingly all over. He *liked* the maid, and for good reason. This was the same woman who would feed the dog when he forgot and bring him candy bars from the market, the same woman who had recently and darn near professionally trimmed his hair for him after the barber had done a lousy job. She would sometimes even pitch batting practice for him in the front yard, lobbing Wiffle ball after Wiffle ball in his general direction, pitches he would smack with a plastic bat to the far corners of the neighborhood. Sometimes he could even get her to fetch the balls. She had *always* been his pal, the last thing he ever wanted to do was get her fired. She was almost like family....heck, he was just trying to do the right thing....he knew, though, at this queasiest of moments, that he had surely done the wrong thing.

The only maid the Barnes family ever had gathered up her cleaning materials in spare yet sinewy-strong arms, without a word, taking care not to spill anything on the somewhat threadbare living room carpet. She left without resistance or conversation.

The boy glared at his mother. "Geez, what'd ya do *that* for?" he said in a weak squeaky voice.

"She had it coming, don't you think?" re-queried Betty Barnes. "After all, you told on her."

Charlie shuffled his feet and mumbled something about how much he liked the maid. He also wondered how in the world he could be so stupid....

"She was a lousy cleaning lady, just awful," the lady of the house continued. She was neither looking at nor talking to him, or to anywhere in particular for that matter. She was just talking: "I've been looking for a good excuse to get rid of her, but it's been hard knowing she has that kid to support." She glared at the kitchen table, which looked just fine to Charlie, but it was apparently still in an unsatisfactory state so she took a wet paper towel and swabbed every square inch of the smooth Formica surface. She wasn't talking like he was even in the room anymore, just a lazy dialogue with herself: "All I can say is it'll be a cold day in hell before I hire another....oh, maybe when things get a little better with the business. He tries *so* hard, I know he does, I just wish....wish he....but God knows I need some help too, with all I have to do around here, and I'm....I'm just not used to getting up and going into an office every day....and I get so tired....it's just that everyone is into everyone else's pocket, I mean *criminettily*! I wouldn't mind it if these people did a better job, but when I have to go back over everything myself it's, it's....well it's just a waste of time and money, that's what it is. I guess I took too big of a chance when I decided to go ahead and hire her in spite of...." She paused, balling up the paper towel and finally glancing over at her son, adding, finally, "well, of everything."

Betty Barnes's attitude was startling. Even for her. Even to him. He may have been just a stupid kid, but not so stupid he didn't know what "these people" or "everything" meant. Man....But he managed to fight off his disgust at his mother's remarks by changing the subject to more pleasant fields of endeavor: "Can you come to my game today?" the boy pleaded. "The game's early, not right at dinnertime like most weeknights," he added hopefully.

"Oh no, baby dumpling, I have a *million* things to do, including cleaning up this whole darn house now, and still making sure dinner is ready for you and your father when you two hard-working boys get home! Some other time. But do go make a couple of hits for me, will you dear?"

Charlie smiled weakly. "Sure. Sure, Mom," he said.

"Now run along, you'll be late." She kissed her son, yawned, and then disappeared down the hall.

Baseball is a game of changing fortunes. Before he got his new Hillerich & Bradsby, Charlie was in a slump. He had been hitting only .349. The problem was basic and timeless; trouble making consistent contact with a pitched ball. And since it is the bat that actually *makes* contact with the ball, he reasoned (in an unusual attack of scientific precociousness) that this, his biggest problem in the world, might well be solved by a brand-new, thin-handled, black-barreled, 28-inch, Frank Robinson autographed special. He liked the Frank Robinson model because of the thin handle. That was the key, he thought, the thin tan handle. The "feel" was just bound to be better. And now, on his way home from the ballfield, he was sure he had been right. After all, he knew he was basically just a garden-variety .380 hitter. In the Major Leagues, hall-of-fame stuff; in Little League, nothing special. But on this magnificent, watershed of a day he had just gone three-for-three, including a triple, raising his batting average to .411! (He'd ascertained the exact figure by badgering his fat, foul-mouthed manager, right after the game, into performing the strange and absurdly complicated task of dividing his total at-bats into his hits, on the back of an old line-up card.) Frankly, it made him nervous being over .400; *I'm just not a four-hunnerd hitter*, he would remind himself over and over. And it didn't matter much that his team had won. Baseball is, truth be told, a game of loosely-linked *individual* performances. As far as he was concerned, the only occurrence of any real significance on this day of days was that there was a struggling ballplayer, in suburban Los Angeles, California, that was finally out of his slump. He owed it all to his new bat, and he stroked it and swung it and hugged it and praised it, and fairly worshipped it, all the way home.

As his house drew near the friendly smells of beef and mashed potatoes conspired to draw him in. Various dinnertime sounds reached out to him faintly through the closed kitchen window. He knew his dad wasn't home yet; the hatchback car wasn't in the driveway. It wasn't quite dark, the streetlights having just come on. Mosquitoes, barely visible, danced and darted in the vanishing twilight, attacking the sweat-soaked ten-year-old without mercy. He fought them off gallantly, like a swordsman of yore, with the aid of the flashing thin handle of his all-powerful new weapon.

"Chaar...*lieee!* Hurry up, dear, dinner's on!" his mother called to him.

"Coming, Mom!" he called back. This was one dinner that was sure to taste big league.

He ran straight to the bathroom and washed his hands, a rare occurrence no matter what the occasion. He even ran a damp washcloth along the back of his neck, and it felt cool against the mild sunburn flourishing above the collar of his uniform. He kicked off his cleats, but left the rest of the uniform on. After carefully tucking his glove and the brave new bat safely away under his bed, he sprinted back down the hall.

By the time he made it back to the kitchen his father was sitting in his designated chair at the head of the breakfast table. He hadn't heard the car drive up, and he couldn't see his face through the front page of the *Pasadena Star-News*, but since his father and older brother were the only ones in his family who ever read the front page, and since the brother was conveniently away at summer camp, he knew it was him.

"Dad, what's Watts?"

His son's voice was enough to lift the father's eyes above the top edge of the paper, but he didn't smile. And he didn't answer right away, either. Roland Barnes was a tall, thin, quintessentially decent sort of a man, a man whose face somehow managed to mix casualness and nervousness within the same expression, a faculty which often rendered him, to his children, inscrutable. He closed the paper up, folded the huge headline in half, glanced unsmiling at his wife, folded it again, and finally, at the end of a silence that made Charlie feel both stupid and naked, his father exclaimed, "Something not nearly as much fun as baseball!"—"*Nuthin's* better'n baseball!" a relieved Charlie doubled him—"You bet'cha!" Barnes redoubled, rolling the newspaper up into a makeshift bat, and when the father finally smiled and ruffled a strong hand through the son's rambunctious blond curls, and whacked him on the butt with the barrel end of the paper, the son was instantly baptized in a feeling that was the only way on earth he ever wanted to feel; and sealed within a cocoon of such sublime and overwhelming security, it is hardly surprising that the boy, any boy, should think it would surely last forever....

The father gathered up his number-two son in arms whose genuine strength was somewhat belied by their lack of size and definition. They laughed a duet, one voice pitched measurably higher than the other.

Barnes hid the newspaper in the silverware drawer. Charlie's little sister had already come a-running, to the sound of her father and brother both in such a good mood. They all sat down. At first the conversation dragged.

Finally: "So how'd it go out there, son—do any good? At the plate, I mean."

"Three-for-three," Charlie said quickly, barely able to contain his jubilation. For effect, he purposely kept his eyes glued to the marinated flank steak that was throwing up knuckleballs of steam from his plate. "Had a triple in the sixth, scored the winning run," he added soberly.

"*Really?* Hey, that's great, Charlie! Didja hear that, Betty? Three-for-three!"

Betty Barnes half-smiled like mothers do, but did not answer.

"It was the new bat, Dad!" Charlie explained, his elation bubbling over now. "It felt so good in my hands, I just *knew* I could hit with it! And I'm the only guy on the team with a bitchin' two-colored one, too. I had three guys come up and try and borrow it, but don't worry, I wouldn't let'm. I've *never* been over four hunnerd before, thanks again for buying it for me, Dad—it's so bitchin' I can't believe it!"

Roland Barnes accepted his son's expression of gratitude with his best fatherly smile. "Well, anything to break out of a slump," he said.

"Watch your mouth, Charlie," his wife added.

Grace was finally anthemed by the mother. Passed-around dishes and serving spoons immediately blurred the table. The conversation soon dissolved into a wordless melody of four mouths mulching food. Minus the fifth wheel of the family, each remaining family member represented one point of a square, and since a square, to a little boy, is little more than a baseball diamond resting on its side, that explains why Charlie now fantasized himself at home plate, the catcher and captain of this Formica infield, and it wasn't the steak but rather his little sister lobbing in the knucklers from second base. Suddenly he was the most skilled of all backstops, and he caught every one. No one dared run on him. He was the complete player. And no crowd was necessary, beyond the grateful, awestruck tumult that had gathered in his mind....It was the second baseman who broke the spell: "What's the big deal about a dumb ol' baseball game?" she wanted to know.

"That's what I say, precious," Betty Barnes said. "I mean heavens-to-Betsy."

"Whaddayou two old women talking about?" an irritated-sounding Roland Barnes inquired of his females. "Fer Pete's sake, I only wish the games were scheduled at a time when I could—"

"When you could go and scream and yell like a wild man?"

"Oh, are we gonna start that again...."

"—And drive those poor kids into a frenzy? I mean it's *no wonder* that by the time they get to be adults they act like maniacs, for goodness sake."

"Maniacs? Oh, come on now, sweetie."

"That's right, I said *maniacs*!" the wife spat forth, in a tone stronger and far more authoritative than her husband's. She was, as usual, gaining the upper hand: "I suppose you've already forgotten about what happened the other day in San Francisco, hm? Well, *have* you? That, that....*animal*, taking that bat and hitting that poor Dodger boy over the head....I say it's no wonder there's crime in the streets! And our son, just starting fifth grade, gets to watch it on T.V.? It's dis*grace*ful!"

Barnes, head down, went to work on his flank steak, two, three bites at a time. "Well all I can say is it's a darn shame when a boy gets to play ball and his old man has to work," he said softly.

"Speaking of work," Betty Barnes cut in, deftly changing the subject back to her, "did I tell you I fired Tillie today?"

Barnes interrupted a gravied bite of mashed potatoes: "Why, honey?"

Charlie had almost forgotten about it. Immediately he realized he was still irritated at his mother's surprising attitude, he had to admit it, but he wasn't going to let it spoil his evening. Besides, he thought, what do first basemen know....

"Oh, it was the last straw, that's all. Charlie caught her gorging herself on our food and it seemed as good a time as any to let her go. You know. Half the time she never showed up and the other half she was spilling something or breaking something, I mean honestly. Edna Rogers told me I was taking a big chance, I mean she *told* me, but I guess I have a soft spot for....well, for women like that. I suppose I feel sorry for her."

Straight-faced, resigned, Barnes resumed his only full meal of the day: "Well, it's your house, honey. You can do whatever you want," he softly said.

Charlie wasn't listening. He was busy thinking about tomorrow's game, wondering if his new Frank Robinson special would see fit to knock out a couple of homers for him.

It was already a warm day when the league's hottest hitter arrived at the junior high school, and he could feel the cotton of his jersey clinging comfortably to his skin. Saturday was always the best day for a game, seeing as how there was no school to worry about or clog up the afternoon. He was early. The hot sun had not yet crept above the brim of his cap. The only real noise issued from the squeaky wheels of the chalk machine, which one of the fathers was just beginning to roll up and down the first base foul line. Charlie drew a deep breath. His nose informed him that the infield grass had recently been cut and watered. The green crewcut of the infield looked cool and sharp against the warm, reddish dust of the basepaths. He stood for a moment, enraptured, behind the chain-link fence in right field. A row of simple frame houses sat behind him, across the street, well out of reach of any ball hit by a ten-year-old. He could feel their presence, looming up suddenly and urgently behind him now, but they weren't simple frame houses anymore; they were the burgeoning triple tiers of Yankee Stadium, they were the double decks of Detroit, they were the rival scoreboards of Dodgertown and Candlestick, growing directly out of bleachers whose fans shared a symbiosis born of the close proximity of Brooklyn and Manhattan, and whose inherited, instinctive hatred of each other could not be quelled merely by separating them with 400 miles of parched desert, rich San Joaquin farmland, and the rugged coastline of Big Sur. It was the Green Monster behind him, all 37 feet 2 inches of it, as suddenly he was standing smack in Boston's Fenway Park, about to be introduced as the starting right fielder (Most every baseball lover knows this storied wall stands in *left* field, and young Charlie sort of knew it, but it was a minor detail and he couldn't help it if he happened to be standing in right field at the time and it was his fantasy and that was that.). Thirty thousand pairs of hands slapped together. And his flesh tingled and his breath stopped mid-throat when this rolling thunder of applause hit him, as the public address announcer proudly proclaimed his name....

The chatter of half a dozen equally hopeful dreamers brought him back to Pasadena. The boys were playing catch in the outfield. Hopefully he could cajole one of them into pitching him some batting practice....

He tossed his glove and the precious bat over the fence, climbed it like a monkey, scooped up the tools of his trade, and headed with singleness of purpose for the infield.

"Hey LeMont, pitch me a few, will ya?" he yelled to one of his teammates in the outfield.

"Sure, Charlie!" the boy yelled back, heading obediently for the mound.

Charlie rolled eight or nine balls from the equipment bag out toward the mound, the last one arriving just in time for LeMont Davis to scoop it up. Charlie liked LeMont. He was the withdrawn type, certainly not the most popular player in the league (perhaps due in part to the fact that he didn't go to the same school as Charlie and his regular friends) but Charlie was proud to consider him his best friend on the team. In fact, ever since he started hanging around LeMont, LeMont had become practically his *only* friend on the team. He sort of thought that was a little weird. But it wasn't something worth dwelling on....

LeMont reared back on his right foot, surged forward, and delivered the first ball at medium speed, belt high, right over the heart of the plate. Charlie—a right-handed batter—stood solidly in the batter's box, well away from the dish, his front foot planted forward a few inches in the direction of first base; a slightly "closed" stance. As the ball dipped into the strike zone he strode into it, whipping the bat around in a slightly uppercut stroke. He got it all. The heavy summer air exploded in a symphony of wood, in the wonderful and completely fulfilling music of bat colliding with ball; to a ten-year-old boy, there is nothing in the world quite like the magic of this sound. The ball departed the bat on a looping line, falling safely into the tall grass in left-center. Base hit. No question about it.

"Hey man, nice poke," chirped the pitcher, wide-eyed, peeling back full lips in a wonderful smile of crooked and missing teeth. "You *hot*, that's fo' sure!"

Charlie threw back an equally adorable smile of relatively straight teeth, and readied himself for the next delivery. For the next few minutes he drove LeMont's pitches with vengeance to all fields. Then, suddenly, LeMont stopped in the middle of his wind-up to wave to someone in the wooden bleachers behind the backstop.

He turned around. She was staring right at him.

"Hey, Mamma!" LeMont called out. The woman waved.

Charlie turned back toward the mound. "That's yer *mom*?" he said in a soft voice.

"Hell yes!" LeMont trumpeted proudly. "She comes t'*all* the games.... that is, when she ain't workin'."

Suddenly he felt very cold inside. Evidently she hadn't told LeMont who was responsible for her being fired, or even who she had most recently worked for....it didn't make a lot of sense, but at least it was something in his favor. He could feel her eyes lasering through the backstop wire, then cutting through his batting helmet, yet he managed to set himself in the box without turning around. His throat was suddenly hot. He cooled it by smearing it up and down with the fresh sweat rapidly escaping his forehead. He quickly wiped off his hands on his baggy pants before re-gripping the magic bat. The ball came in again at medium speed. He took a healthier-than-usual cut—a classic home-run stroke—but got only the top half of the ball, sending it out toward shortstop on two big "charity" hops. Easy out, short to first.

"Alright gang, come on in, on the double! We got a game to play, goddammit, let's go!" a voice boomed from the dugout. It belonged to the typical Little League manager, late-thirties, overweight, determined to make his players pay through discipline for his lack of talent a generation earlier. Charlie had lost all track of time. He'd just gotten mentally into the rhythm of batting practice and suddenly it was game time. Long columns of fathers and mothers, and brothers and sisters, could suddenly be seen filing in from nearby parking lots. He needed time to think.... but the manager called Charlie over to him as his team assembled on the dugout bench.

"Barnes, I was watchin' you take batting practice just now, you been hittin' the crap outa the ball lately," said the manager. His T-shirt had mustard stains on it. "I want'cha battin' third today."

"Third?" Charlie echoed, his voice rising a little.

"That's right, slugger—this is a big game, I'm countin' on a bitch of a day from you with the bat," the manager said with great theatrical urgency. He chewed at the longer hairs of his droopy moustache, no doubt trying to think of something profound and managerial to say. Perhaps to buy more time, he turned back to the dugout and waved his team out onto the field. As the eight other starters rushed by on both sides of their conversation and eagerly out to their assigned stations, the mustard-stained man finally came up with, "Just take it loosey-goosey and go out there and hit line drives, 'kay?"

"Sure....sure, skip," Charlie gulped. The air suddenly tasted funny. It made him look up, and he realized it wasn't such a good day anymore. Yet another skyful of pollution had been cruelly dispatched to this ballfield, as it had been so many days in a row now, an inanimate thing with the tenacious personality of a devout season-ticket holder, and by this time an expected bi-product of this foulest, hottest, smoggiest of L.A. summers. The sun was hiding, and his eyes hurt. And as if he didn't have enough pressure, young Charlie now occupied the most important spot in the batting order, a position stingily reserved for home-run kings and batting champions, the province of Ruth, of Mays, of Clemente and Cobb and Aaron....and of Robinson. All this responsibility for an unexceptional, Punch-and-Judy, garden variety .380 hitter? Under the circumstances, he harbored more than a reasonable doubt as to whether he was up to the challenge....

And on top of everything Tillie Davis, former Barnes family maid, LeMont Davis's *mother* for Pete's sake, was sitting right there in the stands—now crowded with people—right behind home plate. He forced himself to look at her. She was smiling right at him. Darned if she wasn't smiling. It was a curious thing for her to be doing, was his hazy-vague thought.

The manager yelled something dirty and Charlie hurried out to his position at second base.

The bottom of the sixth inning arrived with Charlie's team down by a run. In three trips to the plate he was hitless. He did reach base in the third, but only because of an error by the enemy shortstop. Oh-for-three. Little League games are only played six innings, not the traditional adult nine, so this would be his last chance. It was top of the order due up, so when the lead-off batter singled to left he made his way reluctantly to the on-deck circle.

The on-deck circle can be a lonely place. Usually it provides the hitter with much-needed solitary contemplation of his next at-bat, cordoned off from the jokes and jibes of the dugout, insulated from the chatter of the infield, free of the intense concentration required of the batter's box. But with one man on and his team down by a score of five-to-four, Charlie knew he represented the possible winning run. The worst kind of pressure. Not to mention his being his team's "number-three hitter", which meant he was *expected* to deliver. And so, shouldering the unfair weight of such awesome obligation, the on-deck circle can be just about the loneliest place in the world. He voided the sweat on his palms with the resin bag. With the pine tar rag he coated the thin blond handle of his bat with stickiness, taking care not to touch it to the black hitting area of the barrel. He looked up in the stands, at LeMont Davis's mother. She wasn't looking back at him, for a change, because LeMont was at bat with nobody out and a count of no balls and two strikes against him. She sure was staring in the third, he said to himself, when I hit that weak grounder and reached base on that error....funny thing; she *clapped*! She *never* used to clap when I'd barely hit the Wiffle ball, or when I'd hit a weak grounder on one of her easy pitches—she'd just tell me to try harder....but that was before....before I....God, I wish it was yesterday....

"Stee-rike three!—*yer outa there!*"

The home crowd groaned as LeMont Davis (normally at his best in the clutch, as one might expect of somebody hitting .487) slowly and dejectedly made his way back to the dugout. As he passed his teammate he whispered, "He's pitchin'm all down low, man. Look fo' a low one." Charlie nodded and wobbled out toward his fate.

Just before he set himself in the box he glanced back through the backstop wire and squarely into her eyes. She was smiling again. She began to clap in measured unison along with the rest of the crowd. He studied her as she called out some hopeful staple of advice that was dear to her, but it was swallowed whole by the maddened throng. She knew he was nervous; no wonder she was cheering, he thought. Fifty voices joined her. A hundred hopeful feet pounded the wooden planks in a frenzy of encouragement. His cleated back foot pawed savagely at the dirt to establish a foothold. Then he stepped out. It didn't work, though; with the game on the line, the crowd would not abate its enthusiasm. When he stepped back in he took a couple stiff swings. He felt sick and fluttery inside. The bat felt thick and awkward in his hands. First base looked very far away. He could feel the pressure get to him. He knew he would swing at the first pitch.

The pitch was down low, as LeMont had promised, but targeted slightly, insidiously, outside. This is not the type of pitch to "pull", but in his anxious state young Charlie ignored this age-old baseball axiom. His swing was a violent, frantic attempt to drive the ball over the left field fence. Predictably, he topped it. The ball bounced neatly out to the shortstop on two clean hops, who flipped to the second baseman, who pivoted smoothly and quickly while brushing the bag with his right foot, easily avoiding the lead runner, side-arming his throw to first in plenty of time to beat the slow-moving body of Charlie Barnes by half-a-step. Double play. A tremendous accomplishment for any infield of ten-year-olds, but a double play just the same. It was over. Schoolmates on both teams rushed the pitcher's mound to congratulate each other. Charlie's team had lost by one run.

On his way back to the dugout Charlie retrieved his Frank Robinson special. He looked at it quizzically, as if expecting an explanation. His manager hollered out some foul words he didn't understand, something about batting sixth next week, but Charlie didn't hear him. Oh-for-four. The dreaded nemesis of every batsman down through the ages. He had made the last out, a double play. He had choked in the clutch, in trying to pull an outside pitch at the knees. He hadn't come close to beating the throw. But all these failures paled in his mind when placed beside that awful slang phrase, oh-for-four. It had to be the bat's fault, Charlie reasoned. It wasn't just nerves....after all, he'd been hitting .411 only because of the three hits the bat produced the previous day. Now he was back under .400, back where he belonged....Charlie wondered why his bat had let him down.

The crowd had nearly dispersed now, as only a handful of parents and relatives remained in the wooden bleachers. The victorious opposition sent choruses of *"two-four-six-eight, who do we appreciate?"* ringing through the heavy summer air. Charlie looked out toward second base where LeMont Davis was hitting fungoes, then grabbing his glove and running under the ball in an attempt, usually successful, to make the catch. It reminded him that LeMont's mother still had to be reckoned with. Sure enough, she was still up in the stands, watching her only son run under his own fungoes. Charlie wasted no time in going over to her. He was anxious to get the whole thing over with. He figured he had it coming, even though she was partly to blame for his shrunken batting average....

"Hello, Charlie," she began. "You played fine ball out there t'day, boy. I was proud a'you."

"But I went oh-for-four!" a bemused Charlie stammered. "I didn't get a hit all day."

"How 'bout that one in the third? You made it all the—"

"That was an error," Charlie cut in. "Those count against you."

"The main thing is you tried," she said, smiling again.

Charlie was confused. "Yer sure bein' awful nice ta me, seein' as how I got you....fired," he said.

"You din' get me fired, boy. You din' have nuthin' t'do with it."

"But I *told* on you!" the boy insisted. He was determined to take the blame like a man.

"Lissun, Charlie," LeMont's mother said, taking his hand in both of hers. "Remember that blue vase yo' mamma used t'keep on the piano, 'member when it got broke? And yo' little sister got blamed? Well, that was me that did it. And 'member all them times I didn't show up fo' work this month? Well, I was here a-watchin' LeMont play ball, all them times."

"But I never—"

"That's because I'd watch from the street," she added quickly. "This is the first time I din' hafta worry 'bout someone a-seein' me."

Charlie looked at his shoe tops and kicked a little dirt on them. The woman put her long arm around the boy's shoulders and explained:

"Believe me, child, it din' have nuthin' t'do with you. I jes ain't cut out fo' housework, I never have been. Y'see I had a *real* job befo' I got married an' moved out here, doin' folks's hair. But now, housework's somethin' I jes, I, uh....well. It jes ain't me. Why, did you know I used t'work fo' yo' mamma's friend, Missus Rogers? Well, I was always a-spillin' things, and fo'gettin' t'clean up after myself an' such. I always been clumsy. I don' have no control over it. I guess I musta caused more messes than I ever got rid of! Why, it was a surprise t'me that I even got hired by yo' mamma in the first place, seein' as how they's such good friends."

Charlie looked up at her, finally, and smiled for the first time since batting practice. "You mean it *wasn't* my fault? at *all*?"

"No, boy," she said soberly. "Not yo's and not yo' mamma's. When she told me t'be at work right after lunch time, I guess I talked myself inta thinkin' she meant fo' me t'have some lunch too. I was hungry, is all. But all you did was t'follow yo' conscience, child! You was doin' the *right thing* by tellin' her what you seen. It wasn't no more yo' fault I got fired than....well, than it was that there baseball bat's fault you din' make no hits today."

Charlie looked at the bat again. He felt almost like apologizing to it. Looking back at LeMont's mother he noticed, for the first time really, the intricate network of lines and wrinkles in the woman's soft, friendly, unusually pleasant face. She was obviously so much older than his own mother....At that moment a car's horn signaled him that it was time to go. He couldn't wait to get home so he could have an adult-type talk with her.

"Gee, thanks a lot fer not smackin' me, Tillie—I mean Misses Davis," he sputtered. "I'm glad you turned out ta be LeMont's mom, he sure is a good friend of mine."

LeMont was still chasing his own flies. "I'm glad a'that," she said. "He sho' 'nuff loves t'play ball. He jes cain't get *enough* of it!"

Charlie's face smiled, then assumed an expression of wonder: "By the way, Misses Davis—how come LeMont's dad doesn't come out ta see the games? Does he hafta work like my dad?"

The woman's expression revealed a lifetime: "Well, LeMont's daddy ran off when LeMont was barely two. I ain't never seen him since. It's jes been LeMont and me, all these years," she said quietly. "You should be thankful you got a fine daddy that loves you, Charlie. Havin' folks that loves you is the most important thing they is."

There was a lump in his throat. Two more sharp stabs of the horn got his mouth moving again. "I gotta go now," he said feebly. "Bye, Misses Davis....Bye, LeMont! See ya next week!"

"Bye, Charlie!" LeMont yelled back as he hit the ball. (And then, keeping his eyes passionately focused on the white dot falling from the heavens, he grabbed his glove and reached for the clouds....)

"G'bye, boy," LeMont's mother said.

Charlie ran to his father's car in a full sprint. Even carrying a bat and glove, he ran much faster than he had run out his double-play ball.

ROLAND BARNES (an American's story)

Author's Notes

This is the same general story as *Oh-For-Four*, a companion piece if you will, written from the point of view of the father as opposed to the little boy. Someone who's judgment I trusted and respected read *Oh-For-Four*, liked it, and then years later suggested to me that it might be a very cool thing indeed if I could write a companion piece using the same incidents, the same dialectic between baseball and race riots, but instead told from the point of view of Charlie's dad, focusing on the dad's problems, pre-conceived ideas, and personal prejudices. While also having the two stories intersect a couple times, but only briefly. Just for linkage. It was one of the best ideas anyone ever gave me. *Roland Barnes* is the result.

    Naturally I used my own father as a treasure trove for many of the quirks and characteristics of the title character (this being the only Charlie Barnes story, by the way, where Charlie *is not* either the protagonist or co-protagonist), and that made it easy because my dad was a fascinating man in his own right and I loved him and knew him well. I miss him.

    This is the longest short-story I have ever written, 14,827 words. Nine times the length of *The Black Bee*, for example. Guess I had a lot to say. I do know I was attempting to deal with a lot of different subjects, and needed time to weave it all together. I wanted to make sure that my line-by-line narrative, whether it was rendering a scene or floating a stream-of-consciousness, was never sharper, never smoother, never richer in detail, and so I was in no hurry for the story to end.

    In any case, if this isn't the very best short-story I ever wrote, it's certainly in the top five.

    And it is also—not counting rewrites—pretty much the only story I wrote during the 1990s. Not exactly my decade of literary enlightenment! But I wasn't getting much literary encouragement from anyone in those days, not from agents or publishers, or family or friends, not even from myself, so there didn't seem to be any point in writing anything if nobody was interested. So I didn't.

ROLAND BARNES

(an American's story)

Roland Barnes was a decent man.

An honest man. A God-fearing man. Kind and considerate, dependable and principled. A man of few vices. No major ones, anyway. Friendly as a Methodist minister, moral as milk, loyal as an old hound dog. A decent, God-fearing, considerate, highly principled and ultra-quintessentially good man. Yes, he was all these things. But of all his virtues, it was 'decent' which had been his personal touchstone word ever since he first realized he *was* a man, slogging his way through Italy during The War (between scared-stiff bombing runs, that is), and then later on while faced with the rewarding yet surprisingly difficult task of raising a family. "'Never figured for a *minute*," he was often heard to smile and say, down at his favorite lunch counter, "that something as simple as bringin' up some kids could be such 'gol-darned hard *work*!" But it was. Did a decent job of it, though. For one thing, he wisely chose to raise this typical family of three small children in the Midwest, being a Midwesterner himself, in the prototypical small town of Washington, Iowa, USA, albeit with little money, with no immediate prospects for either excitement *or* money, and yet Barnes managed to accomplish this feat while locked in a state of virtually truceless conflict—which is to say lifelong combat—with an indefatigable foe, a woman, his wife, who in her craving for big-city excitement never could appreciate what perfection in life they had already achieved merely by stumbling upon this small-town Heaven right here on earth and was, therefore, forever nagging at him that they should leave.

"....now for the weather, partly cloudy in the morning but burning off by mid-afternoon, expect another scorcher with highs in the mid-nineties in the Basin, possibly one hundred in the valleys, Santa Monica should see eighty-five *with temperatures reaching as high as one hundred fifteen in the low desert, Mojave, and Palm Springs....and the Air Quality Management District has issued yet another third-stage smog alert for L.A. and Orange Counties, many schools will be closed or open only half-days, and mothers are advised that small children should rest and remain indoors...."*

And so, five years earlier, at the turn of the prevailing decade, they moved. He was, after all, a decent husband, a considerate father. And he was weary of the fight. He could fight the Germans, poverty, his own petty masculine insecurities, but he was no match for his wife. His dream of living and dying in a small town in Iowa was over. They sold the wonderful two-story wooden house, gave away the ancient family dog, loaded up the '55 Rambler Station Wagon, waved good-bye to the most perfect world he knew he would ever know, forever, and headed west.

"....KFWB news-time, seven-forty-four a.m. Recapping the hour's top story, unrest continues in the aftermath of last month's rioting in South-Central L.A., as for the second straight day L.A.P.D. reports a policeman has been wounded....sources close to Governor Brown indicate he is considering declaring Los Angeles a disaster area, and the President reportedly has expressed deep concern over what he terms 'this most troubling symbol of our troubled times'....one final note, L.A.P.D. also reveals that despite several surgeries yet another has died as a result of the fighting, failing to recover after being shot in the chest during an exchange of gunfire with officers on August thirteenth. Identity is being withheld pending notification of next of kin, but authorities have confirmed that the deceased is a local man, approximately twenty-two or twenty-three years old, Negro...."

He absentmindedly turned left, from New York Drive onto Hill Avenue. The tiny hatchback car rolled southward now, and downhill, away from the close ridge of foothills strangely invisible to its rear-view mirror, rolling redundantly, somewhat instinctively, a queer combination of duty and perpetual regret, toward the struggling hardware store on Walnut Street; just north of world-famous Colorado Boulevard, Pasadena, California, USA. He missed the old Rambler wagon. It ran like a dream and it was so roomy and oh it was such a sweet, tangible reminder of his Utopia, something only a man like him could understand, a virtually living link to his beloved small-town roots. It was the perfect car, even better than the old family Model-A when he was a kid in Spencer. That Model-A was the first car he ever fell in love with. The spoke wheels, the cloth roof, the rumble seat....He loved the spoke wheels the best. Accordingly, he often delighted in trying to explain it to his two sons. ("The faster a spoke wheel spun, boys, the more it looked like it was spinning *backwards*. No matter how hard a guy squinted at it. 'Never could get over that....")

And oh how his father had always cautioned him. Or rather *warned* him, predicting with recurrent, iron conviction, that "*There will never be another god-damned automobile built in this country that will ever measure up to the Ford Model-A, and you can put my words in the bank!*", but darned if that old Rambler Station Wagon didn't turn out to be better yet. You bet'cha....'last thing in the world he ever wanted to do was trade it in for something called a 'hatchback'. Nobody who ever had a '55 Rambler Station Wagon would ever *willingly* chuck it for a lousy, no-character.... gad, for an *apology* of a station wagon like a *hatch*back. But a man can walk to work in Smalltown, America. A set of tires lasts forever there. So too, seemingly, does a tank of gas. Not here though, not now, not in Southern California, where Roland Barnes knew he was lucky to have a round-trip commute as short as these eight long miles. Forty-eight extra miles a week. Twenty-four hundred extra miles a year. More than enough good reason to exchange 13 miles per gallon for 37 miles per gallon. And he missed walking to work. He missed the wonderful social geometry embodied by a town square. He missed Winga's, that favorite lunch counter of his back home in Washington. Everybody knew him there. Everybody talked to him there. And the prices were so low. And sometimes the coffee was free. So yes, he missed Winga's. He missed Washington. He missed the birds. He missed the leaves. He missed the change of seasons. He missed a lot of things....

Could it possibly be some sort of nutty coincidence, he often wondered, that things started falling apart just about the time he finally consented to make the move? as punishment for giving in? as the *result* of it? How absurd it is—yet so delightfully human—the way a man tends to boil down the problems of the whole world just as far as he has to, until they finally parallel and reflect his own. So it was with Barnes, an introspective and thoughtful man along with everything else, and he couldn't help but marvel at the timing. Because the 50's were indeed perfect. For both him and his country. Each was at peace, everybody liked Ike, the Yankees always won, a nice Italian fella was heavyweight champ (for a change), and maybe best of all was that the earning of a good living was easy, every man's certain inalienable right, Constitutionally guaranteed. Paradise. And oh how he *loved* it that everybody in town knew him, knew him by his first name, knew him and envied him for both his easy good humor and his fine family of three small children. But now, this current miserable decade only half over, he found himself lost and confused in this the third largest city of his equally miserable nation. First there was the JFK thing.... how could it ever *happen*?...and what would his ultraconservative wife say if she knew he'd always liked him and had even almost voted for him. But now he was gone....and in his place lingered this strange, confusing war. Everyone secretly understood that there was something wrong with this war, maybe not the war itself but certainly the management of it, he knew there was something wrong somewhere, but he didn't know exactly what. Folks were just having trouble pulling together this time. Not like his war. Nothing like his war. It was weird.

(....Why not just try a couple of decent-sized bombing runs over Hanoi? wouldn't that be enough? I mean we bombed Dresden and Berlin and the Germans quit, right? Tokyo and Hiroshima and even the *Japs* caved in, right? So don't we owe it to our boys on the ground to at least *try*? I mean what's changed over the years? Is it really that different a world? What are we afraid of? What the heck has actually *changed*?...)

But his innate lifelong patriotism and governmentally inbred nationalism notwithstanding, Barnes, frankly, was far more concerned lately with the multitude of domestic troubles infecting his own home. And they were many. Not the least among these was the endless worry over money. The cost of living, of simply *being alive* for Pete's sake, was so much higher here, so *unfairly* high, and building up a loyal clientele had been a slow, disillusioning ordeal....How could I have been so dumb as to throw away such a thriving business? he had asked himself a hundred times.... How indeed. How could he have even considered leaving a town where seemingly everyone was a customer, and, of course, knew him by his first name? But leave he had. He had to. He was no match for his wife.

He had to wonder, though....could it be the money? Could it be, really be, that it was the ceaseless concern over the Almighty Dollar which was inflicting this chilly stalemate on his marriage? Well *something* is making Betty all screwy lately....something. In fact she had quite recently—and without actually saying so—called sort of a surprise cease fire in reverse, an undeclared halt to sexual relations, for no good reason that *he* could see, and he had no idea *how* he was going to fix that. Just how does a man bring that kind of thing up with his wife, without begging the question, and still retain his cursed manly pride? For Barnes, the answer so far had been, more often than not, to simply not bring it up. He didn't know what to do. He lacked the tools. And similarly, there seemed to be no easy answer to the problem of his oldest boy, Richard. Sure, he knew that sixteen was a difficult age for a boy, and for that boy's parents, he absolutely knew it would be a difficult time because over the years everyone had been nice enough to warn him about it, but in a small Midwestern town a man does not have to worry about his sixteen-year-old son smoking marijuana cigarettes or talking back to his parents or freely ejaculating words like "bastard" or "tits" or "fuck-head" or "cocksucker" now does he....He wondered if anybody nowadays had the wisdom to be a good father.... Ricky was away at summer camp for the moment, for a whole blessed week in fact, and merely the notion, just the mere conscious thought that this was one blessed thing he would not have to worry about or deal with or struggle through for the next few days fairly saturated Roland Barnes with the warm, welcome prophylaxis of relief. Thank God there were no real problems with the other two kids. They were his rod and his staff. If only they could just stay so blasted cute and unspoiled and respectful and safe, and young, forever....

"....*in sports, the Dodgers take on the Cardinals tonight at the stadium to open a three-game weekend series with the defending champs....going into tonight's action, Walter Alston's boys of summer still cling to a narrow lead over the Giants in their quest to bring the pennant back to L.A., with the hated San Franciscans beginning a three-game set of their own in Chicago....in tonight's match-up, it will be Don Drysdale pitching for the locals, with Bob Gibson on the hill for Saint Louis in a battle of top-quality righthanders....*"

And now this rioting thing. Of all the....and in broad daylight for Pete's sake? looting, shooting, violence in the streets? open defiance of police?....my God, what *is* the world coming to! It's this, this....this *place*, Barnes mused as he crossed Washington Boulevard (into Pasadena now) this so-called 'climate', this heat, relentless heat, year-round heat, and the *air*! He rubbed at his eyes. Already stinging, and not even eight o'clock.... shoot. He blinked up a tear or two to salve the pain. Then, quite bravely, he experimented with three-quarters of a deep breath, stopping only when the dull stabbing in his lungs threatened to reach down even further into his narrow, troubled chest. He could scarcely believe how much the burning in his lungs matched the fire in his eyes. They were twin sensations. Familiar. Like accidentally getting too close to the mouth of an incinerator; breathing in the smoke, blinking away the cinders and tears....and now he tried to remember the first time he ever actually heard the word smog. It actually made him chuckle out loud against the swelling whine of rush-hour traffic. In Los Angeles they'd never even *heard* of trash-burning incinerators (except the bureaucrats down at city hall, that is, who said they were illegal), and back home in Iowa he knew *nobody* believed his letters describing the smog. He barely believed it himself. For his breed of man, from his roots, it was like something out of a science-fiction paperback. Air that can completely block out a killer sun? Air that actually masks the intimidating lurch of the mountains? No wonder they steal and break windows, he thought. They can't breathe.

    Still, it was hard for him to abide anyone not obeying the law. Barnes was not only a God-fearing man he was also a practicing Golden-Ruler, a man who had been raised from the cradle to respect other people, *all* people, respect their space, respect their rights, their property. Do unto others. Heck, it doesn't matter if you're religious or not, just treat people square and they'll do the same to you....or at least they should....Anyway, it was hard for him to understand what pressures might make a good man a vandal, or a killer, or a common thief. He just couldn't believe it was about money, everybody was short of money these days, he'd stack *his* money problems up against *anybody's*, but nobody would ever catch *him* breaking the law. Sometimes he would lie awake on his side of the bed and wonder, wonder how would he ever pay his bills....$45 a month for the tiny hatchback car.... $156 a month for the ugly, one-story stucco box that barely held them....$3.25 an hour just to have some sweet, wonderfully inept old colored lady help Betty with the housework....insane. Not to mention how fast a kid wears out his tennis shoes on these stupid asphalt playgrounds out here, he thought. Maybe grass just can't grow in an oxygenless world....but at $6 a pair? How does *any*body make ends meet in this crazy town?...A man simply cannot afford to have three kids running through shoes every sixty days at $6 a pair, *no way*! It's un-American.

    He turned right onto Walnut Street, and then into the asphalt parking lot of his store on Walnut. Maybe that was the worst thing of all. The business. It wasn't working, and he had to make it work. For a family man, financial failure is not an option. But it was so much harder out here. Back home it was mainly feed and grain, farm implements, fertilizer, but with no livestock or family-run farms or even *grass* to feed or fertilize in this futuristic netherworld he knew he would have to get by with the regular, 'standard' hardware only. Not that he minded a fair challenge. Never had. But the profit margin in a standard, regular line of hardware is so....so *agonizingly* fair, ha! He had to smile at himself in the rear-view. Too bad, he thought, there was nobody around to acknowledge his still-intact good humor. In fact, nobody knew him here. Not really. Even his attempts over the years to get to know his own neighbors had been met with a strange, bug-eyed resistance, people looking at him and giving off vibes like he was invading their privacy, or even trespassing. Back home folks don't even keep their doors locked....Here I might as well be a cotton-pickin' burglar, he lamented aloud. And the result was that there was none of that delightful free business that comes from being everybody's friend. He knew his wife would kill him if she knew about the two bank loans he'd already taken out against the house....but he would not break the law. He would not sacrifice his self-respect *to* money or *for* money. No. Not Roland Barnes. Never. He was a decent man.

"*....recapping our top story, continued violence—*" {click}

As he extricated his long lanky frame from the cramped car, Barnes, his face tightening now against the hot, ash-tasting air furnace of the outside world, noticed the old man. The old man was shuffling (for indeed shuffling is the only way to describe the peculiar method of ambulation this creature was using to transport himself from place to place), shuffling out the back door of the store next door, ever-present broom in hand. The old man could boast of steady work as a janitor at several of the rowed-together businesses on Walnut between Hill and Lake Avenue, his included. Gad he works hard, Barnes thought, and for a lot less than *I'd* ever do it....nice fella, too. But just seeing him standing there, hunched over like he always was, simply sweeping off the back steps of the pet store, the sight of his face alone produced an instant surge of acid in Barnes's empty stomach. He felt it, even recognized it, the what if not the why, and good man that he was he was badly bothered by it. And he felt oddly good inside that he could still be disappointed in himself....

Now he just watched the old man, the old face grimacing between long slow broom strokes. Hard to gauge the age....just a few curls of white integrated into a horseshoe of what reminded him of a steel-black Brillo pad....hard to tell. Sixty? Maybe sixty-five? Maybe even older than that? Maybe. The bald spot in the middle glistened darkly in the morning glare. The man was humming something, and the almost-recognizable old tune threw the only ripple into the flat silence of this early hour, accompanied only by the occasional explosion of an engine backfire floating over from Walnut. No birds were present to whistle their approval; in fact there were *never* any birds on Walnut Street, no dogs, no grass, no apologies to Nature. That was yet another thing distancing Barnes ever further from his beloved small-town Utopia. No birds on the way to work....none....as usual, he found himself missing the birds. And then he noticed it. Fastidious to the core, it was only a matter of time before he noticed that the old man was doing it wrong. Short, quick, efficient little strokes was the right way to sweep, his own father had taught him that, and had reinforced the notion by giving young Roland plenty of sweeping chores during his youth. Barnes naturally became an accomplished sweeper, still was. 'Certainly could teach *this* old fella a thing or two, he thought....but no need. Because even though the old man was a lousy sweeper Barnes could still admire him, for his steady work ethic, for his simple, unsophisticated aura of integrity, and so he certainly didn't mind paying the old fellow a few bucks to sweep up around his own store even though he, Barnes, knew he could do a much better job of it himself and probably needed those few bucks just as bad. No need to embarrass the man. He started to smile, but then, catching sight of the old man's smiling face, it happened again. Another violent injection. More venom spurting from nowhere into his intestines. Now his own thoughtful brow was twisted into mis-shape, a grimace of great urgency. He wished he could just stop thinking about it. But he could not. He simply could not segregate his mind from the no-win war raging not twenty miles to the south. It's true Barnes had been scared in his war, and for good reason, but his war was nothing like this. This was terrifying. So random. So seemingly senseless in its ratio of risk to reward. But it was happening just the same, and the field of battle seemed to be any city street it touched, things were bad enough for him right now, the last thing he needed was for his store to be robbed or vandalized, terrorized, torched. And in a nation of civilized men, *my God*, how did it ever come to *this*! And yet at the same time he felt genuinely lucky; lucky that when he did finally bring his family west, it was to live in a neighborhood that happened merely by chance to be located some twenty miles north of this most confusing unpleasantness. It was about the only lucky break he could remember getting in a long, long time....

"G'mornun', Missuh Barnes. How yuh doin' this fine Septembuh mornun'?"

"Hiya, Jiggs ol' boy—whaddaya know?"

Neither expecting a reply, the two tight-faced men disappeared quickly into back doors.

Almost seven. The hatchback humming, or rather groaning, fighting its way slowly up Hill and finally heading home. The mountains, half-visible in his windshield, grow from formless gray into a grainy brown outline as the sun falls away to his left, the smog losing strength in direct proportion to the sun's welcome flight, but Barnes knows from daily experience that before the thickly wooded foothills he knows are there can then turn from brown all the way back to green the ocean will swallow the sun, and its last redeeming light, and thus he will not be allowed any of it. It is as if all the color of the world is escrowed in limbo—trapped somewhere between the faint memory of that perfect globe Man had been given and the hard reality of his inability to live in Natural harmony upon it—and as a member of the Human Race, and by that definition guilty, Roland Barnes's punishment is that he rarely glimpses the gorgeous green slopes of the San Gabriel Mountains, which he had moved two thousand miles against his will to see. Such frustrating purgatory. The mountains are one of the few really good things about his new world (Iowa, for all her virtues, is flat, mountainless lady) and yet Barnes is so often denied them. He draws a long deep breath to brace himself against his fatigue. Being a devout ex-smoker it reminds him of a dirty ashtray, and tastes as bad as it smells, but it is late enough in the day that at least his lungs are spared. This stale deep breath is at least a full one.

And what a day. Another red-letter tickertape peach of a banner day for the Barneses. Total gross receipts? A little under 200 dollars. Net? What net....He does not even want to contemplate that word. As far as he is concerned all it adds up to, his day's pitiful labor, is merely another frustrating eleven hours spent—or rather frittered away—along the endless, fruitless, thankless treadmill of Life. And hopefully, Betty won't think to ask him to go into it in any detail....

Crossing Washington Boulevard (For Pete's sake, does there have to be a *Washington* Boulevard?) he draws in another deep breath. He is grateful for the absence of pain. They are into Altadena now. The little car's groans grow more pained and irregular as Hill fights its way up the steepening grade. Altadena is the beginning of the foothills, and all northbound streets must gradually rise to that challenge. Barnes down-shifts into low. He approaches New York Drive with the caution of a man expecting a train to cross his path. But he can't remember the last time he was even on a train. Cars are backing up behind him, but he doesn't care. Lousy day....If they want me to go any faster, he muses, well they can just come in tomorrow and buy a lousy wrench or something....maybe a whole new sprinkler system, sure. He comes to a complete stop at New York Drive. He takes his time looking west, east, then west again. Cars are getting impatient. A couple of them blow their horns. He finally turns right.

He goes about a half mile. Deep in thought, he is barely conscious of where he is or is going. At Sinaloa Avenue, purely by instinct, he turns left.

Funny, he thinks now, how he doesn't mind selling automatic sprinklers but he knows he would never install them in his own yard. His little patch of grass deserves better than that....His right hand scratches absentmindedly at a blond crew cut between gear shiftings. Fingertips find easy access to warm scalp sweat through the thin blond flat-top. Damn.... seven o'clock and still hot enough to make a man sweat, wouldn't that frost ya....He reaches for the radio, but remembering the morning news bulletins he thinks better of it and lets the sweatslick hand drop limply to a bony knee. This day is finally, mercifully over, no need to spoil that feeling of relief with more of the wrong kind of news from his adopted mother city. People have been coming here in droves for fifty years, he silently marvels. Hard to believe. How easy, from a psychological point of view at least, the pioneers must have had it. Going from crowded city to quiet wilderness? Shoot, anybody could do that....but going from comparative wilderness to modern super-city, to this ultrafuturistic, speed infected, mechanical push-button world of noise and soot and sirens and tangled freeways, now that *is* tough. It has certainly been a tough five years for Roland Gustav Barnes. He squints hard now, searching in vain for the mountains, which the retreating smog has finally regurgitated, but which now become swallowed virtually whole by the punctual encroach of Darkness. Perhaps he is merely squinting from his own thoughts, as Barnes is typically a squinting thinker. The irony of the 20th century....this reverse migration, a journey westward, yes, just as the pioneers had plunged westward in obedience to the forward thrust of their compasses and dreams, but this time backwards, back to the cities, back into that crowded megalopolis of sin from which their ancestors had so fiercely, freely fled. Being a thoughtful man as 20th-century men go, Barnes considers that very irony even as he pulls the hatchback into its driveway, the eight-mile commute completed eleven and a half hours after it was begun....

"Home again *early*, are we?"

She does not look at him save a brief, purposeful glare. And he knew it was coming. It had been seventeen years since he had first suffered it, way back in their carefree post-war Chicago days. They weren't even married then. It was at a favorite restaurant on south Drexel, one of those tight, comfortable places that can only exist within brief cracks in Time, a place where the whole crowd would hang around, where the coffee was always strong and the danish was always fresh, and he had made an off-hand remark about some insignificant thing like maybe the paradoxical nature of blind religious subservience in a Democratic society, or perhaps the rising cost of latex condoms and other rubber products in a recovering post-war economy and the next thing he knows his face is burning from her eyes, and he doesn't quite know why, but he is no less sorry for not knowing, he *is* sorry, and he finds himself hoping he never has to feel that look, that glare, ever again as long as he lives. Little does he know that he will be disappointed in this regard many times, many times every year in fact, for *practically* as long as he lives.

But this time he refuses the gambit. He will not let her provoke a fight, even though she is patently in the wrong for belittling his pathetic attempt to secure for them a decent living, and she deserves the fight she is asking for. He knows he is the man and she is only the woman, and therefore he must be better than all of that....

"Sorry I'm late, hon. A lot of last-minute customers for some reason," he says, stretching truth all the way into a lie. He follows her retreating nightgown into the kitchen. He can scarcely believe how prominent her once-tiny butt has become over the years...."Sure am starved, though— 'dinner about ready?"

"It was ready an hour ago," Betty Barnes says sharply. "Your daughter is in her room, and your number-two son, get this, is washing his hands without being told. And he won't take off that silly uniform for anything."

"Hey! He must've had a good day!"

"A better one than I've had, that's for sure. There's your paper. Sit down and maybe I'll *finally* get this show on the *road*."

Roland Barnes now begins to leaf through his newspaper with the carefulness of a horsethief. He is as sick of reading bad news as he is of hearing it. What he searches for within the risky labyrinth of the front-page section are the occasional crumbs of Hope and Goodness that a big-city editor will deign to allow him. His seven-year-old daughter runs up from behind and gives his ear a wet sloppy kiss, an affection tool she has just recently learned from the television set, then flees the room with equal enthusiasm. Barnes continues to search through the paper, holding it up in front of him with both hands like it was a giant book.

"Dad, what's Watts?"

The word fairly stabs him. During these last few weeks it has become, for certain, his least favorite word. He peers above the top edge of his paper and standing there, with a quizzical look on his face, is a little boy, all skin and bones under a somewhat oversized head, a head further burdened with thick, heavy-looking tangles of blond curls. The boy is standing in stocking feet, wearing a baseball uniform, the floppy thing more than a little too large for the definitively thin, Barneslike frame. The innocent, cheerful face is crying out for information. Barnes's heart aches. His boy is the cutest little boy in the whole world. He is perfect and pure and unspoiled, and now some stupid jerk has gone and taught him that ugly word. He knows, at that exact moment, one of those rare, mountaintop experiences that stamp and define a man's very existence, that his three children are absolutely the three most important things in the world to him, more important than his own life, more precious, even, than his dear wife, certainly more important than their ever-wobbly marriage, and he knows that he would do anything in the world to insulate at least the younger two from what is becoming a very ugly world. And he knows he cannot. He closes up his newspaper. The best he can do in this case is delay it, camouflage, confuse: "Something not nearly as much fun as baseball!" he says cheerfully.

"*Nuthin's* better'n baseball!" says the son.

"You bet'cha!" concurs the father.

....And then suddenly he felt it.

On the left side of his face. It was her, or rather her eyes, that brief, purposeful glare which he had hated for seventeen years and which now meant that he had, in her eyes, erred yet again, though he was not at first aware how he had, this time, accomplished it. But then her glare shifted from his face to the folded-up newspaper, and it hit him....oh God, the headlines....*damn*!....Instantly he rolled the paper up into a makeshift bat, ruffled the boy's blond hair, and smacked him loudly on the backside. They both laughed. The glare softened against his left cheek, but it did not go away. He gathered up his number-two son in arms whose genuine strength was somewhat belied by their lack of size and definition. He hugged the boy for all he was worth, and the boy laughed louder. His little sister came a-running to the sound of her brother in such a good mood. Barnes hid the newspaper in the silverware drawer. Only then did his wife completely soften her face and sit down to dinner.

They talked baseball. Barnes had missed his son's Little League game this day, as was usual. He knew the boy had been slumping at the plate lately, knew how seriously a boy takes these terrible things, a batting slump being something every bit as terrible to a ten-year-old boy as Barnes's cursed money and marital problems were to him. Accordingly, he tightened up inside with genuine urgency and apprehension over what he was about to say, turned to his right to face the boy, and asked the necessary question of the day in as casual a tone as he was able:

"So how'd it go out there, son—do any good? At the plate, I mean."

"Three-for-three," the boy burst forth, struggling to muffle his enthusiasm, "Had a triple in the sixth, scored the winning run."

And with these words returned joy, order, and purpose to the life of Roland Gustav Barnes. His problems disappeared, and the world made sense again.

"*Really*? Hey, that's great, Charlie! Didja hear that, Betty? Three-for-three!"

Betty Barnes half-smiled.

"It was the new bat, Dad! It felt so good in my hands, I just *knew* I could hit with it! And I'm the only guy on the team with a bitchin' two-colored one, too. I had three guys come up and try and borrow it, but don't worry, I wouldn't let'm. I've *never* been over four hunnerd before, thanks again for buyin' it for me, Dad—it's so bitchin' I can't believe it!"

"Well, anything to break out of a slump," Barnes said slyly.

"Watch your mouth, Charlie," Betty Barnes said sharply, bitchin' being back then a word slightly out of step with the plodding pace of the nation's prevailing moral code, and completely out of step with Betty Barnes's own moral code. She then said grace, whereupon the table was immediately blurred by plates of food being filled, and serving dishes being passed back and forth from Barnes to eager Barnes.

"What's the big deal about a dumb ol' baseball game?"

"That's what I say, precious," the mother said to her daughter. "I mean heavens-to-Betsy."

"Whaddayou two old women talking about? Fer Pete's sake, I only wish the games were scheduled at a time when I could—"

"When you could go and scream and yell like a wild man?"

"Oh, are we gonna start that again...."

....It was at roughly this juncture when the conversation, for Barnes at least, began to disintegrate. In truth, he could scarcely remember the last time he'd actually enjoyed a conversation with Betty. Lately she'd always managed to find some stupid axe to grind....and this time it was her well-documented antipathy to baseball, gad, of all the silly things. How baseball was a waste of time, how baseball was responsible for over-aggressiveness in young boys, how, amazingly, baseball and it's recent attendant violence was somehow at least partially responsible for all that confusing unpleasantness down in the South-Central L.A. war zone...or was it that the Watts thing was somehow to blame for some Mexican pitcher on the Giants trying to use a bat the other day to split open some colored Dodger fella's skull.... whatever. It was always something with that woman. 'Just wish she'd show a little excitement around the boy, as concerns *his* baseball at least....kids can sense that sorta thing....'think she'd at least go and drag her fat lazy butt to one of his games once in awhile, since his old man can't make it....darn it the luck. And as if he didn't have enough bad luck these days, Barnes also learned at this rather unappetizing dinner conversation that his wife had seen fit to fire the maid. Matilda Davis. Nicest little old colored lady in the world, reckoned Barnes; even if she was a little inept as a housecleaner. And just who in the world is going to hire a klutz like Tillie Davis now, he wondered. More importantly, he mused further, just what will be the negative fallout upon *him*, as the result of his wife's infernal temper....a more expensive maid? an even more irascible Betty? Perhaps merely a flood of inexplicable guilt feelings, the way a woman can sometimes make a man feel guilty about something that is not only not his fault, but rather *hers*. As usual, all the problems a harsh world could come up with were collecting at his feet. Darn it the luck, *darn* it the....But at least his number-two son was apparently out of his slump. Three-for-three. Batting average up over four hundred. At least the world made sense again....

Ten-thirty. Roland Barnes is standing in his son's bedroom doorway, watching him sleep. The boy's face is absolutely serene, perfectly unaware of Life's senseless imperfections, oblivious to an illogical, unjust world that will one day swallow his innocence whole. Such beautiful curly hair, thinks Barnes....almost girlish the way it caresses his pillow. He wonders, will this head of wild curls develop a preference for a simple blond crew cut someday, like his old man's? Instantly he is stung by the counter-notion that this beautiful young head might even go *bald* one day, baldness being very much a part of the Barnes family gene history, much more prevalent on his side than Betty's, and that therefore it would be his fault. (All this despite having once read somewhere that it is solely the mother's genes which determine baldness, but all that female chromosome stuff had never made any sense to him so he had rejected the theory altogether.)

Fortunately there are more important things to worry about these days. Like the Little League baseball season....

"Coming to bed?"

He turns around. She is standing in the hallway, in a faded red nightgown. He smiles: He remembers how he'd picked it up in a department store in Iowa City, for their fifth wedding anniversary. Just an impulse buy, very expensive. He remembers what a snazzy, silky, sexy piece of bright red lingerie it was back then, over ten years ago now. Now there is a ten-inch rip down one side, from the hip to just below the armpit....

"Gosh, I wish I could have been there today," whispers Barnes, turning back to look at the boy.

"If you were there watching, he would've probably missed every ball."

"He might've homered. You don't know."

"I don't know?"

"I'm saying you could've been there."

"Oh Roland, he doesn't want his mom there, he wants *you*! Why couldn't you go? You could've taken off an hour or two early, certainly."

"Do I have to explain it to you again?"

"Fine. Explain it to me."

He is angry now. He wants to turn around and let her have it, all of it, vent his fed-up spleen against her indifference. But he does not. He stands silent, rage welling up red in his thin neck and high forehead. He is the man, and knows he must be better than all that....

"Roland, it's late. Come to bed."

Now he turns to her again. He looks her up and down. This time he will not hold back. "What for?" he whispers sharply.

"Oh, suit yourself," says Betty Barnes, casually but with just as much bite, thundering down the hallway to the bedroom.

He follows her into the bedroom at the end of a lengthy interval, designed to let her know he is not following either her or her bland invitation. She has already brushed her teeth and is now brushing out her short thick black hair. Barnes silently begins to undress. He is out of his white dress shirt and black work slacks quickly. Great care is taken to hang the pants so that all the creases are perfectly lined up. As is his curious custom, he leaves his shoes and socks on for the last. She does not look at him as he undresses. He watches her peel the tattered nightgown up and over her head. She is left wearing only panties, no bra, no nylons. She looks awful good for forty-three, Barnes almost says out loud, even with the big butt....even the breasts aren't too saggy, for an old gal!...He starts to step out of his boxer shorts, but stops when he feels the tightness between his legs....darn it the luck....how can a man be so all-fired mad at a woman and still get the itch....stop it, he says to himself; lie down, *get soft*!...damn.

"Turn the lights off, will you dear?" She has climbed quickly into bed. She is lying on her left side, with her back to him. He pulls off the left shoe, then the right, but decides to leave his socks and boxer shorts on.

"Can't you just go and see him play tomorrow?"

"Roland, I have a million things to do tomorrow. I have to take Mother to lunch at Beadle's Cafeteria, I mean I promised her, there's an Officer's Wives meeting at three, and of course now the whole housework thing is back in my lap, heavens-to-Betsy—I get tired just thinking about tomorrow. I can't."

"Alright, alright. I'll pick him up after the game."

"You can't just work a half day and go watch?"

"Betty, we're in trouble, don't you get it? My business is on the ropes, and the one resource I have to fight back with is my *time*! I hafta be there as long as there's enough daylight to bring in a customer. I hafta be there."

"Well you don't hafta shout."

"I'm not shouting, I'm....I'm poor, dammit. We're poor."

Betty Barnes is used to neither her husband complaining nor hearing him utter even such a mild curse word. Either is enough to make her roll over in amazement. When she sees him standing there, in his black, knee-high 'Supp-hose' support socks (*"We don't care how many socks you own. None of them can do as much for you as Supp-hose Socks."*), sees him nearly poking through the thin fabric of his boxers and trying to hide it with his hands, her unfortunate response is laughter: "Oh, my! When did *you* become such a frisky colt?"

"I'm just a man," is an embarrassed Barnes's best and only defense. "A married man, in case you forgot."

Betty Barnes smiles forth a sorrowful expression that can only spell pity: "I haven't. But I'm pooped. Good night, dear," she says dryly, rolling back onto her left side.

Barnes switches off the light and crawls into bed, his front to her back. The tightness between his legs has not abated itself. He slithers up to her, up against her, two spoons in a drawer. Her skin is sticky. He begins by stroking the backs of her legs; she pretends to be asleep, but that is just a part of their little game. The doubt, the not knowing for sure whether or not his clumsy advances will be accepted, is the essence of their sex life and the essential excitement of it as well. Seventeen years they have been rehearsing, refining the same silent roles; they have sharpened them down to a ballet. Barnes moves in closer to her heavily breathing form. His finger massage takes on greater urgency. Still, she has given him no hint as to the outcome. His right hand slides finally over her hip and along her rounded belly. Here goes....He knows if he can only reach the warm, damp crescent of acceptance which had always been there that he has made it....maybe tonight, he muses hopefully, finally....but no. Just as his hand is dropping down to investigate she parries him, a simple roll to the right, placing her flat on her stomach with a solid fold of bedsheet between them. The issue decided, Barnes rolls over to his side of the bed and drifts quickly off to sleep.

The next morning the streets of Altadena were virtually empty, but that didn't make the driving of them any easier. He hated working Saturdays, hated *having to* work them. And the air on Saturday was just as hot and the smog was just as thick and the mountains were just as invisible. So a few less cars between him and his ten hours of routine daily toil didn't really make any difference.

In fact, this time, it was worse. Charlie's game. It was the weekend and there would be fathers in the stands but he, cash-poor Roland Barnes, would be chained to an empty hardware store. What my own boy must think of me, thought Barnes....I'll make it up to him. Maybe I'll take him to a Dodger game next week, sure....'be one more game than *my* old man ever took me to....no....no, that's not technically the truth-------

"*Hey*! Why don'tcha try pullin' yer fuckin' *head* out of yer ass, *asshole*!"

Barely aware of how close he has just come to meeting Death, Barnes did not even glance for the voice, cruised right through the stop sign at New York Drive and Hill Avenue while barely slowing down, then went back to his recollections of the one professional baseball game old Gustav Emmanuelsson Barnes ever took him to. Semi-professional would be more accurate. Major leaguers to be sure, but coming in October with the season already over this game was more of a barnstorming exhibition, Rogers Hornsby and Johnny Mize and a bunch of guys from different big-league teams on one side, a bunch of guys he had never heard of on the other. The elder Barnes had seen an advertisement for the game in the *Spencer Daily*

Reporter, and then asked young Roland if he wanted to go down to Des Moines to see it. Of course the boy said yes. Des Moines was less than a couple hundred miles away, but to young Roland that represented the other side of the world, an adventure of Odyssean proportions. Few memories from his youth were clearer in his mind than that Spencer-to-Des Moines voyage....He recalled even now the exact route they took, first a zig-zag down U.S. Highway 71, then east on State Road 141, finally penetrating the Hawkeye State's capital city from the northwest....'course Interstate 80 wasn't even laid out yet. The old Model-A, the one with the spoke wheels and the cloth roof and the rumble seat, was the perfect touring car for such an assignment, it cruised at forty or forty-five without any wobble or vibration to speak of, and even though when they made the trip that particular October it was starting to get cold out in western Iowa he remembered distinctly that they drove with both windows down. Hard to believe we made it there in under six hours....including that one quick stop for a late breakfast in Coon Rapids, just after we made the turn from south to east....funny. 'Seems even more awesome and mysterious now, knowing you could easily get there in half the time, if you were in a hurry....

He remembered how they didn't talk much on the way. And he recalled how old Gust seemed strangely ill-equipped to handle his usual barrage of child's questions: How come there aren't any big-league teams in Iowa? Why play baseball in October if it's not even the World Series? Why were great players like Hornsby and Mize wasting their time playing guys not even good enough to be in the big leagues?...How come you never wanted to take me to a game before now? Gust Emmanuelsson never was a talkative sort of a man. And when he did talk, the words usually came out salty and profane. But he always preferred to stay away from words, any words at all if given a choice....and changing his name to Barnes because it had a nice folksy, conversational, Yankee ring to it didn't change things any....

(His present-day self turned left off of New York Drive and started down Lake Avenue, having blown the usual left turn at Hill.)

....And they seemed to talk even less during the game itself. In fact, Roland Gustav Barnes now recalled, even at the time he remembered thinking how irritating that was. It was almost as if the old man was *refusing* to answer his questions! *Gad*, that frosted my butt....'good game, too....a slicker, quicker brand of baseball than they play today. It was the other team, recalled the forty-two year old Barnes, his thirteen-year-old brain doing everything for him now but drive the car, man, they were like dancers and waterbugs and magicians all rolled into one: "How can they be better than the big-leaguers, Papa?" he remembered protesting. But the old man sat silent on his wooden plank seat. Maddening. Yet young Barnes somehow managed to convert his frustration into a thorough concentration on the game. How *could* they be better? he had wondered....but they *were*. It was *obvious*. He was only thirteen, but it was obvious. Their grace and speed on the double-play, their dash and daring on the basepaths, gad, just they way they *moved about* set them apart....two of them, especially. Charleston and Bell. The scorecard, curiously, had omitted the first names. Those two were just this side of unbelievable, Barnes recalled now, like players from another planet; *leagues* ahead of anyone on either side, he allowed himself the pun. They were so good it looked like they were just toying with Hornsby's boys....

 Of course even back then it didn't take him long to figure out the primary, defining characteristic of this particular non-league baseball match. That was easy. The guys on the other team were all as black as coal. Literally. He had never seen a Negro before. He had always wanted to. And he just wasn't the type of kid to let such a wonderful watershed experience slip past him like a bad-hop grounder, no way. The surprising thing, even then, wasn't that one team was all white and the other all black, or that the all-black team won the game by a score of 5 to 2, for even a casual evaluation of Bell's and Charleston's performances exposed them as clearly superior to any product the white team could field (especially with Hornsby past his prime), and with Bell scoring two runs and stealing two bases and Charleston singling and doubling and driving in three runs (and all nine of them fielding their positions like some wondrous tribe of charcoal-colored aliens) it was a wonder the final tally wasn't *more* lopsided. No. None of that. What confounded him that day (sitting spellbound on one of those uncompromising wooden bench seats which were the hallmark of *any* ballpark back in 1936, be it major league or minor) *was that players the caliber of Charleston and Bell would actually refuse to play on a big-league team*. Did they enjoy playing so much with their dark black friends that the lure of a big-league club and a big-league contract didn't exist? "How come Bell and Charleston aren't on Hornsby's All-Stars, Papa?" young Roland had queried his father, "Don't they *wanna* be on a major league team? Don't they *like* the white players, Pop?" But old Gust Barnes would not answer. He just stared straight ahead, his sage squint and aquiline nose pointing out towards the center field fence, in the direction of things, apparently, discernable only to he. In fact, the old man uttered not one complete sentence the whole game. Not one....Good Lord, how irritating that was!....'*still* makes me mad, after all these years, Barnes almost said out loud....

(The hatchback forded Washington Boulevard, thereby taking him into Pasadena.)

....He recalled hearing men in the crowd whisper things, like how Hornsby was way past his prime and how Mize was still very green and had a ways to go before he was in *his* prime, and how the boys weren't putting out, weren't giving it their all, that sort of thing. It all rang hollow, though....even then. That's what got him to thinking. Because if there is one quality basic to all men, to Americans in particular, it is a hatred of losing. All real men, all real Americans, are born with a loathing of being 'shown up' by anyone, particularly by someone judged to be inferior. He learned that lesson early in life, as all Americans do, so it was easy to discount the possibility that the major league fellows might not be trying....

He heard other things too. Things the men in the crowd were far less whispery about, for the most part. Things like "*fan* that uppity nigger!" and "hey pitcher, you let a *nigger* get a hit off'n you?" and even "niggers go home!", wherever that was and whatever that meant, but of course he had never even heard the word nigger before, being just a regular thirteen-year-old little kid from Spencer, Iowa, had no idea in the world what exactly it referred to. Naturally, then, the word generated no particular feelings inside of him at the time, negative or positive (Although when he heard his gruff old grandfather use it later that same year, for some reason it generated within him strange feelings of guilt and embarrassment so strong he felt like crawling in a hole.). There was only one thing to do: "What's a nigger, Papa?" he asked his dad, but old Gust, as was his iron conviction on this gray October day in 1936, said nothing. Made me so damn mad, thought Barnes....'never did explain the nigger thing....died without even trying....

The long drive back up to Spencer definitely felt different than the short drive down. His father gave off a strange sort of aura, not of happiness or anything quite so giddy (in fact he never risked a single smile) but rather a feeling of....who knows, of dutiful performance maybe, of 'completion', a sort of stubborn fatherly satisfaction. Roland definitely recalled thinking at the time how his dad seemed, without even smiling or actually saying so, utterly pleased with himself. Even though he continued to steadfastly refuse to answer any of the boy's unending barrage of questions, questions regarding the great and curious game of baseball they had just witnessed. About halfway up Highway 71 he finally, suddenly said, "Son, you just god damn remember what you saw today, 'hear?" And that was all he said. Eleven words. All he ever said about any of it, ever....

When he turned into the asphalt parking lot of his hardware store on Walnut Street the old man was there, a dignified, stooped-over figure under a glistening Brillo pad of hair, and as it did 24 hours earlier the acid spurted and then congealed in the stomach of Roland Gustav Barnes. Realizing this immediately, he made it go away by sheer force of will. The old man was sweeping up around Barnes's store this time, for the first time all week, as Barnes could only convince himself he could afford it but once a week. Barnes didn't get out of the car immediately. The old man did not acknowledge the car's presence, he swept in long slow strokes with his head down, so Barnes took the opportunity to study him. Such a proud, consistent, hard-working fella, thought Barnes....does his job, does it his way, doesn't care what anybody else thinks of him or how he does his work, 'long as, as....Suddenly, all at once, he understood more of what went on in that ballgame back in Iowa in 1936 than he had understood in the sum of the twenty-nine years since it occurred. And this time he was determined to do something about it.

"Hiya, Jiggs old boy—whaddaya know?"

"Missuh Barnes, g'mornin'. An' ain't it a fine ol' summer's day we havin'...."

"So far," said Barnes. "Say Jiggs. Hows about you and I having lunch today?"

"Say what?"

"No, c'mon, how 'bout it? We've known each other for years and we've never once had lunch together. I think it's a disgrace!"

"Now Missuh Barnes, why you all duh sudden wanna break bread wit' ol' Jiggs here?"

"Cut it out, I won't take no for an answer," Barnes substituted for an actual answer of his own, laughing slightly and intentionally to cloud the issue. He pocketed his hands in baggy trousers, then freed the right to scratch the sweat gathering atop the flattened head. It suddenly occurred to him that he had no idea where Jiggs went off to every day, after his morning rounds were completed: "Meet me here around noontime, okay?"

The old man smiled and shook his head. "Well, if'n you feel we gotta," he said tiredly, "I be here 'couple minutes fo' noon." Barnes nodded, and the old man returned immediately to his sweeping.

The hours passed reluctantly through the hot factory-furnace of morning. The day thus forged from this grim coupling of temperature and time was, to put it mildly, an imperfect one. Barnes serviced just six customers in four hours. Times being what they were, he privately thanked God for each and every one. At precisely two minutes before twelve the old man poked his gleaming brown head inside the door. Barnes motioned him in, then held up one finger; as if to say wait one minute, as he was taking care of one last potentially paying guest:

"Let me say it again. All I'm looking for is just one five-eighths socket. I just don't need any other sizes today."

"Sir, we're out of the five-eighths."

"No, *sir*, you are not—and that's exactly my *point*!"

The man across the counter from Roland Barnes was about thirty. His black hair was short and thick, his handsome features tanned and chiseled like a movie star's. Barnes took care to neither glower nor smile at him. He also fought to keep his eyes off the younger man's suit, a marvelous silken-gray garment he figured to be at least a week's current gross income for him. He waited for a moment before responding, making sure his voice came through as friendly and accommodating as possible:

"Sir, please be reasonable. That socket set goes for eleven ninety-five."

"Your internal operation here is not my problem."

"Come on. You can't seriously expect me to break open a complete wrench and socket set for just one socket. Obviously I'd be stuck with the—"

"I don't see why the hell not," the younger man snapped back crisply, his controlled, professional tone more patronizing than angry. "You're the one who has failed to perform here, within this sacred little covenant of commerce. I don't see why you should expect me to pay in time and inconvenience for your failure to make sure your miserable shelves are stocked properly."

"But I—"

"Particularly when the very item which I seek is ensconced most fortuitously, right here, within this handy little *pack*age!" declared the gray-suited man, punctuating the 'pack' in package by slamming the wrench and socket set violently down upon the wood counter. Barnes's head snapped back from the noise and his eyes slammed shut. When he opened them the man across the counter was wearing a smug, closed-mouth smile on his tanned, handsome face. Barnes glanced over the gray silk shoulder and found the old man, whose eyes were still shut from the counter-clap of noise and whose head was down and twisted away to one side. While Barnes struggled to hold his temper, he saw the old man walk quietly behind a shelf of tools, out of view.

"Look, friend. I want to do anything I can to accommodate you. Anything within reason. And you strike me as a most gracious and reasonable man." He barely recognized his own voice. He couldn't help wondering who was thinking up the words. He could feel the old man's eyes on him from behind the far aisle. But he could also feel the weight of those two bank loans, sitting heavily on shoulders far too scrawny to carry them....

"If you truly wish to accommodate me, *friend*, you can accept the fifty-two cents I am more than willing to part with in exchange for that five-eighths socket in this package."

"Fifty-two cents?"

"Certainly. Your empty little bin on that shelf over there, the one that is supposed to be stocked with individual five-eighths sockets, has them priced at forty-nine cents. I calculate no more than three cents of tax on top of that eminently fair price. Which comes to fifty-two cents. The socket is available, the price is fair, you need only tear open this package for us to strike a bargain."

"Some bargain."

"It's a figure of speech. I majored in rhetoric at Stanford."

"Your eloquence is remarkable," Barnes said, walking the thin line between sarcasm and banter. Yet still he was resigned and determined to make a customer of the man. Because the business wasn't working, and he had to make it work: "Tell you what I'll do. We're due to get a whole bunch of sockets of all sizes in here on Tuesday. I get all my deliveries on Tuesday. You come by Tuesday afternoon, I'll give you a five-eighths free. Or I can mail it to you. Socket and postage free of charge. We want your future business. How's that sound?"

"Storekeep, I'll go you one better! If you simply accede to my reasonable request I'll be happy to let you have this entire American dollar," said the man, holding up a one-dollar bill with both hands, not two feet from Barnes's smoldering face, "just so I don't have to wait here one second longer than I have to while you struggle to make change!"

"Hey, young fella. There's no reason to be rude here."

"I am not being rude, you stupid old fool. And being but a simple-minded hardware store clerk I don't expect you to understand the concept that time, literally, is money, but I will try to explain it to you anyway. Every minute I stand here watching you try to master the mystery of basic arithmetic costs me dearly. I am a partner with one of the most prestigious firms in town. I only came in to work on a Saturday because I happen to have a lot on my plate right now, two cases ready for trial, three depositions to complete by mid-week, and of course several wealthy miscreants forever banging at my door, each more willing than the last to meet my standard consultation rate of one hundred and fifty dollars an hour, just to see if I will agree to help them in their time of need. Needless to say I work very, very hard. Some days I don't even take a break for lunch. But today I did. Here I am. So you see, *old fella*, the half hour I am about to waste walking from and to my office at Lake and Colorado, on either side of chewing the cud with you, means you have in effect cost me seventy-five dollars. All right, then. Lesson over. And now I'm anxious to hear what percentage of that precise sum you intend to pay me—as nominal consideration for wasting my time."

Barnes did not change his expression at any time during the younger man's monologue. He had known people like this young man. Growing up on a farm he was accustomed to city folk giving him a hard time, calling him names. So you work very, very hard, huh.... Judas Priest! How he would *love* to tell this proper peacock about hard work, about sweating buckets for fourteen hours a day in the fields under a broiling Iowa sun till his back was all but broke, just so his eleven brothers and sisters could have meat with their potatoes twice a week, or about loading hundred-pound sacks of cement onto freight cars at the Rock Island Arsenal for two dollars a day, because jobs were scarce in 1940 and two dollars was a lot....And to think this wet-nosed punk was spending The War choking on his silver spoon while he was flying through the flak-torn skies of Europe, just so the punk could grow up to major in rhetoric at Stanford....To think that while he struggled along, day-to-day, through a disintegrating marriage, solely for the good of his three precious children. this guy was spending his hundred and fifty bucks an hour on a nightly succession of lean plump women only too willing, only too eager to, to....ah, shoot. He thought it all over within an eyeblink. He would not hold back. Not this time. Funny thing....'wasn't as hard a decision as he thought it would be:

"My loquacious friend, I am going to go you even one better than *your* one better, just to pay for my lesson. Y'see, you had no way of knowing this, but I own this store. Yep. Rusty lock, empty stock, and bottom of the barrel. In fact, I am both the president and chairman of the board of this august enterprise. Which gives me great power to serve you. But great power to make command decisions is nothing, unless a man commands a great network of equally powerful merchants equally willing to serve. I refer of course to the great brotherhood of hardware store owners of greater Pasadena. Let me tell you, friend, this is a magnificent and benevolent association. Why, when they hear me tell them about you—and I intend to call each and every one of them, just to inform them of your incredible predicament—I expect to experience a flood of five-eighths sockets into my store the likes of which has never been seen on the face of the earth. And the very first one that comes in will be sent right over to your office, by special courier, immediately, free of charge. What's more, I intend to take out a full-page ad tomorrow in the *Pasadena Star-News*, just so I can alert the whole San Gabriel Valley about how you have suffered in my humble store. Naturally I will apologize to you publicly therein. You know. For any contribution that I personally might have made to your pain and suffering, unintentional or otherwise. Now then, your golden-throated magnificence; would all of that be sufficient compensation for what you have taught me here today?"

"You miserable asshole," the gray-suited man snarled, then whirled and walked briskly out the door.

"Hey! Come back, Stanford man! That's the most eloquent pearl of rhetoric you've come up with since you crawled in here...."

The old man came out from his hiding place laughing.

"Land o'Goshen, Missuh Barnes! You sho'nuff put that fancy young dude in his place!"

Instantly Barnes was embarrassed by the show he had just put on: "I'm sorry about that, Jiggs, I don't like to have to talk that way in my own store. Guess I got a little carried away! But it just irks me when a grown man forgets his manners."

"Man don't fo-get his manners. No sir. Either he been taught o' he ain't, but a man don't fo-get what he never got to begin wit'."

At that burst of wisdom Barnes looked up smiling, but when his eyes engaged the sad, wistful, definitely non-smiling face staring darkly back at him he transformed the smile into a definitively neutral grimace.

"So yer saying I probably didn't get through to that guy."

"Man's what he is in this here world of ourn. Cain't change what always was."

Barnes grabbed his keys and vaulted over the counter like a much younger man. "Let's go to lunch," he said.

"Fine by me. They's a McDonald's right down the street."

⇶ ⇷

"Jiggs, what year were you born?"

"Ni'nee-seven. Why?"

"You familiar with a couple of old colored ballplayers from the thirties named Charleston and Bell?"

Barnes and his guest were sitting in a crowded McDonald's on plastic chairs. Their lunch was spread out across a metal tabletop. Barnes was working on a fish sandwich and fries, while the old man alternated bites of a cheeseburger and an apple turnover, cleansing his palate between each bite with a small mouthful of orange juice. The old man did not let an insistent Barnes buy his lunch for him, nor did he offer to buy Barnes's; rather, at the time they paid, he had counted out five quarters, a dime, two nickels, and four pennies to account for his share. Dollar forty-nine. Exactly.

"Know'm? Shoot, *every* baseball fan where's I comes from knows of old Oscar Charleston and Jimmy Bell. We called him Cool Papa Bell back then. Lordy, he was fast."

"Yeah, I know. I actually saw them play once. In person. When I was a kid."

"Izzat a fact!"

"Yep. I still have the scorecard."

"So why you go to a Negro Leagues game anyhow?"

"Well, it was sort of an exhibition. The colored team versus one of Rogers Hornsby's all-star barnstorming teams."

"Oh, *Hornsby*! Figures. Dat man was one of the most contraryest fellas they was back then. He sho' din like us."

"Yeah. Sorry."

"Funny thing is, most times a *real* ballplayer woodn' care *who* was tryin' tuh throw it by him, 'long as he was one uh the best."

"So you saw Charleston and Bell play too?"

"Lemme think....well, I played *against* 'em, couple times....don't 'member if'n we ever played on the *same* team, though...."

Barnes stopped halfway through a French fry and widened his eyes. A professional ballplayer....wow. Who would've thought, the clumsy way he sweeps up....

"Oh. So I guess you would know, then. I mean if those two were as good as they looked. I was only thirteen."

"Missuh Barnes, Cool Papa Bell could handle center field easy as dat boy Willie Mays *ever* could—prolly *better*. I'm sayin' Cool Papa was *diseased* wit' speed! And as fo' old Oscar Charleston, well, he was jes about the best all-'round ballplayer God ever did set about tuh thinkin' up. And you may quote me on that, yessuh."

"What position you play?"

"I pitched. Played a little shortstop on my days off."

Barnes smiled and slopped up some ketchup with a greasy handful of fries. As was his custom, he entertained too much food for it to be called a decent mouthful. When he'd swallowed enough of it to free up his tongue a little, he said, "Just think. If things had worked out a few years earlier, it might've been *your* name comin' over a major league loudspeaker, Jiggs! Just like Mays or Hank Aaron or Bob Gibson, or Drysdale or Mickey Mantle or *any* of them. Can'tcha hear it? —'*Now pitching for the Dodgers, number twenty-seven, Jiggs, uh....*'—Jiggs, what *is* your last name, anyway?"

The black man dabbed a napkin carefully and thoughtfully at the corners of his mouth. He finished chewing and swallowing a full mouthful of apples and pastry, completely, and took a measured sip of his orange juice before responding: "Well, Missuh Barnes, fo' starters they woodn' be no mention uh Jiggs anything. That is, I never met nobody acshully *named* Jiggs. That jes be somethin' they calls me up'n down Walnut Street, the white folks I work fo'."

"Huh?"

"Jiggs is jes shote fo' jigaboo, see? But jigaboo comes out less friendly-like then Jiggs. My Chrishun name is Howard."

Barnes could feel his throat tighten. All the times over the years he had called him that....darn it the luck....gad, what he must think of me, of all the so-called decent people like, like...."Well then I'll just call you Howard. And mine's Roland, okay?"

"If'n you say okay, then okay."

"Okay, then."

Barnes figured that this might be a good time to stop talking for awhile. He knew he had to ask him about it at some point, better to do it with his foot on the floor and not in his mouth. So he lowered his eyes, and went after the rest of his fish and potatoes with a relish that comes from simply having lived through something like The Great Depression. Oh, how he loved to eat. Just the bare, unadorned, primal act of eating. The instant biological gratification. Occasionally, between oversized bites, he would glance up at his unusual lunch companion, who was also concentrating hard on the cut-rate bounty before him. Barnes found himself embarrassed at how much he realized he liked the old guy. It wasn't hard to figure out why he was embarrassed: This was the first time that forty-two-year-old Roland Gustav Barnes had ever sat at a table, metallic or otherwise, with a black man. The first time he had ever watched up close as food passed between purple lips, or compared the vein-scratched whites of eyes with the dark, hide-like skin that housed them. Not even during the war....'kept pretty much to themselves at mess, 'never thought of just going over and, well, just never thought of it....and in Iowa? Ha! That's a laugh. The only Negroes he ever saw before the war were on that baseball diamond in Des Moines....and they were better....and they were *banned....damn* you, Papa....ah, shoot.

"Howard, can I ask you something? I was just wondering—"

"You jes wanted tuh know what was up wit' my people down in South Central. 'Zat about right?"

Barnes felt like he had just been stopped by a bullet in the chest.

"No, it's not like that. It's just, well, people like me—"

"People like you don' rob an' steal an' throw bricks an' shoot off guns'n such."

"Well you gotta admit it is a little screwy."

The black man laughed. A couple grim-faced old ladies looked over. Barnes crammed in a few more fries to give himself something to do, waiting.

"I dunno what tuh tell you, Missuh Barnes—I mean Roland. You sittin' on one side uh dat table, an' people like me been sittin' on *dis* side fo' 'long, long time."

"I don't pretend to know what you folks think," said Barnes.

"No, that ain't what I mean," came the swift reply. "My people been on the sorry side uh things in this here country fore'n as long as anybody been here. Prolly differnt in other places, but in the Uni'tee States the white folks is *massa*. Ain't nobody's fault, jes the way uh things."

"Nobody's *fault?*"

"These here riots ain't nobody's fault, neither. It's mainly the *heat*, fo' one thing. Wasn't so damn hot, folks woodn' be so all-fired jumpy down there. Don't take much tuh start a fire, when the kettle awreddy be boilin' an' too hot to touch."

"Howard, you sure have a matter-of-fact way of looking at things."

"I'm jes old, Missuh Barnes. Roland. I seen too much."

"And I'm sorry. I am so, so sorry. Really I am."

"Hell, don' you go feelin' sorry fo' me. Compared tuh my old nigga grandpappy, I'm on easy street!"

It had always fascinated Barnes how friendly and comfortable the word nigger could sound, but only when it was a colored man using it to describe another colored man, or himself. Then it sounded downright charming. But now he recalled again how hearing his gruff old grandfather employ it made his guilty skin crawl, and then the rage he felt thirty years later when his oldest boy let it slip at the dinner table, just last week, a rage that could only be purged by the sweet, satisfying melody of his belt against that sixteen-year-old boy's backside. It was the first time he'd whipped Ricky since he was a runt, first time, but considering the never-ending supply of acceptable, whipping-worthy transgressions this angry teenager insisted in producing, he'd be damned if he could figure out why—with everything that boy regularly threw at him—why it was that friendly, charming, comfortable word that somehow succeeded in pushing him over the top....

"So you think it's just blowing off steam? Like releasing some kind of pressure valve or something?"

"Month from today, you folks never gonna give it a second thought. Believe me."

"You're saying folks....like me, won't think anything of it."

"That's jes it. Folks never do."

Barnes grimaced for the umpteenth time, hoped it didn't say too much.

"It's like in a pennant race," the black man went on. "Like that Giants pitcher, Marichal, swattin' ol' Johnny Roseboro wit' dat bat the other day. Jes the heat. They was all worked up over the pennant race anyway, an' the heat caused 'em to boil over. It wadn't no Dominicans hatin' niggas thing, jes frustration. Jes the heat. No heat, no scrap."

"Marichal's a Dominican? I thought—"

"You jes thought 'dem brown boys all look alike! Like us black boys!"

Now Barnes smiled. He had to, lest he openly admit his ever-mounting shortcomings: "Would you have liked to have played in the major leagues, Howard?"

And now, for the first time, the old man fashioned a look of earnestness, like what he was about to say actually mattered to him. He wasn't angry, he wasn't preachy. Merely impassioned: "Missuh Roland, I *awreddy been* in the major leagues! That's the God's truth, 'what I been tryin' tuh tell you. You saw dat ballgame way back when you was a kid, you saw us play. Was any of us less a ballplayer 'den any of those white boys? No kinda way. But mo' impo'tant, it was *our* game! We played it our way, wit' each other, an' they was never no bad blood. We all happy, fo' most part. The damn game was the thing. Jackie Robinson and innergrashun an' all that stuff, 'worst thing 'ever happen tuh baseball."

"Howard, you don't really believe that."

The black man looked up from his cheeseburger. Finally there was a vague anger etched across his ancient leathery face, but only briefly. Then he smiled and looked upon Roland Barnes like a priest preparing to counsel one of his flock....

"Why 'zat so hard to believe? You think we rilly needs tuh be wit' white folks fo' baseball tuh be baseball? Well let me tell you, puttin' nine white boys on the field wit' nine black boys don't change how they feel. After the game 'white go one way, black go another. An' off the field it's the white folks still runnin' the show. Not much differnt than you'n me, rilly."

"You and me?"

"Yuh see, Roland, aftuh weeze done 'this li'l lunch of ourn, I'ze back tuh bein' jus' yessuhdays old nigga, reckon? An' *you'ze* back tuh bein' Missuh Barnes, 'man I works fo'. It's nobody's fault, sir. Jes been that way fo's long as I can recall. Jes the way 'the world. Not differnt rilly from my old nigga grandpappy's world, 'ceptin I guess it's mo' of a sneaky-bad than a horse-whippin' bad....I means the same folks 'massa now as then, but nowdays we jes caught in a differnt kinduh jail is all....yuh see?"

"No. No, I don't see," said Barnes. "Just because mistakes were made in the past doesn't mean we can't improve as a people. I'm saying you and I can *improve* on your grandpappy's world, Howard! On *both* our grandpappys's worlds! We *can*! *We*, as in you and I. But it means you and I both hafta try. Now I know I'm willing to try, and I'm going to prove it."

"How you gonna prove it?"

"By inviting you to supper, for starters. At my home, up in Altadena."

"Say what?"

"I said you and your wife if you have one are coming to my house for dinner next week. Period. Heck, I figure my neighbors haven't seen a Negro on our street since Hector was a pup, the shock alone'll make 'em better citizens! What night is good for you?"

"Missuh Roland, you'n me sittin' down tuh supper ain't gonna change the world."

"Maybe not, but it'll make me feel better. And it's a start."

"Well thank y'anyway. But I reckon not. No point us puttin' a fancy harness on the same ol' mule. But I thanks you jes the same. Truly."

"You mean you're actually....Are you *refusing* my dinner invitation?"

"That's *okay*, ain't it? You ain't gonna fire me if'n I says *no*?"

Barnes had no answer for either question. A few seconds later, when his slack, wordless expression switched from personal shock to generations of accrued embarrassment, the old man finally continued:

"You a good man, Roland. I knows dat. I knows dat awreddy. An' ol' Jiggs ain't tryin' tuh be uppity. But theys no point tryin' to change a world awreddy set in its ways. You think on it, you'll see I'm right." He dabbed at his full purple lips with a paper napkin as he stood up. He used a different napkin to rid the fresh sweat from his forehead. Finally he made sure to gather up every scrap of trash he was personally responsible for, depositing it carefully and quietly in a nearby trash barrel: "I gotta be getting' back tuh my chores."

"Howard, c'mon. It's just dinner, after all. We're just *people*, man."

"Finish yer lunch. Thanks fo' the chat."

"Howard!"

"See yuh Monday mornin', Missuh Barnes."

The old man shuffled quietly out of the McDonald's, leaving a slackjawed Roland Barnes all but imprisoned in his plastic chair. Briefly, enervated by this watershed conversation he had both enjoyed and endured, he lacked the strength to stand. He looked around the restaurant. They had McDonald's in the Midwest, but not like this. There was noise and commotion everywhere. Two twenty-something men—one white, one Mexican-looking—were arguing about their respective places in line. Over by the bathroom a teenager with tangled and greasy-looking hair down to his shoulders held a transistor radio to his ear, and the utterly nonsensical rock and roll song banging and blasting from it sounded to Barnes like Betty's washing machine sounded on spin cycle, when there weren't enough clothes in it to balance the load. Huge, flab-cloaked women of all races clogged the enclosure and screamed at their children, sometimes seeming as if they were addressing no *particular* children but rather any and all children within earshot. And yet the little urchins laughed and screamed and ran up and down the aisles unaffected, as if virtually unsupervised. He had to smile; it was surely the least relaxed dining establishment he had ever eaten in. And yet it was packed.

McDonald's is no Winga's, Barnes said matter-of-factly to himself….

Five p.m. Heading up Hill Avenue, earlier than usual. Afternoon's awful heat is still trapped inside the plastic steering wheel, but Barnes's absent mind refuses to let in the messages of distress being sent up from his burning hands. Charlie's game. He thinks maybe he can still get there for last at-bats. He asks the hatchback for speed and receives only grudging acquiescence, the road's uphill grade being more persuasive. The engine's shrill whine seems somehow to make the late-afternoon air taste heavier, like excess ashes surrounding a just-toasted marshmallow swallowed by mistake. There are no bird songs to compete with the loud car. There are no mountains in its windshield.

At Orange Grove he turns right.

"*That Jiggs sure is something*," breathe forth the words from his narrow, troubled chest. He means Howard, of course, but for some reason it just becomes Jiggs somewhere between brain and tongue. Doesn't even seem to care that things are the way they….they….gad, what makes a man so 'gol-darned *content* with how things are, anyway….maybe that's the secret…. sure seems happy enough….He seems a lot happier than, uh….happier than, than….

Barnes will not finish this sentence, even to himself.

Suddenly it is 1936 and Barnes is back in western Iowa. He is riding in the passenger's seat of his father's Model-A, heading home, gazing out and over endless fields of corn. His thirteen-year-old mind is replaying the exhibition game he has just witnessed, the only big-league game he has ever seen….concurrently, his forty-two-year-old mind is replaying his bizarre lunch earlier that afternoon with his friend Howard. Could it be possible, he wonders….born in eighteen ninety-seven, huh….yep. He'd be about the right age. So maybe. A little old for it, but maybe. He could very well have been there, Barnes marvels to himself, could very well have played in that very game….Barnes suddenly feels very glad he does not know the old man's last name. If he did, he knows he might have to go up into the attic and dig out that old scorecard, and he is sure that this is one thing in this life he does not ever want to do….

Roland Barnes turned left on Allen Avenue, and a quick right turn at Casa Grande Street brought him immediately to the junior high school baseball diamond. Too late. Game over. It was easy to recognize the familiar choreography of two teams of baggily-clad elves milling about the infield, engaging in various time-honored rituals of congratulations and celebration. One boy, though, was off to the side of the others, hitting fungo flies to himself and then hurriedly putting on his glove to catch them. A black boy. He was actually catching about two of three, the rest falling just barely out of glove's reach. Barnes squinted at this sad, miraculous scene through the harsh grainy air. He could barely see that far. But it made sense to him....

He hit the car horn. When Charlie didn't respond right away he honked again. Soon the boy was running toward the car at full speed. He climbed into the car wearing his oversized uniform and a weak half-smile.

"Hello, son."

"Hi, Dad."

"Was it a good day?"

"Yeah, I guess. We lost, though."

"Get any hits?"

The boy looked down at his droopy baseball socks. "No. I went oh-for-four."

Since the boy wasn't looking, Barnes went ahead and smiled at him. "Well, don't sweat it. That's still three-for-seven over two days. That's pretty good."

"Feels a lot more like oh-for-four than three-for-seven...."

"I know, son. I know. But cheer up. You're a good hitter. There'll be other days to be a hero. I promise."

The little boy smiled the way only a little boy can, when he realizes his father isn't disappointed in him. Barnes put the car in gear and they rolled down Casa Grande. They didn't talk at first. Each remained satisfied with his own smile as they turned right and headed up Allen, in search of the mountains that still weren't quite there.

Finally: "Charlie, who was that colored boy out there hittin' fly balls to himself. I don't remember seeing him before."

"There's nuthin' wrong with him," came the sharp reply, and the smile was gone.

They talked no more on the way home. Occasionally Barnes would glance sideways at his issue, but the glance was never returned. No matter. Charlie's still awful young for this sorta talk, he thought. Heck, he didn't know how to explain the nigger thing to him anyway. Didn't have the first idea of how to go about it. But he wasn't feeling guilty over it....wasn't *his* fault he lacked the skill....didn't mean he wasn't a decent man or anything. And anyway, at the moment, all he could think about was how much he loved the little guy. His son. His boy. His boy was the most important little boy in the whole world. And someday the little boy would be a man, maybe with a boy of his own, and maybe he would tell him about when he was a kid growing up in Pasadena with a friend on his Little League team who had to hit fly balls to himself. And then maybe this would finally be the one Barnes who would at least try to tell his little boy about the nigger thing.

So no need to press him, Barnes smiled to himself. Maybe some things between a father and his son really are best left unsaid. Maybe. Besides, he was late for dinner again. He pushed the gas. Highway 71 raced backwards beneath the spoke wheels. He figured if they didn't waste time on idle conversation, they might just make it back to the prevailing decade before the stove was cold.

LAND OF THE FREE (an American fable)

Author's Notes

I was still a kid when the Vietnam War was winding down. But I did have an older cousin who was a Navy flyer, and he did serve in Southeast Asia. It was on a family vacation to visit him and his own family, at the particular U.S. Naval base in California he was assigned to, late in the war, whereupon I obtained the inspiration for *Land of the Free*.

At 13,795 words this is obviously one of my longest stories, and I believe one of the better ones. More to the point, it bears a close stylistic resemblance to my signature novel which was published just last year; *WHERE GODS GAMBLE, a tale of American mythology*. They mirror each other in so many ways. The use of imagery, the reliance on sensory perception, the rendering of scenic detail through collision and motion, the emphasis on family, the capitalization of words like Boredom and Anxiety to give them personification and thus make states of mind into actual characters, not to mention getting right inside of Charlie's head to make his own thoughts the sounding board for the action and mission statements of the story itself—all of it serves to forecast and anticipate *WHERE GODS GAMBLE*, which takes place in 1980, eight years after *Land of the Free* takes place. To take it one step further, this story is not only the literary precursor of *WHERE GODS GAMBLE* stylistically, but also with regard to the actual subject matter, i.e. our nation's post-Vietnam despair. (Not to mention that *Land Of The Free* plants the roots of Charlie's own personal despair and disillusionment, which by the time the novel takes place, eight years later, are causing him more than a little difficulty....)

Even the title of the story has that same mythological quality to it. It's no accident.

Therefore, for all of that and more, I guess you could say that this so-called 'American fable' of mine, *Land of the Free,* is in essence the father of a far greater literary entity, namely that modern-day epic of American mythology, *my* epic, *WHERE GODS GAMBLE.* And you'd be right. The one does discharge the seed which grew the other. And for that alone, this story shall always occupy a special place in my heart.

LAND OF THE FREE

(an American fable)

"How much farther, Dad?"

"Oh....'bout twenty more miles, I guess. Relax, my boy. Just relax."

A high-school kid leaned back in the front seat—co-pilot's side—of a long blue Thunderbird methodically making its way up Intrastate 99. He was rocking back and forth. Secretly, just a little, but definitely rocking. He was trying hard not to be bored with the miles of parched, obviously barren soil whizzing by on both sides. Sometimes his eyes skimmed disinterestedly over it; sometimes it was easier for his mind to simply block the scorched earth from his sight. He kept rocking. And each of his hands squeezed frantically the plastic handle of a stainless steel spring-hinged hand gripper, endless repetitions, a dedication bordering on compulsion, not so much another weapon against Boredom as it was part of a pre-planned campaign to strengthen his forearms. Strong forearms were important these days. Back then....

His father (not much on exercise, but a paragon of familial shrewdness) had leveled the speedometer off at 75 miles an hour, which, being a figure only five miles over the posted speed limit, was neither perfectly satisfactory to the kid nor particularly offensive to the mercurial Highway Patrolmen of Fresno County. But better to vex his son than irk the whole sovereign state. The kid recognized the underlying genius in all of this. He already had a little of his father in him. They both knew that 75 miles an hour was a figure that would have been *considerably* offensive to his mother, whose wrath, even theoretical, rendered the notion of dealing with California's wheel-mounted Storm Troopers a comparative relief, and so her canny husband had carefully (and somewhat cowardly, it must be admitted) made sure she was stretched out in the back seat, open-mouthed and snoring, before making use of the Thunderbird's considerable engine.

The speed of the Thunderbird (which only last week had been purchased brand spanking new, for the outlandish sum of $4,995) was very useful to its youngest passenger. He wasn't stupid. He knew that 75 mph was fast, just as he was concurrently aware of his ever-impatient Inner Self telling him that *no* interpretation of "fast" could be *too* fast, if it could sooner free him from the surrounding desolation. And he fairly reveled in the sheer pace and power of the actual vehicle, of course; all 16-year-old boys do. But he exhilarated a great deal more thoroughly, albeit privately, in the peculiar sensations he was now experiencing courtesy of his half-open window. It was simply a matter of properly positioning his face to receive the invading jet stream. This man-made wind pushed hard against his forehead, against the thin cakes of sweat layered there by California's unrelenting, late-summer sun. He could feel his undisciplined blond hair being punished, tortured, being blissfully abused by the force of the in-rushing air. For the kid, call him Charlie, this was a feeling of nearly unparalleled pleasure; every nerve in his face seemed to sing with the joy of Life. In other words, it was *"bitchin'"*. And thus the hotter the sun, the faster the car, the sweatier his face, the better he liked it. It was very hard for him to understand how his sleeping mother could possibly detest—or in fact resent the very intrusion of—both the sun *and* the wind. They were, for him, such welcome ministers of delight.

In fact, on a grand scale, lately it seemed that all the world had benevolently conspired to minister to the needs of this one young man. Life was a banquet, and he gorged himself daily on its inexhaustible bounty. Responsibilities were few, school was a breeze, girls seemed to like him, and, if the grapevine could be trusted, he was virtually assured next spring of securing the coveted position of "starting 2nd-baseman" on his high school varsity baseball team. What's more, this was a young man at one with his species. *'Man is good, and nothing is beyond his reach.'* Philosophy being his favorite subject, and being a young man in the market for a personal philosophy serviceable to the government of the rest of his life, it was not surprising that he had come to believe so wholeheartedly in this curious assertion, in the "perfectibility" of Man. It was as good a concept to believe in as any, he'd decided. And the good guys were finally winning the war, the talking heads on T.V. were saying; that was proof enough. Strangely, he had high hopes even for himself. Why not? It's a free country, isn't it? He saw no reason why he, such an obviously fine specimen of young manhood, should be denied charter membership in this "perfect" club, after all it was *his* club, his very own one-man philosophical *junto* for godsake. He'd thought it over....his club, his rules. And so, using himself to confirm his pet theory, he eagerly persisted in squeezing the noisy hand grippers, in order to strengthen his grip, which would improve his bat speed, which would enable him to hit with more power. A 2nd-baseman who can hit with power? How much more proof could a guy ask for that Man, as a species, could actually *evolve*? The incessant squeak and whine of flexing steel rose above the whistle of in-rushing air, and soon it was a song....

"C'mon, step on it, Dad—open this baby *up!*"

A rare road sign came and went, informing them the Thunderbird had finally speared its way up into Kings County. Waves of giddy anticipation shuddered through the kid. He kept rocking. Bare landscapes notwithstanding, he was genuinely eager to reach the town of Hanford. His cousin Earl was there. That was reason enough. Sure, it was unusual that anyone might actually be looking forward to reaching a place like Hanford, just one of the scores of settlement communities unfortunate enough to have been conceived in the blighted ovum of Central California, and one would had to have had a good reason. Case-in-point, neither his big brother nor little sister could come up with one, and so both had elected to stay home. And in Charlie's case, any less-than-spectacular family field trip would have been especially inconvenient, this being the summer of his life when—thanks in part to the mobility now afforded him by his new driver's license—he was discovering such spectacular pursuits as the racetrack and Las Vegas, sneaking into bars, and finding out what 16-year-old girls look and feel like underneath their loose-fitting clothing.

Conversely, cousin Earl had not required a reason, good or otherwise, for actually settling in Hanford. Charlie had the U.S. Government to thank for that. It seems Uncle Sam, in His infinite wisdom, had just recently seen fit to pluck one of His best fighter pilots from the busy skies over Indochina, and, for *some* dumb reason, relocate him to the rank, commonplace armpit of His otherwise most exceptional state. Bad break. California is brilliant beaches, rugged coastline, snow-capped mountains, matchless redwood forests, and ever-fertile valleys. The envy of the nation. But she is also Kings County, and Fresno County, and Tulare, horizon in place of landscape, and for countryside there is only something akin to the aftermath of some great futuristic prairie fire. Several Navy pilots like Earl lived in Hanford because they had to, they had to be near the Lemoore

Naval Air Station, and at least they have an excuse, reasoned Charlie. But he couldn't figure out why anybody else, of his own free will, would actually *choose* to reside in this citadel of dullness. What's the matter with people? Isn't this exactly the type of place that any rational person would try to get *away* from? Hanford....he'd never been there, but if the drive up could be considered a gauge it was already his idea of a ghost town.

He closed his eyes, and commanded his mind give back these sights those eyes had so foolishly loaned him.

Then a sympathetic thought flooded his young head....it was *unfair* for Earl to be incarcerated in such a place....why him? He had much too much going for him to ever wind up here. There was that Annapolis education of his, for one thing....yeah....and then Nam, naturally, where he picked up all those cool war stories, including (incredibly but not at all surprisingly) that fine account of how he ditched his shot-up Phantom in the Gulf of Tonkin and faced death-by-shark for something like seventeen hours. That's when the rumors started...."he's been grounded", "he's not the same kid", "he's lost something"....yeah, right. Stupid fools....all that kind of talk does is prove there are just too many damn aunts and uncles out there who've got nothing better to do than make a bunch of stupid phone calls and stir up trouble with a lot of stupid rumors. Too many old, bored, jealous aunts and uncles, damn it....the guy was *shot down*, for godsake! *Naturally* they sent him home for a rest. And naturally good ol' Earl capitalized, big time, coming back from the war just long enough to marry his most recent conquest, a younger girl, a girl of wit and intelligence who was rumored to be uncommonly beautiful and built like....like a....god, where do guys even *find* chicks like that? Man, can't *wait* to check *her* out....*uncommonly*, they said....far out....must be a fox....damn....

And so it went. There were, in fact, several similar clarion bursts of praise for Lieutenant Earl Savage, sitting waiting in Charlie's head, ever-ready to spring from the youngster's eager throat. The essence of it all was that cousin Earl had seen and done more in his 29 years than most men twice his age, and even prior to his heroic exploits overseas the idolatrous youngster had always regarded him as somehow "better" than regular people. For young Charlie he was, and had always been, living proof of the perfectibility of Man.

He had to admit, though, he wasn't exactly thrilled to death when he first heard about Earl's being sent stateside: "He's prob'ly the best damn pilot they got—don't they *wanna* win?" he had asked his father at the time, just a few months ago, and at the time his father just winced and grumbled something uncharacteristically profane under his breath and, naturally, refused to answer such a ridiculous question.

But thinking about it now, Charlie had to laugh inside. He could just imagine the squawk ol' Earl must've put up when they told him he would have to take a break from the action....

....But one man's bad break is another man's good fortune. The best thing about Earl's R&R was the happy fact that at least until he got another neat assignment overseas, the Savage newlyweds would be stationed only 150 miles north of the Barnes home in suburban Los Angeles. Weekend visits like this one would be easy. Good for him, bad for Earl. But things like bad breaks or tough luck or cruel fate just never seemed to bother Earl Savage, Charlie Barnes secretly marveled, nothing did, and if he knew anything he knew he could count on the oldest and best of his 47 first-cousins to come through....in this case, to come up with something to make Hanford, California seem a little less boring. Up until now, he didn't think there was *any* place in America *this* boring. Another twenty miles of this so-called countryside and he was afraid he'd go nuts. Ergo, it is easy to see why he placed such a high premium on the speed, such as it was, of the new Thunderbird.

"C'mon, Pop, can'tcha make this tub go any faster?"

Roland Barnes did not answer. He simply looked with favor upon his youngest son, smiled his favorite fatherly smile, and then turned his attention back to the endless yawning highway before him. The smile dissolved into a smirk, a profile of quiet confidence, of an ex-officer's controlled self-assurance. An officer and a gentleman to be sure....a man's man. But he did not depress the accelerator.

"It's really nothing, Aunt Betty. Just a buncha tired old mechanics sittin' around a campfire eatin' hotdogs and drinkin' a little beer. Pass the mashed potatoes, Jen."

"I don't want any kid of mine drinking beer!"

"Aw, Mom," the kid whined.

The pilot smiled straight, porcelain-white teeth. His pale blue eyes landed on the matching set belonging to his youthful cousin. Trading the smile for a sorrowful pout to go with an exaggerated shoulder shrug, he said, "Tried my best, partner," and resumed his smile immediately. Charlie didn't smile back, lest his mother might think he wasn't emotionally shattered at the prospect of missing out on one of Youth's great adventures, but he was certain that Earl could not possibly have missed the sincere telegraph of gratitude in his eyes. He could sense that the pilot was eager to participate in his overdue sortie into young manhood. He could tell the minute they arrived, by the way Earl pretended to let Charlie out-handshake him....

"How's the boy ever gonna *learn* anything, Betty?" inquired a careful yet insistent baritone. Roland Barnes was presiding over supper from his place of honor at the head of a small, rectangular, collapsible metal table. His lean, pleasant features were illuminated from above by the spot issuing down from a hanging lamp, Navy surplus, the only light the U.S. Government deemed necessary for this tiny room. "Take *Earl* here!" he continued, turning slightly left to face his nephew, forming that thin, tight-lipped, thoroughly impish grin that Charlie recognized at once as the prelude to yet another priceless story from the Barnes family archives. A frustrated actor and closet stand-up comedian, the elder Barnes positively lived to get himself into position to spin one of these great yarns, and Charlie, leaning forward now, lived to hear them. He especially liked the old stories, the war stories, the way his dad could conjure up from nowhere the ghosts of long-dead regiments of crisply uniformed men, and convince them to parade their colorful banners up and down the dinner table. If an upcoming Roland Barnes tale had anything whatsoever to do with his brief, glorious stint in the service of his country, Charlie could always tell by that wry, tight-lipped grin. And the grin was definitely there, so he knew one of the old stories was coming right around the corner. Betty Barnes, sitting to her son's right and thus her husband's far right, let out an exaggerated groan. She obviously knew it was coming too, and from experience they both knew it might be a long one: "I can remember it like it was yesterday....*seems* like yesterday, in fact," Barnes began, staring off into space, as if spellbound by his own words and the very prospect of recapturing—if only for a moment—the best of times from a bygone era. "It was about, oh, two or three years after the war, I'd only been out of the service a few months. I was staying with you and your folks at the time, in that flea trap of a duplex you had in Moline. Remember, Earl? Can you remember any of that? You were such a *little* shaver!" Barnes said, holding his palm out and down, about three feet above and parallel to the floor. The pilot smiled and nodded, and seemed to blush a little, his new bride hugged his neck and made teasing little baby sounds, and the groundswell of laughter had begun. Betty Barnes, torn, alternately laughed and shook her head. Charlie's eyes momentarily captured cousin Earl's, but the pilot looked away as if something had distracted him. Barnes continued: "Anyway, I was just a broken-down flyer looking for work. A typical post-war casualty. Had no idea what I was gonna do. Hadn't even met your mother, son." (He glanced back to the right, to where Charlie and his mother acknowledged their inclusion in the tale with radically different facial expressions.) "Heck, I couldn't even afford to pay rent. But Grace was just great about the whole thing....y'know Earl, your folks didn't have two nickels to rub together either, but she let me freeload it just the same. She was an awful fine woman, your mother." Earl Savage smiled and lowered his eyes. "And with Mom'n Dad both dead, Gracie, being the only one married, being the oldest sister, and being second oldest of the twelve kids next to me, was certainly the logical choice over the other ten of us so-called adult kids to look after your Uncle Allen....who, of course, was still just a *real* kid," Barnes explained, slowly, skillfully, not omitting even the most minor of details, glancing alternately at Savage and Charlie to create the illusion that he was addressing the words "Uncle Allen" to each nephew exclusively. He was setting the stage. For further effect, he paused to scoop some mashed potatoes onto his plate (having intercepted the mashed potato bowl being passed to the pilot from his new bride), then took a long, well-timed swallow of milk. He dabbed a napkin thoughtfully and theatrically at the dry corners of his mouth. He was masterful.

When his wife shuffled in her chair and made various telltale sounds indicating she might soon erupt into speech, Barnes cleared his throat and took the floor again: "So we got little Al and I in one half of this cotton-pickin' duplex, Grace and Burt in the other, not to mention *this* little squirt (Savage was laughing a little harder now), and I'm telling you we were so all-fired doggone poor that, uh....well, that a big event in *our* miser'ble lives was any time the corner bakery would take pity on us and drop the price of *bread* a couple a'cents." Charlie's light laughter joined cousin Earl's, the pilot's wife made careful overtures to laughter, and the storyteller's wife smiled. But it was a kind of thin, gravely nostalgic, oddly plaintive sort of smile, a half smile, at once plaintive and patronizing, the sort of smile that says more clearly than any words can that there is very little funny about being poor. The sort of smile that can only survive for a moment or two. And in that magnificent moment her hard face had actually softened, and it reminded Charlie that this woman was his mother, and that he loved her. He looked at her soft face and felt sorry for her. He felt sorry for everyone in this stifling room, but for none so sincerely as for her. And now nobody was talking. Seemingly from nowhere he had come, Dead Silence, and now this most awkward of man-made gods reigned supreme. There could easily have been a long, uncomfortable impasse. But when the woman's loving husband leaned across the table and poked a finger into the depths of her ample mid-section, she had no choice but to contribute to the spirit of camaraderie with a reluctant chuckle or two. Once again, Barnes's consummate skill had carried the day. Without hesitating, he spat out, "I mean, let's just say we were *strapped*!", a clear statement of summation. A good storyteller knows when to give his audience an intermission. And now Betty Barnes took full advantage, spewing forth a fusillade of well-rehearsed dogma in all directions, addressing no one in particular, political machine-gun fire. The face had hardened in a heartbeat. The kid now felt sorry for everyone in the room *except* her. Suddenly and forever, all the irreconcilable ills of this world were theirs, their concern, their fault. Their burden. Specifically, though, most of this verbal ordnance was the residue of her dismay over the horrors of the recently completed Olympics, with an occasional deadly, well-timed volley loaded with her equally passionate point of view on the upcoming election ("If that fink *McGovern* gets in, I just *know* something bad is going to happen!"). Her teeth gnashed, nostrils flared, and at times like this it seemed to Charlie as if her bouffant hairdo, a vibrating, upwardly spiraling column of grayish brown, was a beehive preparing to explode.

"Relax, Mom...."

"Don't tell *me* to relax, young man! I've got chores waiting for you back home you haven't even *dreamed* of," Betty Barnes said, more matter-of-factly than one might have thought her capable, and then she kept right on going.

Earl Savage and his wife were at all times touching, fondling, reveling in the inviolate newness of their marriage. Anyone could see they were lost in each other. The wife's blonde hair was a single rope-like braid, allowing the husband easy access to the sweet tan smoothness of her right cheek and neck. Nuzzles, kisses, little bites. They acted like they were hardly listening, and their inflamed aunt hardly noticed, but Charlie, nervous enough to be considerate about such things, figured his own mother deserved at least the illusion of an audience and so he paid some extra attention to her all-too-familiar hot spew of propaganda. She was filibustering the Senate, and he was the only one still awake. Then all at once, in mid-sentence, as if to provide herself with her own intermission, Betty Barnes turned abruptly from her son to the breathtaking young woman sitting directly across from her and inquired, and with far less urgency, "Jennifer, dear—where on Earth did you two ever *find* each other?"

Everyone laughed forth their relief, the pilot's wife smiled, and her tan cheeks flushed with red. "I was in school," she said. "San Diego State. There's lots of naval bases down there, you know. North Island, Miramar....I suppose *I* found *him*! They used to say that about us sorority girls, that we always knew where to find the sailors."

"Baby, how many times do I hafta tell ya, we're not sailors," Earl Savage moaned, a smile of half-serious exasperation creasing his handsome face. "We're naval *aviators*! Just because it's the Navy doesn't make us sailors," he added miserably.

"When I flew, the Air Force was called the Army Air Corps!" ex-Captain Barnes pitched in.

Jennifer Savage hugged her husband's left arm and purred. "Sorry about that, sugar lips," she said.

Charlie was a hundred percent sure he liked cousin Earl's new wife. She was funny and friendly and charming, and all reports of her beauty had been pleasantly understated. Her blue-gray eyes swirled at him like he was staring into the mesmerizing blue flames of a stove. And while her matching blue summer dress was meant to be anything but daring, it happened to be pulled pleasingly tight to her by a thick black belt, giving the kid plenty of clues as to exactly what she might be shaped like.... *damn*.

"So howzit feel bein' married to a genuine war hero?" he finally burst forth.

The tan face narrowed: "I'm not sure there *are* any heroes over there," she said.

"Jen...."

"My wife will handle the politics, thank you!" was Barnes's careful attempt at levity, and his wife immediately threatened him with a fork. But his lighthearted return glance also contained the rare fire of command, in this case for quiet, and the woman obeyed. He then fastened his omniscient eyes to his son, exaggerated his laughter, but couldn't get the boy's attention....

"So how 'bout when he goes back?" Charlie kept on, engaging her in conversation being the best excuse he could think of to keep looking at her. "Are ya planning on, you know, going over with him?"

"Good God, I *hope* not."

There was a sharpness in the young woman's voice. The blue flame reached out from her face and sliced into him, confusing him, and it hurt.

"Jen...."

"I mean I....I hope that won't be necessary," the pilot's wife said. Just like a woman, Charlie thought. But he didn't hold it against her. Bravery and patriotism were hardly the preferred qualities he looked for in a female. He also knew it was a woman's right to get angry every once in awhile, because he remembered his father having cause to say it a lot more than once. Sure. And he certainly couldn't blame her for not wanting to live in some steamy sticky jungle town, or overseas naval base, or wherever Uncle Sam keeps His nieces during time of war. He could forgive any woman for not recognizing the necessity of keeping freedom's enemies in line, simply because she *was* a woman. And especially if she was hot-looking. And man, *is she hot-looking*, the kid caught himself thinking....He tried to share a grin of rugged *machismo* with his cousin, but couldn't establish eye contact. The pilot's eyes were flashing all about the tiny room, everywhere but at somebody, sort of like he'd lost something....

Suddenly Betty Barnes leaned forward, took a deep breath, and they were all under fire.

Roland Barnes spent the break loading up his twice-emptied plate with more food; ham, sweet potatoes, garlic bread; but as usual he rejected the lima beans unconditionally. Occasionally he would "uh-hum" in agreement, drawing loving smiles from his wife of 23 years. Charlie observed that his father was losing some hair on top, but he reminded himself that what was left was still every bit as blond as Earl's. Two generations of flyers....rugged adventurers....patriots (Charlie had long ago decided he liked patriotism.). Do all winners of wars have blond hair? Charlie hoped he, too, could win a war someday....

"So one day I'm over in Rock Island, trying to get work at the old John Deere Harvester plant," Barnes finally resumed, immediately tethering three pairs of eyes, then finally, grudgingly, the fourth, "Grace and Burt are at work themselves, or maybe Gracie was off doing volunteer work at the veteran's hospital, I don't remember....and our hero, ol' Earl here, is stuck at home with Al. Now you gotta remember, uncle or not, Al really wasn't much older than Earl. He was a *fine* one to leave in charge!" Betty Barnes grunted and nodded emphatically up and down, never a big fan of Roland's youngest brother, while the pilot and his wife, hands invisible under the table, giggled their amusement like naughty school children. Charlie, having finally torn his eyes from the pilot's wife's body, now beamed a teenager's grin of approval at his father, his face aching of anticipation:

"Y'see, Jennifer," Barnes went on, "my brother Al was sort of an instigator even then. *Gad*, how his mind worked! He filled yer hubby's little head with a lotta sad stories about how poor we were, and how we were practically starving, and oh how sad the whole thing was, and how there was never gonna be any money, and how he overheard if he didn't—what I mean is he meant that if *Earl* didn't—didn't start helping with our number one day-to-day problem, the procuring of food, we were going to have to give him away. Wouldn't that *frost* ya? He actually told the little squirt we were gonna *give him away*! Gad, what a devious little.... uh, but now Earl, naturally, is only too eager to help out, and so naturally he tells his kind, benevolent, innocent as apple pie uncle that he'll do anything to earn his keep. Anything to keep from being kicked out of the family, right? Yer darn tootin'. And Al, of course, had a plan all worked up, the diabolical little runt. Next door to our property, that is to say Grace and Burt's property, there lived this elderly fella, Mister....Mister, uh....ah hell's-bells, let's just say there was this old guy who lived next door in this green two-story house. And I mean he was one dusty old sonofagun! You got the feeling he'd lived his whole life in that little green house. Sort of a lime green. Lime green, pea green, whatever....'bout the ugliest color green you ever saw. Sorta like these lima beans here. Made me sick just to look at it. But he had this wonderful strawberry patch out back wouldn'tcha know, and everyone in my family, including brother Al, knew how much I liked strawberries. *Still* like 'em. Matter a'fact, and this is just one man's opinion, I personally think that strawberries with whipped cream on top is probably the most delicious thing on—"

"Roland Barnes, will you *please* get to the *point*!"

The table, not having exhaled in several seconds, burst into a grateful combustion of laughter. Charlie used the commotion to sneak a handful of lima beans his mother had spooned onto his plate back into the serving bowl. He caught his father smiling at him. He raised his eyebrows for a question mark, and the father nodded his approval.

"Yes, dear," Barnes said, trading the smile for a far more earnest expression, adding impishly, "Have you already heard this story, dear?", and before she could formulate an appropriate response, he pushed on: "So Al tells Earl that poor ol' Uncle Roland's been complaining up a storm that he can't afford to buy any strawberries, how terrible it is that I'm out of work, how I'm beside myself with grief over the prospect of going without strawberries for a whole summer, something along those lines. What a character....of course ol' Earl swallows the whole thing, hook, line, and sinker, and pretty soon Al's got the little guy all riled up to go on an actual commando raid of old man what's-his-name's strawberry patch. Boy, I wish I could remember his name. Hmm....I can't believe I can't remember it....but I do remember I didn't like him very much. He was really a crusty old fart."

"Roland, stop it!"

"How old *was* he, Uncle Roland?"

"Oh, I don't know, son....I'd guess about—"

"Earl Savage! You're as bad as he is!"

"God I love family dinners," Charlie contributed. He looked up to catch the pilot's wife smiling at him. It felt funny.

"Charlie, stop saying God."

"He was pretty old," Barnes said. "Old enough to fart dust, anyway."

Everyone took a bite or two of food, a couple of the bites muffling laughter. Charlie and Savage shared a brief, fraternal glance the former hoped was more akin to brothers than cousins. But he looked away before Charlie could think of anything to say. The pilot was apparently having trouble containing his amusement; he wasn't smiling, but Charlie noticed his eyes tearing up, and that his cheeks were drawn tight....

"I suppose now you're going to tell me that my husband *stole* those berries, right Unkie Ro?"

"Sshhh! *I'm* telling this story, young woman!"

"Yeah, honey. Shush."

The pilot's wife slapped her husband on the arm, then smiled and rubbed it up and down.

"Well I wouldn't exactly say he *stole* the strawberries," Barnes disclaimed. His expression was quite earnest. "He was just serving his country. Really. Al told him that it wasn't actually a crime to steal food....that is, not if the food was ultimately going to be eaten by a Veteran."

"Oh come on."

"I'm serious! He just told him to be careful, because old man whozits might not know the rules," Barnes went on. He had to raise his voice to pierce the laughter. But his face was still quite serene, marvelously tranquil. He did not smile. He accepted no eye contact. He stroked his chin thoughtfully, looking up and squinting into the government-issue lamp hanging at the end of a three-foot cord. The cord threaded in and out of brass-colored chain links, just as Barnes's tale seemed to be weaving undaunted through the black holes of his memory. Charlie was overcome with the notion that he wished both he and his father could live forever....

"Dad, you kill me."

"I'd sure like to meet this Allen person," the pilot's wife said.

"No you wouldn't," Betty Barnes said.

Her son pretended to laugh. Leave it to her to pick on the one decent uncle in the bunch....'bet she was the one who started all those rotten rumors about him a few years back....probably cooked up those stupid rumors about Earl, too....

"Y'know if I can't remember that old geezer's name I'm gonna be up all night."

The laughing young newlyweds were beside themselves.

"Roland...."

"Wait a minute, wait a minute. I don't *remember* stealing any strawberries!"

"Oh, it was too traumatic. You blocked it out of your mind," Barnes declared, omnipotent, the supreme authority on all things related to any of his stories. "The way Al tells it, ol' Earl here was quite a hero. Made three separate commando raids he did, on his belly. The boy was a natural. Came away with a whole slew of 'em, too. Big fat red ripe beauties. Not bad for a first mission! Got caught, though. Y'see, Jennifer, Earl was sort of a dumb kid."

"Honey, you never told me you were *always* stupid."

The pilot, eyes down, lips pursed against further laughter, was obviously cramping and exhausted from his ordeal. Charlie laughed for both of them.

"Actually, the old man had him in his sights the whole time. When you get to be that age, there isn't much to do 'cept look out the window. Lord, I hope I don't ever get to be that old....okay, okay. That night Gracie got a call from the old man, and he told her about Earl's being a two-bit thief. I remember she was crushed. She really was. I think she cried. At least I'd like to think she did."

"So what became of my little honey?"

"Well, it goes back to Al again. He took ol' Earl aside—the old man was on his way over to see that justice was done and that Earl was properly punished and so on and so forth—he took the little tyke aside and explained that he was wrong about the Veterans Stolen Food Exemption and that it was a bad break and that he was really sorry and that you, Earl, would just have to take your medicine. Now here's the best part. He told you—golly, I'll never forget it—he told you that the penalty for strawberry stealing.... was death. Dum-de-*dum*-dum. *Death*! Hah-hah-hah-hah-haaaaa! Serious offense, he told you; falls under the international rules governing spying! What an imagination. And y'know he wasn't much older than you, either. I think I'll give him a call tonight. What a character."

"I have to go to the bathroom," Betty Barnes said. She left the room in a hurry, not necessarily a hurry to escape the end of the story, but rather like a woman cursed by multiple childbirths with a lifetime of sphincter problems. "Poor old girl," Barnes said.

"That's a very amusing story, Unkie Ro."

"No-no, sweetheart, I'm not finished!" Barnes said, simultaneously pinching his nephew's right cheek between his thumb and curled up index finger. The pilot's wife alertly pinched the other cheek. "I got home from work right about the time—oh! I forgot to mention. I got the job at the John Deere plant. That very day. What a relief! That's why I remember it all, because it was my first day of gainful employment in quite awhile. Heckuva job for a Bee-Seventeen pilot, dipping rake tooth molds for hay rakes. Yep, I said hay rakes, you heard me. I had to dip thousands of those buggers every day, *thousands*, mind you, and all for a lousy buck-twenty an hour. This, after I went to all that trouble to singlehandedly win the war for you ungrateful whelps. But nobody cared. Y'know I figured out once that I was being paid at the princely rate of about a tenth of a cent per rake tooth, can anybody believe that? Gad, that was a crummy job....Anyway, I got home at just the right time, and right away I could see something was wrong. 'Course, the old man was in the room, and that was enough for me. He was terrible. Did I tell you he was, uh....yeah, I guess I did. Anyway, moving right along, Grace and Burt were trying to explain to the ol' duff what a good boy you were, good Swedish stock and all that, always respected your elders, brushed yer teeth every night, all that good stuff. Then you and Al march in, at least *you* were marching, and when you saw me you stopped and saluted. Remember when you used to salute me all the time, Earl? Remember?"

Lieutenant Savage flicked off a crisp salute. Captain Barnes returned it. Charlie laughed and smiled, and then just stared. They looked alike. They could have been father and son. He and Earl could have been brothers. He was as much a Barnes as any of them. He had a different last name, but it wasn't his fault....

"So we're all just staring at the little guy, and he looked so cute just standing there. I felt kinda sorry for him....well, anyway. It was quiet as a tomb at first. Spooky as can be. Nobody knew what to say, least of all a dumb kid like our hero. But then all of a sudden, right out of the blue, he just steps up and in that cute little squeaky voice he had, shaking with fear, but brave at the same time and very militarily, he says 'I am ready to be executed!', and he closes his eyes and squints. I thought I was gonna die."

"I'm ready to be executed?"

"I *am* ready."

At that precise moment Betty Barnes returned from the bathroom. "Ready for what?" she said. Earl Savage couldn't take anymore, and cried out his laughter till he was blue in the face.

"*Ready to die for his country!*" said Barnes and his son in perfect miraculous unison.

And their united laughter was now an explosion, and their squeals of delight nothing less than applause for the storyteller, who laughed right along with them, the way he always did at the end of one of his own stories, and he made a few faces, silly faces not normally associated with a 49-year-old man, and it only fueled and intensified their good humor, but they were soon minus Earl Savage, though, whose laugh died abruptly in a long sip of coffee. When he napkinned the excess coffee from his mouth only a half-smile was left. Charlie barely paid attention, so pleased was he at teaming up with his father in a joke. Roland Barnes continued to laugh at his own memory. Betty Barnes kept laughing because it was the easy thing to do. Jennifer Savage hugged her husband's left arm reassuringly, whispered something, and then finally gave him a long soft kiss on the cheek:

"Would you die for me, Savage? For *me?*"

"Sure he would, Jenny," Barnes opined. "It's in his blood."

"I dunno....I was awful tough back then!" the pilot said, glancing first at his uncle, then his wife. Then briefly, losing the rest of his smile, at his cousin.

"But the point is you *learned* something from the experience, right Earl? You did learn something, right? Tell us what you learned."

"I learned not to listen to Uncle Allen," Savage said, and Charlie very nearly spat up his milk.

"Very funny, young feller," Barnes countered, wasting no time in regaining control of his audience. "The thing was, the old man wound up hiring you to pick his strawberries. Paid you good, too. I remember you ran out one day, without telling anybody, and bought us a couple loaves of bread at the corner bakery with your first-ever honest wages, and Gracie made French toast for us for a week. Boy, could she make French toast....I think she put something in the batter."

"That's a very nice parable, Unkie-dear."

"Now, now. I hereby swear upon my mother's grave, God rest her dear soul, that it all happened just the way I said," Barnes said. He held his right hand reverently over his heart, smiling angelically.

"And if a dumb kid like me could learn a thing or two from stealin' a few strawberries...."

"That's right, nephew of mine. Perhaps young Charlie here can learn a thing or three from a crowd of crusty grease monkeys," Barnes concluded, as his parables generally closed with a moral of such suitable utility.

"Well he's not going to learn anything worthwhile drinking in sin with a gang of dirty old men!"

"Ah, they're not so sinful, Aunt Betty." Savage was suddenly bright-faced and sitting taller in his chair, bolt upright, as if successfully shaking off that particular strain of fatigue made by both laughing and crying. He looked utterly "Navy" in his snug-fitting sport shirt, the tanned arms busting out powerfully from tight short sleeves. The bleach-blond hair was swept back above the ears on each side, meeting in a vertical line at the back of the head, with a slight curl at the nape of the neck. The sudden dynamism of his mood change was perhaps, Charlie reasoned, an indicator that having the floor had energized him. Light seemed to be shooting out from every pore of the pilot's sun-bronzed skin. Charlie decided he looked like a Greek god....make that a Norse god: "They work hard during the day, they deserve to blow off a little steam at night," the flyer continued. "They're really good guys. Really." His wife handed him a large serving bowl of chocolate pudding, which she had just fetched from the kitchenette. It was obviously heavy, but he handled it with two long fingers and a thumb. The kid noticed how clean and well-manicured the officer's fingernails were. He looked at his own nails, chewed and charred with filth. He was embarrassed.

"Jennifer, what do you think of Charlie going with your husband to this....this infernal beer blast!"

"Oh, I don't think there'll be anything there a big handsome stud like Charlie can't handle," Jennifer Savage assured her new aunt. She hit the teenager with a wink. It was a great wink. She was totally bitchin'. He silently complimented his cousin on his choice of a wife. (He also felt the growing embarrassment that often swells up when a boy simply can't help picturing an older, well-built, off-limits female naked. Accordingly, he was grateful to the collapsible metal table for opaquely hiding that embarrassment.)

"How do the enlisted men feel about the officers here, Earl?"

The pilot put down the bowl. "Those men are professionals, Uncle Roland," he began. Biceps knotted and uncoiled as he made the hand gestures. "They're professionals, just like the pilots are professionals. But when they get in a situation where they can't show their competence....y'see, Roland, the night crew here is basically on call, hurry-up-and-wait, hurry-up-and-wait. The day crew has the planes ready, the night guys, well, they wind up just standing around a lot. It gets on their nerves is all. You flew in your war, you know how things are."

"What's all this got to do with—"

"So you don't think these men you'll be with tonight, uh....resent the officers as much as the night crew does," Roland Barnes mused aloud.

Charlie hated being drowned out by so-called "adults".

"Not as much. But there'll be some night men there too. Just the same, I'll be the first officer to make the beer blast in quite awhile."

Barnes was satisfied. "I think it'll be a darn good experience for the boy, Betty!"

"Jennifer, why in the name of God do you let your husband carouse around with these characters?"

"He's not just a dumb kid anymore, Betty," she parried, and everybody laughed.

"I just don't see why the hell ya hafta go fly first," Charlie said, "—not that I don't wanna see you fly," he added quickly.

"Charlie, don't swear."

Earl Savage laughed in between mouthfuls of mashed potatoes. "That's the way it is, young man. Sometimes night time is the best time to fly. In the Navy."

And suddenly they were looking right at each other. They looked at each other for what seemed like a long time. The sparkle was back in Earl's eyes....everything was cool. The kid's stomach finally relaxed for him. *Man is good, and nothing is beyond his reach....*

"Well if you're gonna fly tonight, old man, as your loyal and considerate mate I've just decided you'd better take it easy on the sweets. Sweetie." She then duly confiscated the bowl of pudding.

"Roland, did Aunt Betty start the hen-pecking in your marriage as early as Jen here?"

"Savage!"

"Just kidding, ladies, just kidding."

"Y'know come to think of it, the John Deere plant wasn't even in Rock Island. It was over in East Moline," Roland Barnes said.

Laughter was triumphant.

For what seemed like several minutes, then, they all just ate their dessert (save the pilot), saying nothing, exchanging furtive glances at each other and each pretending not to notice. Without competition, the squishy mulching cadence of livestock feeding filled the tiny room. Finally: "Oh, all right. You can go."

"Outasight! Gee, thanks Mom!" the 16-year-old effused, and a rousing cheer mushroomed from the table.

"But if you come home roaring *drunk*, it'll be all day and *half the night* with you!"

"Don't worry 'bout a thing, Mom—do not worry about a thing."

"Congratulations, son," the father said through a thin, comic smile. With his own smile and the gleam in his pale blue eyes, Charlie thanked him.

"Well, young man, yer halfway to becoming a pilot. How 'bout it, group? Shall we crack a bottle of the good stuff to celebrate Charlie's latest step towards manhood?"

"Oh no you don't," harped the pilot's wife. "You're flying an airplane tonight, remember?"

"Good god, flying a plane at two in the morning!"

"Charles Edison Barnes—don't you *ever* take the Lord's name in vain. You hear me?"

* PART TWO *

Straight, ever-widening, with trees fanning by on both sides, an occasional telephone pole, and with the still-warm midnight air blasting through two open windows, a lonely gray highway led them to the Lemoore Naval Air Station. The moon was a floodlight. They could easily have been rolling through a deserted, well-lit playground. The trees appeared to be running by, so swiftly did the silver Stingray whistle between them. Charlie tried to see the gaps between those running trees, trying hard not to blink as his vision was jarred. It was like looking through a moving bicycle wheel. But the plain was darker than the road, and he could not see beyond the trees to what he had already seen earlier in the day's harsh light. He didn't want to see it. He refused to accept the brown desolation. Instead he saw farms, farms that weren't there, acres and acres of agriculture laid out across the floor of this once-dead valley (yes, in his mind's eye it was now a valley) in what, he decreed, should quite obviously emerge from Night's munificent cloak a sprawling green-and-yellow checkerboard. Yeah, there it is, he said to himself....just another amber, fruited plain to shed grace on and crown with purple brotherhood, or whatever. Yet even with the moon and his imagination both operating at full power, it was impossible to tell for sure what kind of crops they were....

"So when do ya go back to the war?" Charlie said suddenly.

"I don't see how anyone can drive with the window closed," Savage said.

"I like the way the wind tickles my face," the youngster contributed, feeling like an idiot the moment he said it. "Pretty soon, I'll bet. My dad says the only way we can win an Asian war is from the air."

"Yer dad's pretty funny!" Savage declared, slapping his right hand down on the thigh of his bluejeans. "Boy, does he know some good stories. Y'know what, I think I'd like to spend a whole day with him sometime, just hearing what my folks were like when they were my age. Y'know?"

"Yeah, sure," Charlie said mildly. He studied the flyer's profile to find the right moment. He let some time go by before asking him again: "Have they given you your next assignment yet, or anything like—"

"What the hell's everybody trying to do around here, kill me off?" Earl Savage cut in sharply. But he was talking to Charlie without looking at him or even glancing at him, instead lasering his glare into the bleak highway before them. "My goddam assignment is right here, man."

Slapped into silence, he decided not to press it. He figured even Earl must get sick of telling and re-telling the same war stories. Maybe later.

They came to a stop sign. Charlie studied the way Savage expertly toggled the stick shift between the bucket seats. He imagined his cousin up in the cockpit handling the flight stick in much the same manner. Then he remembered he didn't know for sure if Phantoms even had flight sticks....

"This is a funny place for a stop sign. We're right in the middle of nowhere."

"Yeah. I guess the cops figure that if they didn't throw one in every few miles all the fly-boys would for sure be doin' ninety up and down this old road. We would, too." The pilot's body seemed to relax, slouching down a little in its seat. And Charlie smiled inside at the returning mildness in his cousin's voice.

Savage now accelerated his long sleek craft and Charlie secretly mimicked his movements, shifting an imaginary stick inconspicuously into second gear, then third, fourth, taking great care to correctly time the depression and release of his imaginary clutch pedal.

"What grade you in now?"

"Twelfth. I'm a senior. I mean I'll be a senior."

"Drink much beer?"

"Oh sure....all the time," he said softly.

"Well take it easy tonight, partner. You hafta drive my other car back for me."

Instinctively he looked to his left, through Earl's window, and sure enough an empty Mustang convertible shot past them going the wrong way.

"Does it have a stick?"

"No, automatic. Ran outa gas last night, haven't had a chance to pick it up."

The kid, like any high-school kid would be, was looking forward to the beer blast. He *knew* Earl would come through. But he also knew he had his dad to thank, a shrewd counterbalance to his mother, who meant well, but if it was up to her he'd never get a chance to do *any*thing. She could be sort of a drag at times....but he knew he was not the first of his age caught between a rock and a wall, between this familial Scylla and Charybdis, where the mother wants her son to grow up strong and worldly and resourceful but is far too protective to let the process proceed on a natural timetable. The maternal womb stretches with timeless elastic, he knew, from the cradle to the grave, and beyond, strong and everlasting....

The Stingray eased to a stop. A uniformed man in a booth said, "Good evening, lieutenant!" saluted crisply, and pressed a button to raise the bar.

"Evening," the flyer nonchalantly replied.

⇒ ⇐

Airfields at night are like lonely secret factories. The workers mill around like so many bees, silently going about their separate businesses, directing all their energies and affections to their queens, the planes; planes which take off and land, and in between make ten-mile ovals in a dark peaceful sky.

Charlie Barnes watched from the ground, looking up at the lights making ovals in the dark peaceful sky. He stood on a makeshift asphalt runway with metal headgear cupping his ears. Lieutenant Savage's plane would make its oval loop, counterclockwise, straightening out of the final bend and then coming right at him and descending right smack towards him like a firefly growing into a screaming iron monster, to where it would finally drop down between the twin rows of ground lights and touch its wheels for an instant on this imaginary aircraft carrier not fifty yards from its single spectator, one quick, delicate bounce; then lurch majestically upward again. The plane's loop traced the heavens in the shape of a racetrack, with the runway doubling as the home stretch. Charlie stood at the finish line (where he always stood at the track) and gazed upward with jealous, aching wonder. The plane made several perfect ovals, and when one of the landings was a slowed-down triple-bouncer he knew it had landed for good.

"Howd'ja do?"

Savage climbed out of the cockpit and jumped athletically to the ground. His flight suit was baggy and complicated, and if he'd had a large square oxygen tank strapped to his back he would have looked quite like an astronaut. When he pulled his helmet off, Charlie repeated the question.

"Whaddaya mean, how'd I do?"

"I'm not a flyer, how the hell should *I* know how ya did?"

Savage smiled. "Well, for a broken-down fighter pilot I made a few good passes, I reckon," he assured his much younger cousin.

"Shall I have the instruments checked out, sir?" someone said. Charlie turned around to encounter the sudden shock of a bald head. It belonged to a stout, unshaven man. Actually, it would be neither precise nor fair to actually call this man "bald". Rather, the skin on the top of his head was easily visible beneath a few; absurdly few; strands of grayish-black hair, his last defense against the dreaded "B" word, scant, precious, practically individual hairs which had been spaced evenly and meticulously across his bare scalp. The spacing was very symmetrical. Charlie had observed that most balding men develop this naive, misguided penchant for disguising their condition, and it is apparently only they that don't realize how silly it looks. Why fight the natural evolution of Change? Nothing lasts forever, does it? Of course not....not even hair....and Charlie was immediately flushed with pride that his father, for one, refused to camouflage the inevitable....

"No, it's okay for now, Mac. Just put 'er to bed."

"Yessir."

The pilot tossed his bright white helmet to the man, who caught it against his stomach. He held it close to him, in both hands, cradling it like it was a sleeping animal. While his cousin stripped out of his flight suit Charlie pretended not to notice the balding man stroke his fingers across the white crown of the pilot's headgear, where the words BARN OWLS were stenciled boldly in red and blue. Suddenly nobody was talking, and it was an uncomfortable silence. Charlie was still holding the metal earmuffs, and he didn't know what to do with them, so he turned to this portly balding fellow and said, "Ya want these?" When the shorter man looked up his expression was at first a fiery glare, but a glare which quickly softened into a thin, acquiescent smile. "Yeah. Thanks, kid," he said quietly, accepting the ear guards with a hand seemingly permanently discolored from grease.

"You be there tonight, Mac?"

"I 'spec so, sir." He took charge of the pilot's flight suit, eyes down, saluted, and walked away.

Charlie was impressed. "You sure get a lot of respect around here," he beamed.

"Oh, that was Mac Richardson. A good, hard-working mechanic. He'll be at Devil's Landing tonight."

"That's where the beer blast is?"

"Yep," Savage said, running a comb straight back and through his gleaming shock of yellow. "Nuthin' special. Just a patch of hard ground and a bonfire in the middle of some swamp."

"So can we go now?"

"Let's do it."

The Stingray, windows half open, wound it way slowly along a dark dirt road, peering around high, grassy corners, its headlights searching for the firelight of Devil's Landing. The road was in bad shape. It was rich with potholes. Charlie could hear the angry tires kicking up mud. Visibility was poor, and occasionally a fleet of brave flying bugs would engage them. The ones with faulty radar splashed their lives against the windshield.

It was his nose that first assured him they were closing in, the sweet smoky taste of burning wood almost drowning out the droppings of invisible animals. Human voices soon followed.

"There it is," Savage said simply, his finger extended needlessly toward the bonfire.

Charlie smiled and squinted between the bugs. "Sounds like they're havin' a pretty bitchin'-ass time!" he bubbled.

"Oh, yeah. They're a rowdy crew, these old boys....that's what I've heard, anyway."

The pilot parked the Stingray between a pick-up truck and a beat-up Chevy and led Charlie to the fire, striding boldly. The men, one-by-one, quieted down until there was no noise save fire's crackling and popping.

Finally: "Hey boys, look who we have here! Good evening, *sir*!"

"Hey, Bill."

"A *very* good evening to you....*sir*!"

"It is indeed—top of the evening to yeh, *lieutenant*!"

"Joe, Hank," said the officer, nodding twice. It was like a roll call.

"I'm glad you could make it, sir."

"Thanks, Mac."

It was all very formal, very "Navy", Charlie thought. No one shook hands, although a few of the men sort of saluted. But if it didn't bother Earl, it certainly didn't bother him. What *did* annoy him was that he would be the only one there not wearing bluejeans. He looked down disdainfully at the brand-new gray dress slacks his mother had forced him to wear. She had even pressed them for him before she went to bed. He tried to smooth out the sharp creases with his thumbs. He knew he looked like a spoiled brat kid, a sissy, a pussy. God, how he hated feeling out of place....But perhaps the most unsettling contrast he would be a part of was how much *older* they all were, older than Earl even. Ten, fifteen, some of them perhaps even twenty years older than Earl. Perhaps *more*. Wow....He had always thought that everyone in the Navy was supposed to be so young....

"Mac, I'd like you to meet my favorite cousin. Charlie."

"Hello again, Charlie!" boomed the middle-aged mechanic, finally smiling, extending his huge dark hand. Charlie offered his own hand, a mistake. The mechanic's hand was twice as thick as the high school kid's, and it closed hard. Charlie squeezed back as hard as he could, but it only made the return grip stronger. He silently cursed the spring-hinged hand grippers for not doing the job. He sensed that Mac could have broken his hand at any time, and could have done so easily, and this obvious shortcoming made him feel suitably inferior.

"He's a fine-looking boy, sir," Mac said soberly.

"Thanks, Mac, and cut out the 'sir' business, huh? That goes for *all* of you!" he commanded in blustery crescendo.

"You a drinkin' man, Charlie?"

"You bet!" Charlie replied eagerly. He was relieved to discover that the balding mechanic actually had a personality. Mac fetched a beer from one of a dozen full ice chests. He tossed it to Charlie, who gathered it in with the skilled hands one would expect of a 2nd-baseman. He confidently pulled the ring, donned a manly smirk, took a hearty swig….it tasted like hell.

"C'mon, young man, I want you to meet a few of my friends," the pilot said. Charlie thanked the mechanic for the beer, and followed.

The next couple of hours exposed him to a series of firm handshakes and mock salutes, roasted hotdogs and toasted marshmallows, which Charlie liked to eat with one side black and one side white. One of the men (after waiting for Lieutenant Savage to wander off to another conversation) wanted to know "if the lieutenant's wife was everything she was supposed to be", and it initially struck Charlie as sort of a rude question, but under Lord Alcohol's influence any potential indignation was quickly gobbled up by a perverse masculine giddiness, emboldened further by a kid's need to share the inside dope, the scoop, the skinny; and so he rendered the juicy details as best he could. They slapped his back. They made lewd comments. They fetched him beer. It wasn't long before he liked them. Soon he liked them a lot. And finally they were no longer just a bunch of greasy mechanics. No way. They were *better* than that. They were *flyers. He* was a flyer. He refused to accept anything short of this whole wonderful affair being one last rollicking drinkfest in some cozy London pub, prior to taking off on yet another thrilling bombing run over Nazi Germany (His father would be Wing Commander, Mac and Earl the squadron leaders.). Drinking only enhanced the fantasy. He was determined to drink, and so within the first half-hour alone he forced himself to ingest four of the cheap, domestic beers. The beers helped him learn a few Navy drinking songs. And the beer itself was actually starting to taste good. *This was it*! This was being part of the *real* world. This was busting his cherry. This was being a man.

Suffice to say that at that moment the kid was eighty percent sure he'd figured out everything that needed figuring out. You'd need only to have asked him.

Four a.m. The bonfire had settled into embers and blackened boards, making an occasional dying noise like a twig snapping. It had performed well. It would rest during the day, for the following night it would have to work again, like a thousand nights before, and a thousand nights to come.

Charlie was sitting on a log, facing the dying fire. He was holding a half-empty beer can. His seventh. He had used some of the beer to wet his comb, figuring he needed the moisture to mat down his blond curls and form the vertical line in back to match Earl's. It didn't work. Earl was off somewhere, spinning war stories or something. The fire was great, though....it jumped around the black logs like....like....well, like a good mellow fire. And suddenly, *snap*!... crackle....pop—like cereal?...silly. The flames, kinda fuzzylike, then not so fuzzy....then fuzzy again....radical, man, truly radical....god, everybody talking and laughing and talking and singing and yelling....it's a warm fire, too....yeah, real warm....orange and yellow and....so very....very warm and....warm and mellow, yeah....mellow and yellow....mellowyellow....they call me mellowyellow....quite right....they call me—

"Quite a crowd, huh kid?"

Charlie turned. "Oh....hiya, Misser Richards," he said, his cotton-dry tongue tripping delightfully over his teeth.

"Richardson. But call me Mac, everybody does." He sat down on the log, and it rolled back a few inches under the irresistible weight of the two men.

"Whoa there! Hey, we almost took a header that time."

"Almost only counts in hand grenades, kid."

"Or atom bombs."

"Oh, is that right! *Every*body's a comedian tonight," the mechanic said, glancing over to where Earl Savage was holding court.

Charlie was so pleased with himself he didn't say anything. He did smile a little.

"So I take it you'd one day like teh follow yer illustrious relative into the stratosphere?"

"Hunh? Oh! Oh, yeah. God, I jus' think it'd be so cool tuh fly a plane....'speshly in a war....'be able tuh make a dif'runce, y'know? I mean *how else* could we be sure've winning this thing on their home court....y'know?"

"What makes you think we're winning?"

He was gazing straight ahead, with a drunken man's unique passion for living, gazing deeply into the friendly yellow bonfire....

"What? I'm sorry, you say sumpthin'?"

"I said God bless America," the mechanic said.

Charlie smiled and forced down the final swallow of his beer. "You guys come out here often?" he said. It was a dumb thing to say, the kind of thing he might accidentally say to a girl, so he added, quickly and casually, "You know. Just tuh drink'n stuff. Hang out. You know, after a hard day's work?"

"Oh sure, kid. What the hell *else* y'think there is to do around here?"

There was a sharpness in the mechanic's voice that suddenly made the log uncomfortable beneath him.

"I need a beer."

"Don't get up."

"Hunh?"

"I got one right here." Mac revealed the two precious cans.

"Oh....great."

For the next few minutes Mac and Charlie did no real talking, just shooting the bull, basking and radiating and simply wallowing in the strange, inexplicable, yet real and wonderful camaraderie that is two men drinking together.

"Kid, how much yeh really like this beer?"

"Beer? Oh….great, it's *great*! It's just….I dunno," Charlie said, taking a guarded sip of the pale liquid. Then he thought a minute. "Mac, do *you* like the taste uh this stuff?"

"Yeah, I guess it's all right. Don't matter how it tastes. It works."

He tried it again, a slightly bigger sip. Weird….a couple hours ago he was sure he liked it. Now, not so much. In fact, suddenly, just the mere smell of the beer was making him want to throw up. He tried to relax, and reminded himself that he was as much a man as they were. It *must* be a good beer, he told himself. But all his tousled mind could come up with was cold, carbonated, nasty, liquid metal. Just then a huge roar exploded from the crowd.

"He's a great guy, isn't he Mac?"

"Sure, kid. The lieutenant's a *great* guy."

"The guys sure love him, don't they?"

The mechanic spat a mouthful of foam into the mud. "Come off it, junior, they hate his guts as much as—" He caught himself. "Grow up, kid. Just grow up," he finally said. He was staring into what was left of the fire. He wasn't blinking. He was staring at things that were very far away….

Maybe it was the beer, or maybe it was finally fatigue, or maybe he just wasn't too bright, but Charlie didn't follow. He didn't know why he didn't follow. His cousin had laughed and joked and drank with the men all night long, everyone had a smile on his face, and except for the funny salutes and no handshakes there didn't appear to be any….to be anything…."What the hell are yuh *talkin'* about?" he demanded angrily.

Mac looked at him a long time before his jaw dropped open: "They're not the same, kid, can't you see that? We're just not the same."

"Whaddaya mean not the same? What th' hell do yuh *mean*! I don't get it….c'mon, man—*tell me*!"

"They're just a buncha grease monkeys, kid, lifers, every damn one of 'em. He's an officer."

"So what? You prejudiced or somethin'?"

The mechanic laughed.

"Why should they hate him so much? He never did anything tuh *them*...." He was depressed. He could hear himself groaning. He didn't understand. The whole thing was unfair.

"He was a *pilot*, dammit! There isn't a man here who wouldn't give his left arm to be a pilot, they *all* want a shot at those bastards over there, and then a guy like that who did what he did has the balls teh stroll in here like some national hero? How the hell would *you* feel? Huh?" The mechanic's voice cracked under the strain. He didn't try to continue. Instead, he chose merely to drown the excess venom in his diatribe with a cold slug of beer. Charlie, also powerless of speech, absentmindedly gulped down the rest of his beer and stared hard, trying to adjust his flawed focus mechanism on this troubled, middle-aged man.

"But this is a free country!" he finally exclaimed, lamely echoing his beloved history books. "We're all created equal, a guy can do anything he wants—everyone knows that. *You* could have been a pilot, if yuh really wanted to."

It was at this last youthful postulate of wisdom that the mechanic poured out the rest of his beer, tossed the can into the fire, and dripped a tired, insincere smile upon the young man: "How old are you, kid?"

"Uh, almost seventeen."

"Maybe someday."

"Huh?"

"Maybe someday you'll know what I'm talkin' about."

"*Hunh?*"

"The kid talkin' your ear off, Mac?" Earl Savage swaggered. Richardson rose swiftly. "He's a good kid, sir," the mechanic said.

"C'mon, Charlie, we hafta go."

They walked over to the Stingray, where a few of the men were running their hands along the silver paint. A couple of them snapped to a lazy attention at their approach.

"Well men, it was a great party, thanks a bunch. I'll see you at the factory!"

"Yes, *sir*."

"You *bet*, lieutenant-sir."

"Good-bye, Mac," Charlie said. He thrust his hand inside the one twice as thick, squeezing with all his might to measure up to it. "G'bye, kid," the mechanic said, hiding his left eye behind a wink. He looked up and into Charlie's grimace, almost melting it with his far-away gaze.

"'night, Mac."

"Good evening, sir," Mac rejoined with a sharp salute. They did not shake hands.

The cousins piled into the Stingray and retreated into the weeds.

The trees ran by in the dark like wooden burglars. It was hard to see them without the moon, who was off hiding somewhere. Efficient choruses of crickets hailed the Stingray, in their ridiculous unison, but the cousins couldn't quite hear them through the open windows. They couldn't hear anything save the simple song of the engine, muted within the soft cool hiss of in-rushing air. They didn't speak for a time. Savage spoke first: "So, what did you think of the old boys?"

Charlie leaned back in the seat to afford the cool air a better angle to his face, looking up into the pinholes in the ceiling. "Earl," he said, "was Mac ever a pilot?"

"Not hardly!" the pilot said with an arrogant laugh. "He washed out pretty early from what I understand. Lucky break. Would've gone up in Korea, more'n likely. Rough skies in that one."

It was then that Charlie realized he was still holding the last beer can. His fingers were pressed deep into the soft metal.

"Did he screw up or somethin'?" he pushed on. It came out too harsh, so he added, "I mean....didn't he want it that bad?"

"We can't all be pilots," Earl Savage said.

He couldn't think of anything to say, lightheaded and enjoying it, so he concentrated instead on the near nothingness in the windshield. The indefinite boundaries of land and sky bled together in darkness before them. They were driving off into infinity. They were the only people in the world. Charlie turned his head sideways to consider his idol's profile. The pilot's brilliant blond hair, barely discernable in the dashboard light, was dark now, pushed straight back by the wind, a few renegade wisps flying free and horizontal as if in a vacuum. There was the hint of a smirk on his face, a winning gleam in his right eye. *Confidence!* This was a man obviously capable of pulling back on the wheel to where the Stingray would gratefully lurch free of its earthly shackles, ascending gracefully, and irresistibly, and oh so self-assuredly, up and out and off, off into the wild blue-black yonder....

"Bet'cha can't wait tuh get back to it, huh man."

"Back to what?"

"Back tuh *what*? C'mon, man. Bet'cha can't *wait* tuh get back up in one a'those Phantoms. C'mon, admit it."

"I was just in one tonight, remember?"

Charlie laughed like a young man who probably should stop before his eighth beer. "I mean *Nam*!" he said with feeling.

"Y'know for a snot-nosed punk kid, you sure are in a hurry to kill me off," the pilot said softly.

"No, what I meant was—"

"My last mission wasn't exactly anything to write home about," he added soberly. The pilot was staring straight ahead, at the road naturally, but fixedly and rigidly like a man who had no intention of glancing over periodically to create the illusion of conversation. A car's headlights materialized out of the vast darkness. The two pinpricks of light enlarged gradually with the car's approach, then diffused into a single enormous blinding beam, circular, hazy and jagged and circular as it refracted through the windshield and then into the young man's tired, drunken, unreliable eyes, lighting up the inside of their rolling cockpit like a continuum of exploding flashbulbs. He turned his eyes away from it, again toward Earl Savage, whose face reflected a tenseness that one might normally associate with a stomach ache. The eyes glistened in a squint, lips were fighting with each other, cheeks were drawn tight, and then the car whooshed past, light became darkness, and the pilot's profile returned to its dull silhouette. "I didn't drop my eff-four into the Gulf because I had a sudden urge to go for a swim."

Charlie scratched his face hard and rubbed the fresh scratches, the pain making him more alert, and when he looked back at Savage the pilot's face was still determinedly fixed, staring straight ahead. "But I thought—"

"The thing that pisses me off is that none of it does any good. This isn't an air game. We waste 'em by the bushel, but they keep comin'. They just *keep coming*. Knock out a hundred, a thousand more come out of the woodwork. Persistent little bastards....it's *insane*. Like droppin' water balloons on an anthill. Insane."

The pilot's voice was now a distant, inanimate thing.

"It'd be one thing if they let us take out Hanoi, but this thing about fire-bombing dirt roads and patches of jungle....nuttier'n a fruitcake, if you ask me."

Charlie was only half conscious of the engine noise through the half-open windows, fairly mesmerized by the consistent hum of the turbine. He did not hear the wind rushing in. It was cold in their compartment. He felt the dull ache of Anxiety in his chest, and could not organize or assemble the army of stray thoughts running around chaotically in his head. And he could not make himself look at the driver....

"Must've been scary tuh crash in ice-cold water. I dunno how—"

"I was heading back when it happened." The pilot's voice was still but a soft monotone, yet concurrently, strangely, apologetic: "I mean we were *done*. We'd already disengaged, and I thought we were home free. Hell, maybe I wasn't paying close enough attention. I don't know. Anyway, just about the time we made the coast my RIO tells me a Sam is headed our way. I bank-turned immediately, reflex mostly....I didn't even have time to say anything back to him. Man-o-man, it was on us like a duck on a june bug—*shhooomm*! Didn't hit us square, but it blew the canopy clean off just the same. Knocked out the radio, too. Happened so damn fast I didn't have time to be scared. But later....well."

"You, uh, said someone told you *Sam* something?"

"Oh, sorry, a Sam is a surface-to-air missile." He glanced over. It was the first time, and it was only for a moment. "S-A-M, get it? And RIO means Radar Intercept Officer, he's the guy who sits in the back seat and keeps an eye on the radar screen. Kyle Peters. Good guy, a top-class guy. We usta play cards together, me'n Kylie. We'd play two-hand cutthroat poker to kill time before goin' up. He hardly *ever* let me win. He was better than I was."

"He....yer sayin' he didn't make it?"

"When I turned around in my seat, part of him was....was....oh, dear God...."

The air rushed in faster than it had before, whistling through windows which had been rolled up a few inches to cut down on the cold. It was a shrieking.

"Sorry, man."

"Yeah."

"Why'd it take 'em so long tuh get'cha outa the water?" Charlie said dryly, trying not to sound like he was doing an interview, then, thinking things through, "No radio, right?"

"They didn't know exactly where I was. Sort of, not exactly. And my wingman went down before I did, so I was sort of....alone up there. Understand? My fuel was low, I had structural damage....there was *no way* I could've made it back. I had to eject. I mean I *had* to! I had to....I had to....I—"

Charlie believed this conversation to be about over. He knew he wanted it to be over. He closed his eyes and rested his head back against the leather.

"Y'know, it was really *great* tonight!" Savage suddenly exclaimed, almost laughing now. "For the first time it felt like we were really buddies! What a great buncha guys....hell, I'm gonna see if I can get a couple of the other officers to come with me *tomorrow*."

Charlie's head whirled on its axis. He glared hard at his hero's silhouette. The Stingray was going ninety now. Whaddaya know, the high school kid thought….what do you know. He thought about the rumors. He thought about the war. He also thought about what Mac had said. All the beer made it impossible to determine if Mac's words actually meant very much, after all he was only a disgruntled old mechanic, and he thought briefly of struggling his way through it and maybe even giving Earl a chance at a rebuttal, but he decided at the last minute it probably wasn't worth it and, what the hell, he enjoyed the ease of just being drunk a lot more. And besides, Earl was smiling again. So no, he thought. No he wouldn't tell him. Ever….

"There she is."

The Stingray slowed and angled over to the side of the road. The trees came to a halt and stood at attention in a long brown line. Charlie had clean forgotten about Earl's other car. He pushed open the door, and pulled his reluctant body out into the cold night. The crickets now sang without accompaniment; he could hear them all. He was tired.

"How much beer you had, young fella?" the pilot said. Earl Savage practically bolted from his seat, and landed lightly on his feet with a spring already in his step. He began to whistle. It was some sort of "swing" or "big band" or "boogie-woogie" type song, a strange thing to be whistling in the middle of nowhere in the middle of the night, and something obviously about 25 years out-of-date to boot. It was a ridiculously happy song. Charlie was watching him closely now. It was weird….the guy's not tired at all, he thought. Raw energy seemed suddenly to be radiating directly from inside of him, and at first it had a calming effect on the youngster, a reflexive panacea, the kind of reassuring persona people around these parts had come to expect and depend on from their servicemen after a couple hundred years of freedom. "True officer material," Charlie's father would have called it. But then the calming effect wore off, and it made the young man nervous. He'd never been this kind of nervous before. He was confused. Savage found a one-gallon gas can and a funnel in the trunk of the Stingray, and fed the fuel to the Mustang.

"Not too much. Don't worry," Charlie said carefully. His head hurt. He was so confused.

"Who's worried!" said the pilot, tossing Charlie the keys. "But just take it easy, okay? Your mom'll kill me if I don't bring you back good as new. It's easy to drive, no stick to worry about or anything, just follow me right back home. See ya."

The Stingray rolled back onto the highway and flew off into the night.

He stood alone now, on the shoulder of the dark highway. There was a heavy, achy, burning sensation between his legs. He looked down, reflex mostly, and realized that he had to take just about the biggest piss of his life. He couldn't believe he was just now being made aware of it. After all, eight beers. He yanked open his fly and let go, and groaned loudly from the relief. He leaned back a little. He did not use his hands. The arcing trajectory intrigued him, he stared as if mesmerized, and he liked the loud donut of mud it made in the dirt. When he was done he shook the last few drops free, zipped up, and struggled into the car.

He sat for awhile, waiting for some of the beer to wear off. He knew the way back, so he figured it didn't matter that the Stingray was already out of sight. He spent the time in a last-ditch attempt to sort out the words and events of the evening. The crickets were strangely quiet now, as if in their collective generosity they were trying to help him concentrate. The history books couldn't *all* have been wrong, he reasoned. It *is* a free country, you *can* do anything you want....maybe Mac didn't work *hard* enough to be a pilot and he's just *jealous*....yeah that's it, maybe the old guy just didn't work hard enough, because....well, because you can be anything you *wanna* be, in the good ol' U.S. of A....

At least that's what he'd always been told.

(....*strangely crippled ghosts of wars, flags suddenly rent and torn, all the dinner-table fables, all the jingoistic clichés ever spoon-fed to him, all of it swirling and meshing and misting up and finally vaporizing now before his reddened, saddened eyes....and for the first time a reluctance to get older, and indeed a grim reluctance even to wake up, wake up later this very morning, to have to endure the fallout anguish of his own thoughts and theories, to suffer the one-man junto he himself had created, and then the long drive back to civilization and having to deal with the miles of parched, obviously barren soil that he knew would be waiting for him....)*

Finally he shoved the key into the ignition. Too much beer. His brain was "fried", as his generation would say. Perhaps things would be clearer in the light of some future morning. One thing he did know; he knew he would have to get out more. He knew he would have to travel more, read more, do more. Live more. Seemed like the older he got, the less he knew about everything....

He pumped the gas pedal a few times to prime the carburetor. Suddenly, frighteningly, almost amusingly, it occurred to him that it might not even turn over. He didn't have time to sweat it, though, because when he turned the key it started up right away. He could not remember ever feeling so lucky. Or so relieved. For merely the stray, hypothetical notion of being stranded in this God-forsaken wasteland struck Charlie as just about the most hopeless feeling in the world...sort of like having to ditch in the Gulf of Tonkin?

He shoved the imaginary stick into first gear, moving slowly out into the empty flow of traffic. Then second, third, fourth, and then swiftly—if not entirely too straight—down the ever-widening road.

KING CHARLES

Author's Notes

The initial spark for this story came from my admiration for the Ernest Hemingway story *The Three-Day Blow*. Both are stories of high-school love, high-school angst, high-school friendships, and a young man going through the loss of a girlfriend; the notable difference being that in Hemingway's story the protagonist does the dumping whereas in mine the hero is the one *being* dumped.

 The second spark came from the notion of how it's impossible to be completely sure of anything in life. "I was so damned sure about us," Charlie says, thinking of the girl he has just lost. I got the idea from a terrific film about the sinking of the Titanic, "*A Night To Remember*", a 1958 British production starring Kenneth More and Honor Blackman. (I feel compelled to utter and repeat the name Honor Blackman because not only is Honor Blackman the weirdest name ever, for an actress or anyone else, but Blackman later went on to portray that most amusingly named of all of James Bond's paramours, the redoubtable 'Pussy Galore'. Just felt like mentioning it.)

 But I digress. Back to "*A Night To Remember*". More, as one of Titanic's officers, says, "I was so *sure*," right after the great ship goes down. "I don't think I'll ever be sure of anything again," he adds, or something melodramatic like that. It stuck in my head. Just shows you how even a single stray line of dialogue from an old black-and-white movie can trigger something in a writer, enough to spark and shape an entire short-story many years later. Just me 'borrowing' again. Unashamedly.

 My fervent hope is that this story might also trigger a revolution in the libation industry. The alcoholic concoction described in the story was indeed invented by me. I know it sounds disgusting (Eggnog & dark beer, mixed together and heated over a low flame? Seriously?), but trust me, it's *good*! Don't knock it until you've tried it. I wrote the 1st draft of *King Charles* and invented the drink 'King Charles' right around the same time, in 1981, just in time for me to serve the latter at my annual Super Bowl party all through the 80s.

 Consider this story both my certificate of invention and my patent for this unlikely alcoholic beverage….

KING CHARLES

Whenever Ben Craig and Charlie Barnes had a footrace, it was for blood.

It had always been that way, their rivalry, ever since they'd scared up the nerve to become "blood brothers" back in junior high. (They'd chosen the usual procedure. Slash the thumbs, press them together, try to create the illusion that each's blood is coursing into the veins of the other. Try not to faint.) And to their credit, the essence of their relationship hadn't grown a great deal more sophisticated as they had grown older. They were five years older now than then, young adults in fact, but they still found a way to make a competition out of everything; the hallmark of any relationship worthy of the oft-misapplied sobriquet "best friends". This day's race was somewhat unusual, in that it was ten a.m. on a school day, and that each runner lugged a six-pack of beer tucked in the crook of his left elbow, but it didn't matter. The finish line was the kitchen door of Ben's house, and there would be no excuses offered by the loser.

They weren't even tired. Not really. Yes, it had already been a long run, certainly not made any easier by the uphill grade of Allen Avenue, or the unusual weight and dampness of the air, or the gusty autumnal winds which Nature chose this strange spring day to marshal against them. And yes, an armful of beer makes for a heavy football. Running alone, either would have stopped to rest. But competition has a way of easing the ache in a young man's chest, and so, as the willow tree in Ben's front yard on Mendocino Street drew closer, their strides were actually lengthening. With twenty yards to go it appeared that the normally faster Ben held a safe lead, but it was Charlie Barnes's hand that felt the satisfaction of the doorknob. The two combatants tumbled, exhausted only now, into the kitchen of the Craig home:

"Looks like....yer the better man, bro'...."

"Didn't....I didn't....think I had a chance...."

There wasn't much talking for awhile, only a lot of laughing and coughing and huffing and puffing.

"Why don'tcha crack a couple a'those beers," Charlie finally suggested, pulling his shattered body into a sitting position on the linoleum floor. His pal Ben, with a sly grin barely detectable on his face, dutifully obeyed. After all, he had lost.

"I'll never get over my love of ditching school," the loser declared, skillfully prying off the bottle caps with two quick flicks of a can opener. He slumped down on the floor next to Charlie.

"It's no big deal to ditch school."

"Yeah, but to ditch school *and* get drunk before lunch is a *helluva* big deal," Ben explained. "Round One, comin' at'cha," he added, and handed his blood-friend a beer.

Charlie sipped slowly from the smooth smoked glass. Ben elected to gulp his beer like a man who had been denied water for a couple of days.

"Wanna catch the Dodger game tonight?"

"Nah," Charlie moaned. "I don't feel like it. Besides, you know I hate the Dodgers."

"I know, but I just thought it would, uh....I forgot," Ben said.

Charlie, more concerned with the task at hand, took two more slow swallows of their sweet, thick, chosen elixir, and then fixed a thoughtful gaze to the smoky brown bottle. He held it up for inspection as if it were a rare, ancient artifact he had just then pulled from the earth: "Ben, can you understand why everyone we know drinks light beer?"

"Whaddaya mean?"

"You know what I mean. Everybody drinks the regular light beer, chicks'n dudes both. And I mean *every*body. Every drop-in, every party, every tailgater. It's always the same old horse piss, man. I mean don'tcha get sick of it? I don't understand it. Dark beer simply tastes better, I just don't understand it."

"Oh, so you don't mean '*lite*' beer, you mean *light colored* beer."

"Yeah. Light beer."

"As in clear beer."

"Yeah. What the Europeans call *laaa*ger," Charlie droned condescendingly.

"Well, the initial outlay of funds might have something to do with it, bro'. These babies cost a fortune."

"Ah, you get what'cha pay for. Cost, my ass. Ten years from now you'll laugh....about it...." Charlie said, his voice trailing off at the end.

"But what about now, my frivolous friend?" Ben queried ever-whimsically. Which is to say *over*-whimsically: "For now I retain but twelve lonely buckaroos with which to take out, wine, dine, and in general amuse and seduce the fair Debbie after the dance Saturday night."

"Oh you poor guy. Poor, poor Ben. My heart really bleeds for you. *Friend*."

"What?—oh. Sorry, man. I wasn't thinking."

"Forget it," Charlie said quickly, forcing a weak smile. "That's why we bought the beer, remember?" And with that the truant lads repaired to Ben's bedroom, for a morning of some truly serious drinking.

"Boy, these babies are strong. Feels like I've had a *dozen* or so reg'aler beers."

"Yeah, me too....see? They really *don't* cost that much, when yuh think about it."

They were sitting on the floor, facing each other cross-legged as they drank, their voices rising and falling depending on the caliber of rock song blasting from Ben's stereo radio (*'KRLA, Pasadena'*, AM-1110 on the dial, their favorite local station). They kept time by bobbing and nodding their heads to the beat. Or sometimes by drum-slapping their blue-jeaned thighs with open palms. Sometimes they would even sing along. This being an unusually humid spring day, naturally they'd dispensed with their shirts. The air was heavy with moisture, like a damp washrag waiting to be wrung out. Sweat beaded up and funneled down their chests. Each was working on his fourth dark beer.

"This is great," Charlie said dourly. Words came slowly. He was staring glass-eyed through a half empty brown bottle. He fought for control of his own tongue: "I mean this is *livin'*, man. We can do any goddam thing we want, 'slong as we don't leave the house, right? *Right?* I mean it's your house, man. Nobody can tell *us* what tuh do."

Ben leaped to his feet and struck a dramatic pose: "Yes I *am* the president of this house, make *no* mistake about that," he declared, with stunning comic accuracy, hands held high, index and middle fingers spread *a la* 'V for Victory', shaking his head side-to-side and very fast to make his relaxed cheeks flop around like a bulldog's. His affectedly deep, ghostly voice was as familiar as the uncertain times in which they then lived: "And I'm not a crook, make *noooo* mistake about *that*," he added with great feeling.

"Hey! Hey, that's pretty good!"

Ben smiled and grabbed his beer off the stereo. He took a long swallow and let a little run out the corners of his mouth and down his chin. "Ya can't teach talent," he said.

"I mean it—you do old 'ski nose' better'n he does *himself*!"

"I got Dick 'down Pat', you might say."

They both laughed hysterically, like the high school kids they were. Charlie finished his laugh with a long swallow of his own, but the alcohol-induced euphoria suddenly hardened his face into a mask of earnest contemplation:

"Ben....I been thinking....how come all parents seem tuh be....I mean they're all Repelluhcans, but then all their kids, us kids, seem tuh wind up totally Demos....y'know? And then a kid grows up an' changes over to Repulligan. I mean izzat the way it is or izzat the way it is? Well it's stupid. An' we kids *know* it's stupid, which makes it *really* stupid. So 'splain it to me, will yuh?"

"You talkin' wildlife preservation or tough on crime?"

"What?"

"I mean is that the re-*pelican* party or the re-*pull-a-gun* party? Speak clearly, o' pathetic drunkard, for thou dost maketh a fool of thyself."

"C'mon. I'm serious."

"Hell, Charlie, I dunno. I mean how the hell am *I* supposta know? I think you think too much," Ben said, with a shoulder shrug and a swig. But now Charlie wasn't even looking at him, causing Ben to frown and shake his head. He was trying everything: "Well, my dad says it's cuz all kids want sumpthin' fer nuthin'. He says we're lazy. He says we'd *all* vote gee-oh-pee if we took our politics seriously. He says we don't appreciate anything until it's gone. And only *then* do we wise up. He says a man's politics should be like his religion."

"Hmmph. In that case yuh better not let yer old man catch you doin' yer Tricky Dick lounge act, or he might pound you for bein' sacrilegious."

"Big deal," Ben said. "If he doesn't like it....if *they* don't like it....if *noooo*body friggin' likes it, I'll—" He stopped to intentionally miss his mouth with a sip of dark beer. "I'll jus' run away from home and disappear, and then they won't have Ben Craig to kick around anymore," he said quietly, plopping defiantly back down to the floor.

Charlie laughed loud and hard; too loud, too hard. They suffered brief eye contact, and then pretended to drink silently and enjoy it.

"Say Ben, what about old man Larson?" Charlie suddenly blared. Like most young men, he generally talked louder when he was drunk: "He didn't seem tuh care a whole lot that he was sellin' beer to a couple uh high school kids. That wasn't very ruhsponzabull of him....was it? I mean we are still kids, y'know."

"I know, I know. Hell, I dunno. Maybe he was a kid kinda like us once, or sumpthin'."

"Nah! He's too old tuh ever've been a kid."

"Yeah, I guess yer right. At least not in the traditional sense."

A favorite ballad of the times interrupted their lazy discourse, and they used the break to finish off Round Four:

> *"You are the sunshine of my life,"*
> *"That's why I'll always stay around...."*
> *"You are the apple of my eye,"*
> *"Forever you'll stay in my heart...."*

When the song was over Ben smiled and said, "Hey, how come we like KRLA eleven-ten better than ninety-three KHJ? I mean KHJ's got the best dee-jays, right? Charlie Tuna, Humble Harve, The Real Don Steele....and KHJ is 'boss radio', which is the best nickname....so how come?"

"But KRLA's got Emperor Hudson and The Hullabalooer. So it's close. Besides, KRLA is Pasadena, it's *ours*. KHJ is everyone's."

"Oh."

They sucked at their beers some more to consider it all. But the quiet got quieter, and soon Charlie's head and shoulders began to slump ominously. Ben studied his friend a long time before breaking the silence:

"Y'know, bro', I gotta admit. You got a lotta class."

"Yeah? Sinzwhen?" Charlie spat forth.

"Since always!" Ben exclaimed, slumping backwards to lean against the foot of his bed. He draped his arm casually around Charlie's bare shoulders: "Lookit—some lousy girl dumps ya, right? Dumps ya like a load of week-old shit. Now a lotta guys, a lotta guys'd jus' mope around, decide it's the end uh the world'n jus' walk around in a fuckin' suicidal daze—right? How cliché can you get. But look at us! It's eleven in the morning, middle uh the week, and we're gettin' stinkin' drunk on beer."

"*Dark* beer."

"Yeah, and that's another thing. Who else'd buy dark beer? I mean who else *would*? I tell yuh, it's class. Pure and simple."

"Ah, yer jus' tryin' tuh make me feel good."

"Am not," Ben insisted.

"Are too, don't deny it," Charlie said. "You don't hafta deny it," he added softly.

"So? So what if I am?" Ben said loudly. His perpetual good humor was usually a natural overtrump of Charlie's frequent melancholy moods, certainly worth a try: "Why don'tcha just—" He paused. He squinted. He was trying everything: "Why don't you just shut up and go get us a couple more uh these, asshole. Make yourself useful, as my old man would say."

Charlie was perfectly willing—though less than perfectly able—to comply. He got up from the floor slowly, one lanky section of his body at a time, wobbled down the hall to the kitchen, and liberated two more of the dark beers from the refrigerator. Opening them was a struggle. The can opener would not obey him. The effort and jostling required to pry the cap off the second one caused the foam to bubble and rise quickly up the bottle's neck and out the mouth. He quickly wrapped his own mouth around it and sucked in as much of the excess foam as he could. A little of the light brown foam ran down the bottle, and it made his hands sticky. He wiped them alternately on his blue jeans and hairless bare chest. He took another swig and the taste made him smile. Then another. The smile grew bigger. As if, perhaps, his stomach wasn't jumping anymore. He was soon sucking the good taste from both bottles, as if comparing the two. He smiled as if pleased with himself. By the time he returned to the bedroom he was grinning from ear to ear.

"What're *you* so smug about?"

"I been thinkin' again," Charlie said, or rather proclaimed with painful glee. "I *do* have class. I *must* have. I mean nobody but me drinks dark beer. Nobody! You said so yerself. I bet we're the only ones in town drinkin' dark beer right now. Maybe the only ones in the whole damn country."

"Let's not get carried away."

"No, man, I mean it. It's possible, yuh gotta admit. You don't *know* that we're not the only ones in America drinkin' dark beer right now, right? I mean you don't *know* we're not. You don't know....*any*thing, really. For all we know, this roof might fall in an' squash us any minute."

"But my dad just had new shingles put on."

"Ah, but it still might fall in. It won't, but you don't *know* it won't," Charlie said with authority. The dark beer had rendered him very philosophical.

Ben Craig thought for a moment: "So?"

"So that's why I got class! This roof *might* fall in, an' we *might* be the only ones in America drinkin' dark beer right now. And since I thought up *both* uh those things, it not only means that I am a young man brilliant beyond compare but it also means I got *class*....unnerstand?"

Ben Craig thought for another moment. Then he smiled: "I always said you had class," he finally said. He snatched his partially consumed beer from Charlie's hand and sucked a long swallow. "I'll never understand why she picked that punk Anderson over you. Hell, until now I thought he was queer."

"Can you believe it? I mean can you be*leeve* it?" Charlie double-barreled, muffling his own laughter with a healthy slug of beer, adding, "That's why I gotta do something even classier, just to show her who's, uh...."

"Classier?"

"Exactly."

Charlie Barnes sat vacant-eyed and quietly on the bedroom floor, trying to think of something especially classy. He ran his beer-soaked hands repeatedly through his shaggy blond hair without realizing what he was doing. Ben Craig, sitting on the bed now, squinted and watched his friend think.

"Hey....hey Ben—what was that yellow stuff in the jar in the fridge?" Charlie said suddenly.

"Oh, that's just eggnog. Mom makes it for Dad all year round. Why, what's up?"

"Real eggnog, huh?"

Ben nodded.

Charlie's brow furrowed. It was as if a light bulb had been turned on inside the beer-clouded gazebo of his brain. He grinned, and in an instant he was on his feet. "That's the *ticket*!" he yelped, bounding off at once to the kitchen. Ben struggled to his feet, and followed.

Ben Craig arrived at the kitchen just in time to see Charlie Barnes pour the remaining two beers into a saucepan. The saucepan already contained a relatively equal portion of the homemade eggnog. The mixture was a marriage of yellow and brown, soon a rich, tan spiral which Charlie swirled around and around with a long wooden spoon. The swirls seemed to have a hypnotic effect on the two young men. They stared blank faces into the pan, breathed in the sweet, strange aroma, breathed out through open mouths. The pan sat over a low flame on the old O'Keefe & Merritt stove, soon causing the entire tiny room to eddy with this intriguing new smell. A sweet, homey smell. Perhaps (it could be argued) no one who ever lived had ever encountered this *exact* smell. They grinned at each other. Charlie mixed the colors slowly, earnestly, with unfamiliar patience and care....

"So what the hell ya doin'?"

"You'll see."

"I see it, I smell it, I think I already like it a little, but I do not understand it. I repeat, my brilliant yet incredibly twisted and frivolous friend, what the hell are you doing?"

"I'm inventing a drink."

"Yer what?"

"Inventing a *drink*, man, what could be classier than that? I bet there's only, what, about fifty or a hunnerd different mixed drinks in the whole damn world, which means there's only about fifty or a hunnerd guys in history that ever actually invented a drink. Right? It's *perfect*—talk about an exclusive club! Y'know, I bet before you know it this will make me a legend in taverns and barrooms from coast to coast, and my handsome face will soon be a regular staple of the late-night talk shows," Charlie predicted.

"Well if you don't mind, Staple Boy, I'll withhold my judgment until I sample the brew," Ben said, snatching the long wooden spoon from Charlie's grasp.

Ben aimed for effect, then slowly guided the wooden spoon into the saucepan. He then carefully withdrew it and proceeded to tentatively raise the infant concoction to his lips. His eyes widened at the taste. He plunged the spoon in again and lowered his head directly over the pan, taking a bigger sip this time. His obvious delight caused him to snap to a respectful standing position for the rendering of his verdict: "Bro', it's not bad....I mean it's *not fuckin' bad*!" he declared. Charlie took his turn with the eager spoon: "Wow....even *I*, as inventor, didn't think it'd be *this* good," he said, fairly giggling forth his excitement, quickly sloshing some of his brainchild into two mugs. Some of the precious tan liquid spilled on the counter. They ignored it. The blood-friends took seats at the kitchen table.

They drank in silence. Getting used to a new libation is a solemn, ritualistic affair, and neither was inclined to rush through the experience. The heat caused their sips to be even more tentative, more thoughtful, a silent litany of sweet, thoughtful, tentative sips. In between sips each's eyes would seek out the other's, and each time it was Charlie who would pull his away....

"It's good, Charlie."
"Yeah."
"Too good for her."
"You said it."
"Certainly *way* too good for *him*."
"Damn straight."

They were lost in their own little world, these two young men, a one-room world of good conversation and warm, soothing drink, a world sorrowful yet strangely satisfying and perfectly sufficient for the time being. It was certainly a scene far removed from their usual world across town at the high school, where three thousand students were just escaping their fourth-period classes, arriving in droves at the canteen area of the campus for lunch. Those with a more generous lunch allowance could afford the cafeteria's stale cuisine, but the vast majority drifted as usual to the canteen, with its manicured green lawns and steel picnic tables, drinks and fries and hamburgers for sale; hamburgers so bad you were practically coerced into bringing your own brown bag. The school's apprenticing gangsters were patrolling their usual beat next to the lunch lines, where the more faint of heart queued up to pay them their daily protection money. Cheerleaders practiced their routines on the sun-drenched lawn. Admiring male fans sat cross-legged at their feet and gazed up at them. An elite cadre of seniors was holding its daily noontime summit meeting at their favorite table, cooking up some appropriate pre-graduation mischief and wishing, no doubt, that they had ditched school that day with their two absentee members. And a couple tables away a girl, a yellow-haired girl with tan skin, long legs, and a smile that could guarantee a good day all by itself, shared a tuna fish sandwich with a boy called Tom Anderson. This was high school life in Pasadena, the day-to-day realm of Ben Craig and Charlie Barnes in the early seventies. This was their element. They were comfortable here. This was their so-safe, so sugar-coated, thoroughly spoon-fed world of only moderate challenges, a world they cherished, the world which gave them their gentle entrée into adulthood, a still-carefree world to which they would happily repatriate the following morning. But today, for just this one illicit day at least, they were far more content within their sorrowful one-room realm, alone with their talk, wallowing in one's misfortune, and reveling in the improbable, comforting union of eggnog and brown beer....

"Say bro', how 'bout if you'n I head out to the track? We'll miss the first race, but if we leave now we'd probably make post time for the second, 'riders up' for the third at the latest. Sound cool? I mean if we're gonna skate, we might as well do it right, right?"

"It's Tuesday," Charlie sighed. "You know the track's always dark on Tuesday." He was looking down into his mug.

"Oh yeah....I forgot."

Ben drained his cup first and wobbled theatrically over to the stove to ladle in Round Seven. Charlie was lagging a round or so behind. Ben looked at him and squinted. He poured the new drink directly from the saucepan into his mug, and was only half successful. He wound up spilling a considerable portion on his right hand. He made sure his vulgar objections to his own surprising show of ineptitude were loud enough to be heard. But it didn't provoke a reaction. Unlike Charlie, Ben had been blessed with a full thatch of chest hair, and he now made use of this convenient towel of light brown to wipe the excess stickiness from his hand. He laughed at this appearance of drug-induced clumsiness, but Charlie refused to join him so he stopped. Narrow eyed, he stared at the back of Charlie's head a long time without saying anything.

"You happen to get a good look at Kristy Johansson lately?"

Charlie didn't look at him.

"Boy, what a bod," Ben continued. He dipped his half-full mug into the half-empty saucepan. "What a rack. She shouldn't be allowed to wear those tight sweaters."

Charlie still didn't say anything. He was examining the contents of his mug.

"I actually *conversed* with the redoubtable Gail Baker yesterday, in psych class," Ben went on adroitly. His diction had had a short memory all day, switching back and forth from crisp to slow, from slow to slurred, and back to crisp again as the morning bled into afternoon: "You know her? That new superstar bimbo who just transferred in from across town? God, I wonder what *she's* like! That's one hot-lookin' bitch, I'm tellin' you. Ever see a more perfect ass on a chick not in Playboy? If I had any guts I'd ask that hose queen to a movie or sumpthin', 'cept Deb would probably have a cow, or worse, or—"

"You don't hafta do this, Ben."

"Do what?"

"Rap about these random chicks to take my mind off of it. They're just nameless faceless chicks to me, I don't care about 'em. I'm not *like* you, Ben. You've always had tons uh girls, ever since I've known you. Girls always came easy for you. But she was *it* for me, man! She was the first real girlfriend I've ever....Anyway, these other chicks, they might as well be, I dunno, be mannequins or something. I dunno. Just knock it off, okay?"

Ben shut up. He leaned against the refrigerator and took a careful sip of his drink. He didn't spill any. "Say, what are we gonna call this stuff?" he wondered aloud.

Charlie was looking out the window. The willow tree leaned to the left, in deference to an unseasonably strong gust of wind. A light rain began to fall. The wind blew a few quiet sprinkles against the windowpane, some of the water beading up into little droplets. He watched intently as one droplet raced another down the glass. It was close all the way. The drop he was rooting for lost. When it was over he again directed his gaze through the thickening wall of rain: "It's rainin'. It's damn near June and it's rainin'," he moaned.

"I figure we gotta name it after you, seein' as how you invented it. How 'bout....well, how about King Charles, seein' as how it's fit for a king!"

Charlie was still gazing wistfully into the rain, his head resting heavily on one hand. The other hand was rubbing and clutching his stomach. "Wudja say?"

"I said we'll call it King Charles."

"Huh?...oh. Okay. King Charles it is. Does have kinduva bitchin'-ass ring to it."

"Want some more?"

"Yeah, sure. I mean I guess so. I mean what the hell." His voice was very quiet.

Ben took Charlie's mug and filled both mugs to the brim. He was smiling wryly, close-mouthed. He poured directly from the saucepan. Not a drop of the precious concoction was spilled. He poured until there was nothing left.

"Here you go, bro', King Charles, piping hot. Round Eight for me, Round Seven for you. You better drink up," Ben rattled off, much faster than he had any right to rattle. He gave Charlie his mug and continued to stand behind him. Historically speaking, he could always hold his liquor better. Charlie kept his seat. They sipped their drinks without talking. The rain grew steadily stronger, the wind blew markedly louder. If they were paying attention....

Charlie drew a deep breath and warmed his hands on the sides of his mug. "I was so sure," he exhaled. "I was so damned sure about us." There was a long pause while they sipped the King Charles. He stared blankly out the window. The weather had become a belligerent force. Trash swirled, leaves flew. Trees swayed. Rain seemed to fall at absurd angles, in meek, servile deference to the wind. Cold and condensation fogged the window. He could barely see the cars parked across the street. The sheets of rain had effectively curtained the little house off from the rest of the world. Neither spoke for a long time. Suddenly they could hear the rain through the quiet, as it splattered distinctly different percussions against the glass and brick of pane and porch respectively. Nature's music. Generally maudlin, occasionally malicious, and on this day totally, pathetically, indifferent....

"Hey, man, it's no big deal," Ben finally blurted out. "She's not worth worryin' about. It's only a stupid dance."

"Tuh *hell* with the goddam dance!" the young man cried, slamming his mug down on the table for emphasis. Tan liquid flew in all directions. "Dude, you just don't *get* it! I was playing for keeps and she was just playing *games*!" he exclaimed; suddenly the words were coming faster, clearer. He clutched at his mid-section and grimaced like a man with a stomach ache. Nobody who ever lived ever had a stomach ache exactly like this one. He wiped away a stray tan droplet that had landed and beaded up on his cheek. When he spoke again the words came slowly, softly, but every degree as clear: "It's....it's like on third down when a quarterback flips a safety valve pass to a running back when he gets pressure, y'know? She was something I knew I could count on when I was in trouble, when everything else was going wrong....*she was my safety valve*! She was the one thing in this fucked-up world I knew I didn't hafta worry about. We may just be kids but I figured I could at least count on that one thing, man. I was that sure. I just figured she'd....I don't know....always be there for me. For *me*. Man, I was so....so damned....oh god—" He was leaning over the table, his head almost touching it. The ache moved up into his narrow chest, grabbing at his throat, burning.

Ben methodically sipped his drink. He didn't reply right away. Finally: "Yeah, so fucking what? She's not worth it. She's not *worth* it, Charlie! *No* chick is worth worrying yourself to death over, I'm here to tell you. She's not even in yer class, dude. A good running back who can catch the ball on third down is worth *ten* chicks like her," was his analogy.

Charlie raised up, turned in his chair, and looked up at Ben Craig now, finally, quizzically, angrily, then defiantly: "Y'know what? Know what I'm gonna do? Instead uh wastin' the prom on some random, dog-face, blown-out loser of a chick, I'm headin' for Eaton Canyon. I'm gonna hike all the way up to Henninger Flats for the night. Yeah. Dammit, *yeah*. I'm gonna hike up there and sleep out under the stars. And I'm gonna do what *I* wanna do! It's my night as much as...." He paused: "Well I'm going, and that's that. Maybe take summa this weird stuff along and heat it up over a can of Sterno," he announced sluggishly to the world, holding up his mug of King Charles, two-handed, for critical acclaim.

"Bitchin'! *Now* yer talkin'. Can I tag along?"

"Yeah, sure," said Charlie. Then he remembered: "What about Deb? You screw up the prom for her and yer *toast*."

Ben took a long, final swig of the newly named drink. After a protracted search for a plausible response he finally settled for what he usually did, for the comic: "I'm thinking of dumping her. Well, for one night anyway. Or until I get horny."

Charlie forced a mild laugh which eased into a thin smile. Then he said, "Y'know, Ben, I don't care what anyone says—yer not such a bad guy."

"If you think I'd dump a great piece of ass like Deb just for you, yer crazy," Ben rejoined in laughter. "Besides, if she doesn't like it there's always Gail Baker and *her* redoubtable ass, remember?" They both were laughing now. As their laughter died down, Ben rested his hand gently on Charlie's bare shoulder. He gave a gentle squeeze. They each pretended it was no big deal.

Charlie continued to cradle his mug in both hands. He took a last, long, thoughtful swallow of the King Charles. It was gone. His eyes were slits, barely open, lasering his thoughts into the bottom of the empty mug. "Ben," he said, "just how important you suppose girls are, anyway? In the long run."

"Who knows," Ben said. "Depends on if you got one, I guess." He fondled a gold ring on his left hand.

Charlie again looked to the window for answers that weren't there. The rain had thinned into a light drizzle, nearly invisible. He watched it rain. Ben Craig considered him through sharp, bloodshot eyes: "Must hurt like holy hell, huh."

"It hurts like holy hell, Ben….I never wudda believed anything could hurt so much."

Ben frowned into the bottom of his own mug, then smiled. "So then howsabout us makin' another fabulous batch of King Charles?"

"That's a damn good idea," Charlie droned. "We'll hafta get more beer, though. Lucky old man Larson likes us."

"Right."

"You think it needs any changing? A little extra beer maybe, or an extra ingredient or something? I'll name you co-inventor."

"No extras, my man. Tastes pretty darn good just the way it is."

"Okay. If you say so. I guess it's settled then."

"So shall it be written?"

"So shall it be done."

(And so it was decided. They had discovered that there is nothing in the world quite like a brand new drink to make a dry day memorable….or to ease the ache of a lifetime in a young man's chest.)

Ben Craig, teenage humanitarian, his work here almost done, waited as long as he could to push the final envelope:

"Well? Wanna go now?" he finally, casually suggested.

"Right on," came back the dull reply, and then, "We're outa here." But Charlie wasn't moving, not yet. He stayed seated. He seemed paralyzed by something in the window. His eyes blinked several times and he snuffed up, loudly, twice. The rain had stopped as suddenly and completely as a turned-off faucet. Typical for L.A.

"Ready to go?" Ben volleyed again.

"Yeah. Yeah, I'm cool," Charlie Barnes said soberly, standing suddenly and quickly as he said it. His voice mixed resignation with resolve. He rubbed his eyes with the heels of his hands. He slapped Ben's shoulder on the way to the door. "Let's get goin'. You drive?"

Ben Craig smiled warmly at his only blood-friend in the world. He grabbed their shirts off of the washing machine, where they'd thrown them earlier. "Let's walk. I mean I don't think either one of us misguided adolescent drunkards should be doing any driving just now," he opined, "do you?"

"Oh, right. Yer right, Ben," Charlie said. "I forgot."

STRAITS OF MESSINA

Author's Notes

This was a fun one to write, and I certainly think it's a fun one to read. It's got life aboard a cruise ship, exciting ports-of-call (and some not so exciting), and lots of tasty movie references if, like me, you can't get enough of old movies and the wonderful old-time actors and actresses of yesteryear.

Many years after I wrote *Straits of Messina* I stumbled upon an old, little-known story about a few days on a cruise ship called *A Girl in 1941 With No Waist At All,* written by J.D. Salinger, who just happens to be pretty much my favorite storyist. At first I got this enormous rush; I mean holy cow, both stories about cruises, one written by me and one written by one of my heroes? Cool. Suddenly I felt like J.D. and I had a bond. But then I got nervous. The stories are similar in many ways, I said to myself, maybe some people will think I was copying it. Maybe *Salinger* will think I'd copied it! But I didn't. I swear I had never even heard of J.D.'s story till long after I wrote mine. After all, it's a very obscure and practically unknown story. And to prove my point, had anyone *else* out there ever heard of *A Girl in 1941 With No Waist At All* until now, until I mentioned it? I didn't think so….

At this late stage of the game of Life it sounds silly, the idea of worrying about J.D. Salinger reading— and being suspicious of—one of my stories. The far more likely outcome was to live my entire writing life in obscurity, which of course is exactly what happened. And now Salinger is dead, so that's that.

Funny story though, huh? (Maybe I should write a short-story about *that*.)

Straits of Messina would seem to be, on the surface, one of the "L.A. JOURNAL" stories least likely to have been drawn directly from real life. And yet there really *was* a Greco-Turkish War in July of 1974, and I *was* aboard a luxury liner which cruised right into it, and therefore I *did* get caught right in the middle of it….sort of. Let's just say I'm glad they re-routed my ship to other ports to prevent it from docking on Greek soil, so that I didn't have to go join the Greek Army and fight the Turks.

Young American men being impressed into foreign armies in foreign wars? Y'know, the more I think about it, my story and J.D.'s really *aren't* that similar. Oh well. Still would have liked to have met him.

Oh, and it is also true that there *was* a beautiful young girl on my ship who caught my eye, also true that I spent the entire cruise trying desperately to get into her pants. But she was a good girl, for which I am grateful. Because it makes for a much better story that our young hero encounters resistance whilst pursuing such seemingly urgent endeavors….

STRAITS OF MESSINA

Venice is the kind of city Americans pour into every summer, then stagger out of wondering what the hell the big deal is. A breakdown in communication is the villain. Sure, they told you about the great ice cream you can get there, and where an American kid can find the only root beer on the Continent, and where a bigger American kid can find all the American girls (all the things you left America to forget for a few weeks), but they didn't tell you about the dirty air, and the far dirtier water, and the smell, and the crowds (and all the *other* things you left America to forget for a few weeks). It's been said that '*Venezia*' is Italian for 'scam', and that's probably too harsh, but for any American planning to go there it's safe to say that the anticipation is likely to exceed the actual event. About the nicest thing that can be said about the place is that you wind up sympathizing with the people who must actually live there, without a sewage system, and you realize that they wouldn't dump their garbage or discharge their bodily wastes into the canals if there was any other reasonable way to get rid of it. But that doesn't mean you have to actually go there to see it and smell it for yourself.

It was a hot day in July of 1974. Most of the Americans in San Marco Square seemed quite satisfied with the sights that had so satisfied their ancestors that Venice is a remarkable city. They marveled oval-mouthed at the boats passing in and out of the fouled canals. They marveled at the domed majesty of the thousand-year-old cathedral. They marveled most of all, perhaps, at the bell tower, the Campanile, rising straight and high above the square, tapering at the top to a pointed head just above the twin bells. But Charlie Barnes wasn't impressed. There was one just like it back home at college. He wanted no part of anything that reminded him of school, so he did not look at the Campanile. As for the canals, there were replicas every bit as dirty back in Venice Beach; not too far from his *regular* home. No novelty there. And as for the cathedral....well, he had never been able to identify much redeeming value in anything that had anything even remotely to do with that. There were better things to be impressed by.

He was sitting in an outdoor café in "the Piazza". Pigeons gathered optimistically at his feet, but he wasn't eating. And he certainly wasn't interested in pigeons. The café was selected for its vantage point, its tactical utility, not its indigenous wildlife or overpriced cuisine. The best girls were all walking by this café. Women, too. And *so many* of them! Many were American, naturally, but just as many were not, and those that were not were invariably the ones that intrigued him. Especially the French and Italian ones. They were leaner, especially through the legs, and being a devout 'leg-and-ass man' it was this young man Charlie's natural predestination (Charlie himself had decided) to become a 'French-and-Italian-girls man'. Some of the legs walking through the square made his own legs weak and tingly just to look at them. And then, of course, there was the happy fact that these girls were all so incredibly tanned, *all* of them, as though they'd all spent the better part of their lives lying out on Hermosa Beach....but few L.A. girls were *this* tan, the young man marveled, even with the beaches there to seduce them all year round.

Yes, Charles Edison 'Charlie' Barnes was a born French-and-Italian-girls man. It was his destiny. And it was certainly in his post-adolescent self-interest to be so; because he'd heard they were a pretty good way to start. And he wasn't doing too badly. Of the five girls that he'd asked only one actually turned him down, the others just smiled and kept going. But for once he didn't mind the rejection. For one thing, he knew he wouldn't be back in Venice for a week. It would have been awkward to strike gold and then have to make an appointment to come back a week later to actually prospect it. For another, he knew his success ratio figured to be even lower than usual with females he'd never even met and could not even converse with, especially the most delicious of these lean-legged passersby. He wasn't even nervous....*so what* if they said no? Why should *he* be embarrassed? He knew he'd never even see them again. For once, playing the fool came with no downside risk! If anything, he only wished that strangers would be just a little more open-minded to the harmless requests of other strangers, a minor complaint. But they were good. He knew they were good. They had to be.

Occasionally (it should be noted), right in the middle of ogling one of these distant wordless goddesses he would experience a twinge of resentment. It was another minor complaint, nothing serious, but it had always struck him as so unfair that it was so much harder for a guy. A good-looking girl can shed her skin anytime she wants. But for a guy.... well, it was just harder, that's all.

His watch told him it was time, so he stood up and smoothed and adjusted the front of his bright white bell-bottomed pants. He checked his pockets. He had less than two hundred dollars left, but he wasn't worried. He had his return plane ticket and the cruise was all paid for. He'd heard a lot about these cruises; he wanted to take his before he was too old for it to be of any real value. He knew he had to do something. In fact, he knew he should've done something like this a long time ago. His biological clock was suddenly loud and impatient, and he knew he wasn't getting any younger. And that's why he had pursued this enterprise with such blind singleness of purpose, working two part-time jobs, setting aside a little of the expense money his trusting parents sent up to Berkeley each month, even all-but-eliminating his cherished weekend pilgrimages to the track, Tahoe, Vegas, all of it. He had made the big sacrifices. As far as he was concerned it was now or never. He was like Gary Grimes in *Summer of '42*, except that now that he was dangerously older than Grimes *was* he would gladly settle for something somewhat less than Jennifer O'Neill *is*. In other words, his time was now. All that remained was to not be too picky and then to execute the plan. (And he'd already figured the cruise had cost him about ninety-six dollars a day, meaning that wasting time being too selective had just become a very expensive hobby.) He knocked back the final mouthful of cappuccino. He licked his chapped lips at one last sun-bronzed, lean-legged, quickly-passing fantasy. Simultaneously, the metallic throb of the Campanile's twin bells reminded him it was time to go.

The ship was shockingly big. He figured it had to be three football fields....maybe longer. He took off his aviator sunglasses and hung them in the V of his half-buttoned Italian silk shirt, the way Steve McQueen probably would do it. He looked the huge vessel up one end and down the other, squinting McQueenlike in approval. Boy, it looked good; eight decks of pleasure, shiny-white all around. With the single word **APHRODITE** lettered larger-than-life across the hull. "Damn straight!" he said. A history major and voracious reader both, Charlie thought Aphrodite was as good a name as any for a Greek ship, especially one that *he* was about to climb aboard. Aphrodite, the Greek goddess of love, beauty, and pleasure. The ship's very name was clearly a kind omen from the gods. He was suddenly proud of the choice he had made. Could Steve Reeves have chosen any better? Or Kirk Douglas for that matter, or any *other* goddam silver-screen Greeks? And what could be cooler than to do it on a luxury cruise ship? It had become his ideal, the perfect vehicle for what he had in mind. He couldn't wait to fire off a few postcards to three or four friends, the ones who he knew would appreciate the by-god Odyssean perfection of it all. "Damn damn *damn*!" he thrice re-affirmed his good mood, and up the gangplank he went.

(Incidentally, or at least incidental to why he was there, he'd heard that Greek ships were peculiar for their good food, eight courses twice a day, and the crew, he was told, was the loyal type, like a soldier is loyal to his superior officer....Charlie certainly liked the idea of loyal Greeks serving him good food....but he knew that focusing on ancillary things like that was hardly to the point.)

There wasn't as much pre-departure excitement as the young man had expected of a luxury cruise ship. In fact, there wasn't any. He'd expected brass bands, speeches and streamers, girls running around like chickens with their heads cut off, everybody kissing everybody, everything he'd seen in dozens of old movies and imagined he'd read about in the 'Society' pages. But almost before he'd settled into his cramped quarters the great ship lurched forward, moving tentatively and sluggishly, yet hopefully, out into the Adriatic Sea. How hard he hoped it would be a good trip. He was counting on being successful. He could hear his biological clock ticking; no more postponements, no time left to waste. The trip was already paid for, he reminded himself.

II

The first dinner, the so-called 'Captain's Dinner', wasn't for a couple hours yet, so young Charlie was out prowling the upper decks of the great ship, 'scoping' it, thoroughly checking it out. He walked right past the lure of the gaming tables, a nervous irritation which he knew he'd have to come to grips with later. The dance floor didn't strike him as nearly so inviting. And he cruised right through an impressive gallery of duty-free shops without even stopping to look; he didn't come ten thousand miles to squander his meager bankroll on a bunch of trinkets. He finally wound up at one of the many shipboard bars. In fact he was just informed by his faithful cabin steward that there were eight bars in all....*eight*! Eight decks eight courses eight bars? Jackpot. His head fairly throbbed with omens. Pushing his way between two old bald gentlemen in sport shirts, leaning over the smooth wood grain, he loudly and confidently ordered his current favorite drink, Campari and tonic. The bartender, a short, half-bald Greek fellow in a white dinner jacket, mixed the drink and sent it sliding across the glazed wood. *"Efcharisto!"* Charlie said loudly, proud of his one-word Greek vocabulary, and tossed three coins one-by-one to the smiling little man.

There was a girl sitting in the lounge next to the bar. She was looking out the window. She was alone. *Paydirt*! But there was no hurry, no rush.... we just shoved off, he reminded himself. He forced himself to be calm, to scope out the full complement of her charms before actually swooping (In Southern California, young men usually pick up the routine by the time they leave high school; first one scopes, *then* one swoops.). He traded swallows of air and alcohol, and scoured the young woman with his pale blue eyes. She obviously wasn't American. It was obvious. She was too lean, beautifully lean, *achingly* lean, like she might even be French or Italian. And since American girls don't travel alone....yeah....*yeah*! And her olive-dark complexion made it a lead-pipe cinch! But what to say? He reeled his mind through a couple of Cary Grant movies, trying to find the best lines. No luck; he was too nervous. Frustrated, he went back to his leering analysis. He liked her brown hair, the 'continental' way it curled inward at the neck. He liked the far-away range of her Latin-brown eyes. He really liked the snugness of her black backless evening gown. He liked everything about her. No Jennifer O'Neill, but more than acceptable, the young man quickly decided. Yeah.....*a lot* more....

With the casual air of an international playboy he adjusted the knot of his tie, took a last gulp of courage, and sauntered slowly and slyly over to the window as though he'd just inherited the family business.

"Uh, excuse me, mademoiselle, but I'm afraid the only language I sp.... *excel* in, is English."

"Oh, how cute!" the girl said, in her most authentic Midwestern twang.

"Yer American."

"Oh gosh, you sound so disappointed!"

"It's not that," he said a trifle too quickly. He thought *sure* she was French....

"Are you just going to stand there all day looking silly?"

He fell heavily into a stuffed leather chair and set his drink noisily on the glass tabletop between them. The girl didn't have a drink. He looked away, and made himself appear disinterested.

"I'm Stacy Mellano."

"....Hmm? You say something?"

"I said my name is Stacy."

"Oh....Barnes. Charles E. Barnes."

"Charles?"

"Alright, alright. It's Charlie."

"I see!"

"Hey look, can I buy you a drink or what?"

"Thank you, no."

Charlie breathed in a long sip of his Campari. He tried to cast his frustration through the porthole and into the endless salt water, rushing by thick and milky-white. His nerves were fine now. Why wouldn't they be, with nothing to be nervous about: "Well, well. I wonder what the hell makes a small-town girl from the Midwest fly halfway around the fuckin' world, just to sit in a giant floating bar without a drink."

"How did you know I'm from—"

"I plead temporary residency."

"What?"

"Iowa."

"Iowa? Really?"

"Washington County. Born, bred, and completely corn-fed."

"But now you live—"

"Los Angeles. Berkeley. Either or."

"I see."

She dropped her eyes and uncrossed her nylonless legs. Some legs don't need nylons. Hunched slightly over, she looked a long way from comfortable. Suddenly it occurred to him that she might actually get up and leave....

"Listen, I'm sorry if I came off kinda rude there. I don't want'cha ta think I'm a jerk or anything, even if I am—heh heh! Tell ya what. If you happen to have first sitting, I suppose I'd be god-damn happy ta walk you to the dining hall. That is if you want." (What the hell, he decided....)

Her face twisted up uncomfortably at first, but he was relieved to reclaim her smile: "I suppose I'd be gosh-darn delighted," the girl said.

"So what's your table number?"

"Thirty-three."

"Hey, me too—Jesus H. Christ, talk about destiny!"

They both laughed, with Charlie quickly and dynamically gulping down the rest of his drink. His hand folded almost casually around hers, and they walked as slowly as he could to the dining hall.

III

"I love these Greek waiters," said Charlie Barnes, in between quick, noisy bites of a Caesar salad. "They really know how to serve their masters, so to speak."

The waiter, Spiro, had just finished delivery of the first three courses to table thirty-three. Sitting at Charlie and Stacy's table were a Mr. Bruce and his wife, from London.

"Splendid chap that Spiro, don't you agree mum?"

"Yes, dearie."

"Do you take a lot of cruises, Mister Bruce?" inquired Charlie, who was really beginning to like cruises.

"Oh, quite! And they're bloody-good fun, aren't they m'boy!" the old man effused. He was in his eighties, at least, with half a head of thin white hair and a salt-and-pepper moustache. His voice defined 'gravelly', a rich Central London growl. He reminded Charlie of some actor....Cedric Hardwicke? Donald Crisp? He knew it was one of those old English actors who always played the old English aristocrat, he just couldn't remember which one it was. This particular old man considered Charlie through wire-rimmed spectacles and down a long, aristocratic nose....the nose of a member of the House of Lords, probably. Certainly an upper-cruster, he thought, that's for sure: "I say, old chap, 'ow long 'ave you and Miss Mellano known each other?"

"We just met," Miss Mellano volunteered.

"Just met! Oh, that's splendid! Did you 'ear that, mum, they *just met*! Aren't they going to be a *fine* couple, mum!"

"Yes, dearie."

"Whaddaya do in London, Mister Bruce, if you don't mind my asking?"

"No' a'toll, m'boy. I'm a bobby by trade, except of course they don't call 'em bobbies anymore. Was on the force thirty-five years 'fore I retired, and my beat was clean as Christmas all that time if I do say so. Now I just travel about on the gov'ment's money—ha! ho! hoo hoo!"

Charlie felt the usual embarrassment fermenting inside of him, but did not show it. He was having his usual trouble pigeon-holing people. Mr. Bruce, just a bobby, he thought....Bruce the bobby....as in Bobby the Bruce? Good grief....

"Main course, folks."

"Ah, Spiro old bean!"

"How much meat, sir?"

Spiro the waiter, a short, dark, handsome young man with thick black hair and a perpetual half-growth of beard, shoveled the sliced beef onto Mr. Bruce's plate until the latter raised his hand. Mr. Bruce's wife and Stacy had one piece. Charlie split the difference; three pieces.

"Vegetables, sir?"

"You bet," said Charlie. Spiro spooned some leafy-green balls and some yellow balls onto Charlie's plate.

"*Efcharisto*, Spiro ol' bean!"

"*Parakalo*, sir," Spiro said smiling. He then smiled briefly and quite differently at Stacy, then scurried off very quickly to the kitchen.

"Man, what kind of a name is Spiro," said Charlie to table thirty-three, shaking his head as he said it and taking a bite of his vegetables. "I mean fer God's sake."

Mr. Bruce was the only one to laugh: "Actually, m'boy, I understand it's a quite common name down 'ere, especially for a Greek lad. Like that Greek character in that movie! Now *'e* was a Greek Spiro as well. What was that picture called, mum, when they climbed up the mountain and blew off the big cannons?"

The Englishman's wife made no motion that indicated speech was forthcoming.

"The Guns of Navarone," Charlie said.

"That's it! Good show, m'boy! *The Guns of Navarone*, and the young resistance fighter that go' shot at the end was named Spiro—ha-ha, what!"

"That was *James Darren*!" Stacy Mellano declared, the ardor in her voice clear and obvious to all. Charlie looked askance at his shipboard intended, and smiled inside at the knowledge that at least she was man-crazy. The girl continued to smile, her eyes glassy with romantic thoughts. He laughed at her and shook his head. "She's right," he said. "But he's just an actor, and I'm not sure actors count."

"There's scads o' Spiros, I'll bet," said Mr. Bruce, dramatically waving his hands as if these gestures somehow further validated his point. "Besides, you 'ave at least *one* cheeky old Spiro back home, I'm told."

"What? Oh, *him*! Yeah, Mister Bruce, I guess you could say we're stuck with at least one Spiro—although he's not much of a Spiro, if y'ask me. Besides, we call him Ted. Out of love."

"Fairly important chap at one time. Number-two man, what."

"Maybe so, but once the Feds caught him skimmin' we kicked his ass right outa there. We don't let 'em get away with shit like that back home," the American said. "But those are the things I left America to forget for a few weeks," he added urbanely, winked, and kept eating.

"The way things look in the papers his old boss better watch out, or 'e might be *next,*" Mr. Bruce suggested. "He's on the *ropes*, I wager!" He'd tilted his old gray head back a little so that he could view the young American through the spectacles rather than above them.

"No. Dick's too slippery! They'll never catch him," said Charlie.

Again the lion roared, the wire rims wavering precariously on the long, aristocratic nose of the ex-policeman. "Then it's safe t'say you prefer our *own* Spiro roight 'ere to the slippery Dicks and Spiros back in The States, ay?"

Charlie now joined his fellow male in light laughter, but the females—apparently bored by either their *double entendres* or the current state of world affairs—maintained their stony silence.

"Safe as hell, Mister B. Politicians I can do without, but I seem to like little Greek waiters....and Greek bartenders and Greek sailor-boys....in fact, I like *Greeks!*" he said. It was as if he had just made a great discovery. "They're a whole lot better'n the Italians, that's for sure."

"You don't like the Latins, m'boy?"

"Christ, no. They're about the dumbest bunch I've ever seen."

Stacy Mellano appeared uncomfortable: "Do you think it's fair, calling a whole group of people dumb like that?" she finally chimed in.

"The girl's right, old chap," Mr. Bruce said soberly. "We're all individuals, quite right."

"But I *do* take everyone as an individual," Charlie insisted through his chews (he liked the green vegetable ball the best), "It's just that every individual Italian I've run into in Europe happens to be lame or stupid. That's just the way it is. *I* can't help it. I mean hell, it's not *my* fault. I'm just making what we call, back at school, an empirical observation."

"Then you don't dislike Italians just *because* they're Italian," the girl said carefully, like she might have been trying out a question before asking it.

"Oh, Christ no! I gotta *lotta* Wop friends back home. In fact back home, Wop is a god damn term of endearment. It's the Wops over here I wonder about. Of course I don't mean the chicks, just the dudes. Chicks are a separate category."

"I see."

She was looking at her plate. Sitting to her left, it all of a sudden felt quite natural for him to reach his right hand over and put his arm around her, dropping his hand down almost immediately to the bare expanse of her back. The hard muscles coiled there seemed to twitch in eager response beneath the warm tan skin. A Grace Kelly back maybe, or maybe even an Angie Dickinson back....either way a winner....She looked up at him at first with a smile, but then her face resumed its uncomfortable posture and she looked down again. Befuddled, he patted the warm skin like a man might pat his dog, then withdrew his hand.

"You know, you just don't seem like somebody who used to live in Iowa," Stacy Mellano said finally, disappointment softening her voice.

"I must remember to yell 'fer corn's sake' occasionally," said Charlie. He hadn't seen the particular Grace Kelly movie the line came from in some time, and in trying to re-script it to fit his purpose he understandably stumbled over it a little bit. And his Cary Grant impression, admittedly, was a little rusty....

No one spoke for what seemed like minutes, just the animalesque noises of four humans busily eating their vegetables. He hated it when she said "I see" like that, but he was beginning to like her anyway. Lucky break. He had already decided her equipment was more than acceptable. He knew he liked Mr. Bruce, even if he wasn't a member of the House of Lords. But he didn't know what to think about his wife. Do some people actually come without a personality? She didn't seem to have much to say about anything....

"Dessert, folks."

"None for me, old chap. The weight, you know." His wife shook her head as well. Stacy Mellano, her thoughts perhaps still pregnant with James Darren, gazed dreamily out the window and did not catch the waiter's sad smile.

"I'll have some ice cream, Spiro, if it's not from Venice," Charlie said.

"It's Greek, sir."

"Right on."

IV

Dancing had never been one of Charlie's specialties but such a minor inadequacy had never really concerned him until now, laboring as he was to keep from looking too awkward. They were slow-dancing, close together, but when he wasn't worrying about his feet he was enjoying himself, amazingly, more than he ever thought possible on a dance floor. His poor performance suddenly and conveniently divorced itself from all past frustrations. Her body was soft and hard, warm and cool, her scent was by turns sweet and sweaty, and upon closing his eyes he was able to effectively lose himself in all of it. The song seemed to last forever.... When the band stopped playing and didn't start up again, a welcome rest period, he thought for a moment about kissing her, like at dances in high school when a dance is over, or better yet like Bogie might have done with

Bergman at a moment like this, but the young man was no Bogie and thank god the girl was no Bergman. If she was that good he might have risked it and blown it. And since Cowardice was on his shoulder he just smiled the best smile he could think of and led her to the bar.

"Campari and tonic, barkeep!"

"Yes, sir."

"What'cha gonna have, Stace?"

"Nothing, thanks."

Charlie thought it a little strange that anybody would twice refuse a free drink. Especially a girl: "Tell ya what, my friend—give the lady some ice water," he said, proud of his easygoing cleverness, then, turning to his date, "Whaddaya tryin' to do, embarrass me or something?" The girl giggled back, then looked down to watch her finger trace the pinstripes on his forearm. The short, half-bald bartender prepared the drinks quickly, and when he pushed them out to Charlie there was the kind of a smirk on his face that only another man can appreciate. Charlie looked up, caught it, and smiled back his appreciation.

"Thanks, guy....I mean *efcharisto*," the young man said, slapping three drachma on the bar. He winked down at the Greek fellow, with the eye the girl was not in a position to see.

They went and sat down in the same lounge they were sitting in before dinner, but this time he made sure they wound up in a two-seat couch just small enough to be comfortable. They spent the first couple of minutes sipping their drinks, sneaking smiling sideways glances, and making sure legs and shoulders were resting comfortably against legs and shoulders. It was Stacy Mellano who broke this silence: "It's a beautiful night," the girl sighed.

"Yeah, well, we paid for it. So. You were really Nebraska state high school dancing champion last year, huh? Jesus, what a mismatch."

"No, I think you dance very well!"

"Really?"

"Really. I really do."

He confidently gulped down the rest of his Campari. Suddenly his performance seemed satisfactory, and thus he was satisfied....

"Say, how come you never have a drink?"

"Oh, I can't. Not even a soda. It's not allowed."

"Not allowed? Whaddaya mean, not allowed?"

"My faith. I'm a member of the Church of Jesus Christ of Latter-Day Saints."

"Mormons. Yer a Mormon." (oh, god....)

"I suppose you have something against Mormons?"

"No," he said, leaning forward on the couch so that various parts of their bodies disengaged. "No more or less than the rest of 'em."

Charlie felt like a sap. Ten-thousand miles away he picks a Daisy Miller, and a religious fanatic at that....And he was further annoyed that he would now have to watch his language. Damn....

"Let's talk about something else," the girl said.

He finished his drink and wiggled a finger at the bartender.

"Gladly. Whaddaya think about Mister Bruce, isn't he a kick?"

"They're both very—"

"I sure figured him for the House of Lords, though." The bartender hunched over the coffee table in front of them. "Oh, the same, my good man, *efcharisto*," Charlie said.

The bartender smiled and hurried back to his station.

"Europe's great!" the young man exclaimed, through an open smile aimed at no one in particular: "You can drink all ya want and nobody could care less how old you are."

"You sure like that red stuff."

"You bet, babe. There's nothing quite like Campari. Aside from the women, it's about the only good thing Italy puts out that I can think of off hand—except naked statues, that is. I'm tellin' ya, you don't know what'cher missin'." He liked giving her a hard time. And he wasn't really upset that she didn't drink. He had resolved not to let minor setbacks get in the way of his primary long-range objective. Suddenly he found himself combing through his memory, trying to recall exactly how many times he'd let her hear the 'f' word. And the 's' word and the 'p' word and all the god damns. Thank god he hadn't let fly the 'c' word yet; *either* of them.... still too reckless, though....he could've kicked himself....But it was too late to do anything about it now. As an experiment, he rested his hand absentmindedly on her knee, and she didn't seem to mind. The bartender soon brought a fresh Campari and tonic, but no ice water as there was still some left in her glass. Charlie handed him four drachma this time. They exchanged courtesies in Greek.

"I know—let's go up to the top deck. It's such a beautiful, romantic night," the girl sighed.

Charlie grinned, nodded, and stood as if each movement was somehow dependent on the other two. He grabbed his glass with one hand, her cool, delicate hand with the other.

It was on the top deck, standing there in the moonlight, their bodies pressed flush together to guard against the wind, where he first kissed her, or rather she kissed him, her mouth opening first beneath his and her tongue displaying a surprising genius for alacrity and precision that most men can only dream about on rainy days alone. Before he was relaxed enough to fall asleep he lay awake in his bunk, on his back, a good long time just thinking about it.

V

"*Hors d'oeuvres*, sir?"

"Sure thing, Spiro. Plenny of the fried squid, please."

Noon of the second day. Table thirty-three was enjoying an eight-course lunch, procedure and attention to elegance being no different from dinner. The only change was with the passengers; lunch being defined on most cruise ships as 'casual elegance', formal dress was optional. Mr. Bruce was obviously having a great time, clad in a multi-colored Hawaiian sport shirt, talking and eating with equal joviality. His wife ate without expression. Stacy Mellano gazed at Charlie Barnes with soft, doe-like eyes....

"*Efcharisto*, Spiro—efcharisto very much, dude!"

"*Parakalo*, sir," smiled the waiter stiffly.

"Tell me, old girl," Mr. Bruce said. "Is this young man making any progress, what?"

The girl smiled shyly and looked at her plate.

"I'm workin' on it, Mister Bruce," Charlie answered for her. He could feel her left hand investigate his right knee. They didn't look at each other. A little squeeze....He waited, but the hand went no further. Spiro, smiling crazily, lingered a great while over the girl's right shoulder, spooning the *hors d'oeuvres* onto her plate one-by-one. As he was only a waiter, no one noticed the fiery downward spiral of his eyes. When the hand finally left his knee Charlie risked a quick look of his own. His glance angled down to her red and white tank top, hugging the curves of her chest like an extra layer of skin. Her sweet perfume floated under his nose, almost as if his careful scrutiny was what allowed each collateral sense to participate. She smelled wonderful, looked wonderful, felt....man. He knew he had made an intelligent choice.

"I 'ope I 'aven't embarrassed you, Miss Mellano. I suppose I still 'ave an eye for a pretty young bird now'n then!" Mr. Bruce roared. His wife burped, and though eight eyes covertly flew to her it wasn't enough to make her look up from her food.

"You don't have to apologize, sir, I'm very flattered. And please call me—"

"This squid's the greatest," Charlie cut in. "It tastes sorta like, uh.... like bacon, I guess, only about ten times better."

"Hm. Quite roight, m'boy!" Mr. Bruce roared his concurrence, after taking a bite of Charlie's squid.

"I'm tellin ya, I could sit right here'n and load up on tons of chow and gallons of Campari until—"

Charlie's words were overpowered by the portentous blast of a loudspeaker: *"This is your Captain speaking!"* came the voice, in English, echoing and reverberating through the dining hall not unlike that of a public address announcer's echoing blare blanketing a stadium, and Charlie quickly pictured in his mind a football game between two teams of little Greek waiters. But the Captain's words came with a deadly serious tone: *"Turkey and Greece are in a war situation....It will be impossible for us to dock in Eastern Mediterranean ports for that reason....Changes in itinerary will be posted tomorrow morning on the bulletin boards....The situation is completely out of our control, please bear with us....Thank you, enjoy your lunch."*

There was virtual silence in the great dining hall, then tense murmuring amongst the passengers, quiet, controlled confusion.

"A war!" Charlie shouted with glee. "What a lucky break!"

"What would *you* know about *war*," said Mr. Bruce's wife, razor sharply, stringing together more than three words for the first time, with no attempt made to soften the contempt and bitterness in her heart.

"The wife's right, m'boy. War's a bad kettle 'o fish, very bad indeed. I was at The Somme in the Great War, and no' much older than you, lad. Me-mates dropped by the thousands, they did, and all for ten or twenty feet of someone else's mud at that! Very bad, very bad indeed."

"But talk about action!" Charlie pointed out. "All this excitement included in the price of the cruise? Are you kiddin' me? Hell, I think it's a bitchin'-ass break beyond *belief!*"

Spiro, grim-faced and mechanical, was back with the soup course.

"What do you Greek chaps think of this war business, Spiro old bean?"

"We could take them, sir," Spiro said quietly, as he ladled the soup impassively into the bowls. His teeth were clenched, his jaw fixed and tight.

"So ya *wanna* fight, don'tcha Spiro?"

"You should be happy we are turning around," the handsome young waiter counseled the younger man. Skin bunched up on his forehead, and his voice was sharper. He glanced briefly at Stacy Mellano, with a tight-lipped, plaintive expression that spoke volumes of what he might have said to her under different circumstances, and when his eyes returned to Charlie they were on fire: "My government likes to take large American.... *boys*, and put packs on their backs and guns in their hands."

"Impressment! Zounds!"

Stacy Mellano looked very worried.

"You mean the Captain's serious about not going on to Corfu? He's *serious?*" Charlie, with genuine horror in his voice, inquired.

"We are not allowed to return home right away during a war. All the crew, we would enlist. It would be bad for business....sir."

Never in his brief, soft life had Charlie Barnes engaged such despair. He excused himself from the table and walked, head down and hands in pockets, like a disappointed Henry Fonda in *Mister Roberts*, through the middle of the long dining hall. "Would you excuse me, Mister and Misses Bruce?" the girl said, and followed.

"He's a bit like me when I was a lad, ay mum?"

"'Fraid so, dearie."

She found him leaning on the railing, looking out over the restless sea.

"What's the matter, darling?"

Charlie didn't feel like talking. "I wanted to go," he said.

"But you heard what Spiro said—you could get *killed*!"

"I never get any lucky breaks." He took a deep breath. "And I'll never be in a war," he sighed. He felt like spitting into the milky-white foam.

"What is it about boys that makes them want to go to war?" the girl wondered out loud.

"It's not the fighting," Charlie said quickly, trying to articulate the other great unfulfilled passion of his life, "And it's certainly not the killing.

It's....it's the action, I guess. The *urgency*. Everything exciting you ever hear about or read about is outa some kinda war. You can write about war."

The young woman changed course: "What are we doing later?"

"Oh....I'm, uh....I'm playing poker later with a couple guys I met. They're from Austria or Yugoslavia, or something like that. Couple uh pigeons. I told 'em I'd meet 'em in their cabin after dinner. Sorry." She could wait.

"I see...."

"I tell you what," he quickly offered. "I'll meet'cha on the top deck tomorrow, around noon, okay? We'll bag a few rays." He suddenly remembered why he was there.

"Alright," she agreed, kissing him lightly on the cheek. Then she went inside.

Charlie leaned heavily on the wood railing and watched the sea roll by, blue swells white with foam. The water went on forever. Suddenly he was a prisoner, and the water was his jail. He was its captive, just as surely as he was entrapped by the year, the month, the very circumstances within which he happened to live. He couldn't help but think that if he were old enough to be Mr. Bruce's son he could have cruised all over Europe during the *second* great war, and had a *helluva* time....but the reality of the situation was that war was just another untouchable dream. Mister Roberts didn't get to taste his war until it was too late, and now neither would he....The pinkish skin of his bare forearms felt the sun. Without a suit and tie on, its rays were of some small comfort to him. He fired three or four of his best swear words far out over the horizon. Before retreating to his cabin, he slammed one hand down hard on the wood and spat thickly and defiantly into the foam.

VI

The new itinerary, as the Captain had promised, was up on the bulletin boards the following morning:

July 23: Malta.................Departure 9 p.m.
July 24: Sfax...................Departure 9 p.m.
July 26: Palermo............Departure 9 p.m.
July 28: Venice................Arrival 8 a.m.

A crowd had gathered around the bulletin board in the Main Lounge. Some of the people, clearly, could not read English. Charlie Barnes, clad only in red gym shorts and a red, yellow, and green flowered shirt, knifed determinedly through the strangers until he stood in front of the board.

"What's Sfax mean?" he asked the crowd.

"It's an industrial port in Tunisia, sir," a uniformed man said. Charlie turned around and instantly recognized him as the Navigator. He was tall, slim but clearly powerful, with short black hair and beard, and his skin was a deep dark brown as from a thousand tropical suns. He supposedly had a hard-earned reputation for seducing female passengers.

"Tunisia? Christ....well, *efcharisto* I guess."

"You are very *welcome*, sir!" the Navigator said with a bow, and walked—in a posture unusually tall and straight—briskly from the Main Lounge. He sure is a good-looking guy, Charlie thought....no wonder all the chicks lie down for him. (He tried to come up with a brilliant, good-looking actor in his mind to play him on film, but for the moment all he could come up with was James Darren so he stopped.)

The Island of Malta, Tunisia, and Sicily. Charlie had set his mind on Greece, and now he knew he would have to redirect his thoughts to three obscure ports, three unimportant dots on the globe that he either hadn't thought about or even heard of, and, what burned him most, would not have time to research properly. His suitcase was filled with travel brochures and maps and history books on Greece, worthless now, and just the frustration of thinking about it burned him through and through. Who ever heard of a history book on Malta? Who ever heard of Sfax, period? His watch gave him about two hours until his meeting with Stacy.

(After all, he couldn't let peripheral setbacks get in the way of his primary long-range objective.)

There are a multitude of things to do on a cruise ship. Old women can play bingo, men old *or* young can drive golf balls into the ocean. Little boys and girls can swim in a crowded pool. Homely middle-aged women, if they must, can burn time and money at the beauty parlor. Young men of Charlie's caliber invariably wind up at a blackjack table, and in fact he had already decided to there invest thirty dollars over a one-hour period in hopes of extending his Europe trip a day or two. Charlie was a good blackjack player, perhaps very good, but he was also a ham-and-egger, and naturally he felt uncomfortable sitting between a pair of high rollers who would scoff at the thought of betting as little as his entire bankroll on a single deal. They were dark, swarthy; probably rich Arab oilmen (or maybe even sheiks in three-piece suits!). He put out his thirty dollars, and the dealer's agile hands changed it into chips.

"Insurance?"

On the first hand the dealer turned up an ace. Both high rollers insured their bet, Charlie did not. The dealer peeked at his down-card, and when he didn't flip it over everyone knew it meant it wasn't a face card, no blackjack, and that meant the money the high rollers had put up to insure their hands against it being one—50% of the original bet—was lost. The dealer scooped up the insurance money before continuing: "Cards?" he said. The first high roller stood pat on a fourteen. Charlie had sixteen. "Hit me," he commanded, sweeping his hand toward him along the table's green felt surface, and the dealer flipped over a three. Charlie smiled and waved his hand over the cards. The second high roller turned over a six and a four, and pushed forward a chip worth about fifty dollars to match his original bet. The dealer gave him a deuce. The dealer then turned over his down-card, a seven, which combined with his ace made eighteen. The dealer's hands, like talons, snatched up the two high rollers' stacks of chips like they might have been two frantic mice paralyzed with fear. Then one talon pushed a chip worth slightly less than a dollar out to Charlie. He had won. A rush of egomania filled him. He'd played his hand perfectly, hitting a sixteen against an ace, giving himself at least a marginal chance at victory. The first high roller had erred, electing not to challenge the ace with a bust hand. Charlie could never understand why, in that situation, a man would not strive to protect his bet by taking another card. The dealer very likely had a six, seven, eight, or nine down (but not a face card or it would have been blackjack and the insurance would have been paid at a return of two-to-one) and thus already had seventeen or better, and if he didn't an ace is such a versatile card, being at the holder's discretion either one or eleven, that the chances were still quite good that he would be able to eventually make his hand from the deck. So why not at least take a card and hope for a little one? And while the first high roller had been too timid, the second had been too brave. 'Doubling down' into an ace is just as foolish as sitting on a stiff hand, maybe more so (And they had both taken out insurance, which was just money down the drain as far as he was concerned.). Both high rollers had played their hands poorly. But Charlie Barnes had played his hand well, and won. The money involved wasn't even the issue. Money is just for keeping score. Conquest is the gambler's reward.

After an hour the young man was up about eighty dollars. Naturally he was ecstatic. He had watched the high rollers lose hundreds, too much to contemplate. He scooped up all his chips save the equivalent of about thirty-five dollars, which he decided to let ride on a single deal. With at least a 45-dollar profit safely tucked away in his shirt pocket, he figured he could afford the excitement.

The dealer gave him a twenty; king of diamonds, queen of hearts. (....alright, *twenty*!...) He smiled and waved his hand over the cards. The dealer showed an eight, turned over a six, flipped a seven. Twenty-one. It was over in a blink. The greedy talons plucked Charlie's money mercilessly from the table.

"Well, that's all for this cowboy," Charlie breathed in defeat. "*Efcharisto*, dealer," he said, flipping him a chip. It was the first time he had really looked closely at the dealer's face, and when he saw it was a red-haired guy with pasty-white skin and freckles, he felt like a moron.

"Yeah, thanks a lot, *pard*," the dealer said.

As Charlie turned to leave one of the dark-skinned high rollers said, "Where'd yeh learn t'play like that, kid?"

"Uh, b-back home, in Los Angeles," the young man stammered.

"I'm from Toledo myself. Well, see yeh 'round."

He smiled weakly and walked quickly away.

On the top deck a crowd was gathered by the railing. The passengers were taking turns at trap shooting. The Navigator, standing rigidly-tall and straight in his white uniform, was supervising the affair. A girl, or rather a young woman, wearing white short-shorts and a tight white T-shirt with **APHRODITE** spelled in pink letters across the front, was with him.

"How much?"

"One drachma, sir," the Navigator said.

Charlie took the shotgun. It felt good in his hands. It seemed like a lot of money for one shot, but without hesitation he gave a poker chip worth one drachma to the girl and raised the gun to his shoulder. "Pull," he barked, and the clay bird flew. He pulled the trigger and the gun jerked—a satisfying enough explosion—but he missed, and the clay bird dove safely into the sea.

The Navigator grinned. "*Squeeze* the trigger, sir, do not *jerk* it!" was his expert advice. Charlie gave the girl another drachma and yelled, "Pull!", but the result was the same.

"I've never done this before," Charlie apologized.

"Not bad, for a beginner!" the young woman said. She was brown-haired, at least five years older than he, and as she breathed her large and apparently perfect breasts heaved and swelled under the pink letters. He couldn't place her accent, but wherever it was from he loved it. And her face, like her body a tan, perfect thing, could easily have issued from one of the magazines he used to sometimes find hidden under his older brother's bed. He tried to imagine which actress might portray her, but like most girls depicted in these magazines this perfect creature was far beyond any likeness that might be attempted by a real person, even the most beautiful that Hollywood could offer. Maybe Raquel Welch herself, he decided, but she'd be the only one who'd qualify. In any case, she was way out of his league. And he was never comfortable standing so close to something essentially so very far away. Suddenly his shorts felt like they didn't fit quite right. He paid her a third drachma, raised the gun to his shoulder: "*Pull!*" he screamed. He took dead aim, squeezed the trigger, and the charge shot straight and hot from the barrel. But he missed, and the clay bird dove into the sea.

"Like I say, I never did this before," Charlie said, and handed the gun back to the grinning Navigator. There was scattered snickering to quicken his departure. (The Welchlike creature smiled, but at least managed to keep from actually laughing out loud....)

Noon. Finally he was searching the sun-deck for Stacy Mellano. She wasn't hard to locate. Lying on a deck chair, in a bikini, the noon sun caressing her skin, warming it all over, she glistened and gleamed in the sun like a fallen bronze statue. She was half-asleep, and didn't react to Charlie standing over her. He just looked her up and down for a moment, eyes tracing the full, nearly-naked outline. She wasn't the goddess in the **APHRODITE** T-shirt, he thought, but for a regular girl she was pretty spectacular. 'Looks sorta like Natalie Wood in *Love With The Proper Stranger*, he decided....except for the darker skin....more like Wood in *West Side Story*. He bent down and kissed her forehead.

"Oh! Hi, handsome!" she said as she sat up. She smiled a crescent of perfect teeth.

"Hi yourself." He sat on the edge of her deck chair. Without invitation, he grabbed her tube of suntan lotion and proceeded to squeeze some of the slick, buttery contents into his right hand and then massage it into her back, her neck, the tops of her shoulders. He took his time, like it was no big deal. The girl, at first, tensed up from his touch, but then she altered her smile slightly and closed her eyes. He found by experimenting with different techniques that when he massaged her a certain way she would make little sounds to indicate her pleasure, and this principle of action/

reaction—more than anything he could pull from his recent memory—made him feel like a man....

Finally she said, "I saw that girl you were talking to, when you were shooting that gun....was she the Cruise Director? Impressive! What a cute figure."

"Yeah, she'd be a helluva comfort on a cold rainy night, that's for sure."

"Oh honestly, is that all you boys ever think about?"

"Sometimes," he said absently. He stood up. Looking down through the opening in the top deck, his attention became lost in the pool a deck below. The pool was of salt water, and the crowd of tadpole-like children splashed merrily in it.

"Isn't it funny?" Charlie continued, "Those kids don't even care that it's sea water and not fresh water they're swimmin' in."

"You'd....*like* that girl?"

His head whirled in her direction: "Oh, I suppose that's not allowed *either*, huh," he said, not finding it at all difficult to find the appropriately condescending tone. He was beginning to resent, again, how hard it was.

"She's not married! *You're* not married!"

"Is that really all it takes? That's it? Ya gotta wait until some dolt with a white cardboard collar makes you promise in front of God and everybody that you gotta be *nice* to each other, before you ever get to the *good* stuff? Are you *kiddin'* me? C'mon, babe. Let's be real, just this once."

Stacy Mellano sat up straighter in the deck chair and looked out, out far beyond the sea, to a world hidden for now in a far, private cosmos but for her doubtless far more 'real' than this floating world, which in a few days would end. Her words, precious windows to that hidden world, came slowly: "The man who....who '*gets*' me, will give me a diamond ring and a house with a white picket fence, and there'll be a church wedding....and I'll take care of the whole house, and make him a big dinner every night....and I'll plant a garden....and The Lord willing there'll be children, lots of them, because when you get right down to it that's really what it's all about," she concluded; and for a moment her eyes were closed again.

"Exactly how much does the diamond ring hafta cost, Stace?"

She glared up at him for several seconds, changed her expression several times, scrambled to her feet, and stalked off without a last word. He was left standing alone and looking down into the salty pool, still holding in his greasy hand the tube of suntan lotion.

VII

The next four days were a sea of frustrations for Charlie Barnes. Malta was less than satisfying, save for a great piece of cheesecake at a little café in Valletta. Sfax was a land of cripples and dark brown children, all of whom were eager to show him war ruins in return for American cigarettes or any foreign currency he could be cajoled into parting with. And Palermo was probably not the same Palermo that Patton and the 7th Army rolled through in '43. Charlie and Stacy barely spoke to each other at table thirty-three these four long days (one or both of them often choosing room service in place of confrontation), forcing Mr. Bruce to act as liaison, interpreter, and entertainer:

"I 'ear you play a keen game of blackjack, m'boy—'ave you been to the Casino at Monte Carlo?"

"Not yet, Mister Bruce."

"Oh you should, lad. There's nothing quite like casino gambling, you know."

"Yeah, I know. We have some really neat casinos back home, there's both Lake Tahoe and Las—"

"Did you and Misses Bruce go into Palermo today, Mister Bruce?" Stacy interjected.

The old man's wife looked up at the mention of her name, freezing Stacy's eyes with an expression of profound indignation, no doubt piqued at her left-handed inclusion in the conversation. The young girl smiled weakly, the old woman said nothing, and each looked down at her own plate.

"Roighto, old girl. I relish those Italian chaps, you know."

"Well you go right ahead and relish 'em, I still think they're crazy," Charlie cut back in. "Like I hadta take a horse'n buggy thing back to the boat, right? Well, this bus whizzes right by us, and I mean *right by* us. Couldn'ta missed us by more than an inch. So what does my driver do? Nothing! Not a shitty goddam thing," he said with feeling (and with a brief sideways glance at Stacy). "He just drives right on, whistling like a damn canary, like it was the most natural thing in the world."

"Driving on the Continent tins't a*'toll* like motoring around on those fancy roads in The States, m'boy!" the Englishman grinned and guffawed.

"I'll say."

Spiro the waiter, less grim-faced these days, arrived presently with the cheese course.

"Cheese, sir?"

"You got it, Spiro....How's the war goin'?"

Spiro, suddenly tight-jawed, laid a slice each of white and yellow cheese on Charlie's plate. He ignored Charlie's fool question. Outcasts, the Greek's eyes were seeking asylum in all eyes save Charlie's, but their captain would not permit them to land. "Will the lady have some cheese.... sir?" was his bland reply.

"I don't know, Spiro, I will ask. Will the lady have some cheese, sir?" he mimicked in as patronizing a tone as he was capable, smiling idiotically, his hands folded and held in a posture of angelic supplication under his chin. He laughed arrows, and the girl responded by running out of the dining hall. She was crying.

"Uh, excuse me, folks," Charlie said. He felt funny. As he sprinted down the aisle he was sure all eyes were on him.

He found her at their usual bar. She was sitting on one of the leather stools, holding her knees together, bent over, her face inside a napkin.

"Campari and tonic, bartender."

"And for the lady, sir?"

"Oh no, thank you, noth—"

"Scotch, straight up."

"But—"

"Girl, this is one time yer havin' a fuckin' drink—ta *hell* with yer lousy religion."

The bartender soon set the glasses on the bar. Charlie sipped thoughtfully on his Campari. With the ship scheduled to arrive back in Venice early the following morning, he decided he owed it to himself to give it one more shot....

"Hey, I'm sorry about what I said back there. I acted like an idiot."

"I think we're both acting like idiots," the girl said, her sniffling the apparent end of her cry.

"What are we fighting for, anyway? I mean you're a neat girl, I'm a terrific guy, we're both young, at least one of us is probably horny....I mean my *god*! The world around us is at *war*! What the hell are *we* fighting for?"

They both laughed.

"Look," Stacy Mellano said, "why don't we meet on the top deck tonight, hm? Would you like that? It's our final night, and it's so *pretty* up there! We could push a couple lounge chairs together and actually sleep out under the stars."

Charlie's astonished face broke into a lascivious grin: "That is absolutely A-okay by me—*now* yer talkin'!" he declared with a wink, kissing his glass against hers. She took a big swig of the scotch and paid the standard price.

"Yecch! How can you *drink* this stuff?"

"Jesus, girl, *I* don't drink Scotch," he said. "I just ordered it for *you*."

VIII

Time was short. She was up there, already sprawled out across those deck chairs no doubt, and just the thought of it, just the naked *anticipation*, was driving his hormones crazy....*so hurry up*! All he had on so far was a pair of casual slip-on deck shoes. He had just gotten through showering, shaving, and splashing on probably a little too much cologne. He pulled on a pair of just-pressed gray dress slacks that the ship's laundry had charged him double for as a rush job, his favorite pair, because everything had to be just right, just perfect in fact, because she might be just the kind of girl who would notice. He didn't bother with underwear. He didn't put a belt on either. He did pull an expensive light blue cashmere sweater hurriedly over his head, stretching the bottom down over where the belt would normally be. Solid tactics, in *any* country....Then he looked in the mirror. The face that looked back was shrouded in part by lazy, sun-bleached curls. It made him think of a rain-soaked sheep dog. He left the hair wet and combed it straight back, like a gangster. Now the face in the mirror had a forehead, high and nicely tanned. A pleasant, handsome face. Almost movie-star handsome, he thought...."Y'know," he now said to that fine face, which smiled at being spoken to, "yer pretty bitchin'." They winked at each other, smiled again, and left the cabin together.

As he sauntered past the bandstand they were playing *Moonlight Becomes You*. His father had taught him the tune. There were four couples dancing. All of them looked like they were from Germany, or Austria, because of the way they held their hands high and the way the men looked longingly and mechanically and idiotically into the women's eyes like in a 1940's war movie. Yes, they were German all right....One of them even *looked* like Werner Klemperer, he found himself thinking....and not the silly bumbling goofball in *Hogan's Heroes* Werner Klemperer, but rather the suave, classy, good-dancer type in *Ship Of Fools* Werner Klemperer. That cinches it. Definitely Germans. And even Germans get naked and horizontal eventually, right?...He wondered which of them would be doing it later, in the tenuous, thin-walled privacy of their cabins....*stop*! He slapped himself for letting his mind wander, ordered himself to concentrate on being charming, and continued on. Concentrating very hard he didn't stop at the blackjack tables, but did wave to the high roller from Toledo. He ran across the Navigator in the Main Lounge.

"Good evening, Mister Navigator."

"*Squeeze* the trigger, sir!" the sailor said for a rejoinder, through a terrific, masculine smirk, and then, walking tall and unusually straight, headed resolutely for the bridge. He was laughing. Charlie scratched his wet head and headed, somewhat less resolutely, for the top deck.

The night air was soft, restless, and warm. Perfect. There was no moon, but the shore lights in the distance bathed the ship in an equally Heavenly glow. The band four decks down could barely be heard, having the effect of soft music turned down low....double perfect. He made his way to the bow, all the way to the point where port and starboard curved together, thus the only place on the ship where both coasts could be viewed at once. And there she was, lying—as she had promised—on one of two deck chairs pushed together, her beautiful Natalie Wood head resting on one of two cabin pillows, lying under a wool blanket pulled up to her chin. He just stood in the distance for a few moments, alternately numb and tingling, wearing a sly expression revolving around an unfamiliar grin. He was anxious, but in no hurry. He wanted to soak everything in, truly absorb it, make himself acutely aware of exactly what he was thinking and what he was feeling at each successive moment, now that he was finally at the very threshold of shedding the worn and wrinkled epidermis of childhood. He wanted to remember. His legs were weak, he was nervous as hell, but he knew he was ready. Before coming over to her, he had a thought....Maybe even an ultra-cool ladies' man like Errol Flynn would have been proud of him. Certainly Cary Grant would have been proud....but after messing it up before, he decided against using the Grant accent to close the deal.

"The pillows are a nice touch."

"Oh! You startled me!"

She moved over, allowing him to slip without resistance inside the makeshift bed. She wiggled next to him. His heart jumped into his throat, and he almost did something.

"Boy am I glad you're here," the girl said. "One of the officers just walked by, and the way he looked at me I thought he was going to *grab* me."

"Did he look like James Darren?"

"What?"

He made sure to laugh at his own joke to throw her off balance, but then he abruptly leaned over and kissed her, wasting no time, kissing her hard but with genuine feeling as his arms instinctively snaked their way around behind her back, that firm, muscular, Grace Kelly back, his fingers intuitively seeking out the smooth warmth of her bare waist and shoulders. He maneuvered her to where they more or less faced each other (she on her right side, he on his left), and during this necessary horizontal ballet the blanket, for a moment, was thrown clear, allowing him to take quick inventory of her before she repositioned it to cover them. It was a warm night, but the fact remained that she had come to their rendezvous wearing only shorts and a flimsy narrow tank top. Her brazenness relaxed him. Glimpsing again her bronzed, bare shoulders made him finally recall the name of that Grace Kelly movie, *To Catch A Thief*, which he instantly realized was also his favorite Cary Grant movie, *good god*, he could hardly believe that such a perfectly righteous and episodic omen would chance to come his way and that he almost missed it, and it made him want to tell somebody. Soon his fingers began to trace gentle, urgent half-circles across the smooth dampening firmness of her lower back, his mouth concurrently tendering kisses to her face and neck. Her response exceeded even his wildest expectations. She surged into him, spontaneous combustion, her lips sucking at his, her body an urgent fleshy coil begging to meld itself into anything equally hot, sensual, and alive. It was a wet kiss, they broke for air, and never losing eye contact their mouths collided again; but this time softly. Their faces were devouring each other and loving it. Suddenly in a hurry, he sort of matter-of-factly dropped his right hand a little too heavily onto her left breast. It filled the hand up, and his arm felt on fire. Then, deftly, as skillfully as a fencer would parry a threatening blade, she deflected away his forearm with her own, twisting within his arms—in the same motion—to lie with her back to his chest, with her head lodged directly under his chin. "This is nice," she said.

"It's gonna get nicer," said Charlie, kissing the top of her head. She was just telling him not to rush it, he assured himself. And he now knew he'd been right all along....no unredeemable, Puritan-for-life-Jesus-freak could possibly kiss like that, he said inside his own head....this girl's a tiger, a goddam *female tiger*....he *knew* it. "We're going through the Strait of Messina tonight," he added with authority. She moaned her approval. It was a great moan, a Faye Dunaway moan. He wasn't upset. He knew it was a clumsy advance. Think, think....how did Burt Lancaster manage it with that nutty religious chick in *Elmer Gantry*?, he said silently to himself.... yeah, Jean Simmons....and why are your religious chicks always so goddam hot-to-trot?, he might well have been inquiring of his own personal gods.... doesn't matter why....good for Burt, good for me....Reassuringly, he stroked his hands up and down her cool upper arms, squeezing occasionally. She was putty in his inexperienced hands. And he could tell she was impressed with his knowledge of the sea, the Italian coastline, everything. The frustration of the previous four days had at least afforded him the opportunity to research the new route, and now, thanks to the good offices of the ship's library, he was something of an authority on the Strait of Messina; this taboo waterway of Ancient Antiquity guarded by a rock and a whirlpool, or perhaps protected by invisible mythological monsters, a passageway so infamous and fabled for the wrecking and swallowing of so many luckless vessels. Fabled enough for Homer himself to write about. Even as he was explaining to her The Strait's mystical blend of history and legend the head of the great ship was penetrating the forbidden channel, the Sicilian city of Messina on the right, the coast of Italy—Reggio di Calabria—on the left. Lights burned brilliant on both shores. Each shore looked close enough to reach in a long swim....

"Look at these lights, Stace. They're really something."

"I'll take your word for it," the girl said sensuously, eyes closed, twisting her body back to him, and again her mouth opening under his, that precise tongue exploring every nook and cranny, her body curled up tightly against him and purring like a kitten. That's *it*, he thought....it's not a Faye Dunaway moan at all....it's a goddam Julie Newmar *Catwoman* moan, a *purr*....Her hands alternately smoothed and clutched at his hair, his back, his chest muscles. He kissed her back with a fury and a depth not even Batman could have dreamed up, much less Adam West or any mere actor. He couldn't help but covertly ask himself if he thought Batman and Catwoman ever did it, but when he caught himself doing it he banished the thought, and went back to the best kiss of his young life. She moaned, he groaned. They broke, they breathed. She tongued his ear, he tongued her throat, her upper breastbone, her tiny Adam's apple. And then their mouths locked again. Perhaps the best part of this kiss was when he felt her hard thighs surround his right knee and squeeze it tight, release it, and then squeeze again. And then, as the kiss finally subsided, she traced her own sweet circle, around the outside edge of his lips with her gentle, tireless tongue. He played with her hair, ran his hands down her sides to her hips. Her hands found his hands. It was all too good to be real....

Finally she exhaled and relaxed against his body, producing a soft sound halfway between a hum and a grunt, the way someone does when they're exhausted. She kept her eyes closed. When he opened his eyes to breathe (and his heart had slowed and his head had cleared) he saw that the long white ship had pushed its way fully into The Strait, the vessel fully ensconced, no turning back, and Charlie was sure he could now hear the foamy waves breaking milky-white against the shores. He breathed deeply. The sea smelled of salt. He imagined he could actually taste the salt water in the air, his mind taking over where his actual senses left off. Visibility was unlimited. Each coast was a row of sparkling yellow jewels. He caught himself daydreaming, imagining himself as the boldest and bravest of those ancient mariners foolish enough to attempt such a risky voyage. He *was* foolish. He *was* daring. He was more than eager to risk The Strait's twin dangers. A man's gotta do what he's gotta do....for *every* man there comes such a time! His time had come. His time was now. Back to the present....One last survey of the parallel, glittering coasts....He knew at once that this was the most beautiful, the most utterly inspiring, the most significant, inviolate, magnificently singular sight he had ever seen, one in a million, and feeling totally in charge of the situation he was more than willing to delay the final advance for just a moment to pay it the proper respect:

"Stace, ya gotta see this. I've never seen anything like it in my life, it's....Stace? Stacy?"

She was asleep.

IX

"Another one."

"Another one, sir?"

"Wish I'd said that."

"Sir, are you all right?"

"Certainly. And I said another one."

"Yes, sir."

Four tall, empty glasses stood at attention on the bar. The bartender soon set a full one in line.

"Bartender, why do people always drink when they're depressed? I might be a writer someday, it's important that I know."

"I just mix them, sir. I have no opinions."

The comical figure of Charlie Barnes gulped the drink in what must have been record time for Campari and tonic. "Another one," he droned. He leaned his cashmere chest heavily against the bar's brass railing. He was the very picture of Despair. He was his own caricature....

"Make it two, old chap."

Charlie sat up and turned around. "Mister Bruce!"

"Couldn't sleep. This seat taken, m'boy?"

"No, 'course not. Have a seat, my fine English friend." The young man slapped the leather seat of the bar stool to his left with a drunkard's enthusiasm. The bartender, working quickly, set the two glasses on the bar. Mister Bruce eased his eighty-year-old bones onto the stool with apparent great difficulty. Almost immediately, he retreated to a standing position.

"Just what splendid concoction did I order for myself, m'boy?" the old man, wincing, inquired.

"Campari and tonic water, ol' bean," Charlie managed, holding the tall glass up to the light for inspection. "A fine Italian liqueur, light, snappy, not too nasty-tasting....a bitter red treat. Only trouble is it's only forty-eight proof. Takes too long."

"Jolly!" piped the old man.

For almost a minute the two men drank in silence.

"Two more," Charlie said.

"But I'm not through with this one!"

"They're for me."

"Oh....blimey."

The bartender, no doubt tabulating an ever-increasing tip, soon set the fresh drinks in line.

"Mister Bruce, you know much about women?"

"No' much, m'boy." The old man laughed at his own reply, adding, "I neve' actually *met* a man who knew *much* about them."

"You'n me both."

"Troubles, old chap?"

Charlie literally poured a glass of Campari and tonic down his throat.

"Women in general, Mister Bruce. I don't think even if I live tuh be *yer* age I'll ever figure 'em out."

"Don't fret, m'boy. She'll come around."

"I don't think so, man," Charlie lamented. He was sliding the glass around, sliding it along the wood in tight little circles. Displaying surprising dexterity for a drunk, he managed to continually trace the same clockwise circle on the bar without spilling any of the precious red elixir. His eyes were frozen to the moving glass. He was doing his best to concentrate on the pieces of ice swimming around in the spinning red pool. His eyes were lost in the ensuing swirl, and the pieces of ice were the only things in the world that mattered. "It's too late, I blew it," he finally said, with the note of finality of a dying man.

"Just as well, lad. You might not wind up like the old man 'ere, what."

Charlie looked up, and aimed bloodshot eyes at the old man. This being the first time he had seen him in a standing position he noticed, for the first time, that the old man carried a cane. "Aw, you haven't turned out so bad, Mister Bruce. I don't think women could ever be *yer* downfall. I'm guessin' you were too smart for 'em. Too slippery! Ha!"

"All but the wife, m'boy."

"Yer wife?"

"She was a nurse during the Great War, you know. I met her at The Somme. Nicked up a bit I was, during the heavy shelling. Stupid me....I always 'ad a terrible fancy for the nurses! Well, I 'ad her in trouble double-quick, and like a dumb bunny I married the girl. Funny thing—the little tyke died 'fore the war was even bloody over."

"Another one," Charlie croaked.

"So you see, me-dear Mister Barnes, y'rilly no' in such terribly dodgy shape after all."

"But—but things haven't turned out so bad for yuh," slurred Charlie with urgency. "Yuh got a nice fifty-year wife, you two get tuh move around a lot—"

"Do you think I actually *like* traveling about with the old bat?"

Charlie almost gagged on his drink.

"*Don't* you—I mean yuh *don't?* I mean—"

The old man took the last sip of his first Campari. He pushed the wire-rimmed spectacles back up the long, aristocratic nose, coughed, and left a one-pound note on the bar.

"Take it from me, me-old china. You're in tip-top shape now, don't think you 'afta chase after every pretty little bird you find in the brush. Dangerous, you know."

"But what about—"

"Listen," the old man said soberly. The old, gnarled hand, the hand not holding the cane, gripped Charlie's forearm with illogical power. His eyes seared into the young man's, and held them. Suddenly they seemed too young for this old head, as if they were being allowed for one moment to recapture the flash, dreams, and bright virginal promise of Youth: "*Look at me.* This is all there is, all there eve' was. Y'get one chance, m'boy. Don't be an arse. There's plenty o'time t'get wha' you been after over 'ere. I sees the way y'looks at birds—I've *seen* it. *Slow down*! Y'got plenty o'time. Plenty o'time. So think with your *head*, lad, not yer *hobby*. Understand?"

Even under Lord Alcohol's influence, Charlie was impressed that Mr. Bruce was so anxious to make his point that he stubbornly left on the h in both head and hobby. It made it come out clumsy, but it got the job done:

"Yessir. I understand."

"Good. I 'ope so." The ex-policeman tapped Charlie's forehead lightly with the end of his cane, as if he were knighting him.

(Years later, Charlie often found himself wishing he could have loaned him his body, or perhaps a bit of that mis-spent portion of his own youth which every young man fritters away anyway, so that an old man who couldn't be in the House of Lords could at least get to live that lifetime of second chances.)

"I'm really glad we had this talk, Mister Bruce," the young man said. "*Really* glad...."

"Good-bye, Charlie."

"Yeah. G'bye, sir."

The old man wobbled down the corridor and down a stairwell, gone forever. The bartender set another Campari and tonic on the bar.

"Maybe I got a little lucky t'night after all, bartender. In a way, I mean."

"Will there be anything else, sir?"

X

Venice actually looked pretty good to him in the morning sun, but he didn't intend to stay the day. The ship docked without fanfare, as it had departed, and the young man was among the first to disembark. He thought briefly about clearing out quickly, cutting it clean, but waited instead for a running Stacy Mellano to catch up to him.

"You left in a hurry last night."

"You fell asleep. I got lonely."

Her face went slack at first, then forced itself to smile weakly. "That's okay. I was just worried, is all," she said.

"That skimpy outfit looks good on you. With the tan, I mean."

"Thanks."

"So where will you go?"

"Oh, probably straight to my parents' summer home on the Riviera. They're staying there now." She was shielding her eyes from the sun with her hand. It made him think of Deborah Kerr in that scene where she shields her eyes from the sun in *From Here to Eternity*, which also reminded him that he was still no Burt Lancaster....

"You never told me why a nice, conservative, small-town girl from the Midwest cruises all over the Mediterranean alone."

"Oh, that! I get three units of college credit for this trip in history. Didn't I tell you I'm at BYU? And besides, I'm not *really* alone. My parents made sure that when I sailed they'd be close by—the Riviera, I told you."

"Three units," he said softly.

"Maybe you'd like to come with me! Oh, wouldn't that be *fun*? It's such a *beautiful* villa, Charlie. And we have an extra room, so it's no trouble putting you—"

"No," he said quickly, and then, far less sharply, "No, but thanks anyway, Stace. I gotta get, uh....well, I gotta get up to Paris first, meetin' some people there, then eventually head over to Germany. Munich. Bought my train ticket and everything. The Oktoberfest isn't too far off, y'know." A perfectly plausible set of lies, he thought.

"Oh. Too bad. For both of us," she said softly.

The young man said nothing. He wished he was somewhere else.

"Well, good-bye Charlie Barnes," she continued on valiantly, putting her arms around his neck. Her fingers curled and weaved through his sun-blond hair. His fingers found her bare back, the tan muscles, the damp, sweat-slick skin. "I'm sorry you didn't like me as much as I liked you."

"Who says I didn't?" he said, grinned his best Lancaster grin, and they kissed long and hard. But this time, dry. When they broke he grabbed his suitcase and quickly moved away.

"Be sure to write!" she called out. He smiled, waved, and made a relatively clean getaway.

San Marco Square was crowded, as usual. He walked past the cathedral dome, and was instantly struck with the notion that he never wanted to see another cathedral again as long as he lived. He looked up at the bell tower, the Campanile, rising straight and high above the square, and it looked unusually stiff and solid in the sun's early glare. He hadn't really looked at it before, and it occurred to him that it wasn't like the one back at school at all. Berkeley's was gray. This one was more pinkish red than gray, sort of like it had been skinned. It was at approximately this point in time, as he stood transfixed between the cathedral dome and the Campanile, that he knew he would not write to her. For an ordinary girl she was pretty spectacular, but she was no Deborah Kerr.

By the end of the week he had made it to Milan, where he paid sixty-nine dollars for a train ticket to Amsterdam. He should have gone there in the first place. He'd heard the women were good there.

SEASICK

Author's Notes

The day I got the check in the mail for winning the short-story contest for *The Imp of Berkeley* (see my Author's Notes on *The Imp of Berkeley*), in fact right after I opened the letter, my brother and I drove on down to San Diego to board the fishing charter which was the inspiration for this story. That makes *Seasick* the third short-story I ever wrote; probably in late spring of 1977. Unlike *Imp*, which flowed directly from my pen a finished product, I had to rewrite *Seasick* several times over the years to get it right….

One of the lines in *Seasick* is borrowed from an old Montgomery Clift movie. I'll leave it to you to figure out which one.

As a fledgling writer, in those early years, every single thing that happened to me seemed infected with a larger, more special significance than the thing itself. I was finding symbolism under rocks, finding allegories in the mail, and every bland conversation became a thrilling metaphor for something else far more fascinating and far more important. In other words everything that happened to me, every experience large or small, was a potential flint-spark for a story. Throwing up a bunch of times on a deep-sea fishing boat was no exception.

A day of abject misery in exchange for the raw material to weave a solid, socio-political and religious allegory for you good people to enjoy? A worthwhile trade. And so, I do believe my day of suffering was not in vain….but alas I'll never go deep-sea fishing again. I'm not stupid.

SEASICK

....The boat, a juggernaut alternately disciplined and lazy as butter, conceived purely for sport and dedicated exclusively to the abduction of helpless harmless albacore from their saline, god-given home, is typical of its species. It has a galley and a hold, a captain and three strong crewmen. It carries some twenty paying passengers, ranging from crusty, whiskered "sea dogs"—wily fishermen with leather for skin and slits for eyes, invariably the backbone of these well-financed, search-and-destroy missions—to father/son teams drafted directly from suburbia, grinning wide-eyed neophytes just hoping to catch something, which is to say anything they can bring back to their neighborhoods for show and tell. Yes, it is a typical deep-sea fishing boat, this juggernaut of optimism. Too big and too loud. Too confident. And of course it carries no women.....

BOOK I

It was early morning, passengers and crew crowded sardine-close in the stern. They were swapping sea stories and sipping strong coffee, laughing and joking, but always keeping a collective eye on the half-dozen poles that trolled peaceful Mexican waters for the elusive tuna. The boat had been trolling for an hour or so, without luck. No man aboard had yet spied even a single albacore. Which was not surprising. For a tuna's only defense against a boat of such unfair bulk and power is *concealment*! Best to cower safely near the bottom of their mysterious natural domain, they are all in agreement on this time-tested strategy of stealth and home-court advantage, and therefore it is no small occurrence when even one of them, much less a great many at once, surfaces solely for the privilege of being captured and killed by a superior foe. Accordingly, there had been only a couple of stray hook-ups, nothing substantial in the way of numbers to warrant an extended period of fishing, and no albacore; only skipjack and other less-worthy prey. Not enough. A school of good size is necessary to accommodate the blood-thirst of a twenty-man charter, one or two renegade fish simply won't suffice. But the day was young and hopes were high. There was an ambience of impending, guaranteed success hanging heavy in the salt-thick air, and the hook-ups were a glad harbinger of good things to come.

One member of the charter was not in the stern. He was sitting, rather, in the bow, alone, leaning heavily against the starboard side. He was not sipping coffee, he was not eavesdropping on the jokes and sea stories, he was most certainly not laughing. No. For this was a caricature of utter misfortune. Gravity pulled at his jaw, the way it had already pulled the blood from his weakened, insanely throbbing head. His face, accordingly, was completely devoid of color, and the sun to the east—though as warm and comforting against his left cheek as the touch of the gentlest nurse—was a poor doctor. His clothes were already wrinkled and heavy from occasional waves of salt water reaching up and over the rail to sneak peeks at him. Occasionally a low moan would escape his lips, already cracked and chapped from salt and sun. Indeed, the elements themselves seemed somehow strangely allied against him. But this tired young man seemed quite unaware of Nature's cruel minions. He resembled the fighter who has just been felled by a blow he didn't see coming, who neither knows nor cares where he is, and who, consequently, is far too dazed and disoriented to answer the bell for the next round.

Charlie Barnes had never been seasick. Never. He had heard about it, read about it, and had even seen occasional human examples of it, but until now he had never really known the meaning of the word. What's more, he couldn't understand why it was only *he* that Fate had this day selected, from among these twenty paying customers, to be sequestered nearly prone and apparently near death in the bow of this vile, unsteady ship. He had been in rowboats, dinghies, and even a luxury liner. He had once taken the ferry across the English Channel, a voyage far rockier, he was sure, than this one. Why hadn't he been similarly stricken at some point in his past? Why should this random fishing vessel be the vehicle of his Maiden voyage with this horrible malaise, this defeat of equilibrium, this so-called *seasickness*? And again, he wondered, why only *him*? His tortured mind searched the heavens halfheartedly for an answer....

The answer, of course lay within his own personal experience. Or rather lack of it. True, throughout his entire still-brief waltz with Life, the young man had never suffered through this peculiar equation of misery. Yet he had been aboard those other boats. So then what was the X-factor this time? Why the riddle? Well, truth be told, what young Barnes had not taken into account was that not only had he never been seasick, he had never been deep-sea fishing either. That this seemingly obvious correlation was overlooked is understandable; most non-fishermen think one kind of motion is very much like another, motion is motion, a boat is a boat is a good time. But when applied to a sixty-foot tuna boat, this generalization is quickly and easily exposed for the ridiculously amateurish theorem that it is. The quality of motion generated by such a boat is *leagues* deadlier than that of a rowboat or a dinghy or a luxury liner, or even the English Channel Ferry. What sets the tuna boat apart from these other tamer craft is that it moves in two dissimilar, alternating patters, involving two separate and dissimilar actions, thus hopelessly confusing the body into a state of disease. Some brief elaboration on this singular conflict of motion is necessary: When a fishing vessel is moving forward, engines full, the bow and the stern trade up for down, much in the manner of a see-saw. Specifically, when it is the stern's turn to rise, the bow drops quickly, and any less-than-alert soul in the bow will likely find air between himself and the deck before slamming down hard on the latter. This teeter-totter pattern continues until the vessel stops, when, after one of the trolling poles finds tuna, the eager fish hunters take their places around the sides of the boat to begin their unprovoked assault on the sea. Then, with the engines quiet, there is a change from the see-saw motion to a rocking movement, as the stalled boat is now at the mercy of the rolling waves. Back and forth, from side to side, the boat rocks, like a mother would rock her infant child to sleep in a wooden cradle; only much more violently. So it is this *alternation* of motion, from see-saw to cradle, which sets the fishing vessel apart from its more pacific relatives. Charlie did not yet realize this. He had not yet experienced this. He had not yet learned. And not having learned he was losing the battle. All he knew for sure was that in his nineteen-odd years he had never engaged such senseless, baseless torture. His only concerns were to keep his head below the gunwale, so that he couldn't see the ocean, and to always be exposed to the sun's gentle, comforting rays. If he could just do that, his hope was he just might minimize his suffering enough that he just might survive until the charter returned to port that night in San Diego. Just might.

BOOK II

"Hey there, friend. Uh....Charliesomething, isn't it?"

Charlie Barnes looked up. The sun was too bright for him to focus the face in the foreground into clarity, but the voice raining down from the eclipse rang true. There was no reason it shouldn't have. Charlie's cousin Matt had introduced them the previous night, just before the three of them drove all the way down together from Los Angeles. They boarded the overnight charter together. They drank beer together. They played poker together. *Just a few hours ago*, for God's sake....the most annoying people in the world are the ones who manage to combine a perpetually good mood with an inability to remember names, he said to himself. He was hardly in the mood for people *period*, much less people like that....

"That's right—Charlie Barnes. The wonderful guy you drove all the way the hell down here with last night. Have a seat. Lucas." He raised the decibel of the man's name just enough so that he'd get the message.

"Thanks, kid," said the man, as he plopped down smiling on the deck right next to Charlie. (Okay, so he *didn't* get the message, Charlie said to himself with contempt.) "Y'know something? You don't look so good," the annoying man added, as if lending necessary vocal affirmation to some great discovery.

But this recital of the obvious served only to further irritate the nineteen-year-old: "I don't feel so good or smell so good either, Detective. It's a flopped set."

The boat bounced harmlessly on the water, seemingly without direction, and for the moment apparently without plan or purpose, for the moment an impotent vessel of destruction at the very mercy of the hidden currents and mysterious primal forces which both concealed and tacitly protected its otherwise helpless foe....

"Aw, don't feel so bad, little buddy. Believe me, I know just how you feel. I do, I do, I surely do."

"Oh you *do,* huh?"

"Sure do. Puked my guts out the minute I woke up."

Charlie's eyes opened, but he needed confirmation: "Yeah?—I mean you threw up *too*?" was all he could think of to say....

"Yeah what, ya think yer the only idiot in the world that gets seasick?"

There was a pause, and then each shattered man let loose a chorus of sweet, painful laughter. For young Barnes, this was surely the first good news of the day. It is one thing to be near-death sick, but it is quite another to be stuck *in a crowd* and be sick, much less sick by yourself: "So there's somebody else on this goddam boat who's just as stupid and gut-sick as I am," Charlie groaned.

"Prob'ly sicker, little buddy, prob'ly sicker. How many?"

"Huh?"

"How many times 'you thrown up?"

"Oh...." He thought for a minute: "Four, I guess."

"Hey! Me too!"

"Yeah?"

"Yeah, *baby*! How 'bout that, green pea—it's four-to-four. Tie game."

Again both men laughed with ridiculous energy, considering, but Lucas' laughter was cut short when he suddenly bolted to his feet, twisted himself around, practically threw himself against the side of the boat, threw his head over the gunwale, and then vomited, vomited in a horrible crescendo of coughing and choking and wheezing, all the while his left hand clutching at his mid-section. The vomit itself was something of a bile, a dark black bile, thin, laced with chunks, and seemingly endless. He caught his breath in the middle of it all, and readied himself for the remainder of his ordeal. Vomiting generally comes in two distinct waves, and he wasn't through yet. Charlie knew the poor sap would have to repeat the process at least once before he was home and dry....Again his throat would feel like it was clotted shut just below the voice box, a feeling which would be coupled with a light-headed nausea which is distinguishable from all tamer types of nausea. When the actual vomiting occurred, again it would feel like his stomach and esophagus were parts of a dirty sock, and that some invisible hand was reaching down his throat and pulling his stomach inside-out, the way you'd turn the sock inside-out before throwing it in the washing machine. It is a horrible thing, even if only to watch....

In a few seconds Lucas had completed the second half of his punishment, endured this gastric nightmare for the fifth time, and turned around. He plopped back down on the deck next to Charlie.

"Go wipe that crud offa you, man, you look like a slob," Charlie said. The blackish discharge was streaked across Lucas' gray sweatshirt, and a few drops punctuated his otherwise pleasant face. Until now Charlie hadn't really concentrated on exactly what Lucas looked like, but now he couldn't help it. It was a good face. It was smooth and unmarked, very tan, but not a weather-beaten tan as was the mask of most of the experienced fishermen on this ruthless charter. The hair was short and sandy-brown, the eyes clear and pale blue like his own. The overall look was distinctly, and unmistakably, Midwestern....

"Why even bother, little buddy," Lucas said, more a statement of fact than a question requiring an answer, "I'd just have to wipe it off again later. Besides, it proves I'm in the lead."

"Congratulations."

"Thanks. So, 'you always fall apart on trips like this? I mean usually."

"I don't know. I mean how the hell should I know? I've never been seasick before."

"Yer kidding...."

"No."

"Well, then how often 'you come out deep-sea fishing?"

"I've never been deep-sea fishing before, either."

"Yer *kidding.*"

"*No!*"

"Well hey! How 'bout that!" Lucas spat through a gleaming white grin. "Never been seasick and never been to sea? Well dog my cats and pork my chops! This is terrific, I love breakin' in new recruits. So how's it feel? First time, I mean."

"Great, just great," Charlie sighed. "Please just shut up, man. I'd consider it a favor."

"C'mon, seriously."

"I am serious."

"C'mon. Tell me exactly what it feels like, 'first time out."

"How the hell should I know? I've never *been* this kinda sick before, I *told*ja. I can't actually describe *how* it goddam feels."

"Well lemme see if I can help ya. First of all, did ya get real hot in the face? Then break out in a quick cold sweat?"

"I—well, *yeah*, I guess...."

"And then did ya get even colder and dead-clammy all over?—like you were in someone else's body? And then you thought you were gonna faint like some darn fool *woman* or somethin'?"

Charlie was amazed. "*Yeah.* That's *exactly* what happened! Last night when we were playing cards, I'd get real hot, then cold all of a sudden, and real sweaty, but it was like it was *somebody else's sweat*! What was it you called it? Dead-clammy? That's amazing, man, how did you—"

"Take it easy, little friend, it's just that I've been around this block. I'm quite the veteran at this sort of stupidity. Been gettin' sick chasin' fish since I was fifteen," the tan man stated proudly. "Furthermore, I can tell ya exactly what yer gut feels like right now—empty but not empty. Because you know that when ya throw up again there'll be plenty of thick slime and food chunks comin' up from nowhere. We call it 'gravy', in case yer interested. Oh, and I'll bet yer mouth tastes all rusty like it never has before, like ya swallowed some old sheet metal. Right? Am I right?"

Charlie Barnes stared back with an open, rusty mouth. "How—"

"I told ya. I'm a veteran."

"Well, you sure got my misery pegged."

"The voice of experience, lad. Speaking of which, you should put something on yer face, its gettin' red as the proverbial beet."

"Who cares. I feel too lousy everywhere else to worry about my stupid face," Charlie said. He tried unsuccessfully to run the fingers of his right hand through his medium-length blond hair. The salt water had woven his hair into a Medusan tangle, but frankly Charlie currently cared as little about his hair as he did about his ruined face. The latter he reckoned was beyond hope for the day anyhow. The mid-morning sun had already tattooed the salt into his once-fair Scandinavian skin, and by now it had passed pain and arrived at numb.

"Hey, Cuz! How many times you heaved so far? We're makin' *bets*!" came a loud laughing voice from the other end of the boat. Charlie easily identified the sarcasm. Cousin Matt never got seasick, no matter how many beers he guzzled, and took great pains to make sure everyone on the charter knew it. It was as if he considered this lucky accident of physiology as somehow investing him with incontrovertible virtue, irrefutable evidence of God's favor and good will, and he seemed, therefore, to regard the bragging of it as not bragging at all but rather as more or less his inalienable right, the just, ultimate expression and sure sign of his nobility. Yet this 'ability' to avoid getting sick had not translated into any success at the mission; he'd caught nothing all day. In fact the entire charter had thus far bagged only a dozen or so stray tuna, and no albacore at that. "Catch any big bad fishies, Matty?" Charlie managed to bellow back, winking at Lucas, whose eyes were closed anyway. Cousin Matt didn't answer. Lucas grinned weakly.

"That's tellin'm, little buddy."

Charlie closed his eyes, rested his head back against the wood, and smiled. "Matt's got a big ego," he said. "Ex-jock, you know. Swimmer. Never gets sick. But not exactly a born fisherman, 'know what I mean? Fish freak him out. I mean the guy's a goddam *tax accountant* for Christ's sake!" He paused mid-speech to cough and gather his strength. Who knew mere conversation could prove so exhausting: "A squeamish CPA with a rod and reel? Sounds like a miniseries in the making! Hell, he'd probably be more comfortable in there *with* 'em than tryin' to catch 'em and gut 'em. Yeah, too squeamish. Even if he caught one he'd probably wind up apologizing to it, then promise not to disrespect it in the future," he mused, at the word 'with' flicking his head backwards and to the side to indicate the innocent creatures below, being forever and so unjustly pursued....

"If you say so, kid. I really don't know him very well. We just fish together."

"Hey, what time is it?"

"Oh, 'bout eleven I guess."

"Eleven a.m.? As in not four-thirty *p.m.*?"

"Whatsa matter, green pea—'world not turning quick enough for ya?"

"Jesus-God, I'll *never* get off this thing," whispered the young man to himself, and sank back once more against the wood.

BOOK III

"*Hook up! Hook up!*"

A fishing vessel discovering a school is a learning experience. There is a back-stage excitement indigenous to this event which simply must be lived to be appreciated. Almost before the captain can order a halt to the engines each man has one hand on his fishing pole and the other in the bait tank. No man trips. No two men collide. The coordinated performances of the players are fluid, almost graceful. It is a silent clarion call to action that takes place on the deck of such a ship; so quickly are the men mustered around the deck, so surely does each amateur seem somehow to professionally divine his proper place at the side. Yet, for the most part, these men are strangers. They have never met most of their fellow fortune hunters. They will never see most of them again. They are merely responding to their dormant instincts, the instincts which apparently are always there to guide ordinary men when they take to the sea. It is beautiful. It is absurd.

"Leave those damn skipjacks alone, go down deep for the albacore!" came the captain's voice, at once hard and compassionate, knifing through the brassy distortion of the loudspeaker. *"They's down about a hunnerd'n fifty feet, use the heavy sinkers! Do what I tell ya, people, and everything will be fine....."*

To the casual observer, Charlie Barnes might have appeared oblivious to the captain's fervent commands. Indeed, he was still lying in the bow of the boat, eyes usually closed, apparently oblivious to the maritime combat now commencing right under his nose. But Charlie was anything but oblivious. Nor was he himself a casual observer. Of anything. His senses were operating at their maximum level of efficiency: He could feel the sun, directly overhead, burning into his reddened salt-stitched brow. His ears recorded Lucas' controlled breathing a few feet to his right, the exhalations coming in perfectly spaced intervals, exactly seven slow seconds apart. He was painfully aware of the empty, nauseous feeling in the pit of his stomach, which had not subsided, had not abated, had not even decreased in intensity. His nose sorted out the disparate flavors of sea, salt, bait, fish, fowl. And he was aware of the captain's every word. He forced himself to consider each word's meaning, evaluating every syllable, rolling the phrases around and around in his head, backwards and forwards, in a vain and valiant attempt to accelerate the passage of Time....

"What's the difference between a skipjack and an albacore?"

"Well, if yer one a'*those* good old boys, they's a *big* difference," said Lucas, somewhat cryptically, his eyes also closed as he indicated the crowd in the stern with a slight tip of the head. "Takes five or six skipjack to equal one albacore....mosta these boys figure that if ya catch a skippy ya haven't really caught anything."

"Think they'll get any albacore today?"

Lucas paused to prop himself up against the side. He squinted a long, thoughtful gaze over towards the stern, then re-closed his eyes, fatigue finding nothing nearly so interesting as to require them to remain open. "Hard 'say. I know one thing, mosta these naval heroes would give his right arm to pull in a thirty-pounder on a trip like this, simply because nobody's got one yet. God bless 'em. But it's a cinch neither you or I will be the one to bag that first 'core, am I right?"

"Don't know about you. But I'm out," Charlie moaned softly.

Lucas opened his eyes in response to his comrade's slight change of voice....

"Y'know, if ya weren't so danged sunburned I'd say you were lookin' *awful* pale."

"Yeah?"

"Yeah. Sorry, man."

Charlie let escape a long-suppressed sigh of defeat. "I was afraid of that," he said. He rose and made it to the railing just in time, or so it seemed. Everyone thinks that he 'barely made it' to the railing or the sink or the car window. But more often than not that first dreaded reversal of the peristaltic waves is triggered by the mind of the sufferer himself. The anticipation of the ordeal speeds up the natural timetable, to be sure, but the sufferer usually has enough resistance to prevent the embarrassment of the early release. This time Charlie was lucky. He was already leaning over the gunwale when his mind triggered his own body's discharge, and the gravy flowed freely and quickly. But it was still a painful rite of passage for him. He wondered, at this moment, right in the middle of it all and stuck midway between stage one and stage two, how anyone in his right mind could speak of being seasick as if it were some trifling matter. He also wondered if he was going to die that day....

"Five to five. Looks like we's all tied up....*again*!" Lucas said. Charlie collapsed next to him, exhausted; but not before completing stage two. "Well done, rook. Say, you barf like a veteran weak-gut, my man. Well done."

"Thanks a lot."

"Oh, one more thing. If one a'these boys hooks something we're gonna hafta move."

"I'm not."

"Yer not what?"

"Moving. I'm not moving."

"You *gotta*—'we don't move outa the way we'll get run right over."

"I said I'm not moving."

"So what yer saying is yer not moving...."

"I'm *not* moving."

"No matter what?"

"No matter what."

Lucas smiled. "Okay, I'll hang right here with ya, then. I won't desert you in yer time of need, green pea. Just don't say I didn't warn you when we get trampled by a buncha crazy weekend fishermen."

For a couple minutes neither man spoke. It was Charlie who resumed the conversation. And he was laughing: "You know something, man? I couldn't get up even if I wanted to."

Now it was Lucas' turn to laugh a little. Charlie could not join him, too exhausted to maintain his brief good humor. But for the first time all day he didn't feel miserable. He didn't actually feel *good*, but, for one blessed moment at least, the nausea had apparently left him alone. He didn't know why. He didn't care.

"Albacore! Al....ba....core!"

"There they be!"

"Golly, look at the lead—he's a beaut!"

"Git that slimy, slit-eyed sonofabitch, Pete. *Git* eem!"

"He's got him."

"Don't lose him, Pete. Give him room, give him *room*."

At once the entire vessel had become charged with its own self-manufactured electricity.

"What'd I tell ya?" Lucas beamed.

"I'm not moving," said Charlie.

BOOK IV

Albacore fight hard. To the man holding the pole it feels as if a man of equal weight and strength is pulling at the other end of the line. But it is more than mere competition. It is as if land and sea have pitted their champions together in a titanic tug-of-war, all-or-nothing, to determine once and for all the superior domain. In this matched pair, or seemingly mismatched pair, the human combatant was a worthy one. His tanned forearms swelled beneath their tattoos, and he gripped the bent rod in calloused hands even more impressive in their size. "Jesus, he's a fighter," he would whisper from time to time. There was reverence in his voice. He respected the fish, in a way that the casual weekenders funding this charter who were now watching him work never could nor could ever understand. Because this man, whose wisdom, great strength, and vast knowledge of the sea must all be gleaned from thousands of separate, no-surrender skirmishes with its most cunning warriors, surely knew he was in for a fight. He had been battling the great fish back and forth for almost twenty minutes, and was only now beginning to gain the upper hand....

"That's it, Pete, pull eem in!"

"Play with him, boy, *play* with him!"

"*Not too fast, Peter, give him some slack. Let him run a little bit,*" the captain's brassy voice counseled wisely. It is not a good idea to get into a pulling match with an albacore. The fisherman must be willing to give up a few yards of line to his opponent every now and then. All those old sayings about patience being the fisherman's best friend have lasted down through the ages because of their validity. The captain had learned this lesson well. He had learned it long ago, and had re-learned it a thousand times. And he had seen many an eager sea-soldier refuse to give an inch in his time, and the result was always the same; a broken test line, snapped in two like a piece of cheap twine.

So it is part of the captain's job to control his brood, to temper this natural, child-like impatience with a paternal wisdom. And in this respect he had his hands full. The other fishermen had sensed the epic proportions of this singular struggle, this particular pitched battle, and they had all dropped everything to watch their champion spar with this invisible champion of the deep. Not one other hook was in the water. They watched now as Pete, the big fisherman, maneuvered his prey around to the bow, to where they all followed him, trespassing upon the private misery of Charlie Barnes and his fellow weak-gut....

"This is what it's all about, little buddy."

Charlie shifted his position on the deck. "Much ado about nothing, if you ask me," he said. "Some vacation. And to think I actually volunteered to come along, just to keep Matt company." (It was bad enough that he had never been sicker in his life, he thought. But to have to contend with twenty pairs of legs crawling and tripping over him? As if he wasn't even *there*?)

"Whatsa matter, young hero? Are we not having a good time?"

"Cut it out. I didn't expect it to necessarily be fun, but I thought for sure I'd at least get to relax for a couple days. I gotta fly up for *finals* next week, for Christ's sake."

"Too bad."

"I mean I knew going in I didn't know squat about it, I admit it, but from what I understand the practice of fishing is at least *supposed* to be relaxing....isn't it?

"It's supposta be."

"Well I don't see what's so damned relaxing about throwing up all the time."

"Not to mention the hassle of just getting here."

"Yeah, and that's another thing. You call this a vacation? I mean what's the point if you have to drive all the way down to the Mexican border and then take a boat halfway to hell before you even get to drop your hook into the water?"

"Right on."

"Between everyone's cars and the diesel fuel for the boat, I wonder how much precious goddam petroleum we just blew. I mean as a group. Some energy crisis we're supposta be in, huh? And I wonder how much food and beer we consumed. And how much did we hafta pay for the charter, and the crew."

"Quite the sinful waste of natural resources, if you ask me."

"That's what I'm saying, dude. That's all I'm saying."

"I hear ya. I guess the whole thing must seem a little silly to a new boot who's never been out before."

"You're damn right it's silly! All this waste for a few stupid fish? Now be honest, can you remember the last time you saw so many grown men get so excited over something so utterly ridiculous?" He'd been awake for seven hours now, and his stomach was still restless and uncooperative, vexing his speech proportionately....

"It is a little like Nam at that."

"....Nam?"

Lucas looked at Charlie and smiled, then closed his tired eyelids again and rested his head against the gunwale. "I was 'in country' for two years," he said casually.

"In what? What, you mean the *war*? You mean you were in—"

"*There 'e is!*"

"Man-o-man, that sumbitch must weigh forty pounds!"

"He's a slippery old bastard!"

"Not too slippery fer ol' Pete!"

"Naw! Pete's a match fer *any* by-god sea critter *I* knows of...."

"Ol' Pete!"

"Yeah. Good ol' Pete."

The big fisherman had won his battle. His unfair advantage of superior technology and equipment had proven too great a mismatch for the noble fish to overcome. As one of the smiling deck hands speared it with his gaffing pole the rapt spectators roared their approval. There is always ample celebration surrounding the landing of an albacore, and, in fact, the rites and rituals attached to this blessed event are precisely the lure of the sport. But Charlie Barnes, little more than a reluctant volunteer on this voyage of chase and death, was barely aware of the happy screams and shouts that came from men whose legs, only moments before, had caused him such careless grief. His mind was elsewhere. Through a lucky accident of Fate he had unearthed a chapter of his strange, mysterious companion's past that was far more fascinating than some pathetic creature's predetermined capture and execution....

"Was it rough?"

"What."

"*You* know what, the *war*? Was it? Tell me. Tell me everything."

Lucas was sprawled out in the bow, as many sections of his shattered body adhered to the sun-baked deck as was possible. His eyes would have been pointed away from Charlie's stare, if they were open. His chest rose and fell in a controlled rhythm, up and down, up and down, slowly, premeditatedly, the sea air rushing audibly in and out of his lungs. Amazingly, he didn't even look uncomfortable....

"Sometimes they'd go three, maybe four months without hittin' us. Then one day....boom! That was the problem, playin' in their ballpark. We never knew exactly when they'd hit us. Or where."

"What'd they look like?"

"Don't know. I never saw one. Least not up close."

"Didja ever get *shot*?" Charlie queried almost hopefully.

Lucas chuckled, the way war veterans do: "Nah. The NVA were good guerillas, but they didn't exactly shoot straight!"

"The NVA?"

"North Vietnamese regulars. Good, tough fighters, those boys. Never ate, never slept. Never did actually see one the whole time I was there. Oh, except the occasional blowed-up dead one, of course. I'm tellin' ya, we never knew for sure *what* those little guys would do."

For one of the few times in his life Charlie was in a state of awe, though it would have been hard to tell. He was staring dumbly ahead, not at Lucas, but at the deck just beyond his own feet, where the defeated fish had been flung and now flipped and flopped in agony. He was over two feet long. A handsome fish. Charlie realized at once he had never seen a fish this big up close; all the fish he had ever seen or caught had been fresh-water, bluegill and bass, or the occasional rainbow trout. This fish was a beast. He was long and thick and sleek and silvery, and seemed to glimmer and shine in the sun, and this visual image was forever crystallized in Charlie's head by its sharp, accompanying foul odor. The fish bled from a side-wound below his right gill, where the crewman's gaff had pierced him, and in his own reverse way he was gasping for breath. But soon he relaxed. And then he bled quietly. Only moments before he had moved swiftly and powerfully through the water, but the change of element had crippled him, much more so than the gaffing pole had. He lay there seemingly resigned to his fate. He was pacific. He was serene. Charlie gazed at the fish's unblinking right eye, stared at his face. He wondered if a fish was capable of registering facial expression:

"Don't look so tough now, does he kid?" one of the swaggering fishermen spewed forth, his fat finger indicating the fallen tuna. The superior tone of his voice made Charlie angry, for one reason or another. He didn't really know why. But he would not dignify the question, rhetorical or not, with a reply. Instead, he boyishly prodded his newfound personal war correspondent for more stories, anecdotes, anything: "Did *you* ever shoot anybody?"

Again the ex-soldier laughed. "I was a medic. They didn't exactly prefer us bein' the ones *doin'* the shootin'! Wouldn't a'played very well on T.V."

The young man was suddenly no longer lying pinned to the deck of a chartered tuna vessel trolling off the coast of Mexico. He had been, through the generous offices of the Human mind, transported to the other side of the globe, to the steamy, embattled jungles of Indochina, to an epoch and theater that had eluded him by a few chance years. He had never known anyone who had actually been there—save another of his legion of cousins, and that one was a flyer so he was *above* the actual drama—and thus any conclusions he had drawn were the result of transforming media fantasy into plausible reality. And so, he asked questions. And he listened intently. Through Lucas' stories he would come as close as possible, as close as he probably ever would, to actually being there himself. As to *why* he would want to come close, why he would ever even have *wanted* to have been there at all is, well, another story....

"At least you got to go," he said with envy and admiration.

"Got to go....got to *go?*" Lucas said; and for the first and only time all day the strange man appeared angry. In fact, his face looked downright *unhappy.* Charlie grimaced. He could have kicked himself....

"You all-American star spangled idiot, I didn't *wanna* go," Lucas went on. "In fact I went out of my way to *avoid* it. Naturally. Like any sane person would."

"You—"

"Problem was I didn't know the rules. At the time I was in school with yer cousin Matt. San Jose State. We were both environmental studies majors, that's how we met. You ever even heard of environmental studies? Neither had I, until the sixties got aholda me! Very concerned ecologists we were too, gonna clean up the environment all by ourselves. But I got bored with school, and wound up dropping out. So while ol' Matt over there skated by on his student deferment, ol' Luke here was forced to accept Uncle Sam's generous invitation. *'Come with me and see the world, young hero, come to beautiful and exotic Southeast Asia, two years, all expenses paid'*. I just didn't understand the rules, that's all."

As if summoned by the random mention of his name, suddenly the tax accountant was standing directly over them: "Did you see it?"

"Huh?" said Charlie and Lucas in accidental unison.

"That nasty-fat *albacore* we landed!" said Matt, bubbling over with the good news, shaking and gesticulating as if he had masterminded the expedition.

"Yeah, it's a beauty, Matty," said Charlie. He closed his eyes and pretended to yawn. "Good catch. Too bad you couldn't have used your environmental studies degree to help Pete out a little bit."

The accountant swore something and retreated to the stern, grumbling and pouting like the cartoon character he had become. He was not yet even out of earshot when they started to laugh, and laugh, and they laughed until their shattered bodies couldn't take anymore.

BOOK V

"What's the worst thing about being seasick?"

It was late, and the sun was dropping from their view. This might have been a welcome sight, except that with the sun goes its warmth, that comforting warmth which seems to resent the sun's retreat below the western horizon, leaving behind a chilling vacuum of cold and wind. The fishermen were again clustered sardine-close in the stern, talking, singing and smoking, their mood as calm and relaxed as the sea upon which they rocked. They were swapping sea stories, albacore stories mainly. Tales only of victory. They would not be a bother to Charlie Barnes again. But the dreadful malaise that had been his keeper from the outset was still with him. His misery had continued unabated for some twelve hours, during which time the young man had fully studied and thoroughly contemplated his foul predicament, its most ghastly features. He was certain that he had ascertained the answer to his own question....but was compelled nevertheless to ask for a second opinion.

"Well, there's an old saying they have about bein' seasick," Lucas replied. "First yer afraid yer gonna die, and then yer afraid yer *not* gonna die."

Charlie tilted his head back against the wood and laughed in silence. It was a laugh of total, fraternal agreement. He had indeed, though only half seriously of course, entertained thoughts of death on this day. And as he was now staring skyward, he couldn't help but notice a dozen or so seagulls circling over his head. The birds were fat and white, in marked contrast to Charlie's conditioned mental image of scavengers. His preconceptions were confined to a hackneyed vision of vultures, lean and black, circling hungrily over a dying man who had been foolish enough to attempt a desert crossing alone. Charlie's imagination was running wild. The boat was his desert, and the harmless white birds overhead were his vultures, his emissaries of certain death. These innocent fowl were concerned only with the contents of the bait tank, and Charlie was vaguely aware of this, yet still he cursed them. They cawed down to him and he swore right back. Sometimes he would select a particular, individual bird to be the target of his ire, but for the most part his fusillade was directed at the squadron in general. This ludicrous exchange continued for several minutes, and at first Charlie reveled in his fantasy. The misery was mitigated by the madness. But finally it was too much, and he rolled over on his stomach in frustration. It was this chance movement which precipitated a great discovery:

"Hey....hey! Hey, it works! Dammit to hell, it *works*!"

"What works?" Lucas rejoined, the swearing match with the seagulls still fresh in his ears.

"Lying on your stomach! And to think I spent this whole damn day sittin' on my *butt*."

"You mean you don't feel sick?"

"No! Uh, well, I mean not as much, not *nearly*. I guess the deck keeps your gut from wigglin' around, or something. C'mon, man, try it out," Charlie said urgently. Lucas squinted back, nodded his head, and slowly rolled over to lie flat on the deck next to Charlie, very slowly, for any quick movement could trigger a disaster. Finally he was in place. And his elation was his great as his benefactor's: "Well scratch my back and comb my hair. This is one of the greatest moments in deep-sea fishing history!"

he affirmed, "*thee* greatest," Charlie overtrumped him, and they giggled like a couple of schoolboys.

They had been lying prone on the deck for two solid hours when the captain's voice washed over them, like a miracle of deliverance: "*Okay boys and girls, that's it. We're going back,*" was all he said. A simple enough pronouncement, but the nine words shattered the calm ocean air like the crash of cymbals. They applauded their reprieve as best they could from their awkward position—it isn't easy clapping while lying on your stomach—but applaud they did, and with an enthusiasm reborn.

Faster and faster the boat sliced through the Mexican waters for San Diego. The increased speed caused the sea water to cascade over the bow in seemingly timed intervals. Most of these waves landed upon the two men, soaking them to the skin, but they hardly noticed. They knew their ordeal was almost over. The rest of the boat noticed plenty, though, and they watched and giggled and made fun of them the way shipmates do. But Charlie and Lucas, now a team of their own, were impervious to such insensitive derision. They just lay there on their stomachs and talked, their heads facing each other. Their eyes were usually closed from the weight of so many exhaustions. They shivered in the encroaching darkness. They talked about seasickness.

"Dude....You never asked me what *I* thought was the worst thing," said Charlie.

Lucas obliged. "Okay little buddy, I'll bite. What have you decided is the worst thing about bein' seasick?" Just then another waved buried them. When the water's noise subsided a rude, far-away shower of laughter filled the void. But Charlie had his little speech prepared, and wasn't about to let anything so trivial slow his delivery. He had thought out every word, converting every emotion and indignity he had experienced into dialogue. He was determined to present his torture as testimony, and so he began his speech almost before both the water and the laughter had time to drain free of his burned and leathery face:

"The worst thing about this whole damn trip," he began, "isn't the barfing or the puking, or the smell, or the sunburn and the chapped lips or the crappy food or even the jerks in the stern making fun of us, I can deal with all that. Hell, I threw up plenty in high school, I'm used to it. No, the worst thing about this whole experience is that you can't *go* anywhere! Am I right? If you're doing anything else in life—college, a job, a girlfriend, a marriage....even a party someone throws specifically for *you*—and you find out you made a mistake or don't dig it you can at least bag the whole scene and just split. But not on a goddam fishing boat. It's like a prison sentence. No, its worse, because you're trapped and sick to your stomach at the same time. It's almost like being *punished* for stupidity. I musta thought about a million different thing I cudda done today, man....gone to a movie, gone to the track, watched T.V., slept in....I could've even studied for my poli-sci final, if I had a brain in my head....but no. I actually *chose* to get on this bucket. Punished for my stupidity. That's why my mind always drifts back to the same stupid fantasy. Namely, that any minute a big shiny helicopter will just plop right down on this deck and take me off this stupid thing. And the longer you wait for that helicopter that never comes, the worse your gut aches as punishment. Being a prisoner is the worst part, man. A prisoner of your own bad decision-making. And that, my friend, is the worst thing about being seasick....especially if you just happen to be seasick while trapped on a deep-sea fishing vessel lost somewhere in foreign waters," he concluded, satisfied that there was nothing substantially more to be said on the subject.

"Y'know something, man? I may be stupid, but I think I'd rather take on those invisible NVA bastards again than go through *this* again."

"You serious?"

"Yer damn right. This is my last deep-sea voyage, I swear it. Next time I go fishing it's on dry land. You heard it here. Maybe the Sierras, up around Bishop or something."

"Bishop. I hear it's bitchin' up there. All year round, too."

"Yep. Hey! You oughta come with me, green pea."

"Huh?"

"Maybe in the fall, before it freezes over. Whaddaya say?"

"Uh, sure, great," he managed. "I mean that sounds cool."

"Just think, little man," Lucas said, his eyes again closed. "Sittin' on a riverbank, a *motionless* riverbank by God, suckin' on a cold beer and pullin' in those big, juicy rainbow trout—"

"—And being able to leave when we *wanna* leave," Charlie contributed. He looked at Lucas a long time. He had nothing more to say, but his mind, finally, was clear. For nearly fifteen hours his senses had been in charge, but now he was actually thinking. He remembered something about a lame old saying his mother used to employ, something cheesy about there being no such thing as a bad day if you looked for the good in it hard enough.... can't remember exactly how it went....But as he stared at this student come medic come fisherman come friend, he suddenly wished the boat wasn't going so damned fast. A stray thought grabbed him; he didn't even know his new friend's last name....

"Right on, man. I'm with you. From now on my new philosophy is this: If you have to recruit the whole blessed ocean into the plan just to be able to catch a stupid fish, it's not worth the trouble. No more thrill of the chase and kill for me. From now on if a fish wants a fight, he's gonna hafta start it."

"Lakes and rivers only?"

"Lakes and rivers only, that's it. I have spoken. Mark it down as gospel, for future generations."

They laughed like two men actually having a good time....because they were. Finally.

"Luke, you believe in fate?" Charlie asked softly, in a casual tone of voice.

"What'd you say?"

"....nothing. Never mind."

They didn't talk much after that. By the time they were just off the California coast they couldn't see it for the darkness; but the captain said it was there, and so they figured it must surely be so. They were only a few hundred yards from the dock when Charlie Barnes, now officially a veteran of his first and last campaign as a deep-sea fisherman, struggled to his feet. "If you'll excuse me," he said dramatically, then bolted for the rail.

"Six to five. Looks like yer the winner. Buddy."

Charlie looked back briefly at Lucas, who was smiling. Charlie winked, grimaced in pain, and grabbed his gut. Then he smiled back. And then his head disappeared triumphantly over the side.

THE SHORT STRANGE STORY OF HAL HAPPIWELL

Author's Notes

I enjoyed my time at college. The San Francisco Bay area is a great place, rich with awesome natural and architectural wonders, great food, a great climate with its fog and rain and never too hot (everything L.A. is not), there were even a couple of fresh new racetracks for me to discover and explore, and of course I was away from home and on my own for the first time. Berkeley is a fine university, it certainly stimulated my mind to become a serious writer, and Berkeley the city is a fun and festive town in its own right.

But there are some crazies up there. This story is my personal testimony on the subject.

You wouldn't believe how precisely I mirrored the 'Hal' character to someone I actually knew. Someone I actually lived with for 17 harrowing days. At least it made for some decent character development. But it's easy to write a good character when you have the Pillsbury Doughboy, a cartoon hyena, Truman Capote, and Clarence the wingless angel to use as the raw building materials.

This story is not only meant to be a seriocomic look at people, relationships, apathy, homophobia, and mental illness, but I also see it as a metaphor for a cloying, clueless U.S. foreign policy during that period in our nation's history. And speaking of that period, the mid-70s, I wanted to leave behind a look at what was going on in pop-culture in this country, an all-inclusive hodgepodge running the gamut from the *Tonight Show* to Capote to the American League pennant race, to the soul of music and the state of the NFL, to M*A*S*H and the other fine shows which were running on prime-time TV during that era, and of course one man's window into the disillusionment and stark aftermath of that noble, ghastly experiment known as Vietnam. I wanted my son to be able to get a feel for what was going on in the world when his own father was a young man. Maybe that's why I didn't get serious about writing this story and finishing it until thirty-five years after I lived through the non-fiction portion of it, until 2011, right after Rob and I went on a vacation to Berkeley and I got to show the lad the campus and all my old stamping grounds. Including where I used to live, metal-balconied fire escapes and all....

So I guess this story, while fiction, is also something of a letter, a letter mailed from the 1970s all the way to the 21st century. A love letter. From me to my son. As some of the other stories surely are as well.

THE SHORT STRANGE STORY OF HAL HAPPIWELL

"Honey? Sweetie? Sweetie, are you there?"

"Still here, Mom. But I'm hanging up."

"Don't you *dare* hang up on me Charlie Barnes, or—"

"Mom, please...."

"Sweetie, I'm just saying be careful. Just be *careful*, baby dumpling!"

"Mom—"

"That's all I'm saying. I'm—"

"Mom, you've got a much better chance of making your points if you don't punctuate them with baby dumpling."

The woman's voice withered and died at the other end of the line. He could feel her gathering herself. Good. If she could take a moment to regroup, so could he. He took a deep breath and made sure she could hear the exhale. He ran his free hand through dampened tangles of wavy blond hair. Just washed, still wet. The cynical surgeons of M*A*S*H frolicked on the TV screen across the room. He wished he could make out what the hell they were saying....

"I'm just trying to make things easier for you, sweetie. It's a mother's *job* to make things easier."

"I'll be fine, Mom," said her son, smiling idiotically into the phone the way people do, as if there might be special agents armed with hidden cameras, hiding somewhere, somehow secretly videotaping a guy sitting alone and naked in a motel room and watching him watch TV while talking on the phone with his mother 400 miles away. "I'll be fine."

"It's just that Berkeley is *such* a den of iniquity. I don't know what in the world your father and I were *thinking*."

"Take it easy, mom. It's not a den of anything. It's fine."

"And you say you're meeting this strange man tomorrow?"

"I have a ten-o'clock appointment to see the apartment, yes. And I didn't say he was strange. What makes you call a guy strange?"

"I meant strange as in you don't know him."

"Mom, *everyone* is strange to me. I don't know anyone up here....well, uh—"

"Well what?"

"Well except for these three guys from high school who I heard are renting a little house just off Telegraph and Ashby. But that's all."

"Well then why can't you just move in with *them*? At least you *know* them. I mean why *can't* you?"

"No room. It's three guys and only two small bedrooms as it is. And only one bathroom. I hear Theo is bunking on the living room couch. They practically shower and poop in assigned shifts!"

"But you could just—"

"*No room*, Mom. No! Just no. Okay?"

Another intermission. This time, perhaps ten full seconds were allowed to pass into history without dialogue. Charlie started to reach down and scratch himself during the break, but when he remembered it was his mother on the other end of the line, he stopped. He looked at his watch.... almost nine....in a few minutes he would have to make a decision; either leave it on CBS to catch *Hawaii Five-O*, or switch to NBC for *The Rockford Files*....a decision a lot easier to make, certainly, if not encumbered with his mother on the other end of a telephone line. By way of shortening the conversation, he would tell his mother no more tales about these 'old friends' of his from high school. If she knew they were three of the biggest stoners he'd ever known, and had been trying in vain to get him high for years, she would scream bloody murder, audible all the way up from the Barnes family home in suburban Los Angeles, and after picking herself up off the floor she would then no doubt call the Marines and send them up there to save her little boy, snatch him away from that earthly hell for many a mother which the locals lovingly call 'Berzerkeley', once and for all, and have them spirit him safely back down to the blessed blandness of the Nowhere City....

"Your father wants to know if you remembered to pack your Bible."

Charlie smiled again, but this time merely from his own inner amusement. "Tell him yeah," he said with conviction. He didn't like lying to his folks, and was glad he was able to avoid doing so on a technicality. He didn't say he *had* packed it, just to *tell* his dad that he had....

"Just be careful, honey. If you don't mind your p's and q's you'll wind up sleeping on some floor somewhere. Just make good decisions, all right?"

"Sure Mom. I'll be making some of the best decisions of all time. You'll see."

"I love you, sweetie!"

"I'll call you soon. Promise."

"I know you will, son. I know you will. I just wish I felt you *looked forward* to it!"

"I do, Mom. I do," he sighed.

"I *love* you...."

"Yeah, Mom, I know. Love you too. Don't worry about me so much, okay?" He hung up.

Nine o'clock on the dot. Damn her, he said out loud....'missed the whole damn thing....He wished he'd been smart enough to call his mother earlier in the evening, to avoid missing his favorite show. He loved political satire, as might be expected of any political science major who believed television to be a necessary tool for building social and political awareness in young adults, young adults trying to navigate their way through the so-called 'modern', post World War Two world. He'd even read an article recently which stated the opinion that M*A*S*H was the most important show currently running on television, because that while it was ostensibly (which is to say seemingly, supposedly, and superficially) set way back during the *Korean* War it was actually meant to be a political statement concerning the nation's war-weariness over Vietnam. Which certainly made sense to Charlie. Even with that longest and most unsatisfying of U.S. wars now, suddenly, at an end. It was just such articles which conveniently convinced him he owed it to himself to watch shows like these, in order to further his education. But thanks to his mother, he'd just missed out on an important half hour of that education. Damn....can't a guy just *relax* for Christ's sake? He knew he was still a little nervous about tomorrow morning's interview. He desperately needed an apartment. Time was running short. All he wanted was to get it over with and get it done. Junior year would be heavy and hard upon him in less than a week, and he was already feeling its unfamiliar weight. He needed to relax.

He reached down, scratched and stroked himself unabashedly, and then settled in for a relaxing hour of *Hawaii Five-O* before bed. He actually preferred *The Rockford Files*, because it was a newer show and because it made him think and because he preferred James Garner to Jack Lord, but in his current state and prevailing mood he was just too tired and too lazy to get up and change the channel....

The address was on Haste Street, just off Telegraph Avenue. On the corner, in fact. Only three blocks from campus. He found an empty parking space right in front, a good sign. It was a tall, imposing building of gray bricks and old-fashioned metal-balconied fire escapes, of sculpted stone entryways and the intricately tiled lobby floor of a bygone era. Old-school. Beautiful. Perfect. But he scaled the three flights of stairs slowly, his eagerness to get the interview out of the way more than quelled by the usual trepidation that comes from confronting the uncomfortable, from shaking hands with the unknown. He knocked on the door. It was thrown open at once.

There to greet him was a nearly bald little man in plaid shorts and a white T-shirt.

"Hi. Oh my goodness, *hi*!"

"Hi yerself. I'm Charlie Barnes. I called?"

"Yes yes, come in—and *thank* you—thank you for *coming*!"

"Don't mention it." He strode with renewed confidence into the main room. Wood floors thumped beneath his shoes. High ceilings doubled his six-foot-three frame. It was an exceptionally well-lit apartment, the huge window leading out to its own fire escape balcony seemingly drawing in all the light, noise, and ceaseless throb of life the intersection of Telegraph and Haste could spare. All this and only three blocks from campus? He wanted it right away.

"Where would I sleep?"

"Oh! It's great! You have your *own room*!" came the enthusiastic reply. The little man shuffled and waddled over to one of the bedrooms, proudly drawing a hidden pocket door out from within the thick wood wall. "It's *private*!"

For the first time, Charlie really looked at—and allowed himself to study—the little man. The little man's shortness was both accentuated and trumped by his cookie-dough physique, giving the impression he had never run, jumped, or lifted a weight in his life. So white was the skin of this fat little fellow that he appeared to have been dipped in powdered sugar. He could have easily been kin to the 'Pillsbury Doughboy' from the TV commercials, and that notion made Charlie want to poke this living relative in the stomach to see if he'd chuckle in the same cute, childlike, unequivocally happy way. But instead of the chef's hat the Pillsbury mascot wore, this real life cookie-dough man was topped only by a little mat of blond hair, very little, and what little hair he had left was infected with gray, pegging his age (for Charlie, at least) at around forty-five. Maybe even fifty. And the most distinctive feature of this fiftyish face was its red, bulbous nose. Red and round and too big, like a clown's nose, except that the red was not rubber but rather the ruddy residue of tiny broken blood vessels, a clear indicator (to Charlie, at least) of a lifetime of whiskey drinking.... well, maybe whiskey. Who knows. Either way, this was an amazing looking individual. And equally amazingly, this weird, comical stranger looked *familiar*; and not just Pillsbury-Doughboy familiar, but also *real-people* familiar....he definitely reminded him of someone....but who?

"Hey, do I know you?"

"Oh! *Do* you? Do you *really*?"

The little man started grinning insanely. Charlie took a step back.

"No, I guess not....I take it yer not a student."

"Oh no. Golly, *no*. I just *live* here!"

"What's the bite?"

"I beg your pardon?"

"The rent, man. What's the rent?"

He braced himself for the bad news....

"Oh! Well, it's—I hope it's okay, and not too much—it's ninety....no! I mean eighty, it's *eighty*. Eighty dollars a month?"

Charlie couldn't decide what was stranger; the ridiculously low rent for a cool place three blocks from campus, the apparent confusion over the exact dollar figure, or the fact that the dollar figure had been ultimately rendered in the form of a question....

"I thought apartments this close to campus cost a ton," he said dryly. He needed his good fortune confirmed. To kill time he picked up a golf ball and began tossing it from hand to hand.

"I like the way you throw the ball back and forth!"

"Do you play golf?"

"Oh *gosh* no—it's just a little ball I like—I don't *remember* how I got it. Oh *dear*."

It was beginning to strike him as a weird conversation but since he didn't know why and didn't really care, he let it go.

"So it's eighty bucks a month. That's it? What about utilities?"

"Oh, that's all *included*! So when you think about it it's really *less* than eighty! Oh dear....oh my...."

There was no point in looking the rare gift horse in the mouth. "I'll take it," Charlie exclaimed. He was delighted even further to find that he would not even have to sign a lease or leave a deposit, and that all he needed to do was pay one month's rent in advance, now, and the same $80 dollars at the first of every month thereafter. He wrote the little doughy man a check, the man grinned and gave him his key, Charlie told him he'd move his things in little by little over the next few days, they shook hands (the young man taking care to not hurt the delicate white fingers folded softly inside his own), and he started to leave.

Then, when he remembered he'd filled in no actual name on the check, he asked him:

"So roomie, what's yer name? You never told me."

"Oh! It's Hal, Hal Happiwell. I'm *Hal*!"

"Happywell?"

"No, oh no, not *happy* well, *happ* eh well! It's a *short* i—in the middle, the i is right in the *middle*. Four letters, then an i, and then four more letters, get it? But just call me Hal. Okay? Hal. Rhymes with pal."

"Okay, Hal-pal. See ya in a couple days."

"See ya....pal!"

On the way back to the motel to check out it occurred to him. It hit him all at once who the chalk-white, portly, always-grinning little man reminded him of....it was Clarence! Clarence the angel in "*It's A Wonderful Life*"! The wingless angel who helped Jimmy Stewart figure out how goddam good his seemingly dry and crummy life was. He was a dead ringer for him, right down to the huge, bulbous nose. 'Glad I came up with *that* one, Charlie said to himself....wudda driven me crazy....what a relief.

Yes, what a relief indeed. To nail down a cooler than cool apartment only three blocks from campus for only $80 bucks a month, only a week before fall classes started, was well beyond good luck in this particular young man's world. It was all the proof Charlie needed that things were breaking his way. He knew he had to celebrate. And since he had all the clothes and supplies he needed already stuffed into his cramped car, ready to transfer into his spacious, brand new Berkeley apartment, there was no need to bomb all the way back down to L.A. for just a couple of days for stuff he didn't absolutely need and then have to bomb all the way back up again. His folks would understand; even his mom. Only one thing to do, only one place to go....Tahoe. Lake Tahoe. The perfect playground for a young adult male who needed to blow off a little steam before commencing his first year at one of the finest, toughest, most prestigious universities in America. He took Highway 80 up to and through Sacramento and then followed Highway 50 over to the south shore, got there in just a few hours, checked into a motel, got in a late round of golf at the famous Edgewood Golf Course right on the lake that he'd heard about on previous Tahoe trips, got a good night's sleep, played stud poker on and off for two days and two nights and managed to win back both his Edgewood green fees and his first month's rent, plus a couple hundred bucks on top of that for good measure, and he even thought about investing a portion of his winnings in the beguiling opportunities to be found lounging on satin sheets up at the infamous Mustang Ranch, up near Reno, but even though he chickened out he was convinced that just his willingness to even *think* about doing something so far removed from his comfort zone was proof he was busting out in *every* way. By the time he got back to his new Berkeley apartment he was well rested and loaded for bear. And why not? He was nearly twenty years old, bright, healthy, motivated, in love with life, and eager to absorb everything the whole San Francisco Bay Area could throw at him, school-wise and otherwise. And he wasn't nervous. If Berkeley was ready for him, he was more than ready for Berkeley.

In fact he was beyond merely ready; he was prince of the city. A boy no longer. A young man squarely and indelibly rooted in his prime.

The first few days of classes were pleasantly uneventful. He didn't even bother to go to all of them. 'Plenty of time to get serious later he assured himself, he was too keyed up, still riding a high, still thoroughly infected with the rush of simply being out on his own. Friday came quickly. The weekend beckoned, with all its implicit joys. He played a little touch football in a pick-up game in the afternoon and went home right after, having already learned from the local TV Guide that reruns of *The Lone Ranger* came on at five p.m. He got home around 3:30, sweaty, tired, and content. Employing one last spasm of energy Charlie climbed the three flights of stairs like a frisky young billy-goat, unlocked the door, and burst with all the enthusiasm of Youth itself into his new apartment. Hal Happiwell was standing in the middle of the living room, not unlike a butler awaiting instructions. Charlie was startled at first, but only for a second. After all, they did live together....

"Hey there, Hal-pal! What's shakin', bacon? I'm gonna take a shower."

The young man immediately began to pull his sweat-soaked sweatshirt up over his head, in preparation for, and anticipation of, a well-earned shower and quick catnap. The retreating garment revealed his thin flat stomach and thick, prominent chest muscles, all wrapped in smooth, hairless, golden-tan skin; skin slathered with moisture like he had been basted with cocoa butter. Skin which now glistened from the rectangular swath of late-afternoon sun pouring in from their huge open picture window, the window which faced the intersection at Telegraph and Haste. For a moment, the tight sweatshirt was tangled around his head and bunched up over his eyes.

But that didn't keep his ears from absorbing the longest run-on sentence either ear had ever funneled into his brain:

"After your first-period class was over you walked up to Morrison Hall and played the piano for a half an hour and then you walked back down to the Student Union Building and played three games of pool by yourself, by *yourself*, oh dear I *so* much wanted to play, and then you went over to Sproul Plaza and sat down in the Golden Bear Café and ate a big bowl of cream of broccoli soup which smelled *so good*, oh god, and then you talked to two girls who were sitting next to you they looked so pretty but you talked to them anyway, oh god, *oh my god* so pretty, and then you walked south across Bancroft and headed down Telegraph Avenue because for some reason you didn't go to your two-o'clock class but instead you played on the AstroTurf field in the touch football game and you scored a wonderful touchdown oh *my* it looked like such fun and then I knew you'd come home and want to relax before you watched *The Lone Ranger* reruns at five o'clock on channel thirty so I hurried home and drew you a bath—it's already *ready*!—Oh dear, oh my, oh my *stars*...."

Charlie, as startled and confused as would be any living human being, pulled the sweatshirt slowly back down over his tanned and sweatslick torso and stared a startled stare into the weakly smiling face of his roommate.

Finally: "Hey, that's great investigative reporting, Hal-pal. Remind me to have you write my memoirs in fifty or sixty years." He started towards his bedroom.

"Can I watch *The Lone Ranger* with you, Charlie? *Can* we?" Hal Happiwell pleaded.

Charlie didn't quite know what was going on, which wasn't unusual. He was no more or less naïve than any other clueless twenty-year-old. But this was different. And he knew it. He just didn't know why it was or what it was. Yet.

"Uh, I dunno....sure. I guess."

"Great! Oh *my*! *Thank* you, Charlie!"

"Yeah, whatever. Gonna crash for an hour. See ya then."

He retreated into his bedroom and drew the pocket door shut.

"But Charlie! What about your *bath*?!?" came a soft squeal fighting through the wood.

Charlie was already between the sheets, already naked, already thinking. "You take it *for* me, Tonto!" he yelled back. The young man curled up under the covers. He tried to think himself to sleep. But he didn't sleep, and an hour's thinking produced no wise fruit within his head whatsoever. When he emerged from the bedroom he made sure he was wearing long pants and a loose-fitting, long-sleeved shirt. He watched *The Lone Ranger* with one eye on the masked man and the other on the insanely grinning visage of Hal Happiwell.

That night, when he went to bed, he made sure to draw the pocket door shut. Again. Just in case.

But he didn't go to sleep. Not right away. Hal Happiwell was keeping him up. Or rather his voice was keeping him up, or, even more precisely, the *memory* of it....who is this guy....his voice and screwy speech patterns are so eerily familiar, he thought.

Part of it was easy. He had no trouble identifying the whiny, sing-songy, stereotypically gay drone of the unabashedly gay novelist Truman Capote, easily pulled from somewhere within Hal Happiwell's complicated hybrid cadence. Anybody would have recognized that. But there was someone else hiding in there with Capote. Another not-so-famous voice, but for Charlie just as familiar. But who? For two hours he ruminated over the whiny voice's secret identity....

And then he hit on it. An old cartoon. An old skeleton exhumed form his pre-teen youth growing up in suburban Los Angeles. The old cartoon was called 'Lippy the Lion'. But Hal Happiwell was no Lippy, thought Charlie, no, not Lippy....rather he sounded just like Lippy's hyena sidekick, what the hell was his name....there was a song....he tried to remember the words....."*The most laughable, something else, something-something by far—Lippy the Lion, and Hardy Har Har*". Hardy Har Har? Sure, *Hardy*

Har Har! He of the tie and hat, a laughing hyena wearing only a bow tie and a porkpie hat, and very much ironically a laughing hyena because this was one hyena who *never* laughed and was in fact clinically depressed virtually all of the time, that's *exactly* who Hal Happiwell was! A depressed laughing hyena! Perfect! Those cartoon guys are geniuses, Charlie said to himself, out loud this time….even the name fit….Hardy Har Har. Har Har. Sort of like Hal Hal….Har Har, Hal Hal, Har Har, Hal Hal, *stop*! He was laughing out loud now. It was too good to be true. He pulled out a lined, yellow writing tablet and started to write it all down. He didn't know why. It wasn't as if he was some sort of a fledgling, aspiring writer, or anything like that (At least he didn't *think* he was.). He was just a junior in college, a run-of-the-mill political science major. Not much more than a kid. But somehow he sensed, intuitively sensed, that this was exactly the sort of quirky college experience that he should be writing down, for whatever reasons, any and all. So he wrote down what he had seen and what he had heard. That gay-sounding drone. That whiny, depressed drawl. Right down to the 'oh dears' and the 'oh mys'. Hardy Har Har meets Truman Capote and Clarence the wingless angel, and they all merge into one. Perfect. But nobody'll believe it just cuz I say so, he said to himself….so he wrote it all down. Because it was perfect. Ridiculous, hysterical, confusing, perplexing, and perfect.

Right before he dropped off to sleep he was trying to come up with who might, theoretically, play his new roommate on film. It was a game he often played with himself when he encountered somebody both new and interesting. He was pretty sure the guy who had played Clarence the angel was dead….and if we *wasn't* dead he'd be like, what….ninety?

The next morning when he yanked open the pocket door Hal Happiwell was standing right in front of him, holding a cup of coffee. Charlie fairly jumped back a step while his heart got started again.

"Jesus, Hal-pal, you scared the *shit* outa me….How long 'you been standing there?"

"Oh god, I'm sorry Charlie, forgive me, I'm, uh, I'm—I mean I *heard* you, moving around, so I hurried up and made you this cup of coffee. I tried a sip—it's *good*!"

"You made me coffee? And sipped it?"

"Charlie your first class today isn't till one o'clock, so you can—I mean so *can* you go to the Student Union this morning before your class I mean can *we* go, and shoot some games of pool? *Can* we? You *said* we could go shoot some games of pool some day and you'd teach me cuz I never shot any pool games before and I'm no good so *can* we? Oh, dear….oh, my…."

"Uh, no way man, not today. Sorry. I gotta hit the Doe Library and do some research for this stupid-ass poli-sci paper I'm doin'. I'm meeting some guys there. No time. Rain-check, okay?"

Hal Happiwell dropped his head and did not speak. His lips tightened against each other. He fondled the steaming cup of coffee he had just prepared. Charlie studied him. He looked the part of a little boy just denied a piece of candy, or a grown man dropping his head during a particularly tense moment of a funeral. He continued to hold the steaming cup of coffee in both hands at once, out away from him, as if still hoping Charlie would accept the gift, which all struck Charlie as sort of a silly thing to do. It caused him to look at those upturned hands, whereupon he noticed several thick, strange-looking scratches on the white wrists. But he didn't think anything of it at the time. All he could think about was how relieved he was to not have to go play pool with the guy. Funny thing; shooting a few racks at the Student Union was exactly what Charlie had already planned to do before lunch. He'd always loved playing himself in a good game of pool as a relaxing means to a therapeutic end, a chance to unwind, to clear his head, chill. But it was a self-prescribed therapy best practiced alone, and certainly not in tandem with the very source of the tension which required abatement! At least it wasn't serious tension, at least not yet, and he hoped to hell it wouldn't get that way. Just the same, he was looking forward to the day when his roommate's grotesque exuberance would blow over, vanish completely, so he could then concentrate on all the things he'd resolved to investigate during his time at Cal, the local racetracks, the local poker rooms, the streets, restaurants, ballparks, nightlife, and across the bay whatever was most beguiling of San Francisco herself. He went to the Student Union, pocketed several racks with his new favorite cue-stick which thankfully wasn't being used, stopped by the Golden Bear Café for a bowl of cream of broccoli soup and a few hunks of sourdough bread, and made it to his one-o'clock class with time to spare.

But he had to admit he was getting a little paranoid. He found himself looking around from time to time, just to be sure. Thankfully, the cookie-dough man was nowhere in sight.

He got back to the apartment at Telegraph and Haste at around five-thirty. Too late for *The Lone Ranger*, but never too late for an afternoon nap. When he unlocked the door and pushed it open he was again shocked (though ironically not actually *surprised* this time) that the retreating door revealed Hal Happiwell standing smack in the middle of the room, his little white hands balled up into little white fists and tucked under his dimpled chin and shaking:

"When you got to campus you went right to the Student Union and got a table and started to play some games of pool with your favorite cue which I saw you looking for in the holder on the wall and you smiled and so I knew you'd *found* your favorite cue and at first I was really mad cuz I wanted to play *so bad* but then I remembered I really just wanted you to *want* me to play, oh dear, and then I ran ahead to the Golden Bear Café cuz I thought you might want to get some of that wonderful cream of broccoli soup before your one-o'clock class and you did, *and you did*, and it smelled so good and I almost walked up and asked you if I could sit down and have cream of broccoli soup with you but, but—oh dear, oh, oh *my*—and then you went to your one-o'clock class I think it's American Colonial History, isn't it?, and I waited and waited but you must have left from another exit and then I came home and started calling phone numbers all over the country but hardly anybody answered, nobody *ever* answers, so then I, I, I—"

He almost spat out "So then you *what*?" but caught himself in time and settled for merely wishing he was in another country.

"Do you want me to make you a cup of coffee, a *big* cup of coffee this time? I have a really big *mug*!" the cookie-dough man went on. His voice had changed suddenly from sad and urgent to hopeful and happy.

"Uh, no, no thanks, Hal. I'm just gonna take a nap. Coffee keeps me up." He started to peel off his shirt, but then decided to keep his muscular tan torso to himself. "Don't wake me up, okay? I'm beat."

"Okay...." Hal Happiwell moaned.

It was a moment way beyond awkward. Like having to pee in a public place and being uncomfortable and the squirming and no good way to get past it. Charlie knew he had to give him something. Trouble is, he simply didn't know what in the world would be satisfactory.

"And listen, Hal-pal, don't fixate on that cream of broccoli soup, man. It's not that great. I've had better." It was the best he could do in a pinch.

Hal Happiwell smiled weakly. Charlie retreated quickly behind the pocket door.

⇒ ⇐

The next few days were eerily uneventful. Charlie would go to class, come home, Hal Happiwell was usually either not there or was holed up in his room with the telephone and its absurdly long extension cord, making his usual random long-distance phone calls to people he didn't know, but he did so quietly, and for the most part he left Charlie alone.

But then one day, getting home plenty early enough to catch a nap before *The Lone Ranger*—which he now often used as a relaxing, Valium-esque prelude to a hard night of studying—he was about to crawl into bed when he spied a sheet of lined, yellow writing paper sticking halfway out from under his pillow. He felt cold and clammy all over, even before he forced himself to read it:

> My dear best friend Charlie,
>
> I like how you don't always make your bed. I like crawling into your warm unmade bed after you go off to class in the morning. It's so warm and smells so good! I can smell you. Don't worry, I'm not like gay or a gay person or anything. I just like how it smells.
>
> I was looking at and I guess touching your sheets and it was weird because it wasn't wet at all even though I always leave lots of pecker tracks when I masturbate and you didn't so I was just wondering if you masturbate. Do you? I was just wondering.
>
> Can we have dinner together tonight at that place you told me about on Telegraph Avenue, the one you went to with your friend Monte to get the extra-big cheeseburgers?
>
> your pal,
> Hal

He read it again, and again, and was distressed when the words on the page stayed the same. To say that he was now finally worried (or at least a trifle concerned) would be a reasonably accurate assessment of Charlie's general mood at this time. Seeing his old high school friend Monte's name on the sheet of paper gave him the idea that he needed someone to talk to about it, so he called him up immediately and invited him over for a beer the next day, around noon, right after his first class and at a time Hal Happiwell was usually out of the apartment. When he saw him later that night the cookie-dough man confirmed that he would, indeed, not be home at all in the middle of the day the next day, would be 'out of town' in fact, which made Charlie feel better instantly.

The next day Charlie got home around 11:45, armed with a six-pack of San Miguel dark beer. He spent ten half-assed minutes tidying up. He threw all his stray dirty clothes into a wicker-basket laundry hamper, including the T-shirt and jeans he had worn to class. All he replaced them with was a pair of *L.A. LAKERS* purple-and-gold sweat pants. It was a hot day, and he reveled in the notion that his roommate wasn't there to eyeball him. Even so, and even though he knew Hal Happiwell wasn't supposed to be there and had, in fact, already told him he had an appointment all the way down in Oakland at the unemployment office, he found himself going into each room just the same, and he looked around a couple more times just to be sure. He even peeked under his own bed. Which made him feel stupid and safe at the same time. Just before noon there was a knock.

"Hey, queer bait," said Montgomery O'Flynn.

"Hey yourself, you magnificent Irish prick," Charlie rejoined as they shook hands. "Come on in."

Monte O'Flynn was a Mick from toe to crown. The milk-white skin of his face broke into a wide and devilish grin in response to Charlie's playful insult, clusters of freckles rearranging themselves. And he didn't merely enter Charlie's apartment, rather he *strutted* into it, as if he might have been the landlord collecting the rents. As he walked his wild, reddish-brown hair seemed to combust, from merely the friction of brushing against the apartment's humid autumn air. Charlie was no bodybuilder, or even a part-time weightlifter, yet the skinny white arms that stuck out of Monte's purple GRATEFUL DEAD T-shirt were a stark contrast to the bronzed, muscular arms and chest Charlie had brought up to Berkeley, a body freshly cast from a summer of moving furniture for money and lying by his parents' new swimming pool for fun, at their new home in one of L.A.'s richer, safer suburbs....

"Yer folks moved from Altadena to Arcadia, Lester tells me," O'Flynn stated simply rather than asking, by way of catching up. "Is yer dad moving up in the world?"

"Not entirely. More like moving to the beat of my mom's plaintive commands!"

"Ah, the status-symbol house with a pool....the Holy Grail of the suburbs."

"Basically."

"Do yer parents even swim?"

"No. Yours?"

"No."

They moved into the kitchen. O'Flynn sat at the table in the breakfast nook, Charlie freed two dark beers from the fridge. They clunked them together in a poor-man's toast. O'Flynn downed his beer in two great gulps, bounded up, and liberated another dark soldier from its cold dark prison, and rather than fiddle with the can opener he simply opened it with his teeth.

"So this guy wants to play your *skin flute*, huh? I always knew you leaned toward the woodwinds section...."

"Very funny. But I don't think that's it."

"Then what is it?"

"I don't know. That's what I wanna have you help me figure out."

Charlie told Monte O'Flynn the whole story. He told him about how the cookie-dough man followed him around campus and how he watched him eat his lunch, about the endless run-on sentences, about meeting him at the door with freshly-brewed cups of coffee, the whole sad, silly, psychotic saga. He did not tell him about the guy's looking like Clarence the wingless angel or sounding like Lippy the Lion's sidekick doing a Truman Capote impression. He didn't want it to come off like *he* was the one who was crazy, or obsessed, or sick or whatever the cookie-dough man was....

"But has he ever put his hands on you? Ever?"

"No, never. Oh....well, there was this one time, sort of. It was last week, Monday Night Football was on and it was Raiders versus Bengals, which means it was Ken Stabler versus Ken Anderson, two really good quarterbacks goin' at it so naturally I wanted to watch it and he asked me if he could watch it with me and it seemed harmless enough so I said sure. And so he sits down right next to me. Okay. So we're watching the game, it was early in the first half, and he starts pokin' me. In the stomach. Just playfully *poking* me, man! Again and again, trying to get me to horse around with him. I told him to cut it out and that I was trying to watch the game but he wouldn't stop and it was really buggin' me cuz I couldn't concentrate hard enough to make sure the Raiders were winning so during a commercial I started rough-housing him back, pushing him around and roughing him up a little, he was laughing and giggling like a little kid, but I was getting annoyed as hell and then the Raiders fell behind so I finally turned it up a notch and landed a short hard punch to his belly. You know, as if I was still just playing around? But I really let him have it. Well, that got him to finally stop pokin' me. But he didn't even get mad! I think maybe he *liked* it. He just caught his breath and went back to watching the game and asking me all sorts of stupid questions about football. It was easily the worst time I've ever had watching a football game in my whole fuckin' life."

"Okay, that's not so bad. But why do I get the feeling yer holding something back?"

Charlie took a deep breath. He got up, pulled two more beers from the fridge, darted over to his bedroom, and came back with the yellow piece of paper. He sat down and pried the caps off the beers.

Then he showed him the note.

"Okay, Barnes, now this is fucking ridiculous."

"I know."

"*Pecker* tracks?"

"I *know*! It's like I'm Alice and I've gone through the looking glass and this is where I wound up. I don't know what to do, man."

"But he doesn't grab yer dick or yer balls or yer sweet ass, and he doesn't try ta *smooch* ya?"

"No! That's what I'm talking about. It's not a gay thing, it's weirder than gay *ever* was."

"Could be he's both weird *and* gay."

"You think so?"

"I dunno. But I tell ya what," said Monte O'Flynn, leaping to his feet and gulping down his third beer to Charlie's two in one final, giant swallow, "I've got a bio-chem lab comin' up so I gotta jet, but come on over for dinner tomorrow night. Lester's got a quiche recipe he wants to try, and we got a coupla dime bags of Jamaican to go with it. We'll twist a few scoofers and hash it out....no pun intended."

"You twist, I'll drink."

"Oh, that's right. I forgot it was you. Okay, we'll twist and toke, you drink and complain."

"Okay. I'll come by. But soft-pedal it on stuff like that note about crawling into my bed, huh? The guys'll never let me hear the end of it."

"Don't worry, dude. That's yer biggest problem y'know. You *worry* too much."

The two old high-school friends talked in the hall for a couple minutes. Then Monte O'Flynn bounded jauntily down the stairs and Charlie went back inside the apartment, closed the door, and secured the deadbolt. When he turned back around to head toward the kitchen for another beer Hal Happiwell was standing in the middle of the living room.

"*Aaagghh!*"

His heart jumped and his legs stopped working, and he almost fell to the floor. Suddenly he was conscious of being half-naked. Even in this fleeting moment of sheer panic he was strangely aware of having no underwear on beneath his purple-and-gold *L.A. LAKERS* sweat pants. He felt more naked than if he *was* naked....

"Jesus H. Christ, man, what the hell is yer fuckin' *problem!*" Charlie nearly screamed. "Where the hell did you *come* from, you psycho?"

"I was out on the fire escape," Hal Happiwell whined in despair.

"You were *where*? Out *there*? *Spying* on me?"

"Yesterday when you asked me if I was going to be home tomorrow I mean be home today I had a feeling since you didn't seem to want me around that you were going to be doing something fun or secret or interesting so I made up that story about going to the unemployment office so I could watch you and see if I was right and I was right I was right I was *right* because your friend Monte came over and you had those nice-looking beers together and it made me want to have a beer *too*, a beer with *you*, oh my, but I had to stay on the fire escape because I told you I was at the unemployment office and you would of got mad and I was scared maybe you'd throw me off the fire escape or something or just get mad and oh dear you two sounded like you were having *such* a good time, such a *wonderful* time, even though I couldn't quite hear everything I knew you were having a wonderful time and I wanted to have some dark beers too because I've never you know I never had one before, a dark beer, ever, and and and I, and I, but you never and I, I, I, are you mad? Are you mad at me Charlie? Oh *dearie* dear...."

There were tears at the corners of his eyes.

"Hell no, I'm not mad. But Jesus, man, just stop sneakin' around all the time, willya? It's givin' me the creeps. And if you wanted one of my goddam beers all ya hadta do was say so."

The cookie-dough man smiled wide, like a pale jack-o-lantern: "Can *we* have a beer together? Like *now*?"

Charlie scratched the wavy blond hair of his confused head in search of answers. The last thing in the world he wanted to do was have a beer with the same psycho-case who just got done spying on him from the fire escape. But he sensed that this was no time to ratchet up the tension. In any conflict, when things get really tight, sometimes a tactical retreat is what's called for. Besides, hadn't his father told him once that, what was it, that the day you can't break bread with a stranger is the day you've stopped being human? Yeah….'something like that….okay. One beer.

"Tell ya what. There's only one left, but there's no reason we can't share it," he declared with forced enthusiasm. "Really? Golly, that would be *great*!" Hal Happiwell responded with even greater enthusiasm. He ran to the cupboard and fetched two glasses, grabbed the can opener, liberated the last San Miguel from the fridge and opened it and poured equal portions into the two glasses in a startling blur of motion. It was like a sped-up cartoon, the animation accelerated to simulate frenetic action. Charlie would have laughed, of course, but when he realized he was still half naked he ran to his room and threw on the longest baggiest T-shirt he could find.

For about ten minutes they sat at the kitchen table where he and Monte O'Flynn had sat, sipping their shared beer in silence. With every sweet swallow of the dark nectar Hal Happiwell's eyes would roll contentedly back in his head. Like a shark's at feeding time.

"Gotta go now," Charlie said suddenly, setting down his glass, gathering up his book bag and tennis shoes and keys and moving quickly for the door, "Gotta hit Doe and study for a stupid English test, I'm way behind. You stay here….okay? I mean I need to concentrate."

"Sure. I understand. You have to study."

"Okay. See ya."

"See ya. Have fun! And thanks for the beer….pal!" Hal Happiwell said.

Charlie flew down the stairs, jogged down the street, and actually hopped on a bus just for a couple blocks, just to make sure he wasn't followed. Yet all things considered, he found himself in a fairly good mood. Maybe, he wondered, it was because he left Hal Happiwell in such a good mood. Funny, he thought, how the dude managed to switch himself right back from 'French fried' to 'nearly normal', and all within the blink of an eye….just because of half a measly beer….man….'dude looked downright *happy*. It was the only time he'd ever seen that strange, twisted, uncommonly white face actually look happy.

And he actually did have some studying to do. He stayed at the Doe Library till late, grabbed a bite, stopped for a cup of coffee on the way home at a cool coffee house he'd heard about west of campus and not too far from the Berkeley Marina, and by the time he made it back down to his south-campus apartment Hal Happiwell was already asleep. Which was always a relief. Before he went to bed Charlie made one phone call. To his brother, in Toronto. He had never called this particular phone number before. The man who answered the phone spoke in strangely cryptic tones, said he didn't know any Ricky Barnes, but that he would leave a message on the refrigerator in case anybody there knew the guy. Charlie thanked him and hung up. It took him an hour to drop off to sleep.

"I don't know about that, Les. I've already seen a couple of halfway decent-looking chicks walkin' around campus. The really hot ones can't be far off."

"You just transferred here, dude. I been here two years, and I haven't seen one chick yet I wanted to do the horizontal rumba with."

"I'm sure they feel the same way about you," said Monte O'Flynn.

"That's not the point—and besides, who cares what a *chick* thinks? Seriously, I'm trying to make a point here."

"Keep trying."

Dinner was good, as their dinners always were. Double-onion quiche, spinach salad with hot bacon dressing, and homemade banana bread. The dishes were all washed, the leftovers were already put away, and now the four old high-school friends were positioned around a large wooden living room coffee table. The table—fat and designed to resemble a redwood tree stump—was covered with Zig Zag papers, matches, and seeds. Theo, the most wasted, was lying fully stretched out on the couch. Lester and Monte sat on the floor cross-legged, like Irishmen impersonating Indians. Their guest occupied the only chair, regrettably an uncomfortable, high-backed wooden one. The roommates all puffed and dragged with gusto on their tiny hand-rolled marijuana cigarettes. The tips glowed in the darkened room like three fireflies. Charlie Barnes sucked on a *Budweiser*, apparently the only brand of beer the roommates kept on hand....

"I'm serious. I think it's the climate."

"You might have something there, Sigmund. That's definitely one thing L.A. has over the Bay area, the hot babes. Ten to one."

"Ten to one as good or ten to one as plentiful?"
"Right."
"No, which one?"
"I dunno....both, right?"
"Right."
"You see that article in the *Examiner* on Sunday? It was pretty good."
"What article?"
"It was in the editorial opinion section. Some guy was trying to explain Vietnam, our role there, why we did it, why we keep showing up where we're not wanted, that sort of thing."
"Geezus, we pulled outa there five months ago—can't they just let it go?"
"You never pulled out in your life."
"Hah!"
"Yeah, very funny....yer right, though."
"So what was the guy's point?"
"Aw, it was somethin' about how the U.S. wants to be everybody's friend, and they all resent us for it. Like we want extra credit for imposing our will on 'em. And they sense it. And so they don't dig us. Something."
"Everybody resents us."
"What, just for trying to be their damn friend? More'n they resent us for blowin' up their countries and shit?"
"In a different way," Charlie chimed in. "We're dealing with this sorta thing in one of my poli-sci classes, world affairs one-oh-one. Our 'prof' shared this one anecdote about some nineteenth-century Austrian prince, who said about the Russians helping them out in some war against Hungary or something, '*They will be astonished by our ingratitude*'. Cool, huh?"
"Aw, cut the classroom crap, willya? School makes my head hurt."
For some reason this exchange produced a smattering of light laughter from all four of them. It was a giggling sort of intermission, elongated by much impassioned smoking and drinking.
"So Barnes, how come you never toke?" Theo finally contributed as he sucked loudly on his doobie. It was practically the first thing he'd said since dinner. Charlie squinted in his direction. It was hard to make him out clearly in the dark. Shirtless, Theo's hairy chest seemed sunken into the couch itself, which was brown to match his brown corduroys. Since

the brown 'cords' blended into the color of the couch, his bare feet seemed to be growing and sprouting out directly from cushions....

"Cuzza guys like you guys," Charlie responded, perhaps a little too quickly. He wasn't getting personal, it was just his pat answer for such an oft-asked question: "It's the peer pressure thing. My protest against the great, late-twentieth-century *uber*myth of our times. Everybody gets high. Like if you don't get high you don't qualify to be a member of the post World War Two free-thought generation. You're a square, as my dad's generation would say."

"But you drink."

"Sure. Because drink tastes good. If you get high you're just gettin' high. But if you drink, you might just like the drink itself, the taste. Right? Beer, scotch, wine, it's all bitchin', as in *tastes* bitchin', I'd drink the shit even if it *wasn't* alcoholic. So I go to a party and have a drink. And I like it. So then maybe I have another. And another. And *then* if I get a buzz, sure it feels good, but it's just part of the natural fallout. It's not the goal. Besides, I've always hated doing something just because everybody else is doing that same something and the doers crave company...."

"Hunh?" Theo rejoined with a squinty expression.

"Exactly."

"Okay, Barnes, you drink we'll toke," Lester cut in. "So what gives? Monte says this quack you live with wants to smoke *yer* joint, 'zat so?"

"Jesus, Monte, you told me you'd keep it light with that shit," said Charlie.

"I'm undependable," said Monte O'Flynn.

"Iss' pos'ble, dude," Theo managed. As the highest of the three, he was edging closer to complete incoherence with each dreamy drag on his flaming god: "He might be gettin' set tuh jump yuh. Yer so *cute*."

"He crawls into Charlie's bed looking for gism," Monte added casually, like it was just a lazy afterthought.

"Thanks, Monte."

"What? *Geezus*, Barnes!"

"He wants yer jizz! He wants yer jizz!"

"Cut it out, guys. This is what I'm talking about. He's never acted, you know, just plain gay. He's never touched me. It's more like he's....I dunno.... like he's *curious*. It's creepy. Creepier than gay."

"Sounds like gay to *me*."

"Sounds more like *crazy* to me."

"He might *be* crazy, I don't know. I just don't think he's gay," Charlie said.

"What about his friends? Flaming gays?"

"I dunno. He never has any of his friends over," Charlie said.

"But he never has chicks over either, right? That tells ya something."

"I'm tellin' you, it's not like that. He's just weird is all."

"Gay is weird."

"No, it's a different weird. He does odd, crazy sorta stuff, besides climbing in my damn bed."

"Like what?"

"Well, like he follows me around. Everywhere. He watches me. He likes to watch me eat *cream of broccoli soup*, for Christ's sake."

"He eats yer soup?"

"No, he likes to *watch* me eat soup."

"What?"

"It's hard to explain."

His three hosts each took a drag on a fresh 'dube', their second of the evening, in ridiculous accidental unison, almost as if each's shut-eyed sucking required the symbiotic participation of the other two. Charlie took a long sip of the awful beer, by way of fitting in. But he kept his eyes open. In fact he was fairly studying his old high-school friends by this time.... all very white, all very skinny....weed, coke, crystal meth, 'must be quite a strain on the system to keep all of that up, he mused....no wonder they stay skinny....and they eat like pigs too. He wished he understood more about it....

"I still say he's gay," Monte said.

Light laughter now punctuated this mass intoxication, but only for a moment: "I say *yer* gay," said Lester, resuming his impassioned sucking on the smoking idol of worship he had so lovingly created.

Charlie realized that he couldn't tell them about Hal's spying on him and Monte from the fire escape. He knew that in their shared, stoned, paranoid altered state, they'd freak out. He could tell they were already a little freaked out as it was. He decided an acceptable retreat was to tell them about his discovery:

"I admit he sounds gay," he began. "Like Capote sounds, when he cuts up with Carson on *The Tonight Show*. But the other half of him is the funny part. Sounds like Hardy Har Har."

"Huh? Hardy hardly who?"

"No, Hardy Har Har! Don'tcha remember that old cartoon? The one with the lion and the laughing hyena who never laughed and they were both so stupid they—"

"Lippy the Lion!"

"That's the one," Charlie affirmed, adding with joyful clarity and enthusiasm, "—and the non-laughing hyena was Hardy Har Har."

"And wasn't there a wee little song?" Monte O'Flynn queried in his whimsical, ancestral brogue, pointing his impish gaze and wide Irish smile towards the ceiling.

"*The most lovable, laughable loonies by far....*" Lester sang out,

"*....Lippy the Lion, and Hardy Har Har!*" Theo warbled, finishing the jingle for him.

And now the laughter was a tumult. There was no holding back now. They roared forth their delight, all four of them. Charlie had to admit to himself that even the *Budweiser* was starting to taste good, accompanied so well by the warm, sane fellowship of rational—albeit heavily medicated—old friends. And so Charlie changed his mind. He figured their galloping good mood could stand the whole truth, and so he told them of Hal's spying on him and Monte from the metal balcony just outside the big picture window. It was just too juicy a slice of the story to keep under wraps. Why not, he figured....as threats to Humanity go, Hal Happiwell was harmless enough....in fact, thinking about it now, he realized the cookie-dough man had never actually done anything bad to him whatsoever, nothing mean, nothing malicious, and in truth he had been uncommonly kind and generous to him....making him coffee, cleaning up after him, filling up bathtubs for him....even his low rent, he had always suspected, was probably far less than an even fifty percent of the *total* rent....ah, Christ. Jesus H. Christ. All the little guy wanted, probably, was someone to hang out with....pal around with....shoot the breeze....why was it so hard for him to reciprocate in kind, he wondered....*why not* split some soup and share a couple games of pool, he wondered....what would be the harm, he wondered....to the young man's credit, at least he was asking all the right questions. Just not out loud.

"You mean the guy was watchin' us from the damn fire escape? *The whole time?*" Monte O'Flynn exclaimed.

"Yep. He sure was. I think he likes you."

The laughter was more tentative this time. Measured. Less intense.

"Well I guess you can stay here for awhile, Barnes, if he ever tries ta hump ya. Okay, dudes?"

"Sure, Les, iss' cool. And no rent, Barnes. Don't know where we'd put'cha, but you'd be our guest. You can jus' buy us lotsa beer. Food, too. And uh course cigarettes....ah hell, we'll work it out."

"I need a beer," Lester said.

While Lester climbed to his feet and managed to walk slowly and carefully over to the refrigerator, their rectangular conversation ceased. Just for a moment. Charlie leaned his head back and rested his eyes. Monte O'Flynn hummed something soothing and catchy by Crosby, Stills & Nash, Theo smiling his approval. Breezes whistled outside from the night's dropping temperature. Dope fumes smogged the air. Shapes and shadows danced in the translucent frosted glass of the window pane which comprised the upper half of the front door:

"Who 'zat guy in the winduh?" Theo said, gazing at that translucent window-pane portion of the door.

"Nothing," said Lester. "Just some shadows from the streetlights."

"No, iss' not. Thass' someone's face...."

"Geezus, you always get so damned paranoid when you toke, Theo, chill out. Barnes, want another beer?"

"No, thanks."

"I'm telling yuh, iss' somebody's face. Thassa *person*!"

"Naw. Les is right, yer just high."

"No I'm not, Monte....well yeah I am but I mean thass' not it, issa *face*, dammit...."

At that chance moment the blob-like shadow turned sideways in the frosted TV screen of the window. Which transformed the blob clearly into a face, a most definitively recognizable face, a profile. A profile with a huge, bulbous nose....

Charlie started laughing. "My god. Now I've seen everything," he said. But his three friends were frozen, fearing the worst, their mouths open ovals incapable of speech, so he continued: "Guys, you know who that is? It's the fat little guy I was telling you about, my roommate. It's *Hal*," said Charlie as-a-matter-of-factly. He purposely said it calmly, casually, almost quizzically, rather than investing his words with any great calamity or alarm. But it didn't work———

"*Oh my god*!!!" one of them screamed.

———for suddenly it was another old cartoon. It was frightened characters fleeing in all directions. Like Bugs Bunny, or an old Tom & Jerry one-reeler, it could have been any one of a hundred dormant, animated vignettes suddenly unearthed from over a decade of being buried in his child self's memory. It was vapor trails of exhaust in the wake of where his friends had been but a moment before, humorous puffs of smoke lingering in the air as if the characters had been blasted from the room by jet-packs hidden up their butts. This is hysterical, he thought even then, even in the excitement, even as he tried to make sense of why and how Hal Happiwell's face could possibly be silhouetted in that translucent window, a window over a mile from their apartment at Telegraph and Haste. The cartoon characters were of no help. Monte was hiding behind the refrigerator, Theo had rolled off the couch and having crawled to the kitchen now took cover behind the stove in a fetal position, while Lester had quit the scene altogether, finding glad sanctuary behind the locked door of his bedroom. Charlie, suddenly alone at the table, realized he must have done a good job of describing the cookie-dough man, in order to make three grown men flee in fear like that. You would have thought he had just announced that there were Nazis at the door, Nazis who didn't like to be kept waiting....

Needless to say the dire mood of his three high-school friends was not lightened when the silhouette began to pound on the door and call Charlie's name.

"Fer Crissakes, Barnes, do something!" wailed Theo.

"Yeah, *do* something!" wailed Monte.

"He's gonna kill us all!" wailed Lester from his locked bedroom fortress.

Charlie started to laugh again at his stoned stoner friends but stopped, realizing that since the object of their fear was right outside and had evidently stalked him for over a mile, all the way down to their formerly-safe little rental house, and was literally pounding on their door, that for all concerned his personal amusement might best be delayed till another time, and would doubtless be more gratefully embraced a year or two from now. Or perhaps thirty years from now. But not *right* now. He got up, moved quickly to the door, opened it, and slipped outside while closing the door behind him in one fluid motion.

"Hal, what in God's name are you doing down here? Are you nuts or what?"

The cookie-dough man was crying. He was shivering and shaking as well, and though his mouth was open no words were coming out. His eyes were wide and round as golf balls, quivering insanely in their sockets. The silence was the worst of it....

"Hal? C'mon, Hal-pal, what gives? Are you all right, dude?"

Finally, all at once, like water bursting through a cracked dam: "Why can't I have nice dinners with you and Monte and your other neat friends? Why don't you ever want to be with me? Why can't we ever go have cream of broccoli soup together? Why do you think I'm a jerk or a turkey?—*do* you think I'm a jerk or a turkey? Why do you look at me like I'm some sort of a freak or a bug or a weirdo, oh god, *why*? Why is everything so hard? Why can't you at least *pretend* I'm your friend or something, please? Why is everything so hard, Charlie? Oh dear....oh my...."

Charlie had never had anyone ask him nine questions in a row before. It wasn't until later (when he sat down and wrote it all out) that he realized one of the questions was a duplicate....

"C'mon, man. We barely know each other! I only met you a couple weeks ago! Seriously, dude—relax. C'mon. Take it easy, okay?"

Hal Happiwell had stopped shaking, and Charlie Barnes's deep steady voice was surely calming him down, but his eyes were still leaking. He snuffed up. Charlie put his hand on the older man's shoulder.

Then: "Before I followed you down here, I....I called 'Suicide Prevention'."

"You called who? You called *what*?"

"It's sort of a hot-line they have here in Berkeley if you think you're going to, oh my, want to commit—"

Charlie did not wait for Hal Happiwell to finish the sentence he already knew the end to. Suddenly he was two people. The first was the one in the moment, the scared one who couldn't believe that another human being might seriously consider taking his life over him. The other was his out-of-body self, who was watching the scene from a few feet away as if he was a movie director, and who knew that this was a once-in-a-lifetime opportunity for his in-the-moment self to act out a scene usually reserved for those who act for a living. And now both of these personas drew back their shared right hand, merged themselves into one, and whipped the open hand swiftly and violently against the cookie-dough man's left cheek, and then slammed the backhand against the right cheek, and then repeated the process, four solid, meaty flesh-claps which hit the dull autumn air like muffled gunshots and took less than two seconds from the first to the fourth, from the thought to the deed. He would find himself forever unable to explain, to himself or anyone else, the exact nature of the exhilaration of that moment....

"Hal, you better get it together, man. You'll never be any good to yourself or anybody else until you get some help. This is *no answer*! People *care* about you, man, don't be selfish. Don't be stupid."

"You mean you, uh, oh dear, you—do *you* care about me Charlie? *Do* you?"

"Well I care enough that I don't wanna see you kill yourself. Put it that way."

The eyes had narrowed and the short stout body stopped shaking immediately. The face managed a weak smile. Suddenly the once-shivering figure before him seemed almost happy. Charlie glanced back to the house's front picture window, and spied three wide-eyed heads bunched close together.

"Now go home. Pull yourself together. I'll be home soon, and we'll talk about it tomorrow morning."

Hal Happiwell snuffed up, wiped his huge nose with his tiny right hand, and walked away. He didn't say anything.

Two hours later. Charlie had calmed his friends down, forced down one more beer, and then walked home as slowly as his long legs could manage it. But now he was finally standing at his own front door. He took a deep breath. When he opened the door to their apartment his roommate wasn't waiting for him in the middle of the room like he expected. Not this time. He was busily flitting from this to that, dusting, organizing, casually cleaning up. "Your brother called," he said.

The voice was normal. There was no whine in it. There was no desperation or fear in it. Charlie could scarcely believe it was a voice coming out of the same person who just two hours before was shaking and shivering and crying his eyes out in front of Monte, Lester, and Theo's dark cramped rental house. Charlie said thanks, grabbed the phone off the kitchen table, and courtesy of the long extension cord was able to retreat into his bedroom with phone in hand, safely behind the pocket door.

He painstakingly ran his finger clockwise around the old-fashioned, circular, 'finger wheel' dial plate. Eleven times. The phone rang seven times before being picked up:

"Yeah...."

"*Yeah?*"

"Yeah yeah, who 'zis?"

"Is that any way for an adult to answer the phone?"

"Blow me."

"That's better."

They began the conversation with a silent intermezzo, no rush, the way few conversationalists save brothers can. The only difference between this and past pregnant pauses was an awkward absence of nervous laughter. As if chased away by fond memories of a shared youth, or perhaps by an adolescence wholly absent that fraternal interaction, memories exhumed now only by the stab of a familiar voice becoming less familiar with each passing year. Grist for another conversation. Perhaps....

"Why the largesse? Hit it big at the track?"

"Whaddaya mean?"

"If Dad knew his hard-earned dough was going towards long-distance calls to the not-so-prodigal son, he'd crucify you," Rick Barnes said.

"He trusts me. I'm a fine student," said Charlie. He forced a smile through the phone.

"Are you?"

"Not really. But they think I am."

"Well, say hi to Mom for me....him too."

"How's Toronto?"

"It's okay. As good a place as any for a noble expatriate to get lost in. Clean. Friendly. Big and crowded. Lots of crummy jobs available to support my poor uneducated ass."

"You could get lost just as easily right here."

"Too risky," Rick Barnes said.

"Maybe not. Now that it's over maybe things'll finally loosen up."

"We'll see," Rick Barnes said.

Enough, he thought. Time to back off of that one. Time for his own troubles to take center-stage:

"Ricky, I got a problem. The problem, though, is I can't really explain what it *is*."

"Hunh?"

For the next five minutes Charlie did his best to explain to his brother exactly what he had endured during his first two weeks of major college life, explain what Hal Happiwell was, and wasn't, just reporting the news mainly. It wasn't that he figured Ricky would, or could, come up with any great crumb of wisdom which might successfully defuse the cookie-dough man, no, this was merely a chance to air it all out, to tell somebody important what he had been going through. Just to have it on the record....

"I dunno, man. Just watch yer jewels. That's all I can think of."

"My jewels?"

"Yer *dick*, asshole. My best guess is that this guy is as queer as Christmas. If I'm right, he's gonna jump you at some point. Just be ready."

"No, I really don't think he's a fag," Charlie said.

"Hey, *you* called *me*, remember? You wanted my opinion. Queer bait is all I got. Either that or he's just plain crazy. Imagine wanting to spend all his free time with *you*. Hell, I spent the better part of my childhood tryin' tuh get *away* from you."

"I know," said Charlie.

"Gotta run. Anything *else* I can do for you in the next ten seconds, ass-bite?"

Charlie stopped before answering. How he wished he knew how to keep him interested, how to make him *want* to stay on the line. But he didn't know how. For there was plenty of mutual cud he could gladly have chewed with his brother, his only brother, this brother he hadn't seen in six years, this brother whose voice stayed fairly familiar but whose face was fading fast....they could have discussed the Red-Sox on the verge of a World Series, or the start of another football season....he could have asked him if he missed America....if he ever got lonely up there....and was it all worth it....but no. Another time, maybe. Never now, always later. Another time....

"What about you? Need anything?"

"I asked you first."

"No. I mean I guess not. Everything else is fine. College is great, Berkeley is great, the cooler climate is great. I love it here."

"Then don't blow it."

"Huh?"

"It's a gift, little bro'. Don't blow it like I did. Suck the most out of it. Make Mom and Dad proud they spent their precious middle-class money on you, and don't worry so damn much about me. I'll turn up down there one uh these days. You'll see."

"Okay, Bonehead. Thanks for the advice and everything. But I don't think he's gay."

"Yeah, yeah. I think *yer* gay," Rick Barnes said sternly. He rang off without waiting for a reply.

Charlie was exhausted. It had been quite a night for the young man. Too much drama, too much beer, too much second-hand dope fumes, and definitely too much Hal Happiwell. But it would all be over soon. He knew now he had to get out, get a new place. He sure didn't need the hassle of getting a new place mid-year but the situation had gone too far, had morphed into a righteous case of brain damage. Not a cool way to start junior year at a new college, he lamented....what a hassle....but it would all be over soon. Tomorrow he would begin to find a new place, or the next day, or the day after that at the latest. Yes, the worst was over....

He opened the pocket door, his roommate was in his own room behind his own closed door, so he quickly walked the phone back over to the kitchen table, went quickly and quietly back into his bedroom without saying good-night, closed the pocket door carefully and tightly and went right to sleep.

bam bam bam bam bam

He looked at his watch. Four a.m. He was trying very hard not to dislike the little guy, but the cookie-dough man was sure making hard work of it. "Hal, what the hellya doin'? It's four in the goddam morning!" he cried out.

"Open up!" a man's deep voice said.

He found himself unable to speak.

"Berkeley police, open up!" the strange voice repeated.

Charlie bounded to his feet, pulled on a pair of blue jeans, threw on a dirty yellow T-shirt, and flung open the pocket door. The two cops were young, in their late 20s. Each had a well-trimmed brown beard and surprisingly long hair in back. They were smiling close-mouthed, as if trying not to laugh. If not for the uniforms, they could have easily come straight from a 'Democrats For Peace' rally. Hal Happiwell was standing behind the two officers, using them as a shield. His lips were tight, and his eyes were round and twitching side-to-side....

"Is this about the footnotes I fudged on my last poli-sci paper?" Charlie quipped.

One of the cops laughed. The other smiled open-mouthed and said, "Okay, Mister Joe-College, this other guy here, whose name is on the lease, says you made a couple hundred expensive long-distance calls on his phone this week without asking him and then broke the damn thing, and unless you make it all good he says he's gonna sue your ass in civil court."

Charlie glanced at the phone in the cop's hand. Half of the circular finger wheel dial plate was broken off.

Perhaps he shouldn't have started out by mixing sarcasm with irreverence but he couldn't help it. "Are you gentlemen aware it's four in the morning and neither of you live here?" he said laughing.

For the first time neither of the cops was smiling:

"Give us a break, kid. It's a dead-slow night, we hafta respond to any destruction-of-private-property call, so just tell me yer story so we can get the paperwork out of the way and go catch some *real* bad guys. Whaddaya say?"

His response was essentially one long sentence but took him three full breaths to complete it: "Men, what we have here is a crazy-ass pot callin' his own kettle black, don'tcha get it?—*he's* the one who makes all the random long-distance calls, *he's* the one who broke the damn phone, he's a wacko from way back who follows me all over everywhere like a lost puppy dog, he followed me down to my friends' house just last night, he follows me all over campus, he crawls into my damn bed when I'm not here, and if you guys don't *do* something he's gonna make me eat *cream of broccoli soup* with him sooner or later and believe me that's something you wouldn't wish on your worst enemy so why don'tcha let me get some sleep cuz I've got classes tomorrow, or should I say today. Okay?"

(He thought about saying oh dear or oh my, or both, but he just didn't have it in him.)

The two policemen looked at each other. They both glanced at Hal Happiwell, whose mouth was wide open, and who was starting to shake. Then they both looked at Charlie, who simply rolled his eyes.

"Uh, look here, little fella," began the officer-in-charge, looking at the cookie-dough man but pointing at Charlie, "We believe *this* guy's story not yours, and since he's gonna move out in a day or two anyway—you are gonna clear out of here, right?"

"Yes, sir. Maybe even today if I can swing it."

"Y'see? Maybe even today. He's gonna move out and you'll be rid of him and he'll be rid of you and everyone will be happy. So why don't you just drop all this nonsense and go back to bed?"

"*I want to sue him in civil court!*" Hal Happiwell said.

"Be our guest. But we're not going to cite him."

"Can I have your card, officer?" Charlie said. The policeman gave Charlie his business card. "Sorry about this, men. Thanks for coming out," the young man added professionally.

The moment the cops were gone and the front door was shut, he glared fire into Hal Happiwell's white, doughy, now-frightened face. His movie-director self was back, and he had always wanted to say something like this, and knew right away that this might be the only time in his life he would ever come close to either saying it or meaning it: "You come through this door tonight and I'll kill you," he said gravely. Hal Happiwell smiled weakly. Charlie disappeared behind the pocket door and further barricaded it with books, half-eaten bags of chips, and dirty clothes.

He was out of the apartment by noon that day. Thankfully he didn't have much stuff to move. What he couldn't store in his car he and Monte stacked in a corner of Monte, Lester, and Theo's kitchen. Which is also where he slept for three nights, until he managed to find a place available mid-semester, sharing a furnished one-room studio north of campus with a glowering, shaggy-haired and heavily bearded chap who claimed he was Jewish but struck Charlie more like an Arab terrorist hiding out. Being a one-room studio, there was no wall between their beds. But at least he *had* a bed. This Jew/Arab hybrid rarely spoke to him, rarely did either dishes or laundry, liked to walk around in his underwear, chant, and clip his woolly black beard over both the bathroom and kitchen sinks which he rarely cleaned up after. Still an improvement.

But that was later. For now, for three nights anyway, he had shelter but was nevertheless homeless. As an ex-kid from the suburbs, it was understandably difficult falling asleep that first night on the kitchen floor. He'd never employed linoleum tile for a mattress, and a backpack of books makes a poor pillow. It gave him time to think, about everything, but it didn't do any good. All he could focus on was something his mother had said....something about him sleeping on a floor somewhere if he wasn't careful. Well, he thought he *was* being careful, but he still wound up on a floor, which confused him even more. Strange, he thought....'turned out just like she'd predicted. How do moms know stuff like this in advance? he asked himself. But he was finally asleep before an answer ever came to him.

⇒ ⇐

Charlie Barnes never saw Hal Happiwell again. He did, however, hear from him again. Sort of.

Not long after he moved out and found the north-campus studio, which was just off of Euclid Avenue (and which was just about the time he was beginning to accept the notion that since his old roommate's place was *south* of campus he was thereby rid of him), he and his hairy new roommate started getting strange phone calls. From men only. Young men. They all identified themselves respectfully, and in approximately the same manner: "*Hi, I'm responding to the advertisement I saw today, in the bathroom of the Doe Library?*" After a few days the frequency of the calls increased. Charlie took most of the calls, but his roommate did field more than a few of them (which of course rendered the Jew/Arab hybrid man even more antisocial), and they each told all the callers the same thing; wrong number.

Until one day, when Charlie fielded the following call:
"Hello?"
"Is this two four two, seven five four three?"
"Yes...."
"You know what I'm doing right now?"
"No...."
"*Enjoying* myself!"
"Good for you. Keep it up." {click}

He hot-footed it down to the campus library that same day. He went into every men's bathroom in Doe, eyeballed every urinal, went into every toilet stall. If someone was using a stall, he waited right there till the user was done. Finally, in the bathroom on the lowest floor of Berkeley's stately old Doe Memorial Library, the basement floor, in the very last stall he investigated, were printed pretty much the words he expected to find in indelible purple ink: **HANDSOME YOUNG MAN WITH BEAUTIFUL BODY WISHES TO HAVE SEX WITH SAME, PLEASE CALL 242-7543. THANK YOU.** He always was a polite little fellow, Charlie thought. This is actually pretty fuckin' funny, he thought. Ah, revenge is sweet, he thought. And so he wasn't even upset. It's easy to change a phone number....He just wished he could figure out how in holy hell his *old* roommate had discovered his *new* number....He never did figure that one out.

So yes, Charlie Barnes did indeed suffer some left-over, ancillary contact with the cookie-dough man. But he never actually saw him again.

Perhaps the closest he came was right after the holidays. It was a dark and dreary winter day a few months later, which is to say a few months after he moved out, he had placed his old car in storage and was idly riding his new bike around just south of campus after his classes were over for the day, inevitably he found himself gravitating to Telegraph Avenue, and so he rode over and down towards the intersection of Telegraph and Haste. Just to see. Just to see, well, he didn't know what. But he wasn't even able to get close to the gray brick building he had lived in for seventeen harrowing days. There were too many people. And too many vehicles. Emergency vehicles. Cars and trucks with red and blue flashing lights and sirens and thick rings of people surrounding the front of the building and clogging the intersection and all apparently looking at something. He parked his bike across the street. There were too many people to be able to see what the ones in front were looking at. He started to push his way through the crowd. But at the last minute something inside of him stopped him. Then his eyes drifted up to the balcony. All the way up to the metal fire-escape balcony, the same balcony from where his roommate once spied on him as he drank dark beer with a friend. Then his eyes panned straight back down to the huge crowd. And then a cold shiver vibrated right through him, dying in the skin of the shoulders and the back of the neck which had lost its L.A. tan. Yes, back then Charlie was no more or less naïve than any other clueless twenty-year-old. But he wasn't stupid. And when it came to side-stepping guilt and avoiding the yoke of responsibility, he was actually something of a genius. He knew that sometimes in life it's important *not* to know. This was certainly one of those times. In fact if ever there was a single solitary time when he didn't want to know what happened, and couldn't *afford* to know what happened, this was it....

So he hopped back on his bike and headed up Telegraph, due north, then straight through campus and then north on Euclid and then home. And then straight to bed. That's the one thing major college life had thus far succeeded in teaching him. That no matter how late in the day it is, it's never too late for a late-afternoon nap.

THE IMP OF BERKELEY

Author's Notes

Second story I ever wrote. Also one of the very few stories I have never *re-*written. And I mean I didn't rewrite it either *during* the first draft or rewrite it *since* that first (and only) draft. In other words, you are seeing here the exact first draft I wrote start-to-finish back in the winter of 1977, every word. Only took me a few days. It worked out well for me, though. I entered a short-story contest with it—and won! Fifty bucks! I'd been a fiction writer for just a couple months and I'd already won a contest and made fifty bucks. That makes *Imp* the first work of fiction I ever got paid for.

It got a little harder after that, though. I never would have believed it, 'never would have dreamed that it would be twenty years until I got paid again, but another two decades would indeed pass into history and fade into oblivion before I would make my next dollar with my work. Over twenty years between dollar number fifty and dollar number fifty-one? Funny how life works out....

If someday one of your kids were to come to you and tell you he wanted to pursue a life of writing fiction, tell that story. You might stand a good chance of dissuading him.

The Imp Of Berkeley is also my tribute to one of the masters of the short-story, O Henry, a.k.a. William Sydney Porter, he of the sprightly tone and the twist ending. As with *The Beggar Drives a Metal Horse*, wherein I endeavor to suggest traces of Thomas Wolfe while wrapping Wolfe's voice within my own voice and vision, in *Imp* I tried to employ aspects of Mr. Porter's celebrated tonal qualities while still allowing the story's pulse, pace, era, and metaphoric messages to be mine. At least that was my mission.

Whether or not I succeeded, dear readers, is up to you.

THE IMP OF BERKELEY

Stuart Tidelman was fit-to-be-tied. It was already the end of the week, Saturday, and the mailman (after finishing his daily sermon on the virtues of right-wingism) had failed to provide Stuart with his weekly copy of *Sports Illustrated*. *Time* had come for Barry Gilchrist, *Newsweek* had arrived on Thursday for David Cohen, and *The Progressive*, addressed to Clint Murdock, had long since found its way into Stuart's modest Berkeley apartment—but the sports magazine, Stuart's favorite, was late as usual. Stuart knew that the delay could not be attributed to his alias, Harry Agannis in this case, because Agannis, being an "A" name, would be among the first names to be mailed; this, of course, according to the law of alphabetology. So, Stuart vent his wrath on the true culprit, his nemesis, the mailman: "Your service is as bad as your *pahlitics*!" he shouted in his thick New England accent, and closed the window behind the gust of his angry vituperation.

Harry Agannis was Stuart's favorite alias, which was only natural. The name Agannis is a sports legend in Boston, and Stuart, being a native, had a soft spot in his heart for the local hero. Considering that Stuart had the presence of mind to ally Harry with a sports magazine, and not some dreadfully boring news rag, it is likely that Harry would have acquiesced to Stuart's using his name as an alias. And Stuart considered his "alias system" the finest and safest stratagem yet created for the free procurement of popular periodicals. He knew that these huge corporations, whose profits *surely* soared into the millions, couldn't possibly care that little Stuart Tidelman, in Berkeley, California, was ripping them off for a few measly dollars a year.

Warm, humid waves of steam wafting in from the bathroom told Stuart that his roommate, Charlie Barnes, was taking his morning shower. He could also hear the drum-like pounding of the water on the shower curtain. Stuart didn't much like his roommate, and in fact didn't see eye-to-eye with him very often at all. He didn't trust anyone who hid behind a "smoke screen" of high principles; too unrealistic not to be hypocritical, he had long ago decided. But Stuart acknowledged that Charlie served a useful purpose, in that the very presence of the latter reduced Stuart's rent by fifty percent. And then there was the food and other household conveniences that Charlie brought back regularly from his parents' home in suburban Los Angeles....yes, Charlie was very useful indeed.

"Hey *Bahnes*, where are my shoes?" Stuart asked loudly.

"Under the coffee table where you *always* throw 'em, you curly-haired imp!" came the reply from the shower. Charlie Barnes had described his roommate perfectly. Stuart Tidelman was short, maybe a head shorter than Charlie, though it was hard to tell exactly how much shorter, because of the inches of ropable brown curls that grew, unchecked, around and above Stuart's head. The shoes he pulled from under the coffee table were of the rare type that elevates the toe above the heel, giving his feet a distinctive elf-like appearance. His walk, a curiously quick, pigeon-toed gait, did little to diminish Charlie's caricature; it was thoroughly impish. And Stuart now made use of that impish gait, as he walked through the cloud of steam that now filled the little hallway between the living room (which also served as Charlie's room) and his bedroom—where he donned a button-down shirt and pulled a pair of tan corduroy trousers over his unusual shoes. This was his standard costume.

"You goin' to the game?" asked Charlie, who was now free of the shower.

"Maybe. I gotta work the *pahking* lot," rejoined Stuart, in that New England whine. "It's gunna be crowded with Oklahoma in town. I should clear at least twenty today."

"Don't you ever feel guilty, ripping off the school like that?" Charlie asked, though not in a condescending tone.

"With their budget? Nah! What's a few bucks to a major university? Now, if I was rippin' off some poor guy on welfare, or sumpthin'....well, that's different."

Charlie Barnes did not respond to Stuart's analogy. Instead, he turned his attention to the more pressing matter of clothing his naked frame, as there were no drapes on the windows.

"Maybe I'll see ya at the game, after you're off work," Charlie said.

"Yeah, maybe," said Stuart, picking up his new *Time*, which he intended to peruse while minding the campus parking lot. A piece of paper fell to the floor. Stuart picked it up and glanced at it, his twisted face betraying a puzzled mind.

"Can you believe this?" he began. "They're billing Barry Gilchrist for six ninety-five in back fees! You'd think they'd have better things to do than *baather* poor guys like me!"

Stuart tore the bill in half, threw both sections into the fireplace, and walked, impishly, out into the street.

Except for the fact that Oklahoma's gridiron gladiators were in town to battle Cal's inferior mob, it was not a special Saturday in Berkeley. The air was clear, the sky a cloudy blue, and the temperature was fixed at that sublime level that gives the human being no cause to complain that it is either too hot or too cold. Brisk winds, bringing with them the familiar scent of the sea, rolled over the flatlands and caromed off the Berkeley Hills to the east. Telegraph Avenue was alive with its usual hustlers and heroin addicts, its pushers, panhandlers, social malcontents, and down-and-outers, as well as legions of those regrettable individuals who, somewhere along the way, have jettisoned their senses. These dingy denizens flock to Telegraph in dizzy droves, because in Berkeley, to a degree unmatched in Western civilization, craziness is a badge of legitimacy.

Stuart Tidelman hurried northward along Telegraph, the fact that he was late for work lending wings to his elf-like shoes. He was in such a hurry that he passed right by his favorite panhandler, an able-bodied soul with a sad expression on his face, without dropping a single coin into his wooden cup. In a matter of minutes Stuart had reached the campus, where Telegraph spills out into Sproul Plaza. The Plaza is Berkeley's political soapbox. Stuart couldn't see, for the crowd, who was speaking that day. Very likely it was a Eugene McCarthy or a George McGovern or even a Teddy Kennedy, telling his story to a thoroughly receptive future plebiscite. It is certain that the speaker was *not* one of their enemies. But it could have been President Carter himself up there on the steps of Sproul that day, and Stuart Tidelman would have been obliged to walk right on by.

When he reached the north end of the Plaza, Stuart turned right, scurried past Sproul Hall, cut between Morrison Hall and the Faculty Club, huffed-and-puffed past the Hospital, arriving at his parking lot booth just in time to greet six or seven honking autos. He hated giving directions on game day: *"O.K., go up to this street here, it's called Piedmont, just follow it south a couple blocks and the stadium's on the left, big stadium, can't miss it."* But as much as he hated the people, Stuart loved their money, and an inconspicuous percentage would be his at the end of the day.

⇢   ⇠

"Hey *Bahnes*, you home?"

"I'm in the kitchen!"

Stuart Tidelman slammed the door behind him, and was able to reach the kitchen in just eight or nine of his pigeon-toed strides. There were smaller kitchens in Berkeley, but it was still fortunate that neither Stuart nor Charlie suffered from claustrophobia.

"Who won the game?" Stuart asked.

"You didn't go?" re-queried Charlie Barnes, his face displaying all the time-honored symptoms of surprise.

"Nah! I sawr this special at the Pancake House, two bucks for cakes, ham 'n' eggs, and 'fee. Too good to pass up."

"I was wundrin' why I didn't see ya there. They killed us."

"Yeah? What was the score?" Stuart asked numbly. He was not loyal to his team like his roommate, and really couldn't have cared less about the score. But he asked just the same, just to maintain the flow of dialogue.

"I don't even remember," Charlie lamented, obviously fatigued from three hours of observing Cal's lamentable lack of aptitude in pigskinnery. He was sitting with his elbows on the table, his hands cupping his head under the jawbone to prevent the tired orb from falling on the toaster, wherein an English muffin was slowly turning brown. "Let's just say it was a dark day for Cal and her Golden Bears!"

"Well, it was a *great* day for me. I cleared twenty-two bucks, even more than I counted on."

"Don't you think the school might get wise to you someday?" asked an annoyed-sounding Charlie Barnes.

"No way!" Stuart responded, in his I've-got-it-all-figured-out tone of voice. "Every third or fourth car, I just don't stamp his voucher. Then at the end of the day I re-set the stamp for about an hour *earlier* than those particular cahs actually left. I pocket the difference. It's foolproof. I'm tellin' ya. Besides, the lot took in over ninety today, they're not gunna miss a lousy twenty-two bucks."

"Well all I can say," Charlie philosophized, "is it'll all even out someday." Charlie's muffin was sufficiently toasted now. He gingerly removed the two halves from the toaster, and ladled a terrific spoonful of plum jam on each one. He noticed an attractive-looking black and white mug next to one of his muffin halves. "Where'd ya get the cup?"

"Pancake House."

"God, I don't believe—"

"They got millions of 'em!" Stuart yelped. Charlie was getting on his nerves now. 'How could *anybody* put up such a moral façade?' he asked himself. But as much as he felt like dropping the whole thing, Stuart decided it was more important to put the coffee cup into what he felt was its proper perspective. "*Everybody* steals dishes from restaurants, you know it and I know it, the same way everybody, uh….well, the same way everybody rips off insurance companies. Nobody cares. It's a good investment for *both pahties*, everybody's happy."

All Charlie could manage was a muffled, "Huh?"

"If I can get away with rippin' off, say, this cup, the owners know I'll tell my friends that it's easy to lift dishes from their place," Stuart began his explanation. He filled his new cup with chocolate milk Charlie had just bought at the corner grocery store, took a big swig, and resumed the tedious task of enlightening his roommate. "And *then* they know that my friends will come in and eat at their place, just to rip off a cup or a spoon, or sumpthin'. A cup doesn't cost the owners much, but for a decent meal they charge *us* plenty! Now, let's say I file a phony insurance claim for, let's say, a couple hunnerd bucks. You think they care? Hell no! They know I'll tell people what a swell company they are, and then they'll do more business. They're not gunna let anybody clip 'em for, say, ten thousand, but they're happy to let me have my couple hunnerd. It's all good public relations, don'tcha see?"

Charlie's tongue refused to move. He sat motionless for several seconds, staring blankly at his roommate. Then he forced his attention upon his English muffin, devouring it quickly before it could get cold.

Arcadia is not at all like Berkeley. The air is not clear, and, courtesy of the automobile, it is not even pure. Though a suburb of Los Angeles, which everyone knows is on the ocean, Arcadia has formed no Berkeleyan attachment to the sea. The climate of Arcadia, of all of Los Angeles for that matter, is always a little warmer than it should be. And, instead of lying in the gutter of some cold and impersonal city street, people in Arcadia lie in the sun, in perfect languor, beside the peace and security provided by very expensive swimming pools.

Charlie Barnes was lying beside just such a pool, putting the finishing touches to a turkey and mayonnaise sandwich. The Thanksgiving bird had been a plump one, and Charlie was able to draw from its bounty all weekend long. It had no doubt been a good weekend for Charlie; four days with no scholastic worries, tolerable relatives and fast friends for company, and, most important, all his favorite football teams had won. It had been a fine weekend, but in a few hours his plane would leave for Oakland, and by nightfall he would be back in his tiny Berkeley apartment, with Stuart Tidelman.

"*Chaa*rlie, *tele*phone!" harped Charlie's mother from inside the house. Like a rubber band, Charlie snapped to his feet, sprinted across the driveway, through the open sliding-glass door to the rumpus room, and into the kitchen; a kitchen at least four times as large as its counterpart in Berkeley.

"Hello?"

"Yeah, it's me," came the voice of Stuart Tidelman over the phone.

"What's happenin', man, whaddaya callin' long distance for?"

"I had to. Listen, I—"

"Hey, I'm not ready for finals, man, why don't *you* take 'em for me?" Charlie smiled into the phone.

"Very funny," replied Stuart in a sarcastic manner. As usual, Charlie was getting on his nerves. "Listen, I got clipped over the weekend."

"What?"

"*Robbed*, man! The T.V., stereo, my tennis racket, all gone. I still can't believe it."

"Did they get any of *my* stuff?" Charlie asked.

"Nah, your stuff's all here," moaned Stuart, making no attempt to conceal his irritation over the imbalance. It just wasn't fair that he should get off without losing anything, Stuart thought. He felt like telling him so, but since his composure would be of use later, he suppressed his innermost feelings. "Remember I told you I'd be spending Thanksgiving in Frisco, with Dearben and his family? Well, while I was gone they must've cased the joint."

"Too bad, man. You got insurance or anything to cover it?"

"Don't need it. I figure we can use your old man."

"My what?"

"I've been thinkin'. We can just pretend it's *your* stuff, nobody'll know. Your dad's policy has to cover you too, right? I figure the stuff's worth about four or five hunnerd, but we can tell 'em the crooks got away with, say, seven, to cover your dad's deductible. I don't think there'll be any *prahblems*, do you? We *might* even turn a small *profit* on the deal!"

For a couple of seconds there was no response. Then Charlie Barnes began to laugh. Slowly, at first, the laughter came, happy peals of suppressed emotion which quickly cascaded into guffaws of great joy. He was wheezing now, uncontrollably, which necessitated his putting down the phone and going to the sink for a gulp of water.

Stuart Tidelman was confused. "Whaddaya laughin' at?" he demanded quizzically. "Whaddaya laughin' at? *What the hell are you laughing at?*"

THE GOOD OLD DAYS

Author's Notes

I wrote this story in 1981, then completely *re*-wrote it in 1988, 2006, 2011 and 2012. I don't consider it one of my major 'signature' stories, and its short length and straightforward subject matter were probably not worthy of so many rewrites, but I just never felt totally comfortable with it; until recently. I guess that's why I rewrote it four times. Which makes it probably the most altered, tweaked, tinkered with, torn-apart, and thoroughly beat to death story on my shelf. I hope I haven't ruined it....

By the way, here's a revealing word or two regarding Ben Craig. Ben is obviously Charlie's best friend, a key player in both *The Good Old Days* and *King Charles*, and he is also prominently featured in *WHERE GODS GAMBLE*. Ben is also what I call a 'catch-all' character. He is an amalgam of several of the guys I grew up with in suburban Los Angeles; some of them close friends, some not so close. Anyway, Ben is proof that I did grow up with some interesting fellas. There was Pete, who was always so gregarious and charismatic, there was Torrey, always the wisecracker, Paul, world-weary and wise beyond his years, Bill, always finding new ways to screw up, Mark, sloppy and profligate with his women, Dick and Steve, each gifted with early facial and chest hair, Bob, in bed with intemperance and addicted to the gluttonous and glorious spirit of excess, and Kevin, who pretended to be lame and goofy but was in fact uncommonly shrewd and was always there when I needed him....All of them have found glad sanctuary in the variegated and multifaceted personality of Ben Craig. My favorite catch-all character. He cracks me up.

As part of the structural detail work which makes any good story better, by making it more relevant to the time in which it takes place, I write in *The Good Old Days* of how the lead character laments that rock bands he likes, like The Beatles, have given way to bands he loathes, like Led Zeppelin and Black Sabbath. I realize not everyone will agree with my ragging on rock groups who play the heavier, noisier brands of rock and roll, but that's the way it goes. As the celebrated author and essayist Joan Didion once said, a writer is always selling someone out.

I just hope my boy Rob—a fine guitarist in his own right who loves both hard rock and 'heavy metal'—won't hold it against me.

It's just fiction, son....

THE GOOD OLD DAYS

...he just stood there and took it...and he KNEW that barrel pointing at him meant business, he had to know...hell, we'd been shootin' at sparrows all day long...but those robins...they gotta be tougher nuts than sparrows, that's all there is to it...so he knew...he knew his number was up and so he just stood there and took it, that's all...no point in trying to get away...but nobody in his right mind, not even a bird, just stands there and waits for a hunk of metal to cut him right through the throat, that's just plain crazy...god, the way it spurted out... little red jets all over the place, all over the garage roof...a little darker red than his red belly, I think...wow...with each heartbeat a spurt...beat, spurt...beat spurt beat spurt beat spurt...took too long...didn't make a sound, not even a final flutter...what a great bird...wonder if I would have had his guts...wonder if I would have had the———

Suddenly his heart stopped. His right hand instinctively pulled hard at the wheel. White light hit full on his face, a horn stabbed into his brain, and in the same quick convergence of terrors the swift black form swept close by on the left, disappearing just that quickly, quite passively, behind him and quietly into darkness....

He glanced alternately at the road in the windshield and at the old elementary school running by through the passenger's window, realizing there would have been more than a little irony involved if he had picked that spot to die. Coming back to Altadena always stirred up the nostalgia in his system. For Altadena was not only his old home town it was also his Brigadoon, his own sleepy little hamlet that never changed, never grew older, stayed safe, predictable, familiar, and as he drove past the school's yellowed facade, its brick stanchions conspicuously in support of a decaying roof, gray vignettes from his youth fell, like in a nickelodeon, in chronological sequence through his mind. The dying bird was one of the most vivid daguerreotypes of that youth. Always would be. But just the sight of his little old elementary school was enough to jar the cold gray tintype to life, and in so doing lent it depth and movement, color and sound. "*Idiot!*" he scolded himself out loud, and then made a mental note to stop daydreaming at the wheel....

The little red Volkswagen Bug turned left off of Allen Avenue and onto Mendocino Street. The great pink mansion on the corner appeared in the rearview mirror. Huge. Celestial. It was therefore somewhat grossly out of place in a middle-class L.A. suburb like Altadena, but it had always been there. Charlie Barnes inhaled deeply. It was not an attempt to steady himself after a close call; no, he was beyond that now. He was thinking about the party, and a hundred other parties, and how he habitually returned to these stupid, stupid parties without ever knowing why. The ghosts of high school. The same faces, the same stale dialogue....a sad attempt to preserve something already dead. Funny thing: Ordinarily he would have been totally in the mood for a little relaxation, what with his mother nagging at him about both his flagging grades and burgeoning leftist ideals, and what with his father practically begging him to come down and help out at the hardware store just like he begged him *every* time Berkeley broke for summer, Thanksgiving, Christmas, or Easter, only lately more so than usual. It wasn't like his father to be more annoying than his mother. So the idea of a little well-timed tactical partying was hardly anathema to him. But not with dudes he no longer knew. Not with chicks he had no shot with even when they were available. Not with ghosts. He felt stupid even telling Ben he'd be there. It *was* stupid, *he* was stupid, but he was going there just the same, and so it was his own self-loathing that had made him mad. And so, accordingly, as he slowed to a stop in front of Ben Craig's house on Mendocino Street, he slammed one hand down on the wheel and swore, very softly, at his reflection in the mirror.

Outside the front door he recognized the high-pitched laughter of several girls he used to know. He hurriedly pulled a short black pocket comb through the uncooperative curls of his long blond hair, and quickly stuffed it back into the back pocket of his gray corduroys. Okay....no problem....emergency hot chick alert....fine.

"Hey! Look who's here!"

He stood heavily in his shoes, just inside the door, and waited patiently for all the worn out greetings and salutations to evaporate into mutual lack of interest. As a matter of good form he exchanged a few words with his host.

"Hello, Ben."

"Howzit goin', bro?" Ben Craig queried his reply. "Where ya been keepin' yer gloomy old self?"

"Oh, I've been lurking," Charlie sighed. "Still up at school. You know."

"That's *right*—it's Mister College now, I forgot! Howzit going up there, my man? You actually learning anything useful that might be applied to the *real* world?"

"Sure. Humility," Charlie said dryly. "You should try it sometime."

"Like to, bro'. Can't afford it."

"Can't afford it?"

"Or the humility either!"

"C'mon, it isn't *that* expensive to—"

"No, man, I mean I can't *afford* to screw around at some dumb-ass college. Makin' too much damn dough down at my dad's shop. Can't afford it."

"Oh...."

"Listen, dude, I'm glad you came. Wouldn't be the same without'cha. Look at the chicks we got here, horn-dog....we got Johansson, we got Baker, Black, Eggert, Scalzo....it's like an all-star team of primo tail from the old days. Unbelievable, huh?"

"Yeah. Unbelievable."

"Hey hey *hey*, like I always *say*—when the wife's *away*, Ben Craig will *play!*" the poet Ben Craig declared to half the room. Pockets of laugher reported back. It reminded Charlie that after Ben's mom died Ben and his new wife had moved in to keep the old man company. But he didn't expect Ben to still be living there two years later, and now he was wondering what Ben had done with his wife and father for the evening, so that he could retreat into yesteryear and hurriedly throw together a high school type drop-in. He almost asked him. But no. Too much work. He looked around for escape routes...."Charlie, loosen up. Go get yerself a drink, you up-tight fag. I think you'll find the bar facilities, shall we say, satisfactory?" Ben blustered on, and then he disappeared into his sweet, personal coterie of familiar sycophantic humanity.

Charlie worked his way over to the bar. No easy task. The room was small, and eager drinkers were in abundant supply. As he slipped and burrowed between the bodies he realized how a fullback must feel on a run up the middle. He couldn't decide what annoyed him more, the crowd or the noise. This was a young man who never could figure out why his generation insisted on playing its music so loud as if the intent was to test the very limitations of the human eardrum. He missed The Beatles....Black Sabbath and Led Zeppelin made his head hurt, made him practically want to kill himself. Between the music and the elevated conversation the noise was near to deafening. Every light in the house was on, everyone was talking at once, and the whole scene was indeed a football stadium in miniature. He very nearly turned right around and left, but the lure of free alcohol was too much for him.

"What'll it be, Chuck-a-luck? Can I interest you in a little Scotch, perhaps?" nearly yelled the bespectacled young man behind the card table.

"No thanks, man, never touch the stuff, you know that," Charlie barked back. The smell of Scotch whiskey mixed with sweat and too much armpit odor nearly caused him to barf, but he held steady. "Just drop a little of that Burgundy in here," he continued, holding a handy plastic kitchen tumbler at arm's length. The bartender filled the tall glass to the brim. Charlie inhaled a quieting draught of the red wine, sniffed the rich, fruit-sweet aroma as an antidote for all sour aromas within nose-shot, and swallowed its tart, bitter bite just as a delicate finger tapped his shoulder.

"Say, big boy, buy me a drink?"

Charlie grimaced and managed, "Pour," to the bug-eyed, open-mouthed fellow behind the card table. As much as he liked girls he had never thought them to be particularly funny creatures....

"Where you been, Charlie?" the girl cooed. Their faces were so ridiculously, movie-screen close that she didn't even have to yell. "I never see you anymore."

"Perhaps because we're never in the same room anymore," Charlie said dryly. She didn't laugh, but at least she didn't look mad. "Been keepin' pretty busy up at school, I guess. You know, doing *real-life* things," he added sarcastically.

"I guess *so*! You know, you haven't called me in *ages*."

"I've never called you."

"Well that's what I *mean*. Ever since high school it's like I got *leprosy* or something. What's the deal?"

"I think you've confused me with someone else," Charlie said dryly.

"Stop it! I wanna know how come you never hit on me."

"Like I say, girlie-girl, busy busy *busy*."

"Well my feelings are hurt just the same," the girl said. "I always thought you were such a cutie. How long have you had that moustache?" she rambled on, using the question as an excuse to gently touch his face and work her other arm around his waist. Charlie didn't fight her, but he didn't contribute either. Instead he simply looked her up and down, from head to toe, frisking her with his eyes. He didn't want to but he did. She was more than attractive, tall, with especially long legs growing out of her ultra-short jean-shorts, and a suntan that fit her like a light brown body stocking. Her red tube top barely covered the twin swells of her womanhood, and covered nothing else above her denim waist. Her hair was blonde, though not as sun-fried light as Charlie's, and it fell straight down her bare tan back like a waterfall. He knew this girl a little bit in high school, but not enough to amount to anything. Truth is, just a few short years ago, this kind of chick was way out of his league....way *way* out of his league. Back then a female of this caliber, with this kind of only-in-your-dreams chassis, well, suffice to say such a girl would rarely consent to even speak to him much less touch him. And when such females did actually deign to acknowledge his presence on the planet, they always wanted to talk about boring things, like buying clothes, and getting money from their parents, and going out with college dudes and getting high, while he was consumed with more lofty pursuits....like 18th century Enlightenment philosophy and the National League pennant race.

He hated the way he felt just now. He hated being so fiercely attracted to somebody he didn't even like. Just because she was a girl....or rather a woman....even a superbly cobbled together and undeniably well constructed woman like this one. The twin aromas of her breath and perfume were almost too much for him; both equally intoxicating individually, in combination they became a drug that he could actually feel making him weak and light-headed. Anyway, he didn't much like himself at moments like this....

He backed up slightly and nervously fingered the end of his moustache. "I don't keep track of hair," he finally said. Suddenly it was quieter. Charlie looked around the room. There weren't nearly as many sweaty bodies as before.

"Say lover, they got some dope in the other room. Hear it's some really good hash. God, hash makes me horny! Whattaya say we go and check it out."

"Oh, I don't know if—"

"Oh come on, boy scout, *everybody's* in there! You don't want to be left on the outside lookin' in, do you? You know it's about time you figured out a few things, Charlie Barnes. You want everybody to think you're weird or queer or something? It's bad enough you don't even try to *do* me, after I give you every opening imaginable, but turning down free pot, well, that's beyond geekville. C'mon, let's *party!*"

"When did you become so interested in me, anyway?"

"Hm? Oh....well, uh....well it's just that everybody else in there is just so, well, uh....oh shit, what difference does it make about before! You like me *now*, don't you?"

Charlie wiped a thin layer of perspiration from the front of his neck, wiping it off on the butt of his gray cords. "I don't know," he said flatly.

"You don't *know*? Well maybe later I'll let you take me down to The Salt Shaker and buy me an early breakfast, and we can *find out!*" the tan girl said suggestively, "—or maybe right after we blow some hash we could just blow this whole scene, and I could let you buy me a drink or two in Old Town before everything closes. And then we could go somewhere. Would you like that? I could make it worth your while!"

There it was. Finally....

"Okay. I'll be along in a minute," he lied. Drugs and brain-dead chicks....he never could decide which one bored him more....

The girl smiled and hurried off to join her old friends, leaving Charlie relieved, alone, a little confused, and more than a little frustrated at the bar. Time passed. He filled his glass again. After awhile he succeeded in prying himself away from the card table and walked slowly, nowhere in particular. Ben being his closest friend all through high school the Craig home was as familiar as his own, and so there was nothing new to discover, nothing surprising to see. Boredom was beginning to beckon him towards the mobile sanctuary of his car, only a few quick strides beyond the open front door. Then a voice said: "Charlie? Christ, is that the one and only Chuck Ed *Barnes?*"

He spun away from the front door as if yanked back by a rope. The familiar voice was coming from the den, adjacent to the main room but sunken down a few feet below it. He walked over and lowered his head into the sunken room. It was dark inside.

"Don't tell me you don't even recognize an old friend."

"Scott? Scott Chapman? Ha! Well I'll be damned...."

"No you won't. But I suspect *I'll* be. Have a seat, Kimosabe."

Charles Edison Barnes stepped carefully down and into the dark room, walked past the piano and sat down on the piano bench, setting his plastic tumbler on a few of the white keys. Scott Clayton Chapman sat behind him, surrounded by the high arms of a light brown rattan chair. Charlie spun 180 degrees on the bench so he could face him. His old friend was illumined by a vertical scythe of light slicing in from the doorway. A yellowish liquor bottle was in one hand, a plastic kitchen tumbler in the other, so they didn't bother to shake hands. He appeared to be squinting behind his sunglasses, and a red turtleneck sweater held his head up at the chin. His hair needed cutting.

"I can't believe it's you, man," Scott Chapman said, his smile thin-lipped and sly. He was something straight out of yesteryear. A vision, a memory. Living proof of the best of times. Undisputed leader of the pack: "So where'd the years take ya, Charlie-boy?"

"Up'n down, all around. You know."

"You've changed."

"Have I?"

"No," the young man said softly. "No, I guess not." He raised his glass to his thin lips and tilted just a little of the clear liquid into his mouth. "Let's drink to not changing," he said.

Charlie reached back for his tumbler. He swung it back around, quickly, and the two plastic cups collided in a dull thud. The wine crept up the side of Charlie's tumbler, almost spilling over into the other glass, but instead withdrew, swirled, then settled into a fine red pool.

"To the good old days!" Scott Chapman proclaimed.

"The good old days," said Charlie.

The party continued to exist outside the dark, sunken den, but they did not attend it. There were many years to account for, much nostalgic red tape to cut through, and two old friends must necessarily do this before beginning an actual conversation.

"Tell me what'cher doin' with yourself, Scott. You couldn't possibly be earning a living."

Chapman reached under the rattan chair and re-produced the half-empty bottle of Scotch whiskey. He poured a shot or two into his plastic cup and took a big gulp before answering. "I'm trying to be a salesman," he said.

"Yeah? Where's that?"

"Some dumb hardware store. Pasadena."

"Pasadena? So you moved back?"

"That's right. About a year ago. Want summa this?" he extended the yellow bottle out toward Charlie. Charlie shook his head. "Your funeral," was Chapman's response.

...his mind flashed back to a more idyllic time, when school didn't mean work and work meant nothing more than idle play. Scott was the leader then; there was no confusion or equivocation over that salient fact. He was born to lead, maybe because he was born to live. Certainly nobody loved the very fact of life itself more than the young Scott Chapman. Charlie Barnes was thinking about that most perfect time of life, as he eyed his best boyhood friend from face to toe...

"Since when did you decide you were a salesman?"

"I'm not. I said trying."

"Wait a minute....a *hardware* store?"

"That's right. Yer dad's a cool guy."

"But why the hell didn't he—"

"I asked him not to," Chapman said.

Charlie smiled. Scott was right....his dad *was* a cool guy. Clever, too. Sneaky old bastard....

"Man, these drop-ins are so stupid—we could sure use a little light in here," Charlie said, figuring a change of subject was in order and having grown weary of both the party and its unnecessary near-darkness. He reached over Chapman's right shoulder to flip the switch.

"*No!*" Chapman said sharply, grabbing Charlie's forearm with his left hand. "No. Leave the lights off. No need to turn the lights on. I....I mean no need, right?" His hand trembled as his grip tightened on Charlie's forearm.

"Sure....sure, Scott. No need to turn the lights on," managed a very startled Charlie Barnes. What the hell is wrong with lights, he thought.... what's going on....Chapman finally relaxed his grip and Charlie quickly took a swig of his wine to collect himself.

"Let's not talk about me," Chapman said, a hugely exaggerated grin suddenly taking over his face. He appeared to have immediately calmed down, amazingly, all the way back to normal. "How's college life? I hear you're up at Berkeley."

"Yeah."

"Yeah? Just yeah?"

"It's okay. I guess. I mean it's fine. I mean I'm not sure it's worth the money, I dunno."

"Yer pop can afford it."

"Oh, is that right? Well, since you're so up on my dad's finances and such a trusted family confidant all of a sudden, maybe we should just trade places!"

"Yeah. Yeah, maybe we should," Chapman breathed in reply. Again he filled his plastic drinking cup from the yellow bottle. "What else?"

"I'm a writer."

"A writer! You? Well *that's* certainly one for the books...." Chapman deadpanned, then grinned again.

"Hilarious. Very funny, Scott. I bet you kill 'em behind the counter," Charlie droned. He'd had enough of cheap canned humor for one evening.

"Sorry. So what kind of writing 'you do?"

"Fiction. Just starting out. I don't even know if I'm any good."

Suddenly Scott Chapman leaned forward. He came close enough that Charlie could see a watery glaze glistening across his old friend's widened eyeballs: "Whaddaya do when they....*don't like* what you write?" Chapman asked quietly. The words came slowly, and carried the urgency of genuine concern.

"Well, I suppose I *have* already piled up my share of rejection slips!" Charlie proudly revealed through a weak, casual smile. "I don't let it bother me, though. I mean I *try* not to let it. No point in worryin' about stuff I can't control. I just keep writing and re-writing and sending stuff out, that's all."

Scott Chapman buried his face in his hands. "God, I don't know how you *stand* it!" he wailed. Charlie's brow tightened. His eyes narrowed. It suddenly seemed hotter in the sunken den, and his T-shirt was starting to cling to him. "You kidding?" he wondered aloud, afraid of the answer. But Chapman didn't answer. He didn't even appear to hear the question. He just sat with his head in his hands, shaking visibly, violently. The next few seconds were an eternity. Finally, all at once, Chapman sat up board-straight in the rattan chair, adjusting his heavy-looking sweater at the neck with one hand, resuming his drinking with the other. Then he slumped back down in his seat, the rattan chair's high arms swallowing him.

"Sorry," he said.

"Don't worry about it, man."

> *...As he stared bewildered at the quivering figure in front of him, Charlie could not believe it was the same Scott Chapman he once knew so well. He preferred to imagine that before him was his twelve-year-old counterpart, leaning against a brick stanchion at the old elementary school, eyeballing a couple of the school's more physically advanced females as they walked by. "How far do you go?" he would say, and more often than not they would tell him. Or show him. And young Charlie was there too, apprenticing, observing, learning but never really being able to learn fully what simply cannot be taught. But in the end perhaps Scott learned his lessons a little too fast, he reasoned, although at the time Charlie thought his old friend had it made; a good-looking girl with piles of money. So what if they made a little mistake? "Ah, to be financially and socially secure at sixteen!" Charlie used to kid his old chum, his superior officer, his mentor. Who knew then that the price of social maturity was so high...And as he stared with sadness at the shattered figure in front of him, Charlie Barnes was glad he didn't learn too fast...*

He finished his wine and leaned back against the piano keys. He lowered his eyes. He thought about what words he would use to terminate the conversation with as much tact, and speed, as possible. Chapman beat him to it:

"Those were good days we had growing up, weren't they Charlie?"

"Yes. Good days. Every damn one of them."

For several agonizing, intolerable seconds silence prevailed in the dark, sunken den. The kind of silence found in a hospital waiting room, or at a funeral, or at some weddings. Or when boyhood memories fall prey to the ruthless realities of adulthood....

"Charlie," Chapman finally said with a shudder. "Remember that bird we shot?"

Charlie Barnes now forced himself to look directly at his oldest friend.

"Remember that day?" Chapman kept on. His voice was louder.

"What about the bird, Scott?" Charlie demanded. He too was shaking by this time, just not as much. "What about him?"

Scott Chapman did not hear Charlie Barnes. His ashen face betrayed this fact, a face which pointed straight ahead but clearly saw nothing. The cup fell from his hand. He spoke: "Poor little bird....he didn't wanna die....poor little sparrow....he tried to get away, he tried....flapping and chirping....he tried....poor little helpless bird....oh God, he didn't have to die, did he? *did* he?...we were just kids, I was just....a *kid*!...not my fault, not me not me not my, my....that awful chirping! Stop it! Stop it! I didn't mean to, I didn't, I'm sorry, I'm, I'm....it was only a sparrow, that's okay isn't it?...okay?...is it *okay*?...only a sparrow....doesn't matter, doesn't matter, doesn't, doesn't....nothing matters....nothing...."

The remainder of Chapman's monologue was largely unintelligible. Words came in bursts and slurs, and he shook like an epileptic. Sweat beaded up and poured from his brow. Dampness began to soak and show through the red belly of his sweater, making the thick red wool appear to be a darker red, as if he had spilled something on it. His continual moaning was somewhere between a whine and a song. Through it all his hand clutched and re-clutched at his throat, gripping and releasing the flesh beneath the heavy material. Charlie Barnes watched this scene in horror.

"It was like that, wasn't it Charlie?" Chapman finally pleaded. "Wasn't it just like that?"

Charlie drew a deep breath. "Yeah, Scott. That's just how it was," he exhaled.

At that Scott Chapman plunged his head into his hands and sobbed. Charlie watched for as long as he could, and then he left him alone.

The living room light forced his eyes closed for a second, and when he opened them nobody was there. All the alcohol had been consumed, all the hash had been inhaled, all the old stories had been retold, and the good and not so good young people of Altadena were gone. They had returned to the real world of the present, and would wake up the next morning next to women they didn't know or men they didn't like, each to then resume his or her agonizing pursuit of happiness, each to suffer through the normal, essentially predetermined course of a present-day life. Like nothing had happened. Like Brigadoon.

Charlie was stopped at the door by Ben Craig.

"Looks like yer ol' buddy's had just a teensy weensy too much ta drink, bro'!" Ben said laughing. "Maybe one of us should drive him home, he looks like a pretty weak kitten from here."

"Guess yer right," Charlie said. He was looking in the direction of the sunken den. Funny how things reverse themselves, he was thinking.... It had just occurred to him that Scott had called him 'Kimosabe', when that had always been his nickname for Scott. Scott had always been the leader, the Lone Ranger, therefore the *real* Kimosabe, while he was merely the loyal sidekick. Just a dime-store Tonto. And yet tonight he called *me* Kimosabe, damn....how could so many years have slipped by unnoticed, he wondered in silence, for such a wonderful and awful metamorphosis to have occurred? Too many years. Too many. Yet he would be damned before he would compound his own mistake: "Can't be me, man. I'm kind of in a rush. You might say I....I made a late date with a lady," he lied.

"Oh. That's different," Ben said through his trademark, winning smile. "Chicks take precedence, that's what I always say."

"Thanks, dude. Owe ya one."

"Ah hell, I guess maybe he can just crash on the couch for the night, why not. He's really fried. He's toast, dude. I'll hide his keys. No point in sendin' him away like that, he might kill somebody....Hey, thanks for stoppin' by, bro'. Big college man! Big college dude lowers himself into our corrupt little web of sin! Thanks for coming. Just like the good ol' days, right?"

"Sure. Sure thing, Ben. The good old days."

"Pop on by next time yer in town, bro'."

"You got it, rich boy."

A handshake later he was out the door. The night air tasted cool and moist, and for this he was grateful. He ran to his VW Bug and it started up right away. He took a different route home.

THEATER-IN-THE-ROUND

Author's Notes

I wrote the first draft of this story in 1982 (it takes place in December of 1980), and have been tinkering around with it ever since.

On the subject of tinkering, apologies to my sister Marji. Like me, Charlie does have a little sister (see *Oh-For-Four*), and she is in fact the star of my as-yet-unpublished short novel *A VERY L.A. EASTER STORY*. But there is very little evidence of her existence in the "L.A. JOURNAL" collection. Part of the reason for this is that originally she was supposed to be featured in *Theater-In-The-Round*, mainly to round out the Barnes family of five I established in *A VERY L.A. EASTER STORY* and *WHERE GODS GAMBLE*. To that end, the little sister character was indeed included in the early drafts of *Theater-In-The-Round*. But alas, in the final analysis, as the story developed I just couldn't justify her place at their grandmother's dinner table, couldn't give her enough useful lines of dialogue without disrupting what the other four characters were saying, and I guess you could say she wound up on the cutting room floor. Ah, this thing writing....such a ruthless process! Sorry, sis.

(Just remember, these stories in Part One are not about me and my family, they are about Charlie Barnes and his.)

Theater-In-The-Round is, of course, a satirical poke at religion. This is obvious from the get-go. From page one. Christianity has played an important role in both my life and my work, which I suppose was inevitable, having grown up in Bible-belt Iowa in the 50s and 60s and being the son of deeply religious parents. And while my point of view on the subject is usually cynical, often derogatory, and always tongue-in-cheek, it is not entirely a negative one.

I'd like to think that throughout my formative years I absorbed certain wonderful elements of the Judeo-Christian ethos which, hopefully, helped make me a better person than I would have been had I not been exposed to them by my wonderful parents. In other words, I'm probably more religious than I think. There. I said it. How about that, Mom? Did you hear that?

As for the rest of it, the rest of religion that is, I'll just keep hammering away at it until somebody—including God—gets it right.

THEATER-IN-THE-ROUND

"I tell you it's dis*grace*ful the way these heathen young people *drive* nowadays!" spit-barked Charlie Barnes's grandmother, a fiery old woman who carefully minced her pork chops but never her words. "Everyone in such a *fright*ful hurry to meet his *maker*."

"But didja actually see it?"

"I should *say* I did! Bodies flying through the air, the screaming and the yelling.... honestly, in all my years I've never seen anything *like* it."

"Now now, Mother, don't excite yourself. Remember what the doctor said about your heart," Betty Barnes said. Her husband sat to her left. He dissolved a faint smile with a forkful of potatoes.

"Well, I guess it happened that way if you actually saw it with your own eyes," Charlie said slowly and sensibly. A recent convert to the satisfying principles of Empiricism, he was testing the words on himself more than he was on his elders. But he wasn't completely convinced: "I just find it pretty damn hard to believe he couldn't make that measly little curve, no matter how the hell fast he was going."

"Well he *must* have been going over sixty miles an *hour*!" rifled back the old woman. "It's just a dis*grace* the way these young people drive. They ought to be put in jail for driving that fast."

"And by the way," said Charlie, "if these kids are so damned heathen, why would they give a flying crap about meeting their alleged maker?" He then laughed out loud at his own cleverness.

"Well of all the—"

"You young people think you're so—"

"—Of course thee, uh....the *rains* this time of year have a lot to do with it, son," a suddenly contemplative Roland Barnes said, cutting off both his wife and mother-in-law in mid-froth. Charlie and his father smiled and winked at each other across the table.

"It's not the kids' fault there's so many accidents, Granny-baby, everyone just drives faster nowadays. It's not the thirties anymore, y'know. No 'Keystone Cops' jalopies or anything like that. There's more people, faster cars, better roads—"

"—You're a *fine* one to talk with *your* driving record, young man."

Charlie Barnes fired a keen, lethal glance into his mother. A wide, wry smile dominated his face. It was the smile of a blackmailer. A silent reminder of all the times he had been sitting next to her when she had run red lights or made illegal left turns, or had gone over the speed limit just because there was no bored policeman below his quota in sight. Charlie loved to catch his mother in this kind of mistake. He lived for moments like this. If she pushed it any further he'd crush her, he'd annihilate her, he'd never let her hear the end of it. And she knew it. And he *knew* she knew. And he knew she knew *he* knew. And he knew she had to be thinking about it, all of it, as she meekly avoided his grinning glare. Her way of changing the subject, she shredded a pork chop into oblivion.

"A fine one to talk indeed....And please don't call me Granny-baby. I don't even know what that means."

"It means it's *hot* in here for Pete's sake," grunted Roland Barnes, his comic timing perfect as usual. "Hot as hell's fire itself. Can't we please turn down the heat just a little bit, Ethel?"

"We can *not*, young feller, you just keep quiet and pass me those potatoes."

Barnes complied with his mother-in-law's request, picking up the serving dish with long, bony fingers and setting it down in mock defiance on the old woman's plate. The loud bang of colliding porcelain set various startled eyes to blinking. He winked at his son.

"Well I agree with you, Mother. These kids should be locked up for driving that fast, lock them up and throw away the key, that's what I say.... and it serves them right when they finally get in an accident. It's the Lord's will, sure as anything."

"Hey, how come when anything bad happens it's always *the Lord*, stickin' his nose in where it doesn't belong. Christ, you'd think he'd have better things to do than screw around with *our* miserable little lives."

"Because for the thousandth time everything that happens is part of His plan, that's why. And watch your language, young man, you're still not too old to have your mouth washed out with soap!"

"Aw geezus, Mom...."

"There you go *again*. I mean it, I *won't* have you taking the Lord's name in *vain*. Honestly, sometimes I don't know why we ever sent you off to that college, they brainwashed you so."

"Mom, I'm twenty-five years old for Christ's sake."

"Twenty-five isn't too late to accept Jesus as your Lord and Savior."

"Not me. I can't chalk everything up to some harebrained god. Too damned easy."

"Hey, speaking of brainwashing, did you see that whatchacallit Unification Church is in the news again?"

"Moonies? You mean those awful *Moonies*?"

"Yeah-yeah, the Moonies! Seems that some girl they had under their spell got loose and spilled the beans to the authorities about all the mind-control stuff they supposedly do to their converts. Gad, how those guys crack me up."

"Supposedly? *Supposedly*? There's no supposedly *to* it, Roland Barnes, those people are nothing but a cult, a dirty filthy *cult*!"

"Watch your language, young lady," Barnes said. He smiled covertly at Charlie, who smiled back a little less so.

"Don't joke about it. It's cults like that that give religion a bad name."

"Well personally, I think it's religion that gives religion a bad name."

"Why you blasphemous little—"

"Actually, son, in the same article, I read that the Reverend Moon himself is going to be our new Vice President's personal guest at the Gipper's inauguration. Arm in arm with the Vice President of the United States! Don't that beat all."

"Well I, for one, *don't* believe it!"

"Neither do I, Mother. Not a good Republican like the Vice President, I should say not."

"Oh, God...."

"Charlie Barnes, I'm warning you—"

"It's not just the Veep, Betty, there's a long list of important people who have endorsed Moon. That's what makes it so funny! Fulbright, Hatfield, George Wallace, John Lindsey....President Carter himself gave him some sort of proclamation not too long ago. And there's even a picture of him with Humphrey, Strom Thurmond, and Ted Kennedy."

"Sounds to me like he's a fine American patriot. For a godless Korean, that is."

"Hush your mouth, boy."

"Mother!"

"I know he's your child, dear, but it's still my house."

"Son, when you were up at Berkeley, didn't you get approached by the Moonies a couple times?"

"What? You never told *me* that."

"Oh, my stars!"

"Couple times, yeah. I knew they preyed upon kids in their early twenties. I wasn't a very promising recruit for them, though. You and Mom never had a thing to worry about."

"Not your style, huh?"

"Not hardly. I mean if I refused to accept a good ol' meat-and-potatoes religion like yours, Dad—a really nice, safe, friendly religion where they at least *pretend* to give a guy free will, a religion with cool holidays and cool movies where they always get smooth-talkin' British guys to play the Romans—well, there was no chance I was gonna fall in with one that wouldn't let me make at least *some* of my own decisions."

"Why of all the—"

"Plus I heard they forbid beer. It's downright un-American."

"Charlie!"

"And they don't let you pee for hours at a time and they sit around all day long singing goofy Korean hymns."

"The Korean angle is kinda weird," Roland Barnes mused. He was staring off into space, his eyes landing on no one: "Moon is a native Korean, of course. Moonies believe that Korea, not Israel, is now God's chosen nation. He says that Israel had their chance and blew it."

"Honey, please stop."

"He says part of the reason God chose Korea to rule the world is that Korea is a peninsula, and therefore shaped like the male sex organ. That part of the article wasn't entirely clear to me. I don't know. Some sort of wacky symbolism."

"Roland...."

"He also says that God actually *caused* those six million Jews to be killed in the Holocaust, as sort of a punishment for the nation of Israel for rejecting Jesus."

"Roland!"

"Oh, and get this, Son—he says Christ is not a product of any sort of immaculate conception, but rather a regular biological child of Mary's adultery. Says he's the bastard son of Zachariah, John the Baptist's father.

Which would make Jesus and John the Baptist half-brothers! Isn't that a scream?"

"*Roland Barnes!*"

"Don't blame me, my love. I'm just the messenger."

"I know what'cha mean, Pop. I enjoyed talking to them. I mean I like good comedy as much as you do. But the truth is, I've just never found any religions out there willing to meet my personal minimum standards of moral rectitude. When I do, sign me up." He struggled to maintain a straight face.

"Just what you might expect, from someone who—"

"Let's talk about something else," Roland Barnes said with quiet authority. "Betty, you saw the accident too, was it a beaut?"

"Where did we go wrong with you, Charles?" Betty Barnes cut back in. "You were taught to love the Lord and his teachings."

"I *thought* I was taught to think for *myself.*"

"Charles Edison Barnes!"

"Betty? The accident?

"Oh, I'm sorry, dear," Betty Barnes cooed. She patted her husband's right knee under the table. "It was about, oh, two or three weeks ago, I think you were working late so I came down to see Mother. And well it was just awful, like Mother says. We heard this awful crash, I tell you my blood just ran cold. And these two bodies flew through the air, uh-*huh*, and some poor elderly man was killed—I tell you, I didn't see the *whole* thing but I've just never seen anything *like* it!"

"You say a man was killed?"

"Well, that's what the paper said."

"But it's really nobody's fault, right Mom?"

"Well, I—"

"Because no one had any control at all over the outcome."

"Well, no, what I mean is—"

"Because it's all God's will."

"And I suppose *you*, young man, think everything in the world just sort of *happens.*"

"Maybe it does. Maybe everything just happens."

"*What?*"

"I said maybe there's no rhyme or reason for anything. Is that so terrible a thought? Maybe we're all just poor ignorant creatures scattered throughout a doomed planet, four and a half billion lost and deluded souls. Duped for centuries by religions east and west, take your pick. And in the end we're left with no accurate idea of why we're here or why anything happens. Maybe the joke's on us, Mom. Maybe the joke's on us."

"Well I was going to say that's just about what you'd expect, from someone who bets on stupid *horses* for a living...."

"It's been a pretty damn good living lately, Granny. Paid for that beautiful knit shawl you're wearing....baby."

Charlie and his father laughed out loud, while the two women just silently shook their heads and muttered.

"Where did we go wrong, Lord?" Betty Barnes said softly. Her head was bowed in prayer, and her eyes were closed. Her mother joined her.

"Fer Pete's sake, you two, can't we have just one cotton-pickin' meal where—what was that?"

There was a screeching sound, the haunting cry of tires grabbing in vain at the road, followed by the dull thud of metal demolishing metal. Then nothing. Charlie Barnes almost didn't hear (through the deafening, disbelieving silence) his mother's familiar scream. He was through the door in an instant, his father not far behind.

The first thing he noticed was the cold. Unusually cold for Southern California, even for December. The same light drizzle that had lifted the oil from the pavement now coated Charlie in a chilly blanket of moisture, quite a contrast to the cramped crematorium of his grandmother's apartment. The second thing he noticed, finally, was the total and absolute quiet. He didn't know quite why it surprised him so, he just figured that more noise, more fanfare, should accompany so spectacular an event. But there was no noise. None. Just a brown Pinto hatchback molded into a guardrail, and the bodies of a young man and woman lying in the rain, all quiet and motionless beneath a single overhanging streetlamp. It was a black night void of any Heavenly illumination, a starless sky, an absentee moon, and so that lone streetlamp—absurdly well-placed—was allowed to cast down a perfect yellow cylinder through the blackness, arriving at the pavement as a perfect yellow circle to completely surround and reveal the players. With nothing else man-made to bleed light into the void, it was the only light of the world. Too perfect to be a coincidence?...maybe. He let out a deep breath, saw it cloud up and then disintegrate in front of him, revealing again the two still bodies. The whole thing was so utterly theatrical, thought Charlie at that moment. The opening scene in some gruesome one-act play. And he didn't know his lines....

He had been standing mute between the bodies for only a few moments when his father caught up with him: "*Go call an ambulance, son, I'll take care of things here*!" Roland Barnes declared in taking command. He was carrying blankets. Charlie was thankful for some direction. He had never arrived "first at the scene" before. It is a difficult time for anyone to know what to do, and the younger Barnes was hopelessly unqualified. So now, cast in a more welcome supporting role, his heart instantly slowed down, and he fairly flew up the stairs to his grandmother's building feeling both relieved and important, two grateful steps at a time.

He arrived breathless at his grandmother's apartment door, pushed it open, injecting himself reluctantly back into that unbearable hot-box of a room, only to find the old woman on the floor. Her daughter was applying a damp rag to her chalk-white forehead. "What the hell's wrong with *her*?" he said.

"Oh, she's fainted again!" Betty Barnes wailed. "What's going on out there, Charlie—is anybody dead?"

"I dunno, Mom. Gotta call an ambulance. There's a girl and a guy lying out there, they both look pretty bad."

"*Young* people?"

"Dunno. My age, probably. Maybe younger. Dunno."

"Oh, dear God. Oh, dear *God*!"

Charlie dialed 911, had the operator connect him with the fire department, and then managed to render all the details with reasonable alacrity and dispatch. By the time he hung up the phone the old woman had come to.

"mnmmn....unngh...."

"Take it easy, Granny. Dad's got everything under control out there, just relax."

"*What*? *What*? How can I relax with all this, this....this infernal commotion right outside my *window*," the old woman moaned. "Ohhh....I'll bet it's some young kid out drinking and....joyriding....ohhh!" And she was unconscious again.

He grabbed his jacket this time and flew out the door.

"Charlie! Tell Roland not to move them until the ambulance arrives. Tell him not to *touch* them," Betty Barnes exclaimed. "—and tell him to say a *prayer*!" She then went and yanked the blanket off the bed, and draped it carefully over her mother's limp body.

⇒   ⇐

The corner of New York Drive and Allen Avenue was now a bloat of humanity, people finally spilling into the street and pouring out of houses that suddenly lit up the sleeping town of Altadena like lights on a switchboard. It seemed like a dozen people lived in each house, so effectively did they populate the intersection. The rain had stopped. Charlie ran down to where his father was attending the injured. His water-crisp tennis shoe slaps seemed to slightly silence the crowd's muttering. The young man was conscious now, and sitting up, shaking his head, slowly reclaiming his senses. But the young girl lay perfectly still on the asphalt. She was on her back, her belly distended upwards into the yellow cone of light. Roland Barnes had spread a blanket over her body. He had already stripped off his best cashmere sweater to fashion a makeshift pillow for her. Someone stepped forward with an umbrella, which Barnes now positioned at the proper angle so as to act as a pup tent for her head, to deflect both sympathetic stares and insensitive rainfall from her face. Then, clearly in direct response to studying that face, Barnes' right fist closed around the left shoulder of his white dress shirt, yanked hard, and the garment tore loudly. He dabbed the blood from that ruined face as best he could with the white shirt-arm, delicately coaxing as much gravel as he could from the deep gouges and cuts. The girl did not move. Her eyes remained closed.

"You get ahold of that ambulance, son?"

"Sure did, Dad. Gave 'em the address twice. Said they'd be right over." Even as he spoke their ears received the faint, distant whine of sirens. The shrill reports sent cold chills up his spine and through his scalp. Roland Barnes did not look at his son during this brief Q and A. Rather, he peeled off the rest of his white dress shirt and quickly fashioned a makeshift tourniquet for the girl's left leg, having alertly spied a deep gash running, or rather leaking, from knee to calf. Charlie tore his eyes from his father and directed them left and right, front and back, astonished at the sheer swell and volume of the vast and growing multitude. The crowd had encircled the area, completely, a ridiculous yet tragically real theater-in-the-round....

The intersection was now almost totally blocked. Traffic was starting to back up on New York Drive. "Son, go turn those cars around until the police arrive, there's too much debris and commotion around here as it is. Go on, *move!*" was Barnes' next order. Charlie was again grateful for a commander, again relieved to have something to do. He jogged over to the first car in line, whose driver, an elderly woman, already had her head sticking far and crazily out the window, craning her neck for all she was worth in order to glimpse the proceedings.

The young man hated it when people got all giddy and excited about a car accident. He despised these ambulance-chasers, for him the modern-day equivalent of Old West townspeople coming out of the woodwork only *after* the gunfight was over, just to stare at the dead bodies: "Nuthin' special here, lady, just yer typical goddam violent collision," he snarled. The woman extended her head even farther out the window. She appeared not to have even heard Charlie's strict admonishment. She did not look at him. But he found himself looking at her. Then studying her. Her manner was strange. Almost trancelike. There were a couple of fresh-looking scabs glistening wetly on her white forehead. Her oval mouth was an expression of abject wonder. Finally she managed to alter it into a thin, valiant smile: "My, but that's funny," she said, but not to Charlie, and really to no one in particular. "My husband was....and at this very intersection....only.... three weeks ago."

It began to rain again. It was a steady rain, more punishing than the prevailing drizzle of half an hour earlier, and it began to fall more rudely on the multitude gathered at New York and Allen. Charlie muttered a lame apology and politely turned the old woman around. The other cars in line followed her, their detour a slowly oozing letter U, every one of them heading back reluctantly from whence they came. Police and paramedics soon arrived in tandem, relieving Charlie and Roland of their duties.

He returned to his father's side amidst a buzz of excitement and confusion:

"Did ya see it?"

"*See* it. I was the first one here!"

"Like hell. I was first."

"You liar—I bet I beat'cha down here by twenny seconds."

"Oh, what difference does it make."

"Boy they sure were lucky to be thrown from the car, huh?"

"Yeah. Real lucky."

"You know what I mean."

"Hey, y'think anybody's dead?"

"Dunno."

"Me neither. The girl, maybe."

"Sure is exciting, livin' around here....y'know it?"

"No wonder. Seems like there's a crack-up every other week."

"Most dangerous corner in Altadena, that's fer sure."

"Bet'cha most dangerous corner in Pasadena too. Or Arcadia or Sierra Madre or Temple City for that matter."

"But we're not *in* Temple City, you moron."

"You know what I mean."

"Man...."

"Yeah. Man-o-man is right."

"Maybe we should all say a prayer. Let's join hands."

"Ah, cut it out, willya?"

"It's a stupid corner, that's what."

"You'd think somebody'd at least put up an extra stop sign or somethin'."

"Or a speed bump."

"Yeah. I hate those things."

"Wonder why there's no reporters, or anything like that."

"No reporters."

"Why? Not big enough?"

"No. No, I mean that's not how they do it."

"Then how *do* they—"

"Boy, I sure hope nobody's dead."

"Wudda*you* care...."

"You see her head?"

"If that girl's not dead she'll sure be messed up good."

"You see her *belly*?"

"I know I know. I saw it. Shut up, willya?"

"Okay. I'm just saying."

"—and stop *touchin'* me."

"So sad. Makes you think."

"Yeah. Happy Holidays."

"Yeah."

"Y'know even if she makes it she's probably screwed."

"Prob'ly be a vegetable."

"I'll bet she's a paraplegic....or a....hey, which one means you can't move *any*thing?"

"Shut up."

"That's a quad."

"A what?"

"Yeah. I mean no. I mean the vegetable thing is more likely."

"Prob'ly right."

"Either way it's not milk and cookies."

"Oh god, what the hell difference does it make...."

Roland Barnes, lean and bare-chested against the elements, a bald pate wet and glistening where blond hair used to be, pursed his lips and draped a wet wiry arm around his son. "This whole thing must seem incredible to you, Charlie."

He looked out to where the elderly woman had spoken to him. He could feel his flesh tingling again beneath its wet outer layer of skin. The paramedics (there were three of them) continued to apply their vast collective knowledge and render their considerable healing gifts as best they could, hampered though they were by the rain's inconsiderate persistence. Two of them worked feverishly over the young woman, the girl. The third applied a gauze-thickened, oversized bandage to the forehead of the young man, who was standing now, shaking, shivering, crying. Charlie looked down at the girl lying on the rain-slick asphalt, wondering if she would ever stand again, knowing in his heart she would not.

The Barnes men, as was their custom, talked it out:

"This whole thing's not fair, Dad. Makes me mad. And it doesn't make sense."

"You mean because the boy was driving and he's okay?"

"No, not that. I mean two bad accidents right here, right at this same damned corner, within a month of each other. How do you explain that?"

"It's a mighty dangerous corner, son."

"But doesn't it seem like there's more to it than that? Jesus, we were actually *talking* about the first one when the second one happened! I mean the *very second* it happened! Sort of almost like we caused it somehow. I mean can something like that really be just a coincidence?"

"Well I tell ya, son, when I was a kid, what I had a heckuva time with was getting my mind around the idea of God being everywhere at the same time. God is everywhere at once, my mother used to tell me. Gave me a fearful headache." They both laughed. It was the necessary tonic, laugher where laughter is uncalled for, the aspirin they both needed. As usual his dad's timing was pinpoint-perfect, his touch light as talcum powder. But this time it wasn't completely enough: "I'm serious, Dad. I'm serious. This thing really bugs me. Jesus H. Christ, man, it really creeps me out."

"Charlie my boy, these are the types of questions you were always going to have to ask yourself eventually. Something like this happens, well, it's just a wake-up call," Roland Barnes explained, sounding very much like a father. He even looked the other way at his son's having twice more taken the Lord's name in vain, something he would not have even considered letting slide as recently as a couple of years ago. Perhaps he knew he was losing that battle, and didn't want to fire his last shots at it in the face of defeat: "Things like this—God, fate, destiny....predestination—they're very personal notions, son, everyone has their own ideas about them. I wish I could help you. But nobody can. Not me, certainly not your mother. Charlie Barnes is the only one in the world who can make up Charlie Barnes's mind on anything important, really important. It's what makes a man a man. Remember that."

Charlie looked directly at his father now, for the first time really since the ambulance had arrived, and was reminded (it surprised him every time) that he, not the father, was finally the taller of the two. Barely.

"Will you remember saying that, the next time Mom tries to make me into a Methodist to help me fight off the Moonies?" Charlie said, forcing a smile.

Barnes laughed. "I'll take care of both your mother and the Moonies," he said.

Two of the paramedics lifted the girl into one of the ambulances. Her eyes were closed, but Charlie convinced himself he could see her chest rise and fall. They had drawn the wool blanket up to her chin, no further, not yet. While one policeman diverted the remainder of the backed-up traffic his partner interviewed the shaken young man. The cop then made the young man do things like touch his nose with his eyes closed and say the alphabet backwards. He looked at the man's driver's license and wrote some things down. Rain was coming down in sheets, the hardest it had fallen all evening. All but the most tenacious spectators had gone home to spin their stories of the great event, probably as many stories as spectators. The ambulance rolled quickly away. Sirens on.

Roland Barnes exhaled deeply. He used his long bony fingers to wipe the rain and perspiration from his face. His performance had been excellent, virtually professional. "You okay, son? You all right?"

Charlie nodded. Out of the corner of his eye he noticed the remaining paramedic running up the stairs to his grandmother's apartment, carrying his bag like a football. But his attention was quickly reclaimed by the young man sitting, again, on the curb. It was his crying. Or rather his pathetic, rhythmic moaning, an almost musical refrain. His head bent low, and his face was completely covered by both hands. A thin white T-shirt was all that stood between him and the angry, driving storm. Charlie studied him, trying hard to imagine what it was like, what must have been going through the young man's mind. The police had finished with him, and had also moved quickly for the shelter, stifling-hot as it was, of his grandmother's apartment. "Dad, I'm gonna go see if I can help him," Charlie said, but his father was suddenly nowhere in sight.

All Charlie could think about now was the old woman in the car. He asked himself: How could she possibly be first in line at that intersection, at that precise moment, under such absurdly theatrical circumstances? Why was she even there? Was she there at all? He couldn't stop thinking about her. He didn't ordinarily believe in either cheap coincidences *or* the supernatural, and he certainly didn't side with either one. He liked not knowing who or what was calling the shots. If anything, he leaned toward coincidence over predestination, if only to fight off the encroachment of religion. But this? A coincidence? No way....but if such a comical coincidence was impossible, doesn't that leave only the supernatural? His brain was a battleground, the logical versus the mystical, the supernatural, and the divine. And the divine was winning. All he knew for sure was that this was something he would never tell his mother. Ever. Because she would never let him hear the end of it. Because it was too cute, too convenient. Because it was too much like the whole thing had been arranged for his personal discomfort and everlasting doubt. Because it was exactly like everything his mother had been telling him since he was a little kid....like what goes around comes around, like sowing what you reap....like as a man thinketh in his heart so is he, like you are what you are when you're not watched.... and like everything that happens is the Lord's will, His plan, His bat and ball, just like all the great and unfathomable miracles of the Almighty, incomprehensible and sublime.

Like some harebrained god stickin' his nose in where it doesn't belong....

Suddenly the rain stopped dead. Lightning flashed once in the western sky, and its thunder took six seconds to report. Then a black curtain of quiet fell gently down upon the little town, not to be lifted again until morning. Charlie walked over to the young man and helped him to his feet. "Here," he said, offering up his jacket. "Let me give you a ride to the hospital."

"Just take me home," the young man said.

WELCOME TO MISS IDA PARROT'S BED & BREAKFAST

Author's Notes

This story is also included in my other short-story collection, "U.K. JOURNAL", which was originally published by my first publisher, Boson Books of North Carolina, in 1999. It takes place in England but it is clear that its protagonist, our own ubiquitous Charlie Barnes, is still a Los Angeles resident and is merely in the middle of an extended working vacation in the U.K. Indeed he reflects upon his native L.A. many times during the story. Of course since it's a Barnes story, I would have wanted it in "L.A. JOURNAL" regardless of where Barnes was living at the time....and would have given you whatever convenient excuse made the most sense.

It is the only short-story which appears in both of my short-story collections.

Ida Parrot was begun (or at least conceptualized) in 1987, during one of my many trips to England in the 80s to gather material for "U.K. JOURNAL", and the first draft was probably completed around 1989 or so. I consider it to be one of my better stories. It's a nice combination of the literal and the allegorical. Not to mention the historical. There's certainly a lot going on there, both on the surface and beneath it. (If you want to play detective, you might want to start by reflecting on what was going on and, more importantly, what was coming to light in America back in 1987. Do you remember? You'll figure it out.)

One more thing: Regarding the scenic detail of the story, if you are planning a trip to the splendid city of Salisbury, England, any time soon, I personally guarantee you won't need a map or a brochure. Just take a copy of this story with you. It's all in there. You'll get around just fine.

WELCOME TO MISS IDA PARROT'S BED & BREAKFAST

It had been forever since he'd flattened his ear to a door.

"Come-come now, young man, listen *veddy*-veddy closely, I haven't *got* all bloomin' *day!*"

....her accent isn't so sharp, he thought, but that tongue is a razor....

"Now then, perhaps if I go slowly. What—do you take—for *breakfast*?"

....make that a loud, sarcastic razor. He couldn't help but be pleased at how easily he could pick her up, even through thick English oak, but quickly lost that smile somewhere within the concentration required to catch the soft reply....

"Uh....vee vill have....how you say....oggs?"

"*Eggs*! It's *eggs*, in the name of bloody God, not *oggs*! You've simply *got* t'learn t'speak our language better if you're to *get about* over here! Oggs. Bloody unb'lievable. Now then. I'll just put you down for scrambled eggs, bacon, mushrooms, toe-*mah*-toes, and a spot of cold baked beans, my usual. And of course tea and toast....unless you'd seriously prefer coffee?"

"Cafe, si—uh, yes. Coffee, yes. Yes-yes, coffee eeza vetty vetty good. Gratzi!"

"No no no *no*! Say *thank* you, for bleedin' heaven's sake, not *grat*zi! Go ahead, *say* it!"

"Thank you," came the young male voice, louder this time, vibrating the wood with near-perfect Shakespearean diction.

"Veddy good. Now then, that wasn't so terribly difficult, was it?"

At that well-chosen moment the American, smiling again, emerged from his tiny upstairs bedroom (which he had not ten minutes before checked into) intending merely to enquire, in a tone as innocent and respectful as he could manufacture, about proper and timely use of the shower facilities (and thereby thrust himself, of course, squarely into the middle of the action).

"Mister Barnes! Can't you see that I'm conversing with this *Italian* chap at the moment? Now go back inside y'own room for 'bit, put on a bloomin' *shirt* f'godsake, and I'll be right in to mark down *your* order for tomorrow morning. Go on then, *get on* with you!"

Not used to being caught so completely off guard (even by a woman) the American remained speechless, exaggerated the sheepish smile, removed his glasses to give him something to do, and then backpedalled a somewhat cowardly retreat into his assigned quarters. He had to duck his head. He did, however, remember to take a quick reading of her dimensions....no more than five-four, but no less than one-eighty?...hell, round it off to thirteen stone. He did not get a good look at the Italian....

"I *am* sorry, Mister Constantino, you know how *pushy* the Americans can be, but I've *so* much work t'do and only *so* many hours in which to do it. Now then, I suppose your young friend will have the same as you? Hm? Good! Less to remember. Breakfast is at half-eight, and I must ask you to please, *please* be prompt, I'm on *such* a shedjule, and the little girl I have helping me must be out the door'n gone by ten o'clock to catch the bus back up to Amesbury," the squat proprietress concluded, talking very fast, and with the y in Amesbury barely free of that quick mouth she thundered frantically down the stairs to answer the telephone.

"Thank you so very much, for every....thing," the Italian man said, slowly and carefully and near-Higgins perfectly, but probably not quite loud enough for her to hear.

The resounding *thub thub thub* of a thirteen-stone woman climbing stairs was all the signal he needed that he'd be next. He scrambled from his narrow, child-sized bed, stood 'at ease' as far away from the door as he could get, about twelve feet, which placed him next to the room's one window, which, like the bed, was unusually narrow, and which, at some not-too-recent juncture, had been rendered permanently closed by too many coats of black paint. She knocked and entered in the same motion.

"Now then, Mister Barnes. What shall *you* require tomorrow morn?"

Per her order, he had hurriedly pulled a gray *Lacoste* sportshirt over his wide square shoulders, and all the way down, down over the suddenly adventurous waistline finally fed up with three-plus decades of living within his lanky frame. The house was kept unreasonably hot, blotches of sweat already beginning to seep through the belly of gray cotton. He'd tucked the damp shirttail into a pair of faded beltless bluejeans. He now tucked his hands into the front pockets of those jeans, leaning slightly forward in reply:

"Well, I uh....Missus, uh...."

"*Miss* Parrot, young man, Miss Ida Parrot—you *can read*, can't you?"

"Read?"

"Oh honestly, Mister Barnes, how I *wish* you Americans would try to be more re*spect*ful!"

....confused and in enemy territory, best to play along:

"I'm truly sorry, Miss Parrot, I certainly didn't mean any disrespect," said this confused American, this Mr. Barnes, Mr. Charles Edison Barnes, thinking it had been a long time since anyone had called him *young* man. "Scrambled eggs, bacon, mushrooms, toast and coffee, yeah. That'd be just fine for breakfast, thank you. But you can *lose* the tomatoes and baked beans!" he chuckled; but when she didn't join him he soon stopped, coughed, let his hands again borrow the glasses from his head, and continued: "Listen, I was gonna ask you before, is it alright to take a shower pretty much anytime I—"

"No no no it is *not* alright t'ave a shower any bloody-well time you please! This isn't the States, we're not *made* a-money here! That's the *trouble* with you blinkin' Americans! You think *your* way is the way o'the whole bloomin' *world*!" She was shaking. He squinted to make sure. Sure enough, her eyes were quivering insanely in their sockets. He imagined he could even see the sweat bead and gather above thick, blurry eyebrows. She stopped just long enough to draw a new breath, briefly close her eyes, perhaps calm and organize her thoughts, and noticeably (which is to say grudgingly) modulate her voice; and when she began again the eyes were, for a moment, still closed: "We have an economy hot water system in this house, young man, and that means we don't *heat* the water during the middle of the day. And that's *another* thing. During the middle of the day, I would *veddy* much appreciate it if you would *not* be around while we are trying to clean up. If you stay in your room all day that's your business, I suppose, but you *won't* get a clean room and you'll *just* be a nuisance....now then, is that clear?" Though less violent in her delivery, she had nevertheless discharged these concluding words at a rate of two to the average tongue's one.

"Perfectly clear, Miss Ida," said Barnes, feathering a delicate arrow of sarcasm covertly through his words.

"Best 'go into Salisbury, that's why you're *here*, isn't it? Salisbury is a veddy fine city, a *wunde'ful* city in fact, capital city of Wiltshire and one of the *finest* little cities in the whole of England. No point in coming all the way *over* if y'going to just stay in *bed*!"

Barnes employed a tight-lipped smile to hide his thoughts, a flat, courteous smile. His squinting pale blue eyes were equally bright with congeniality, but they, too, were a sham. Behind them lurked plots, twists, paper schemes. They were not eyes to be trusted. He dropped his head just long enough to return the glasses. The lenses were two perfect circles, like a fashion-conscious owl might wear. Still smiling congenially as he looked up, relieved at no longer having to squint the world into focus, he now took a more thorough inventory of the woman who would be his landlady for the next three days. Her hair was an equal crime of black and white, not so much gray as just plain worn out, hanging down not very far and in no particular style. It was so nondescript he knew even *he*, a professional, would have trouble describing it. He ran his eyes swiftly through the deep grooves in her sunless, pasty-white face, and around the crow's feet, predictably, that flanked each bushy eye. It was a delightfully homely and perfectly unattractive face, just wonderful. But it was the face's resultant collective physiognomy which played flint to his dulled mind, not its component parts. This sternness of expression seemed to him cemented in place by an almost fanatic self-assurance, as if the years of thankless toil had case-hardened the mold, or perhaps some higher authority had long ago convinced her of the unchallengeable rightness of her views. Life had obviously trampled all over her. And all these things made her marvelous raw material for Mr. Charles Edison Barnes. People like her, he mused, must be why their two countries once went to war....make that twice.

(As an appendix to these quick thoughts, he couldn't help feel a little sorry for her. Her having to work so hard. But not as much as he could empathize with his own sorry plight; that of paying twelve pounds a day just so some annoying old lady could order him around....)

No doubt weary of waiting for him to contribute something, the old woman turned to leave. "Miss Parrot...." said Barnes finally; and misrepresenting himself again he smiled innocently and respectfully in her direction: "You may continue to call me Mister Barnes. For the sake of propriety, you understand."

"Veddy good," she said, in total agreement, and without the slightest hint of hesitation she added, "Remember, breakfast is at half-eight, and

I do mean half-eight *sharp*. Please do *not* try my patience by being late.... Mister Barnes." And then she left the room.

But the oak door had barely clicked shut between them when right back through it came the muffled postscript: "And *do* put on a clean shirt, man—y'sweatin' like a bloody *pig*!"

Eight-thirty comes early to the American on vacation, especially this particularly reluctant owl-breed of American—nocturnal by necessity, not choice—and it was a groggy and discouraged Mr. Barnes who made a careful descent of the stairs. This being a so-called 'working vacation' he was more tired than he might otherwise have been, having been up most of the night wondering why he couldn't get any work done. (On nights like this, he would have mortgaged his soul to the devil to get something accomplished.) He remembered looking at his watch as late as 5:30 a.m. Awake at that wee hour, he made sure to re-set his alarm clock for exactly 8:27, providing for maximum slumber and still allowing for a couple minutes to slip into what he considered proper breakfast attire; faded bluejeans, sweat socks free of shoes, and a gray sweatshirt with LOS ANGELES RAIDERS lettered large and aggressively across the front. It was unusually dark in the house and Barnes, a myope, wished he hadn't left the round-lensed glasses in his room, but he decided during the same brief brainwave that he was far too tired and lazy to think about it much less actually do anything about it. He took his time going down the stairs. A hunched-over walking style was necessary, due to the low ceiling clearance. He was well aware that most of the old houses in this country weren't constructed with people over six feet tall in mind, but was just as sure that this staircase represented an extreme case of shortsightedness even relatively speaking. He made a mental note.

He pulled open the French double doors to the breakfast lounge, and was immediately greeted by his first splash of sunlight of the day. It angled in through the large bay window as a single narrow beam, where the tiniest of cracks had been made in the drapes, and banked off a white china plate before hitting him in the face. He took a step to the side and his eyes adjusted quickly, and it became, again, a dismally-dark room. The bay window was the only window, and none of the lamps were on. Even the French doors leading in were curtained top-to-bottom. His first inclination was to fling the drapes hiding the bay window wide open, let rush in the eager light of the world, but he was besieged by a strong, intuitive feeling that this was the very last thing in the world he should do, and so he didn't.

He took the seat at the head of the table, at the plate that had temporarily blinded him, the one seat facing the window. There were two seats on either side of him. The two on the right were empty; the two on the left were already occupied by the two Italians.

"G'morning," he said, extending his hand. "I'm Charlie."

The older and larger of the two Italians shook Barnes's hand in a firm, confident vise and said, "Allo, Challie, I am called Silvano!" His skin was dark, his hair jet black, and he was built like an Olympic swimmer. He could just as easily have passed for Central or South American, the North American decided....or maybe even a run of the mill L.A. Chicano. "Thees eeza Paolo," Silvano said.

Barnes reached for the smaller Italian's hand and shook it, gently, as it was a soft, delicate thing offering no resistance whatsoever, and there wasn't any point in hurting the little guy: "Howya doin', Paul," he said with a big brother's smile, and the young Italian gratefully smiled back but said nothing. He was scarcely half Barnes's age, decided Barnes, and at least half a dozen years Silvano's junior.

"Heeza Engleesh, Challie, eeza notta vetty good."

"No sweat," said Barnes, his mood brightening from the anticipation of food and the proliferating notion that he was awake. "My Italian's lousy, so we're even."

A young English girl about Paolo's age, perhaps younger, entered the room next carrying a large Tupperware container filled with something that looked like granola.

"Please 'elp y'self 'ere t'muesli, gent'lmen!" the girl said in a pert Wiltshire accent, smiling creatively. The American grinned back the way he supposed an aging, dissolute rake should grin, and threw her what he hoped was a suggestive wink. (Concurrently, he wrote himself a quick mental note that the accent was much stronger than that of her boss. No h's.) The Italians did not look at the girl. She walked very slowly from the room, looking back once over her shoulder at the American.

"So Silvano, are you guys here on a holiday or what?" Barnes inquired, just to create the illusion of conversation.

"Oh no, Challie, I—uh, I mean *vee* study. Si—atta' university!"

"Oxford?"

"Si—uh, yes. That eeza correct, yes."

"I'll be darned," Barnes said, simply because it seemed the correct conversational rejoinder in that situation. It had always seemed silly to him that strangers should try so hard to converse at the bed-and-breakfast table, especially when they did not even share a common language. He found himself *wishing* he spoke Italian, because that would mean he could extract that much more data from this particular stranger, but since he did not he knew he would simply have to use his imagination to render the stranger worthwhile. And he needed the work. Perhaps his dulled mind did not lack the flintspark of inspiration so much as it required the whetstone of practice. (As a pleasant afterthought, he decided he couldn't help but like the guy.)

He poured himself a full bowl of muesli, splashed on some milk, and munched up a concert with the Italians. It hit the ear like horses at feeding time, and the three traded fraternal smiles with one another. In a blink, the American imagined that the three of them were partners in some wild international intrigue, a sinister *quid pro quo*, everything hinging on the ultimate cooperation and rational disposition of their wildly eccentric proprietress (indeed their common adversary) but realized just that quickly that his compatriots back home would probably not support such fantasy at the bookstores. His mind tended to wander like this when he was struggling. He knew he was a slave to the public, what they wanted, what they would believe. And who'd believe a crotchety, provincial old broad like this would have *squat* to do with helping out a blunt, pushy American, much less the lowly unwashed of some *other* screwed-up foreign country....though he did smile inside at the delicious absurdity of the idea. Some people will believe anything, he reminded himself, if it's written down....yeah, wait a minute....don't forget who you're dealing with here....but no. No, in the final analysis, he was convinced that even the gullible constituency he served would treat this half-baked notion with rejection. And as if to underscore his fears, this perfectly tranquil breakfast atmosphere was shattered by Miss Ida Parrot's entrance into the room. She fairly flung open the French doors with her free right hand, as she was balancing three plates on her left arm in a manner which suggested that she had, once upon a time, endured quite a lot of penance as a waitress. She was muttering like a crazy person. His back to her noise, Barnes dropped both the smile and his spoon; and instinctively hunched his shoulders up around his neck....

"There you are Mister Constantino, Mister Delacorte, and here *you* are Mister Barnes, eggs and bacon with mushrooms—no toe-*mah*-toes, no *beans*!" she rattled off barmaid-style, setting the three plates firmly down, one-by-one, in front of each corresponding border. The American dissembled his amusement behind a neutral smile, secretly quite pleased with himself. She was just too perfect. Immediately upon seeing her, his eyes fired off crisp, urgent dispatches to his slumbering nose. Still a little groggy, he only now succeeded in matching the room's familiar, overwhelmingly foul odor with the proper corresponding compartment of his memory....it was his grandmother's house, equally stuffy, equally gloomy, the international, unmistakably acrid aroma of old people growing older in dark, cooped up, hermetically-sealed quarters. For an instant it was the early 60's, he was a boy of seven, and the four other chairs were occupied by his father, mother, sister and brother, the five of them being served some endless 4th-of-July meal in the hottest, dreariest, mustiest house in Peoria, Illinois, by an old woman he didn't really know and could barely understand. This sublime union of memory and fresh experience produced sweet electricity in his brain, and awakened him more thoroughly than would have a bucket of cold water in the face. And the operative word to describe the overall sensation, DECAY, jumped into his mind as if the letters had been scratched into the thick atmosphere in front of him. Oh, the familiar decomposition of rotting, roasting, aging human flesh....*stop*! He stopped and shook himself out of it. He ordered his sense of smell to concentrate on the bacon and eggs. The Italians traded whispers of seemingly great import. Miss Parrot, at all times broadcasting an aura of complete authoritarian control over her brief domain, glanced about in silent, frantic rage. Something was terribly, inexcusably wrong:

"God almighty! Which of you, you, you *people*, has gone and opened the bloomin' drapes—*you*, Mister Barnes?"

Barnes started to laugh, then thought better of it. He shook his head.

"Mister Constantino, I would *veddy* much appreciate it if you would *please* refrain from playing with the drapes as *long* as you are a guest in this *house*! Me-eyes *don't* take well to the light anymore, and those drapes are drawn shut ev'ry morning for a *purpose*! Do I make myself *clear*?"

"Yes yes, uh, I....apologize Signora, scoozi, scoozi!"

"No no no, not *scoo*zi, my dear young fellow, *I'm sorry* is perfectly acceptable 'round here if you are trying to *say* you are sorry, please at least make an *effort* t'speak our language while you are in residence, I, for one, would *greatly* appreciate it, thank you veddy *much*!" the old woman somewhat wearily exclaimed, but nevertheless in an astounding partnership of pace and perfect enunciation. She leaned over and re-closed the drapes. Instantly, the house returned to its eternal state of gloom, the only light to speak of having to fight through the translucent cheesecloth of the cheaply-made curtains.

"Miss Parrot, could you tell me where the racecourse is from here?"

The old woman now regarded Barnes with a pinch of disgust mixed with a dash of old-world provincialism: "Mister Barnes, I suppose only *God* knows why a perfectly intelligent young man such as yourself, with all of Salisbury at his disposal, would choose to fritter away both the day *and* his hard-earned readies on a flock of *dumb animals*! Why, did you know that the spire of our Cathedral is the tallest in England? And I don't suppose you could *spare* the bloody time to drive *seven* blinkin' miles up to *Stone*henge, it just *happens* to be one of the true wonders of the ancient world, and a *whole* lot more interesting I'm sure than which *farm* animal can outrun *another*!"

"I'm sorry. I'm so ashamed."

The Italians snickered quietly, then whispered amusing comments to each other.

"Well if you absolutely must know….go south on Exeter Road, through the round-a-bout, and then get on the A-3094, which goes through Harnham. It's about five or six miles southwest 'the city, I should imagine there'll be signs posted to guide you along."

"Why thank you, Miss Parrot, thank you *veddy* much," Barnes said, rolling his eyes as he said it so only the Italians could see. And again they both giggled, two disobedient schoolboys.

The old woman snorted, muttered, and brightened the room with her departure.

Breakfast was winding down when Miss Ida Parrot and the young English girl returned. The minute the French doors opened, all vestiges of attempted conversation ceased. Miss Parrot carried a steaming fresh pot of coffee, while it was the girl's job to clear the table.

As she poured a cup for the older of the two Italians, Barnes could tell from the way her grooved, pasty-white face was squinched up that she was dying to say something. It was a quality of the human face that over the years Barnes had observed almost exclusively in the female. And when the Italian's dark smiling face finally went up to her, she simply could not help herself: "Mister Constantino, just why is it you *Italian* chaps refuse to make any effort a'toll t'speak our *language*? It *is* our country, you know."

While Silvano Constantino struggled to formulate an appropriate response, Barnes studied the young girl tidying up the breakfast area. When it came time to take his plate, he picked it up and handed it to her. "Why thank you, guv'nah!" she said with a sly half-grin. Barnes nodded suggestively for a reply. He had reached that stage of life where girls half his age could legitimately be imagined his illegitimate children, and it made him feel particularly lecherous for an attractive, fresh-scrubbed girl of this ilk to call him "guv'nah". At once—two halves of the same fantasy—he felt a father's studdish pride and a prospective lover's tingle. He couldn't help it.

Finally, Silvano was ready to reply to his landlady's question. His reply was a question of his own: "But-a Meeza Parrot, do you-a speak Italiano?"

"I don't *hafta* speak Italian!" Miss Parrot was quick to rejoin. "There's *no reason* for me t'speak Italian! I neve' *go* anywhere, let alone *Italy*....in fact I have no *social* life a'*toll*! I work veddy-veddy hard 'round here, from dawn till late ev'ry night, there's simply *no* time for me t'do *any*thing, let alone take the time to travel as far away as all that. So you see, young man, there's absolutely *no* reason to waste me-valuable time learning to *speak* a language I'll neve' bloody *use*!"

The young girl was busy clearing the plates and silverware from the Italians' side of the table. He squinted, wishing he could see her better. But she's obviously a pretty little thing, the American did observe, her shoulder-length blonde hair continually falling in front of one eye in a sort of 'peek-a-boo' style, every time she would lean over their shoulders to pick something up. The occasional pearl of sweat running from temple to cheek did nothing to diminish her appeal. The blonde hair and fair skin meant that she could, theoretically, indeed have sprung from his very loins, and he smiled at this easy self-confirmation of his theory. She smiled back. In leaning over, various parts of her body would rub against Paolo's right shoulder and Silvano's left, but again they took little note of her presence. In fact, they both seemed perfectly spellbound by Miss Ida Parrot's dissertation on the Italian language:

"Please don't misunderstand me, gentlemen, I'm as aware as anybody else what a beautiful language you have, it's the most beautiful language in the world for opera, when I get the time, which is ex*treme*ly rare, but that doesn't mean I should bloody *learn* the language if I am *not* going t'be required to *speak* it! Surely that distinction from *your* situation cannot be all that difficult to perceive."

Now it was Barnes who couldn't hold back: "Oh I don't know....I myself have always preferred Italian sausage to Italian opera," he said. He rolled his eyes again, and again the Italians giggled in stereo.

"Well there's *no* reason f'you to openly make *funna* me. I suppose you don't think I already *know* yer takin' the Mickey outa me the *moment* I'm out 'the *room*!" the old woman said, stomping a loud path to the door. But just before she withdrew, an ingrained sense of duty compelled her to ask the obligatory question: "Now then. Have you....gentlemen, enjoyed your breakfast?"

The younger Italian, Paolo, as fate would have it, was at precisely that moment biting into a terrific piece of dark toast, which he had taken considerable time to coat meticulously and liberally with lime marmalade. He'd been saving it. Out of involuntary reflex probably more than anything else, and in the first thrilling example that he was capable of the faculty of speech, he exclaimed (albeit somewhat squeakily), "*Molto bene!*", twice, to no one in particular.

She was muttering vows and curses as she squeezed through the French doors.

Traffic oozed along the A-3094 like ketchup from a just-opened bottle, but Charlie Barnes didn't mind. He'd just beaten the races for a pound or two, not much mind you (especially for a man who had once made his living at it), but he had reached that stage of life where just being at the races, and winning at all, were far more precious commodities than the bottom line itself. To be sure, he was bemused as to why the bottom line wasn't bigger, all gamblers participate in such lifelong wonder, but at the same time he was vaguely aware that it was his own fault, for convincing himself that he could beat all six races on the card and then wagering accordingly (And twice, a character flaw that was a source of eternal bewilderment and chagrin, he had actually changed his mind at the very last minute, right at the betting window, jumping off a winning animal and—financially, at least—onto a losing one.). This time, he blamed his chronic indecision on the fact that he'd never been to the Salisbury course before. He'd never wagered over a course shaped like a needle with an eye. It was as good an excuse as any. But for Barnes, win or lose, racing was one of the really good things about England. Each grassy racecourse has its own distinctive shape, unlike American dirt tracks which are all shaped like an oval, and that curiosity alone was always worth the inflated price of admission. He liked not knowing what to expect. And he liked not knowing whether it was success or failure that was conspiring covertly with his destiny....

It was a brilliant day. The five-o'clock sun was alive and working in the western sky, behind him as he drove west-to-east, operating in that manner peculiar to English summer suns that involves burning brightly without actually generating much heat. (In England, summer is the season that got lost.) It had drizzled a bit around 3:30, as it always seems to do in the southern counties, leaving behind a world of misty-clean air and a sunribboned sky full of interesting gray-on-white cloud formations that Barnes was rarely exposed to in his native Los Angeles; where the sky can be cloudy without any clouds. As traffic picked up on the A-3094 the clean-tasting air rushed in through his open window, fogging his sunglasses, pushing back his wavy light brown hair. He sucked it in through his nose and then his mouth, alternating, trying to decide if it was more akin to menthol steam or a vanilla milkshake.

(Whichever it was, he found himself asking whichever gods might be listening if they might perhaps inhale a houseful of it, and then mercifully displace the infernal miasma of his prisonlike barracks with a collective blast of their nostrils.)

Miss Parrot was right about one thing; Salisbury was indeed fine, a magnificent little town. Or actually a 'city', because for some reason a little town in England gets to be called a city if it happens to have a cathedral in it. The cathedral spire was indeed magnificent as well. As he approached the Exeter Road turn-off it towered above him on the left, and looked even taller than its 404 feet due to Salisbury's obviously intentional dearth of buildings over two stories. He couldn't stop his mind from playing upon this conspicuous digit, this impertinent, thrusting thing. Does a city not officially achieve its manhood until it erects for itself a gigantic, skyscraping sexual structure? The way this one ripped the smooth, chaste skyline asunder couldn't have helped but affect a mind like his. He was at once reminded of its many relatives throughout the world which he himself had seen; its campanile brothers in Berkeley and Venice, the needlesque nephew in Seattle, its patriotic penile clone in Washington, and the hundred-story arrogance of its many famous Manhattan cousins. Paris had always suffered from a sort of split personality....the painfully stiff, metallic fantasy of Monsieur Eiffel; the circumcised simplicity that is Concorde. San Francisco has the same problem, he thought....the Transamerica Building is larger, stronger, more magnificent, and therefore just not as realistic as the softer, stubbier Coit Tower (short for coitus?). And of course there were the stubby, square-bodied mutations of London and Pasadena, two hands forever circling each brick face, neither structure very attractive but both at least able to tell time. The way the subconscious mind can manage it, the car was left to drive itself while he pondered the absurd linkage of these cities. That was one thing about L.A., he mused....one town far too laid back and apathetic, and downright shy for that matter, to embarrass itself by erecting one building that might somehow stand out from all the others....But even though Salisbury's erection is—in its discrepant height from all buildings that surround it—the most conspicuous erection of them all, for some reason it struck him this bright damp day as the most fitting. In its conspicuousness it had become strangely natural. It wasn't merely the symbol of Salisbury, he decided, it *was* Salisbury; as it will forever be for any foreigner who will ever venture here....

St. Andrew's Church, Pasadena, CA

Finally, as more or less a brief epilogue to his musings, he amused himself by reflecting on how Silvano and Paolo would probably attach 'special' significance to the spire, laughed out loud at his own cleverness, rubbed the tired, reddened blue eyes hiding behind the aviator-type prescription sunglasses, and resumed control of his vehicle.

He followed a pre-planned route home, north on Exeter, which soon became St. John's Street, then a quick left on New Street and a right-turn acceleration up High Street. Upon weaving through those pedestrians courageous enough to cross High at New Canal he immediately down-shifted into second with his left hand, decelerating and leaning into a right-hand turn onto Silver Street, then a quick left lean onto Minster Street, thus effectively zigzagging between the old Poultry Cross and the Haunch Of Venison Pub. Again heading north he pushed the gear shift lever back up into third, swerved left, then slalomed back to the right to shoot right through the alert, scattering shoppers infesting the flea markets along Blue Boar Row (there really aren't any traffic laws in Britain, regardless of what anyone tells you), which placed him on Castle Street heading north again.

Castle Street is lined on each side by irresistibly quaint pubs but this time Barnes resisted, his left hand instead pulling the shift lever down into fourth. His new car, a used Ford, with an enthusiastic rebuilt engine, virtually stolen from a Surrey mechanic via some fancy Yankee horse trading out behind the mechanic's garage for 200 pounds and no questions asked, responded with a generous burst of speed, accelerating the wind through his window, the cool air coaxing his right elbow back inside. He approached the Ring Road round-a-bout by down-shifting from fourth to second. The Ford lurched over its front axle from the sudden change of orders, objecting vehemently with a prolonged whining sound, but obliged its master just the same and handled the round-a-bout nicely, hugging the outer edge while circling in the familiar clockwise search for the correct exit. Barnes kept a cool eye to his right, always aware of the high likelihood that some crazy local in one of the inside rings might try to cut him off, in a frantic, foolish, routine effort to make his exit within the first revolution.

But the good thing about round-a-bouts, Barnes knew, was that if you missed your exit you could always catch it the next time around. Or the next time. Or the time after that. There had even been occasions, in less-familiar territory, when he'd had to circle three or even four times before finally veering off left and onto the proper carriageway. But this time he knew exactly where he was going, Salisbury being one of those mystical little towns (or rather cities) where you wind up knowing your way around practically from the day you arrive, almost as if you'd grown up there. And since he was perfectly placed in the outer ring of this three-ring round-about, all he had to do was veer off left when the proper sign approached him, and he was heading due north again.

Immediately north of the round-a-bout Castle Street changes its surname and becomes Castle Road, for reasons Barnes was never able to discover, strangely enough, even from interviewing several of the friendly local pub crowd two nights running. The bill-o-fare changes, too. The pubs abruptly disappear, only to be just as abruptly replaced by bed-and-breakfasts. Lots of them. As he roared up Castle Road they were everywhere, on both sides, seemingly every other front yard displaying a sign with the familiar insignia B&B next to the name of the establishment. There were cute, clever names like 'Wiltshire House' and 'High Wycombe' and 'Tudor Manor', names obviously designed to impress the tourists with their authentic 'Olde English' quality. First-time tourists, he figured, probably can't help but be impressed. The signs approached his advancing windshield like the billboards which line the freeway leading into Las Vegas….He stopped counting at forty. The more there were, the more ridiculous that made the odds, he lamented, that he should wind up at the very one he did.

When he finally approached the outskirts of town Castle Road changed its name again and became, simply, the A-345. Almost there. A couple more miles, almost to where the houses finally disappear into endless dunes of tall, sandy-colored grain, and finally he spied the dull, paint-chipped, somewhat grayish black facade of his temporary work cell. He down-shifted into second and turned into the makeshift gravel parking area which might have, under different circumstances, been some nice family's grassy front yard. Just before he got out of the car he noticed a cardboard sign taped to the lower left corner of the outside surface of the bay window. A large and conspicuous sign. Strange. He hadn't noticed it before. Printed freehand, in a small child's crooked capital letters, were the words:

WELCOME TO MISS IDA PARROT'S BED & BREAKFAST

He couldn't help but laugh at that. For good measure, in response to a practiced discipline to document his material, and because he was sure that no one would ever believe it if the story ever came out, he snapped a picture of it with a Polaroid instamatic before getting out of the car. The side door of the house was unlocked. Standing just inside this absurd dwelling place, the stifling heat already attacking his outraged lungs, his sunglasses conspired with the eternal state of gloom to render him nearly blind. He removed the dark glasses but it didn't help; it got a little brighter, but without the prescription lenses he lost visual acuity. Screwed either way. He was just about to gallop up the stairs to prepare for a late afternoon nap (his usual preface to a night of pub crawling) but stopped himself when he heard the low buzzing prattle of someone muttering urgently to herself. It struck him as almost a religious chattering. He walked around behind the staircase to where the old woman, in a white bathrobe, a damp towel wrapped tight like a beehive around all but the most renegade wisps of nondescript gray hair, was fervidly and feverishly composing something at a compact wooden writing desk, which fit quite naturally under the stairs in the acute angle the staircase made with the floor. A single narrow candle provided the only threat of illumination.

"Why, my dear Miss Parrot, I didn't know *you* were a writer!" he exclaimed. The track, as always, had placed him in remarkably good mood.

"Oh! Mister Barnes! You startled me....Good God, young man, I would so *veddy* much appreciate it if in the future you would *please* refrain from sneaking up behind an *old woman* like that! I find it *most* discourteous, most discourteous indeed...."

"I'm deeply sorry, Miss Parrot," said Barnes. "I'll refrain, I promise."

"I hope so. Well then, there's tea and biscuits in your room, if you require more milk please let me know....but not *too* late, I have more important things t'do 'fore I retire than run to the kitchen ev'ry few minutes—oh, and if you happen to be awake when those *Italian* chaps finally drag themselves in, I would be *most* grateful if you would tell them I would like them *out* of here *before* breakfast....I've had enough, I've simply had *enough*!"

Without his regular glasses (which in his haste to make the first race he had again forgotten and left in his room) it was too dark to make out the detail of her facial expressions, so all he could do was squint in the general direction of her blurry, turban-toweled head.

"Is that really necessary, Miss Parrot?"

"Is it *necessary*? Mister Barnes, do you have *any* idea how difficult it is to run a bed-and-breakfast? *Do* you? Well I'll *tell* you. I don't have any social life, *none*, because I'm bloody-*chained* to this place sixteen *bloomin'* hours a *day*! Why? Because guests the like of your *Italian* friends bloody-in*sist* on coming in late, so I hafta be up to lock the door behind them, not to *mention* the late phone calls from bloomin' tourists, like yourself, calling at *all* hours attempting to find a *room*!" I can put up with just about all of it, Mister Barnes, just about all of it, but when those, those....those *foreign* chaps insist on making funna me behind me-back....well I've had enough I have, and that's why I'm writing this letter to the Dean of Students at *Ox*ford!" It was a prodigious speech, yet Barnes, employing ears to lend strength to faltering eyes, was unable to detect the intake of a second breath, indicating, incredibly, that she had managed the monologue with a single blast of hot air.

"So yer writin' this guy about Silvano and Paolo?"

"Not that it's any of *your* business, Mister Barnes, but yes. Yes I am. I bloody-well guaran*tee* you that I will see them disciplined for their behavior, and I *further* guarantee that I shall cause as much commotion as possible to prevent these wet-nosed Oxford whelps from coming down to Salisbury and polluting our fine little *town*!" She meant city, of course, but because she was so upset Barnes naturally assumed that she didn't know what she was saying....

....Then something jerked inside him. It always did in situations like this. Her attitude reminded him that he had never been that impressed with his own species, as much as he enjoyed certain individual products of it. Like Silvano and Paolo. They're not hurting anybody, he said to himself, all they want is to be left alone....He could feel his face flush violently red with anger. He'd promised himself he wasn't going to rock the boat, he had promised, but, what the hell, he now rebutted himself, who would know? After all, he was what he was; just a blunt, pushy American....

"Listen, Ida, couldn't you at least *try* and be a little more pleasant? I'm only gonna be here one or two more nights, at the most, and since I actually gotta *pay* to stay in this stuffy old-world morgue, can't you at least *try*?"

The old woman, perhaps not used to being angry to the point of speechlessness, puffed up at the gills like a 180-pound blowfish. Brows bristled, white cheeks flushed red, drops of sweat lining the forehead soaked up the irregular dispatches of candlelight. It was several wonderful seconds before she could blow her stack, but blow she did, and Barnes knew he was in trouble when he suffered a plosive salvo of Olde English profanities he had never encountered before.

"No, I guess you can't...." he said, this time with intentional impishness, pleased and proud to be an American, scurrying up the stairs very quickly and locking his bedroom door behind him.

Before slipping out of his clothes and into a much-looked-forward-to nap, Barnes was compelled, like all worthy practitioners of his craft, to chronicle the events of the day. He ferreted out a simple yellow writing tablet from his suitcase, a tablet marked U.K. JOURNAL at the top, and commenced writing while lying on his belly:

<u>August 17, 6 p.m.</u>
Won L25 at Salisbury. Turf quite heavy
and yielding from all the recent rain. Rumor
has it that it's August here too, but I'm happy
to report that it's still cool enough during
the day for my old letterman's jacket (summer
here is a joke, thank god). Guess I should've
bagged a lot bigger elephant than 25 pounds,
actually found some real decent plays out there,
but I just made too many bets. Didn't lay off a
single race. Damn. Just couldn't help myself.
Being disciplined at the track sure is harder <u>now</u> than
when it was my <u>job</u>! As for the course
itself it's strictly minor league stuff, horses
bottom-of-the-barrel cheap, nothing special.
And the other jocks just can't stay with
Cauthen and Eddery. Those two just keep taking
turns, per usual (Makes a guy wonder if they take
turns at night!). Love the screwy layout,
though, a mile-long straight gallop with a loop at
the end. Of all the ones I've toured this trip,
this is the one the hacks back home would be
the least likely to swallow.
Should make Newbury no later than the day
after tomorrow, York by the end of next week.
(That'll make 7 courses in 16 days. Not bad.)
*****

The two other guys staying here are pretty
decent joes. Silvano is quite friendly and
outgoing, he's apparently doing some graduate
work at Oxford, while his sweet young traveling
companion Paolo is/////well, let's just say
he seems devoted to Silvano. Luckily the landlady
is too stupid to realize what's going on, or she'd
no doubt give them even more grief than she

currently insists on giving them. Which brings me, again, to my ever-charming proprietress.... Miss Parrot, who continues to challenge the imagination. Her picture should appear in the dictionary next to the word 'crotchety'. Maybe she just seems ornery because everybody else in this ridiculous country is so compulsively nice, who knows. Sometimes I could just slap her. She's a hard-headed idiot, but unfortunately she's also great material; 'like to blow this tube right now, but the way things are going I've got to stay at least one more night. Can't afford to run away from anything even remotely inspirational. Who knows, maybe she'll come through for me and show me some sort of an angle. I could use a break.
*****

That's all for now, dear journal. Very tired. Must catch a quick nap before I hit the Castle Street pubs. Folks in the pubs here are very chatty, by the way. They'll tell you anything. And I think if you asked them they'd give you the folding money right out of their own pockets. I will always love the English people....But I'm going crazy waiting to be able to work. Experiencing withdrawal symptoms from lack of baseball box-scores. Would kill for one decent cheeseburger. And I'm sick to death of hearing about this Iran/Contra thing. If just one more self-righteous prick comes up to me and asks me what we were trying to pull, I might not be able to keep from punching him in the nose....

His eyes were shot. He made one last attempt to get some work done, just a haphazard little sketch about the Italians, but it was no good. Certainly not something he would ever let anyone see. So he shredded it into little pieces and fed it to the trash can. On this occasion, the updating of his journal was the best he was going to do. He stripped naked and crawled beneath the amazing warmth of a goose-down duvet, realized at once that he could roast alive under such circumstances, peeled the duvet back down to his waist, replayed the day's six races in his head, cursed himself, and was asleep in ten minutes.

Eight p.m. His Ford skidded to a stop on the rain-slick cobbles, into a parking space in the town square close enough to the Haunch Of Venison Pub that the fresh spray of merriment could whisper to him. Laughter was just the tonic he needed for his nerves. The nap he had so craved gave him but the cruelest illusion of sleep, a war of anger and frustration, specifically his nemesis' treatment of his adoptive Latin allies versus his inability to render it. And so, denied his rest, he had decided the next best thing was a few more pints than he might have managed had he reached this destination at 9:30, as originally planned.

As fond as he was of Salisbury, Barnes had a problem with her town square. He stood now in the middle of it, in a sea of asphalt, glancing in all directions, trying to understand. What were they thinking of, he wondered. A square formed by four of the most quaintly-named streets in the world, and all the modern-day city planners could come up with to fill the inner quadrangle were a hundred parking spaces and a couple of underground toilets? And while he applauded the preservation of Ox Row's City Arms Pub (est. 1780), as well as the charming and equally well-preserved Duchess Of Albany, it was difficult to countenance the incursion of Kentucky Fried Chicken on Oatmeal Row; so close to the old Poultry Cross that it was not so much ironic as it was offensive. And how was he supposed to stomach the sight of Blue Boar Row's new Pizza Hut franchise? Barnes had nothing against these sacred cows of American junk food, but finding them here challenged—no, *violated*—his concept of historical integrity, and made him wish he was born and had died in a prior century. He could just imagine, years from now, some as-yet-unimagined child skimming over something of his and asking, "What's this town Salisbury like, Daddy?", and he responding, "Well, little one, I don't know about now, but back in the 80's it was a place where a fella could drink a beer on a street called Ox Row, pick up a bucket of chicken on a street called Oatmeal Row, then take a stroll through the town square, go pee-pee right in the middle of it without even getting in trouble, put the chicken in the car, then head over to Queen Street and then up to the travel agency on Endless Street to make an airplane reservation home—all in less than half an hour! And by the way, sweetie, if it's got a big church you must say city, not town." good god....

He fled the square in a purposeful jog, fearful that he might drive himself to distraction with his own imagination.

Of the several score pubs, bars, taverns, watering holes, and assorted hostelries of drinking that Barnes had personally researched and chronicled in his many tours of the island, none shone brighter in his mind than the Haunch Of Venison. Built centuries ago (the sign says 'about' 1320, so as to be vaguely precise) its 20th-century proprietors had the good sense not to poison with progress the establishment's essential character, though Barnes certainly wouldn't have minded if some far-sighted chap had at least raised the ceilings a trifle, simply to accommodate the gradual, relentless growth of the species. He had to hunch over and duck his head just to clear the door. But even then there was no relief for his spine. The ceilings in each of the astonishingly tiny, cube-like rooms could not accommodate a full-grown man, observed Barnes, at least no full-grown man exceeding the average height of his 14th-century ancestors. Glancing about the front room, he was delighted to spy grinning handfuls of ale-crazed men, all stooped over, their equally jovial female companions leaning against them at impossible angles. And with the walls and ceilings painted as black as the Middle Ages, the scene titillated his creative palate as would have a roomful of drunken Normans driven mad by the confinements of their malevolent Saxon dungeon. A chamber at once so stark and theatrically surreal....he couldn't help but be delighted.

{Actually, though indeed quite low, the ceiling in the front room wasn't nearly so low as those in the back rooms and the kitchen, indicating that at some point in the pub's history it had indeed been raised; however slightly. But as a result of an optical illusion caused by a couple of low-hanging, iron candle-chandeliers, the room's truly astonishing smallness, and the beer about to be swirling mischievously in his head, Barnes had convinced himself, wrongly, that the ceiling was scarcely five-and-a-half feet from the floor—as subsequent entries in his journal confirm.}

Moving forward with the improvised gait of an arthritic old man, the American proceeded directly to the bar. "Courage," he said. It was dark in the old pub, and his myopia certainly needed plenty of abatement, but he sheathed the round lenses in the pocket of his gray sportjacket anyway. Just to look cool and appear younger at the same time. The bartender, a chatty, compulsively nice youngster with red hair and freckles, short enough of height, amazingly, to be able to stand fully erect at his station, drew a pint of John Courage Bitter Ale and set the glass frothing on the bar. "Seventy-one pence," said the short English lad, interrupting his own discourse with at least half a dozen customers on at least half a dozen topics that were dear to him, and then grinning open-mouthed he cheerfully soaked up the excess foam with a wet rag. "Nice round number," said Barnes. He dropped a one-pound coin on the bar and told the boy to keep it.

There was a vacant seat over by the window. A tiny wooden plank that resembled a miniature picnic table, to Barnes it might as well have been the throne of England. He waddled over to it as quickly as a severely bent-over man can waddle, lest it be taken from him. He sat down. His lower back offered up messages of praise. Much of the beer having been spilled from his irregular gait, his right hand was sticky. He wiped it on his jeans, and took a huge gulp of the bitter ale. Wonderful....and his window-seat view was equally so. The Poultry Cross sat right across the street, Minster Street foot traffic provided a fine free theater, and the ever-quaint Oatmeal Row was only half a block east of the pub, in case he should be seized by an uncontrollable urge to stroll himself into sobriety along its cobbled sidewalks. Satisfied with the exterior view, he now examined the interior of his drinking cube. He liked the musket on the far wall, while the long brass horn above the south wall mantel, displayed just above the fireplace that heated his left leg, reminded him of the hornblowers peculiar to American racetracks and made him, briefly, think of home....Looking up at the ceiling, at the rows of low black beams, he noticed that the recessed gaps between the beams were painted orange. Fueled by the incessant buzz of close-by conversations, his imagination was able to conjure up the threat of a giant drunken bumblebee, and, pleased with himself, he smiled. This is truly a pub, he mused, complete inside and out with its own singular, custom-built atmosphere. He wondered how many more beers he would have....

Suddenly they were staring at each other.

"Oh!...'ello there, guv'nah!"

He was astonished at how different a teenager could appear when liberated from her daily work station. The 'peek-a-boo' hair style was the same, one eye always covered, but he couldn't tell what was affixed more snugly to her torso; her tight red sweater or his unchaperoned stare. And there was a welcome, wild look in the girl's green eye. She was the prisoner on weekend furlough, the kid alone in a candy store, the vamp. He loved it.

He beckoned her with a sideways flick of his head, and, after disengaging herself from a young man's formidable-looking arms, she came over.

"Good to see a familiar face," said Barnes.

"Tha' makes two!" said the girl. She sat down next to him, surprisingly close.

"What's yer name, anyway?"

"Lesley. Lesley Anne." Her voice was deeper than he suspected it could be, and her eye was half-closed. "An' there's a dash in between, guv."

"Lesley hyphen Anne, huh. Like Lesley-Anne Down."

"Tha'sit! That's why I *put* it there! I din' think a *Yank* bloke would know who she is!"

"I liked that movie she was in with Harrison Ford," said Barnes, smiling with the purely masculine pride that comes from a man thinking he has a girl right where he wants her. "You know, the one where he plays this American pilot who has this steamy affair with the wife of a Brit spy? You see it?"

"More than once!"

"That girl was so hot she was cool," Barnes amazed himself by saying.

"An' 'e was *cute*!" contributed the girl.

"By the way, no more a'that 'guv' stuff," Barnes rejoined quickly. "Call me Charlie. It'll make me feel better."

"Okay, love. It's Charlie, then."

"Beer?"

"Lovely. I'll joost 'ave a spot a-yours." Barnes stared with rapt delight as she raised his glass to her rose-glossed lips, flicked her hair aside, and entertained a man-sized mouthful of bitter. Her tiny Adam's Apple bobbed up and down in steady swallows. What she couldn't hold in her mouth drooled nonchalantly down her cheeks, chin, and thin white throat. Were only her American sisters so unabashedly free, he said to himself.

"Say, Lesley hyphen Anne, aren't you a little young ta be out drinkin' in a place like this?"

"A place like this?"

"A bar," the American said.

"Oh, f'pittysake, love! Doon't be such a dinosaur!" She took another drink of his drink. "Sorry. My error," he said, and timing his move accordingly he draped his right arm around her shoulders and casually kissed her forehead. "Umm!" she said.

The young man who only minutes before had been the lone target of the young girl's affections was watching them, sending over scornful expressions from the fireplace mantel he was leaning against. His mates either sat or crouched around him, whispering suggestions. Barnes returned his glare, but took care to fashion no expression that might indicate either too much self-satisfaction or too little indignation. He wanted to maintain his neutrality. The rejected one was not the biggest of the lot, and Barnes was sure he could take him, but he knew that fighting them all *and* their home-court advantage would be foolhardy. But he did not lift his arm from the girl's shoulders.

"Do you think yer regular boyfriend's mad at me?"

"Y'mean Randy there? Oh, *'e's* no' me-boyfriend, no' *really*....And even if 'e was, what could 'e do? The bloke bloody-*knows* if I want 'im back 'eel *come* back. The bloke's joost no' masterful enough t'sort me out! Besides, I already told 'im yer a guest at Miss P's, so as long as we no' doin' anythin'.... roight in front of 'im, I doon't see—"

"Yeah, whaddaya think of Miss Parrot? What's the deal with her? Isn't she more than just a little weird?" He tried too late to hold back. The last thing he wanted to do was conduct an interview. He knew if there was one thing all females hate it's being interviewed. He could've kicked himself....

"Aw, she's alright, love." She wiggled closer, apparently not at all put off, and as if to prove it ran her hands along various surfaces of his body. "Miss P's alright. She treats me good, she gives me things....I suppose she treats me like 'er own."

"She treats everybody else like dirt."

"She's changed, she 'as," the girl rejoined, and there was more than a hint of loyal defensiveness in her voice: "All them poxy tourists, they *changed* 'er. She wasn't always this sharp....it was *them* tha' did it."

His ever-wandering eyes floated out the window. The old Poultry Cross, less than fifty feet away, was lit up to resemble a great stone monument against the dark background of the city. It was a hexagonal stone gazebo supported by six stone pillars, with a hexagonal stone bench surrounding the post in the middle. Charlie knew from his own research that in olden times the Poultry Cross, as did poultry crosses in other towns, served as the center of Salisbury's marketplace; a designated, town-sponsored, open-air supermarket for poultry merchants to trade their fowl for cheese or linen or coin of the realm. His eyes climbed up the middle post, through the inverted-cone roof, up the stone spire to finally settle on the cross forty feet in the air. He remembered that he'd read somewhere that the Poultry Cross was built around 1335, and gazing now up at the stone crucifix he imagined he was suddenly living in that year, having a beer, observing the construction of this future historical landmark. He knew he could theoretically do this while sitting in this very pub, because the Haunch Of Venison, of course, was built fifteen years earlier. How he suddenly *longed* to have been born in about 1280! If so, he would have had the requisite youthful energy at age twenty to properly celebrate the turn of the century, and later on he could have easily raised the first flagon of ale at this venerable pub, and could perhaps have even been commissioned, by the town council, to chronicle the construction of both the pub *and* the Poultry Cross for posterity. (And since he also knew that the cathedral was completed way back in 1258, thus officially qualifying Salisbury as a 'city', his stubborn use of 'town' speaks volumes!) Getting a job would be no problem. He knew there wasn't much of a market for his material back then, but he figured every town in the 14th century could use a good 55-year-old historian. He'd sort of been *feeling* fifty-five lately, weary of fighting the pitiless encroachment of age, and so he didn't mind all that much losing two decades of his life in transit...and since he certainly wasn't getting any work done in the *20th* century....

Finally he squinted, and the stone gazebo immediately fled the clarity and simplicity of 1335, returning with regret to the dull, mottled spotlight of 1987. He couldn't tell where the illumination was coming from. With the beer and without his glasses, it could have been either the moon or some well-placed streetlamp. There were two human forms sitting on one of the stone benches.

"Seventy-one p, mate!"

He whirled back around, and the ruddy freckled lad had left his post at the bar and was standing over him. Another pint of bitter sat sweating on the table.

"What gives?"

"Oh! You were done, love, an' y'kept starin' madly out tha' window, so I 'ad Terry bring over anotha' pint. Y'do *want* it, right?" The girl and the bartender shared a sly smile.

"I dunno....sure. Thanks, I guess." He gave the lad a one-pound coin and told him to keep it. "Cheers, me-old knob-end!" said the lad. He winked at the girl, and his red-orange hair seemed to paint the ceiling as he walked away.

"Knob-end?"

"Tha' means 'e likes you," she said. She turned to him, leaned against him, pushing her breasts enthusiastically into his chest and right shoulder. So young, he thought. Firm as rubber....

"Oh look, Charlie. It's y'friends!"

"My friends?" he said quizzically. "Where?" He followed her eyes out the window. "Why in the old Poultry Cross!" rejoined the girl. He looked back over his left shoulder and out the window. It was the two formless blobs in the gazebo. They were alone. He squinted, but it wasn't enough. Reaching inside his jacket he produced the glasses, and when he put them on the characters of Silvano Constantino and Paolo Delacorte crystallized before him.

"Oh yeah. My friends," said the American. Even through eyeglasses, his instinct was to squint at something he was concentrating on. The two young men were sitting next to each other. They were sitting close but they weren't actually touching, and it surprised him. And he was both surprised and disgusted that it did surprise him.

"I think they *fancy* each other, don't you?"

"Why doesn't Miss Parrot just leave them the hell alone," he said without a question mark.

"Oh, it's no' that, love. She's joost 'ad the most terrible luck with foreigners, y'know. It's either that they leave without payin' or else they lift lit'l trinkets from the breakfast lounge or take the towels out 'the loo. She joost don't trust them, that's all."

She mashed the left breast again against his right shoulder. He could feel himself beginning to stir.

But in spite of the unrefined genius of her technique he continued to study the Italians, still sitting alone in the Poultry Cross. Funny....In days of yore it was a place wherein merchants could sell their chickens, now it was merely a sitting room for confused tourists. Sitting by themselves, it reminded him that they were in trouble. Suddenly it was important to him that they leave before Miss Ida Parrot followed through on her promise to make even more trouble. It was an intrigue, and he was the key player. He wanted to help them. He wanted them to blast their proprietress—verbally, at least—and take her down a peg. He wanted the drama of a confrontation, for his own selfish purposes. He wanted, at the same time, to find a way to avoid getting involved. He didn't know what he wanted....

"I live up Amesbury way," the girl now said to his left ear.

He turned back to her. "Is that so," he said dryly.

"Only 'bout fi'teen minutes from 'ere," she said a little more musically. She took a big swig of his caramel-colored ale, licked her lips, smiled. Her fingers fumbled through his short, wavy brown hair. His right ear now the one more accessible to her, she traced the ridges and furrows of it with her tongue. He fought both her and his own body for control of the situation:

"And you're thinking that maybe you'n I could make that fifteen-minute drive together, in the interest of improving foreign relations.... hm?"

"If y'mean what I *think* y'mean!"

"But are you sure you've had enough to drink?"

He didn't hear her confused response. He was glancing over to where the gang of young toughs was plotting his demise. Her foreplay continued unabated, lips, tongue, and fingers doing equal work. Finally she whispered, "Shall we go now?"

"I'm not sure your current not-really boyfriend over there would understand," he said with a rakish smile.

"Aw, 'e get over it! I already *told* 'im why I fancied the idea. He knows it's joost f'kicks."

"What idea?"

"Why *you'n me*, love! I told 'im it sorta set me to *quiverin'*, the idea a-doin' it with a bloke old 'nough t'be me-father."

Suddenly, instantly, he was through with her. He had reached that stage of life when a man (perhaps to the actual surprise of the women who utter them) becomes overly sensitive to such comments. She wiggled closer and said something, but for him she was no longer useful. Abruptly, then, and without preamble, his allegiance had shifted wholly to the Italians. He looked out the window. They were still sitting in the darkening solitary of the Poultry Cross. Silvano's arm was now draped over Paolo's frail shoulders. He stared until it didn't bother him. He wanted to help them. It wasn't completely in his creative self-interest to help them, but still he wanted to. Perhaps it was the intrigue. Or maybe he was simply a more inherently decent person than he suspected he was. He hoped so, but he didn't really know. Perhaps, like most everything else in Life, it was something he had no real control over....

The young girl having defused any incentive to remain in the Saxon dungeon, Barnes suddenly bolted to his feet, bent to avoid the ceiling, and dug into his jeans for another one-pound coin.

"I'll see you at breakfast tomorrow," he said.

"What? But wha' about….oh, y'joking!...yer not joking?"

"Here," he said, tossing her the coin, "have yourself another one of my beers. Tell your accomplice to keep the change."

"Did I do something wrong?" the girl said ingenuously, and then, "I mean is there really something wrong with me?"

Part of him felt like blasting her to smithereens, making her a paying example for insensitive females everywhere who believe that the swells and crevices of their bodies somehow indemnify them against the consequences of anything flippant they might say, but her youth was indemnification enough so he did not. But he also figured she deserved at least *something* sharp, something *somewhat* punitive. Perhaps, he mused, something in the guise of a compliment. So he drew a deep breath and split the difference: "Not really. You're quite likeable, Lesley hyphen Anne. In fact, your melons are really quite rubbery. Downright vulcanized, in fact. Where I come from you'd be very popular." And then, retreating behind the phoniest smile he could imagine, and taking quick little hunched-over steps, he freed himself forever from the Haunch Of Venison Pub.

"Hey! Silvano!"

It felt good to stand up straight again. His lower back rewarded him with a warm surge of blood. He didn't hurry his way across the street to the Poultry Cross. He needed a few seconds to come up with a line, an angle, something which would serve the situation better than the truth….

"Challie! So vetty, uh, wonderful to see!"

The Italian rose to shake the American's hand. He's no Olivier, thought Barnes, but at least he's trying….good for him. Paolo, smiling shyly, remained seated.

"Howya doin', man," Barnes said. Busy with covert thoughts, he stalled with silence and a smile. He wanted the Latin to know he liked him. And suddenly it had become equally important to torpedo Miss Parrot. So he needed to aid his new foreign friends, and at the same time put this tyrant in her place, but only in a way that would effectively ameliorate his own difficulties. Quite a complicated puzzle. He was confused. He wanted to safeguard the feelings of his allies, but not nearly as much as he needed the confrontation. And if the whole thing didn't wind up ultimately benefitting *him*, of course, there was no point. It was almost too much for one man to figure out. He wished he had more time to think it through…."Listen, Silvano—I'm afraid Miss Parrot's got a problem."

"Meeza Parrot? Challie! What is wrong?"

Barnes looked down. He put his left hand in his pocket, and with the right he ruffled the waves of light brown hair into a tangle, stroked and massaged the various puckered regions of his face, doing everything as convincingly as he could.

"Well it's like this, my friend. Miss Parrot was checkin' her appointment book earlier, and she noticed that she'd....accidentally booked another family in your room, yeah. Yeah, that's the story. These other people called her to confirm the appointment, and she realized she'd made a mistake and that she doesn't have room for both of you. I know you were there first, but evidently that doesn't make any difference to the old bitch. I'm sorry, man."

"But-a Challie! I no understand!"

"Silvano, you and Paolo hafta go."

"But—"

"It's simple, man. Either you or these other people hafta go find someplace else to stay, starting tomorrow, and Miss Parrot has decided that that's you. She's kickin' you out."

The Italian leaned over to discuss the situation with his companion. They spoke in their native tongue. The smaller of the two Italians remained seated, and rearranged his facial expression very little, despite the expressed urgency of the situation. Barnes glanced over at his car, alone in the rectangular parking lot, and noticed its open window. He turned up the collar of his gray jacket. It reminded him of just how cold a cold Wiltshire night can be....

"Gratzi, Challie, uh, thank you. Thank you, my friend. I vill—"

"No-no, I don't wanna know what'cher gonna do. That's yer business." Oh, how he *loved* not knowing what to expect! "I told Miss Parrot I'd give you the word if I saw you, and I did my job. So now I wash my hands of the whole mess. But if you ask me, it's a pretty lousy thing to do seein' as how you guys were there first."

(Perfect....either a confrontation with the landlady or they leave without paying....perfect either way. What a scheme. He couldn't wait.)

Silvano Constantino, his smile as broad as the distance between their two countries, again reached out to shake the American's hand. "Thank you, Challie. Gratzi." Paolo Delacorte, still disinclined to stand, tugged at Silvano's sleeve and muttered something: "Oh, Challie. Paolo, he vant-a me to say you, uh, how you say....you are most exceptional friend vee have heer!"

The American dissembled with a sheepish smile. "Don't mention it," he said. He left the Italians alone in the Poultry Cross and jogged to his car.

He tried to continue his drinking up on Castle Street, but found himself no longer in the mood. Something out of his distant past was calling to him. First thing they teach you back home, he chuckled to himself, from the time you're a kid till the day you die; don't get involved. What was it the history books said, something about no entangling alliances?...Two sips into a Mann's Brown Ale he knew he had made a mistake. But then he remembered Miss Ida Parrot, the way she looked, the things she did, the way she was, and then he remembered how desperately he needed that fleeting spark of inspiration which might at least justify sharing the same roof with her, and when the dust finally settled in his head he found that he had decided that she 'deserved it', which made him feel 'better'. He was alternately in and out of control of his emotions. But he knew that if nothing happened soon to quicken his pen, if nothing happened soon, he would have to pack up and go try it somewhere else. He sure needed something....and she *did* deserve it! And thus he allowed himself to be satisfied that his actions, in this case at least, were justified. Sort of.

But he was no fool. Regardless of what she was, he knew his actions had boiled down to the black, oily residue of his own self-interest. Period. He knew it. But at least he admitted it, to himself.....

He left the rest of the brown ale standing useless on the bar and quitted the establishment. This was a man who had never been good at drinking through a depression. Besides, it was after ten-thirty, and he knew the pubs would be closing in a few minutes anyway. His drive back was thoughtfully slow. A key had been taped to the door, and he let himself in quietly. He went straight to bed. He did not attempt to add to his journal.

"....oh my God....*oh my God*!"

It was a high-pitched scream, or at least the voice carried the all-or-nothing urgency of a scream, the type of desperate shrill cry that commands all within earshot to come a-runnin' and that's just what Barnes did. He'd taken two or three steps out of his room before he remembered he was naked, retreated, grabbed his robe and put it on even as he bounded hunched-over down the stairs.

 The sobbing was coming from the breakfast lounge. He stood transfixed and cloudy-headed at the French doors, trying to decide whether or not to go in. Having barely adjusted to the unwelcome circumstance of being awake he was still a touch disoriented, and in point of fact wasn't entirely sure what time of day it was, such was the eternally gloomy state of this hermetically-sealed establishment. He looked around. Although no light was allowed in, there were plenty of clues pointing to it being very early in the morning; the welcome, cool taste of forbidden moist air, the faint wisp of coffee nibbling at his nose, muffled bird songs barely fighting through the stark, forbidding walls. Too early. He reached into the pocket of his robe and found, luck finally with him, the round lenses. Before putting them on he rubbed some feeling back into his face. Somewhat more in charge of his faculties now, his pause at the French doors was an utterly conscious one. He had intended, naturally, to burst upon the scene as he was summoned to do, yet now the closed doors seemed to him a reprieve, a warning, a last chance to remain isolated from foreign difficulties that didn't concern him, a chance to finally succeed in not getting involved....but no. Not he. He threw them open anyway and stepped inside.

 The curtains of the bay window had been parted halfway, amazingly, allowing dawn's earliest light to flood the breakfast table in yellow. Miss Ida Parrot was slumped heavily in one of the chairs, staring blankly at a card of some kind. On the table, bathing in the warm swath of light, was a bouquet of flowers. A fiery, stupendous bouquet. It was as if the flowers were an irresistible vacuum for the light that angled in, or that perhaps, in grand, chromatic opposition to this eternally gloomy enclosure, the twin forces of Gaiety and Reason had conspired to light this room with a collage of spontaneous floral combustions. Barnes didn't know beans about flowers, but he did have a professional's appreciation of color, and there was plenty of it exploding from this out-of-place centerpiece; reds, lavenders, whites, pinks, yellows....and green foliage to tie it all together. The colors didn't seem to go together, but that's the way it always was with bouquets and he reminded himself that he was no expert and that it probably wasn't the point. It was a welcome aberration. The more he looked at it the prettier it got. But his proprietress continued to cry. He approached her cautiously, not sure of what to make of it. She seemed genuinely unaware of his presence. Even as she whimpered he lifted the card from her fingers:

Signora Parrot,
Me and Paolo, we musta go back a school.
So very sorry for short notice. You hav a
very nice place heer. Good food to! You
will finda extra night of money in onvelop.
Many thanks for thee good lessens in Engleesh!
Thank you so very much, for every
thing.   Silvano

"I mailed the letter!" she cried, pathetically aware of him now. "Dear God, I mailed the bloomin' letter...."

And suddenly he knew why he was there. This pitiless old woman was finally piteous in her unfamiliar grief, and the contrast touched him, touched him as deeply as anything had touched him in over ten thousand miles. With the sterile walls of authority torn away he saw her as a microcosm of what is most essentially, most definitively, human. He couldn't help but feel sorry for her. He felt sorry for all people, for all the flawed and frail members of his species. He now realized that this insubstantial old soul had no more control over her frailty than she did over which phylum her personal, sovereign germ of life happened to be born into. Had she been born a dog she would have bitten people and cats and smaller dogs; had she been born an insect she would have freely spread some epidemic plague with her bites, not maliciously, perhaps, but spread it she would have just the same. And he knew she could have no real, lasting control over what she did, anything she said, anything she thought, what she was. He knew that no one really does. Standing right next to where she was sitting, sobbing, quivering, he reached for her, half intentionally half involuntarily, cupping her head in his hands and drawing it to the yellow terrycloth of his robe. Her face disappeared into his stomach, the cries became muffled, the tears finding sanctuary in the towel of his garment. She sobbed and she sobbed. His hands stroked her unkempt hair, a petting stroke, smoothing it again and again while he rocked her back and forth, while he cradled the haggard head of this old woman, who through it all seemed strangely unconcerned with his being a stranger, a border, a temporary intrusion upon the mediocre crawl of her life.

In this respect, too, he realized how fully consistent she was with her race. She was not unlike the rest of this planet's chosen creatures; reactive rather than proactive. And reacting only within the limitations placed on her by her Creator. She was the cop on the take, the housewife on the make, the priest no longer on the wagon but keeping it between him and his wrathful god. She was the kid stealing quarters off his father's dresser, the father embezzling corporate overflow profits to supplement his six-figure salary. She was the 'best friend' who consistently lies to the other half of this ironic label, lying simply because it happens to be convenient, or hangs him out to dry and twist in the wind because it's personally expedient and because his subconscious mind is sure the fabric of the friendship will withstand it. She was the drunk. She was the oh-so-sure gambler and the oh-so-self-righteous bigot. She was the sad soul whose unrequited love of the needle will always supersede the love of mere human beings. She was the politician who changed his platform because the voters demanded it, who lied to his country because the times encouraged it, who changed back to his old platform when a new generation of voters insisted on it. And she was just as surely the man who cheats on his woman because society expects him to, and the beautiful woman, or girl, who eventually cheats on all her men because she knows her beauty means she can get away with it; and get away with it as many times as she needs to.

Indeed she was even the 'artist', the storyteller, who would cultivate a friendship simply, or at least primarily, because it might one day make a good yarn....

She was anybody and everybody who was ever compelled to do anything deceitful or despicable or petty or wrong, and then must one day go mournfully and melancholy to the grave without ever discovering why. She was every man and every woman. She was Mankind. And it was Barnes's job to see it, and then to know it, and then to tell it. And then move on.

Not used to being ignored, a redundant telephone called out its brassy indignation from the hallway. An unattended frying pan sent messages from the kitchen. A gathering of invisible birds played loud and derisive tunes from the tree beyond the bay window. The notes grew louder in their ridicule, as if the thick, forbidding windowglass was temporarily powerless to mute them. Presently, the sun shot its glare over the top of the curtain rod, a half-inch horizontal scythe that split the ceiling in two. Blessed dawn. The kinetic reprise of morning, a daily second chance for every darkened corner of the world. The young man released her head from his benign grasp, barely conscious of his one final stroke of her hair. His compassion had a short attention span. Already his thoughts were thick with the grassy loam of Newbury. Post time for the first race was two o'clock. No time to waste. There were farm animals yet to be wagered on, stories yet to write, castles to see, meals to savor, pints of dark beer to swill, grown women to prospect, and he needed to go and ingurgitate it all. He couldn't help it. Nor did he wish to help it. Time to move on. He mentioned something about smelling something burning, but Miss Ida Parrot didn't seem to even hear him. She continued to whimper, a raw, pathetic dirge, then looked out the bay window for a long time, then finally up and into the strange, distant face of the American.

"Those poor boys!" sobbed the old woman. "Those poor, sweet, dear *Italian boys!*"

A YANK IN WINDSOR

Author's Notes

This is one of the most-recently-started and therefore one of the most-recently-finished stories in the collection. In fact I wrote the whole thing in August of 2011, a full quarter century after the incident upon which it is loosely based, a short cab ride west of London, occurred. I wanted to have a handful of stories written right around the same time the "L.A. JOURNAL" collection was published to actually *be in* the collection. Ergo, this is one of six stories written (or at least finished) between 2010 and 2012 that you'll find in this book.

    The incident between the cab driver and my dad really happened, during a 5-hour London layover on our way to an African safari back in the mid-80s. All the scenes in the L.A. portion of the story are contrived, for artistic purposes, but the portion of the story which takes place in London transpired almost exactly as I have rendered it here fictionally. It remains, to date, one of my two or three favorite memories of my father's simple yet exceptional life.

    I wrote the rough draft of this story in only one day. I wrote it straight through. Took just a few hours. It was easy. All subsequent rewrites of this story aside (rewrites being both the really fun part and the really time-consuming part about being a writer of fiction), I have never written the complete rough draft of a short-story in one single solitary calendar day before, and doubt if I ever will again.

    A Yank in Windsor is unique to this collection in another way, besides being the most-quickly-written tale herein, in that it is the only Charlie Barnes short-story told in the 1st-person. I'm not entirely sure why I chose that method of narration, why I chose Charlie's voice over my own. To hit the right emotional note maybe. Just felt right.

A YANK IN WINSDOR

Good evening. First of all, I'd like to thank all of you for coming. Or, more accurately, thank you all for inviting me. Just goes to show ya—a guy lucks out and publishes a couple books and sneaks on a few late-night talk shows, and people will fall all over each other just to hire him to make a speech.... even if he doesn't know what the hell he's talking about! Thank you, thank you—but please, in lieu of applause, just throw money.

Seriously, all kidding aside, that was me not being entirely fair to me. Fact is I *do* know about it. A lot more than most people do, that's for sure. Just not from experience. What I mean is, World War Two had been over for ten years and I still wasn't quite born yet. So it's not like I lived through The Blitz or Pearl Harbor or Auschwitz, or anything like that....

And I'd also like to thank you for holding this year's annual Fifteenth Air Force Reunion right here, in my adopted home town of Los Angeles. Pushing forty, the lure of travel isn't half as seductive as it was when I was a much younger man. Oh, and all you out-of-towners who are staying in hotels around here just so you can be near the airport, please don't hold so-called suburbs like El Segundo or Inglewood against us, okay? There's more to L.A. than the strip clubs on Imperial Highway, or a 'rubber chicken' like this one at an ugly hotel on Century Boulevard. Make sure to go see some of the sights while you're in town. Take in a Dodger game. Afterwards, drive up and down Hollywood Boulevard and count the transvestites! Spend an afternoon at the La Brea Tar Pits. Or in Chinatown. Or up at the Huntington Library in San Marino, near Pasadena, staring at The Blue Boy. Go somewhere. Do something.

Anyway, it's great to be here. My dad loved these annual reunions. He loved the Fifteenth. He loved traveling around the country seeing his old war buddies, swapping stories, reliving the best times of his youth. And that's the whole point, isn't it? Isn't that's what makes these gatherings so much fun, so much joy for all you wonderful veterans? It's the remembering. Remembering when you were young. Remembering what it was like to be in your prime, lusting after adventure, scared stiff, never more alive. I myself have often regretted never having served in and survived a war. I imagine that recalling your dubya-dubya-two days must be like remembering what the essence of just being twenty or twenty-one years old was like. Like maybe how it felt getting an eyeful of a dazzlingly beautiful woman, what it felt like in your twenty-year-old gut wanting to have her so bad you almost jumped right out of your own skin. Is that what it feels like, men? I'm a lot younger than all you fellas, and *I'm* having a hard time remembering what that feels like....

Anyway, my father told me that these reunions were some of the best times of the final few years of his life. For which I am grateful to all of you.

Having said all that, I now hasten to add that there is lately a prevailing mood around this cockeyed country of ours that what you crusty old chaps did doesn't matter. That everyone has forgotten. Or never knew, or was never told, or just doesn't care. That our nation has retreated in both tangibility and spirit, over the years, retreated from that victory of victories you brave men achieved for us fifty years ago today. Even here, in this very room, I have this very evening suffered the cynicism. We were all having cocktails a couple hours ago, and I was milling about, saying hello to some of the members of my dad's squadron in the 459th Bombardment Group, shaking hands with some of the guys in his own plane's flight crew who I recognized, getting into little conversations. Listening in, mainly. And all I seemed to hear from you debonair captains of the air was *complaining*! Nobody cares, nobody knows, nobody respects us, blah blah blah. Pretty depressing stuff, guys. I have to tell you, I was disappointed. It felt like—to me at least—like my dad's entire bomb group had become infected all at once, and through and through, with all those old worn-out clichés having to do with how 'nothing in the modern world can compare to the good old days', and 'everything has gone downhill since *I* was in the service' or 'nothing we did for these ungrateful young whippersnappers matters a tinker's damn anymore', is that about it, men? Did I get it right? Feeling a bit tender and sad are you, that what you risked and won in the flak-torn skies over Europe fifty years ago no longer matters?

Well, old men, I'm here tonight to tell you that you are wrong. You're as wrong as you can be.

But rather than me just giving you a stern lecture you about it—after all, I am an old American History major with a snooty Berkeley degree, maybe that's why your treasurer hired a non-vet to be your keynote speaker on V.E. Day—I think I'd rather tell you a bedtime story which even the oldest, crustiest, and most cynical of you officers and gentlemen will appreciate....

It was about ten years ago. Almost ten years ago to the day, in fact. My mother had just died, Dad was pretty depressed, and I was looking around for some way to take his mind off things and cheer him up a little. Must be a tough thing, I said to myself, being in your sixties and having your wife of thirty-six years die on you. Then I remembered something Dad had always told me. He was always saying how much he wanted to see Africa before he died. "Son, I bet'cha it would be just great to stand there smack in the middle of the Serengeti Plains and just stare at all those tens of thousands of animals in one place, *gad*, it must be *unbelievable!*" he would grin and bark in that familiar Midwestern twang. For years I never thought a thing about it. But after Mom died, suddenly it was like the most natural thing in the world to not only think about it but actually *do* it, because there I was, without even asking him if he still wanted to go, hastily putting together an eight-day African safari for my dad and me, and before you know it we're updating our passports and getting our shots and packing our bags and before you know it we're on a plane and off to Kenya we go.

The problem is that there are no non-stop flights to Nairobi. We had to lay over in London. Just as well. Each leg was eleven hours long, and I'm not sure I could have stood being on a plane for over twenty hours straight with my old man, listening to him gripe away and complain about everything like *you* old men.

So we land in London for a five-hour layover. We get off the plane, we start to walk through the terminal, and my dad suddenly sits down on a bench. What are you doing? I say. He says he's waiting for the plane to Nairobi. I remind him it won't be taking off for another five hours, c'mon Dad, I say with great urgency, get off your ass, let's go do something. He says he's not going anywhere. I say what the heck are you talking about? And it soon becomes clear that he intends to just sit there on that bench for five hours, for fear of missing his connecting flight. No, I'm *not* kidding! Sure, you laugh now, but he was serious. He was so conservative by nature that he was perfectly content to just sit there on that bench for five hours doing nothing, just to 'make sure' that he didn't miss his flight. Anyway, that was my dad. What a worry-wart....

Anyhow, after much prodding and cajoling, I am finally able to convince him that we are *not* going to miss our connecting flight, and that we are *not* going to just sit here for five hours, and that since he's never been to England and probably will never come here again we are damn well going to go out and *see* something. Anything. He finally, grudgingly, agrees. I'd already been to England a couple times by then, many more times since, and I realized at once that the most interesting thing in the area, not too far from Heathrow Airport and not too boring, is Windsor Castle. One of the Queen's many weekend getaways, five hundred servants and all. And only a few miles away. Fine. We hail a cab.

Dad was so nervous during that cab ride. In his mind, he was only a few hours from realizing his lifelong dream of seeing the Serengeti Plains, and so he was sure that he was tempting fate by leaving the airport and that some great catastrophe would surely befall us and we would miss our connecting flight. As for me, I remember what an absolutely gorgeous day it was. Balmy, breezy, lots of puffy white clouds mixed with dark, foreboding black ones, dreamily cool and overcast even though it was late spring, typical England. A picture-postcard day. Truth be told, part of me was wishing that we *would* miss our connecting flight, so that we could spend our whole vacation in England instead. I'm not much of a wildlife guy. I figure if you've seen one zebra or hairy wildebeest or stupid sleeping leopard you've surely seen them all....

Neither one of us said much at first. Dad just sat there, nervous as a cat. I remember glancing at him occasionally, trying not to laugh out loud. It was, oh, only 'bout half an hour to Windsor I think, not a long drive, I don't remember exactly how long. Anyway, we were almost there, when we drove right by this old abandoned airfield:

"Son, lookie here—that's an old American bee-twenty-four bomber!" Dad suddenly yelps.

"Isn't that what you flew, Dad?" I volleyed back.

"Darn tootin'. Bee-seventeens and bee-twenty-fours. This must be one of the bases we occupied during the war, before the invasion. You know, as a launching point."

"But you yourself flew out of Italy, right?"

"That's right. Cerignola, Italy. Gad, that was a crummy little town...."

Suddenly, after not saying a word and barely moving a muscle, our cab driver finally comes to life. He turns halfway around, showing us his left profile, his right eye thankfully still on the road. At least I assumed it was on the road. Frankly he appeared to be driving more by feel than by sight. He was a good driver.

"You was in the war, guv?" he pipes up. He had a very pleasant cockney-ish accent.

"Yes sir," Dad says, adding, very militarily, "Roland Barnes, captain, at your service. I was attached to the four hundred and fifty-ninth bombardment group, Fifteenth Air Force. We bombed ball bearing plants and railroad yards in Germany and Czechoslovakia. Flew nine missions, 'was in my plane getting ready for the tenth when the pink flare went up. That was some day!"

The cabbie's face went dark at first. Very depressed-looking. It set me to studying him. It was a very worn-out face, no doubt a very white face in its youth but lots of broken blood vessels and acne pockmarks had rendered it darker, redder, ruddier. His nose was a mess, like it had been caught in a garbage disposal. I figured it was either from endless drinking or a lifetime of getting in fights in bars. His clothes were old, ratty and smelly, but his hat was immaculate, an old-fashioned flying officer's cap in very good condition. That should have clued me in right away that something was up. You'll have to forgive me for going on and on about this guy. It's the writer in me. Over-active imaginations are our crosses to bear. It could be worse. I *could* be a bitter old man who complains all the time. Like *you* guys.

Finally, after a few seconds of silence, the guy turns his whole face back to the road, and says, or rather sort of mutters, very softly, "I wanted to go....'was only sixteen at the end, but I....I *cudda* gone, they woodn' *let* me go....I cudda done it." I barely heard him. But I heard him.

Dad and I then sort of forgot about our cabbie for awhile, we leaned back, and we just enjoyed the final few minutes of our drive to Windsor. We had the windows down, it was loud, the wind was whipping in, it was cool without being too cold, it was marvelous. And we got to talking about the war. Dad never had any trouble talking about the war. He loved it. I guess that's the difference between slogging right through the muck and horror of war and flying *above* it all. He went on and on about all the USO dances, about his pre-flight training in Columbia, Missouri and Lubbock, Texas, his nerves, how he actually failed his first couple flight solos, then the going overseas for the first time in his life, meeting the fellas, forming a nine-man flight crew, the missions, how cold it was in the planes, "*colder than Sam Hill*" he liked to say, and on that subject he told me about the time he forgot his electric gloves *and* his electric socks on this one mission and his hands and feet froze nearly solid, and of course he told me all my favorite stories that he had told me many times before, like his selling chocolate on the black market between missions to Italian kids on the street, his going AWOL to go see Rome and not getting caught, getting promoted, going *back* to Rome, how he marveled that in Rome men would just up and drop their pants and pee in the streets if they felt like it, how every day was a once-in-a-lifetime adventure. Once in awhile our cabbie would cock his head a little, as if trying to angle his left ear to be able to hear us better....I can see some of your confused faces, wondering why it wasn't his *right* ear. Remember, this was England. They drive on the wrong side of the road and the wheel is on the wrong side of the car! That's why it was his *left* ear he was using to try to eavesdrop on us, his *closer* ear. Anyway, I could tell he was doing his best to hear what we were saying. But he never turned around or glanced back. Or said a word.

Well, we finally pulled up to Windsor Castle. But before we could make a move to get out of the cab the cabbie suddenly spins fully around in his seat, facing us, he looks Dad right in the eye, and extends his hand. Dad had no choice but to shake it.

"I just want to say thank you," he began. There was a plaintive, far-away look I his eye. He kept talking, his thick accent getting thicker the more emotional he got: "I knows we'd never've 'ad a chance without you Yanks comin' over 'ere. I knows it. A lot of me-fellow Englishmen like to take the Mickey out've the Americans, it's bloody-good sport i'tis, but they bloody-well knows it too. They joost don't like to *admit* it! But I knew it even then, even when I was but a sprout of a lad. I only wish they'd a-let me go off and fight the bloody Jerries me-self."

Neither one of us could say anything. I know I couldn't. I looked at Dad, and there were tears running down his cheeks. The two of them were just staring at each other. And neither was letting go of the other's hand.

With no reply forthcoming, the cockney cabbie continued: "And me-mum fancied the Yanks as well, guv. She took in two or three fly-boy pilots in forty-four, to 'elp pay the rent, and they treated her joost like proper gentlemen would treat a lady. Very respectful, they was. And at night they would let me wear their flight jackets and caps before me-mum shooed me off to bed. Roight nice blokes."

It was at that point, when I heard him say the word "caps", when I realized his cap wasn't a *British* flying officer's cap. It was American. Complete with that familiar metal shield of an eagle clutching a handful of thirteen arrows while the other talon clutches an olive branch with thirteen leaves. *E pluribus unum* inscription and all. I only wish I'd had my camcorder with me.

"Well, I don't know what to say. Nobody's ever thanked *me* for winning the war!" my father finally managed to spit out. He was always trying to lighten the mood with a joke, you know.

"But you did, guv. It *was* Yanks like you 'won that war. We Brits joost 'elped out a bit, didn't we—ha-ha! Anyway, I say to you now for all of England, thank you very, very much. You saved us, mate. Sorry the thanks be-comin' a bit late."

"God bless you, my man," Dad said, "God bless you." And he quickly exited the cab.

At this point it was I who was shaking the cabbie's hand, and I thanked him for making my Dad's day....or rather for making his month, his year, whatever. By this time I'm sure I was crying too. He said not to mention it and that he was only telling the truth.

"How much do I owe you?" I asked him.

"Oh....six pounds and ninety p," he said, "But no charge. It's my honor, i'tis."

"Nonsense," I said. He'd already provided me with one of the greatest experiences of my life, I wasn't about to make him pay a fee for it. I handed him a twenty-pound note.

The cabbie stared at Mr. Shakespeare's face like he'd never seen a twenty. Yes, I said Shakespeare. As some of you who were stationed there know, that's something else that's different about Britain, compared to America. Over there they put men of achievement on their money, like artists, writers, composers, and scientists. With us, other than Ben Franklin, it's only the damn politicians! Anyway, "This is too much, lad," he said, "And I can't make change for a twenty anyhow. Seriously, it's on me."

"You don't need to make change," I said. "Just tack it up on the dashboard for a souvenir if you don't wanna spend it. Besides, I could never actually give you enough for what you did for me today. Thank you, my friend." We locked eyes for a couple seconds. I'm fairly sure he'd never cadged a two hundred percent tip before. But before he could come up with another rebuttal stating why he couldn't accept it, I got out.

Life is funny, isn't it? How one thing leads directly to another? When I think of how hard Dad tried to get us to stay put in that airport terminal, and what we both would have missed....

Well, that's all I have for you tonight, gentlemen. And thanks to an old cockney cab driver with an American flying officer's cap, I suspect I earned my fee. So don't you dare think what you brave men did fifty years ago doesn't matter. It matters. It will always matter. Don't ever think it doesn't. And don't let me hear any of you ever *say* it doesn't.

Or I will personally wash out the offending officer's mouth with soap.

Thank you again, survivors of the Fifteenth Air Force. Thanks for having me. And allow me to thank you all for the very same thing that cab driver thanked my father for, for winning the war for all us young whippersnappers.

Y'know, you are some very lucky people sitting there. And not just because you survived the last 'good' war in Human history. You also got to experience the greatest *adventure* in Human history. I'm jealous. I'm jealous of each and every one of you. God bless you all. Good night.

A COMMUNITY OF HOLINESS

Author's Notes

My son (Robbie then, Rob now) was only six or seven years old when he uttered the phrase which became the title of this story. The minute I heard that sweet little boy utter such a strange, mystical, adult combination of words, I knew I just had to write a story to go with it. Even though at the time I didn't have any idea what the story was. Probably the only time I ever wrote the title of a story before the story itself.

Of all the Barnes stories, this is the last one. The last one as in Charlie is older here than in any other Charlie Barnes story. Late-forties. Of course that could change later on, if I live long enough and something really interesting happens to inspire me! At which point I might just drag ol' Charlie out of mothballs for one last go-around. You never know.

A Community Of Holiness was begun in earnest in 2007, put away for a few years, exhumed, and then finally finished in September of 2012, just before this book went to the printer; one of the shortest stories in the collection finished nearly five years after commencing it.

I guess I got sidetracked….

But I'm glad I got back to it in time for it to be part of this collection. Because at the end of the day, *A Community Of Holiness* just happens to be my favorite short-story. By any author.

A COMMUNITY OF HOLINESS

"Why don't you just stop thinking about it? You're just a little *boy*."

The man leaned slightly forward in his favorite living room chair and stared. Staring back with wet eyes was his son, his only child. Eight years old. Even though the chairs they sat in were identical twins it was tacitly understood that the one nearest the T.V. was the son's, while the one under the reading lamp belonged to the father. Neither ever sat in the other's chair; it was understood. The chairs swiveled, allowing them to point their tense countenances directly at one another without twisting their backs or craning their necks. They were good chairs. Stuffed, efficient, comfortable. But the chairs were surely the only relatives of comfortable inhabiting this room, on this black Sunday evening in November....

"I'm *not* a little boy."

"I know you're not, son. I know. What I mean is, why don't you just—"

"Don't you think I've *tried*? Don't you think I *want* to be happy again? I can't stand this, Daddy, I can't, I *can't*. I just miss him. I miss him *so much*. Help me, Daddy....*help* me! I don't know what to *do*!"

"Everybody dies, son."

"I know, Daddy, I know you always taught me that. But I mean *so soon*."

"Soon?"

"Remember when those bad men drove the airplanes into the buildings and killed everybody I told you I had a broken heart in my stomach because I thought maybe they killed Uncle Rick too because he lived in New York City? But he was okay and so I felt better, and now it's only a couple years later and it's so neat he's living out here with us even though he always said he always hated Los Angeles even back when he lived here when you guys were little kids like me and then he *dies*. It's not *fair*! Why did Uncle Rick have to die *now*, Daddy? I'm only eight! Why *now*?"

"He was a stubborn man, son. And he wasn't very lucky." Vague enough, he thought....'plenty of time to fill in the gaps down the line. He wondered how many more times they would get to sit in the big stuffed chairs together....he started to calculate things in his head....but it was a depressing equation, and he banished it from his mind before he drew his next breath.

"I miss him so much. And I'm sad all the time. It makes me want to die too."

"Don't talk like that, Gust Barnes! That's *silly*. You've got a great life ahead of you and I won't have you talking like that, 'you hear me?"

The boy started to sob again. He was quivering. The man felt sorry right away for snapping at the poor kid like that, especially in his hour of need. But it was the boy who said, "I'm sorry, Dad," and that just made him feel worse. What do you do with a confused little kid who says out loud he wants to die, he asked himself....

"Life is a miracle, son. You need to treat it that way."

"Doesn't *feel* like a miracle."

"Sure it does. Life is full of miracles every day."

"What miracles...."

"How 'bout the Red-Sox? Hadn't won the World Series in eighty-six years until last week. I bet'cha the folks in *Boston* think it's a miracle. And how 'bout when you ask me to punch something you're curious about into the Google page on my computer? Doesn't it always pop right up like magic?"

"I'm serious, Dad."

"So am I, son. So am I."

"I really miss him...."

He was running out of ideas. Time to break out the heavy artillery:

"Son, would you like to go visit Uncle Rick's grave sometime?"

The wet face brightened at once: "*Could* we?"

"Of course. I've just been waiting for the right day."

The little face tightened up and the eyes went side-to-side. It was his 'I'm thinking' face....

Finally: "What about *Grampa*? Could we maybe go to Africa together someday, and see *his* grave? I've never been to Africa."

"I know you haven't, my boy. Because if you'd gone off to Africa, I think I would have been one of the first ones to notice it."

"How come Grampa's all the way in Africa, Daddy?"

"It's a long story."

"But I *like* your long stories."

"I know you do, son. I know you do."

"So can we? Go see him?"

"Sure we can. Some day we will. I'll introduce you. He'd be happy to know you wanted to stop by."

"Daddy, do you think Grampa would have liked me?"

The father started to lose it, but somehow he caught himself in time.

"You bet he would have liked you, son. You guys would have gotten a kick out of each other. After all, I did give you his middle name, and you *hafta* like somebody if they get named after you. I think it's a rule."

"So you think he would like me cuz we have the same name?"

"Sure. Plus there's one other reason."

"What."

"Because you're a great kid. That's what."

The eight-year-old face broke into a smile. Not an ordinary smile, but one of those once-in-a-lifetime smiles which stick in a father's brain forever. He couldn't remember the last time his son smiled any kind of smile, it had been days, maybe weeks, and his heart ached with sadness, love, and joy. And for the moment at least, relief....

"Thanks, Daddy. So can we go see Uncle Rick *tomorrow*?"

The man smiled back. He took off his glasses, pretended to bend and adjust the temples of the huge black plastic frames, and then put them back on. "How 'bout next weekend. You have school to go to tomorrow, remember? Now let's both go to bed. I'm tired."

"You don't have to walk me to school, Daddy. I can do it by myself. You're tired."

"I know I don't have to, son. I want to. Now c'mon, quit stallin' and go to *bed*!"

The boy ran upstairs to wash his face and brush his teeth. He was well trained in these areas. The father followed him slowly up the stairs to supervise. The boy's mother was already fast asleep in the master bedroom, behind closed doors, so she would be of no use to them this evening. It was a slower stair-climb than usual. He was a tall man and, at this stage of his life, a big man as well. Not fat, but big. And he'd begun to feel both his age *and* his size the last couple years....like now....a painful clicking in the right knee on every upward step, fatigue halfway up like he'd just sprinted fifty yards, even though, ironically, the clicking knee meant he would never be sprinting anywhere, not ever, ever again....sure does hurt....damn. This is one thing at least, he thought now, he would not regret about moving to a one-story house. One thing he would not miss. Stairs.

The boy raced past his father and into his bedroom, whereupon he dove face first into the bed. His dad flipped him over onto his back, tickled his ribs for a few seconds, which tickled them both into laughter, ruffled the blond hair that had not yet begun to turn even a little bit brown, and then pulled the covers up and into place.

"Thanks for talking to me, Daddy. I think I feel better."

"You'll feel even better tomorrow morning, my dear Master Gustav Barnes. Bad things never seem so bad the next morning."

"Okay. Thanks again. I feel better, I think."

The man leaned down and kissed the boy on the forehead and on each soft white cheek.

"Your new beard is weird, Daddy! It *tickles*."

"All dads are a little weird, son. In one way or another. Just be patient with us."

"Daddy?"

"Yes, Gust."

"I love you, Daddy."

The man smiled down upon his only son. The way his own father had smiled down upon him, so many, many times, oh so very long ago. He smiled very hard, so as not to cry. So as not to betray *all* his sorrows. Not now....not the right time.

"I love you too, son. Some day you'll understand how much."

"I hope I'm not scared when I'm standing right next to Uncle Rick's grave...."

"You won't be. Good night."

He switched off the light, slowly and carefully descended the stairs, and curled up on the couch. He was asleep in ten minutes.

The next morning they let the boy's mother sleep in and had cold cereal for breakfast. They started out from the big yellow house at around 7:15. The school was only a few blocks away. Just a short, pleasant walk. *Everything* is walking distance in Sierra Madre, the man mused....'not many L.A. County towns you can say *that* about. The boy wore a red sweater under a purple backpack, and as he walked he intermittently bounced a small basketball which he would routinely conceal in the backpack right when he got to school so as not to get into any trouble. The man wore a black sportcoat. He wanted his son to know, or at least sense deep down, that all the other kids could see he was one of the classiest dads because he was wearing a sportcoat, which despite his expanding waistline he held together with the middle button only. But since he liked wearing suits and sportcoats anyway he convinced himself not to feel weird about it, about putting on airs. They were about halfway there before either of them spoke:

"Daddy, do you ever wonder where we go after we die since we don't believe in God?"

The man started to smile but realized at once it wasn't the time.

"Son, just because I don't believe in God or pray to a god the way a religious person does, doesn't mean *you* hafta think that way."

"Daddy, we don't believe in God," the boy repeated, gravely, as if affirming a widely-understood truth or handed-down father/son rule. He was always doing things like that....

"Okay. Well yeah, I think about it sometimes. Don't have any answers for you, though."

"That's okay. I think I've got it."

"You've got it? Got what?"

"What *happens*."

"Well don't keep an old man in suspense, let's have it."

"Well....the first thing is Heaven. I don't think there is a heaven. It's more like *guvvament* stuff."

"You mean like a government with God as the President and Jesus as the Vice-President, and maybe all the Disciples as the cabinet members? Sort of like that?"

"Sort of. But not as religious. But it has to be *sort of* religious. So it can last forever."

"You mean like reincarnation?"

"*No*, Daddy. Not reincarnation. That would ruin *everything*."

....A scene from a Woody Allen movie darted into his head...."*Hannah and Her Sisters*".... something about reincarnation and Nietzsche and the theory of eternal recurrence, and Woody worrying about being reincarnated and having to see the Ice Capades over and over again....little Gust wouldn't be a Woody Allen fan for years, so the father had no idea why reincarnation would 'ruin everything', but the why wasn't as important as the what, and so for the moment, despite his fatherly curiosity, he let it go:

"So religious but not *too* religious, huh? Sounds like sort of a tough problem."

"And it's more like a *town* guvvament than the whole country and president type thing. Like a community. I like that word, don't you Daddy?"

"Community? Sure."

"I like the way it sounds to my ears."

"Me too. Community. One of the best-sounding words we got," the man said, smiling secretly.

The boy dribbled the basketball a couple of times, then tossed it out in front of him a few feet while spinning it backwards, just to see if after it hit the sidewalk it would bounce right back to him. It did.

"So you know what I wish? I wish that it's sort of a *partly* heaven, because even though I'm like you and I don't believe in God I still sorta think there *is* God, or, I don't know, something *like* a god, you know, and maybe there's a place *like* Heaven, for everybody, but what I want it to be is something *different*."

"Okay. If you say so," the man said. "Tell me."

"We just need a place where all the dead people who we know, or that are like loved ones of ours, can stay together. Sort of a community! But since everybody's dead it has to be a *different kind* of community, like, I don't know exactly....maybe like a community of *holiness*? Like maybe a holy meeting place? Like a holy meeting place in a community for people who die so that they don't have to be alone forever. But not *too* holy. That way they won't feel like they're being told what to do all the time, like when they were alive. Daddy, do you think there might be something up there like that?"

"Don't see why not, my boy. I've never heard it explained better. I don't see why it wouldn't be *exactly* like that."

They walked a few more steps without saying anything. Only about two more blocks to go....

"Doing this helps me get through, Dad."

"Get through what?"

"The day."

"You really have trouble getting through the day sometimes?"

"Don't *you*?"

The father paused to consider the son. He took a moment to remind himself that just because he was only eight didn't necessarily mean he wasn't as smart and shrewd as anyone. Best to answer an unwanted question with another question: "Exactly what is it I do that helps get you through the day?"

"This, Daddy. *This*. Caring enough to walk me to school. Most of the kids wouldn't be caught dead being seen with their parents on the way to school. They're so dumb."

"Well I'm flattered you enjoy my company, Gust."

The son glanced up at his father with exasperation splashed across his perfect, porcelain-white face: "Sometimes you don't get stuff at all, Daddy."

"*Now* what did I do...."

The boy stopped walking in order to better answer back, but with his face and eyes still pointed straight ahead. The better to get through it, no doubt: "Daddy, don't you think I know you're hurting *too*? First your brother, and now you having to take some crummy job you don't even want because we need the money and because Mom nags at you about it when you think I can't hear you and you normally wouldn't do it for even one day or even for a *whole bunch* of money, because you know it's not good enough for you and it's just because the world *makes* you do it? But even though you're having a bad time you still think of *me* before you think of *you*."

A monologue worthy of an eight-year-old Hamlet, the father found himself thinking, while at the same time hoping he'd be able to remember it all. As in word-for-word....

"Don't give me too much credit, son. Maybe that's just what a father is supposed to do, 'walk his kid to school. Or take a crummy job to pay the bills."

"But don'tcha see? It's not the actual walking of me to school, it's that you want to do it *for me*. It makes me feel really important. So thanks, Dad. It really calms my stomach down so it doesn't jump all the time."

"Good. Little kids shouldn't go around with jumpy stomachs!"

"I'm serious. I'm trying to tell you I think I'm fine now. I figured it out."

"Oh, you *did,* did you? *What* did you figure out?"

"I don't know....life, I guess. You were right, Dad. Life is really the cool little things, not dumb ol' big things. Just like you've always told me. Big things are just for lucky famous guys. You walking me to school when you're trying your hardest to be unhappy in secret *is* one of the cool little things. Makes me want to live again."

The boy looked up at his father, finally, and his father grimly stared back. He pulled his eyes away when he felt them tearing up from the inside out. He fastened them to the eavesdropping mountains just to the north, just to give them something to look at while he digested everything. Remarkable, he thought. Remarkable. They started walking again. He put his arm around the boy's shoulders and slowed his stride so they could walk in step. The boy stopped dribbling the basketball and just held it under his left arm while they walked. They didn't say anything more for the final two hundred or so yards before they reached the school crossing guard. Before crossing the street and running to his classroom the boy stuffed the ball into his backpack and zipped it up.

The man squatted down so he could kiss the boy on the forehead and look him in the eye.

"Work hard in school, son. Always do the best you can. Make a difference."

"Okay. You too, Dad."

"Me too?"

"Make a difference. Do something *big* today, like you always tell *me* to do."

"Like what?"

"I dunno....whatever you think you can do best. Then when I get home we can sit in the big chairs and both tell each other what we did!"

"Okay, son. It's a deal. I'll do something big. I think I finally have an idea that may qualify." He stood up by first pushing the ground with his fists, to take the strain off of his knees until he was halfway up. His legs took over from there. Then he smoothed out his black corduroys and re-buttoned the black sportcoat. The middle button only.

"And we def'nitly can go see Uncle Rick? You promise?"

"Definitely. I promise."

The blond head broke into a smile, and the boy who it belonged to ran across the street, past the slowly-walking crossing guard holding up a red octagonal stop sign, he then ran all the way up the hill to the school's huge front door and then disappeared inside.

When the man got back to the house he was relieved to discover that his wife's car was already gone. She's even more eager to avoid basic human contact than I am, he thought. Good....the last thing he needed to deal with on this particular morning was her. Especially now that everything had been decided. And exactly how in the world will I tell the boy about *this*, the man now asked himself....how do you tell a boy who hasn't even had time to recover from the death of someone close to him that his parents are splitting up, that his dad is moving out of the big yellow house, that they'll never sit across from each other in the big stuffed chairs again....yet one more row of hurdles to help the boy over....and still such a *little* boy.... such a sweet....sweet little....*damn*! Hasn't that kid been through enough? Just how many more hurdles would he have to help him clear, he wondered, how many more blows would he have to soften, how many more, before his son would be old enough and tough enough and sufficiently jaded enough to suffer Life's cruel, unprovoked blows on his own? Gust is right, he said to himself....it *isn't* fair....none of it. It never is.

He poured himself a huge glass of red wine, forced his legs to take him up the stairs, went into his private office, and sat down at his desk. His writing desk. One of the few things he would take with him in a month or two (after the holidays, of course) when it was time. He looked out the window and northward, to the San Gabriel Mountains looming in the near distance. They were beautiful. So beautiful. So close he could practically reach out through the window of his office and touch them. Practically every day of his life he had gazed upon them, even if some of those days it was only for a few seconds. Oh sure, there were days when he was a kid—those strange, science fiction days before automobile emissions controls—when he could barely even see the mountains through the smog. Some days he *couldn't* see them. But he knew they were there. They were always there. As the northern picture-border of every town in Los Angeles County he had ever lived in—from Altadena in the early years, to Pasadena, to a Downtown L.A. high-rise right after college, from Van Nuys and Studio City to the west to Bradbury and Arcadia to the east and half a dozen towns in between—they were always there. They were the mountains which had been the controlling mistress-landmark of his entire life, ever since he was Gust's age, younger even. Ever since Gust's grandfather, and namesake, brought the family out from Iowa to Southern California over four long decades ago. Looming so close, they always struck him as so much larger and taller and more awesome than they really were. These were no Himalayas these hills, hell they weren't even half as high as the Rockies, but for him it would forever remain the mother of all mountain ranges. After all, wasn't the very name of this quaint, obscure little village which for the moment he still called home, a tiny town folded neatly and covertly between Arcadia and Pasadena and unknown even to thousands of his fellow L.A. County residents, indeed Spanish for 'mother range'? Yes. Sierra Madre indeed. This he would miss. He would miss this utterly gorgeous, utterly sublime, so-perfect-it-looks-phony picture postcard of a view. Turns out it *wasn't* perfect....turns out it *was* phony....like most things.

But for now, amazingly, while no less concerned with what to do about his boy and how to do it, or with what his new life would be like and how he would live it, his momentary thoughts were only of excitement. Anticipation, purpose, and excitement. And it felt like Heaven....or whatever damn thing Gust was telling him was up there in place of Heaven. But that damn thing was the whole point! He had to get it down, right away, before he lost the thread of it....It had been a long time since he'd played the student, and he was grateful to a nameless, faceless, surprisingly forgiving god for providing him with the best teacher a disillusioned, middle-aged man could ever have. A boy. A little boy. *His* little boy. His own son. He couldn't see the way out of his wilderness not twenty-four hours ago, not to mention twenty-four weeks ago, much less twenty-four or forty-eight or a hundred and fifty months ago, and suddenly he knew he was never really lost at all. He just needed something to remind him of why he was put here in the first place.

And therein was the miracle.

He placed his hands on the keyboard, and for the first time in fourteen years he prepared to type out letters of words for the purpose of creating something. And not merely the words of a man more worried about creating a paycheck than he is committed to creating something worthwhile. Not words to pay the bills, not comically made-up yarns reeking of commonplace pulp. Not the kind of cheap formula writing that any skilled sell-out could do (and from experience he knew usually *would* do), but rather actual fiction. Literary fiction. Art. *Literature*! A feeling of lightness, airiness, and virtual electricity filled his fingertips and traveled deliciously up his forearms. It would be a short-story, he decided. Novels are usually the discharge of barely creative arrogance (he now mused in a purely self-critical moment of easy self-deprecation), or the insatiable need to get into print, not so much Art as entertainment. But not stories. No money in stories. No glory in stories. In fact, the very fact that a short-story is generally doomed to mass public indifference is part of what often makes a good story great; its very obscurity the proof of its purity. Yes, the short-story was, is, and will forever be the world's greatest Art form, he silently decreed to no one but himself. If this thing 'Art', this thing Art as in capital A, is a means to leave behind scraps and crumbs of truth, history, philosophy, and genuine wisdom for people to use to provoke themselves into worthwhile thought (thought the artist now), if the true definition of Art is any creative vehicle designed to leave behind lasting vignettes of the history of a time and place for future generations, then lesser Art forms like music, sculpture, painting, film, and yes, even the novel, would all have to be forever content to ride in the back of the bus. Yes, this was too important, he decided....too important for a novel....only a short-story would do.

His fingers began to type letters. Slowly. Solemnly. He usually, which is to say typically, would not begin work on a new piece with its title, preferring instead to write the rough draft first, maybe even the second draft as well, and *then* let the title fill itself in, fill itself in naturally, near the end of the process, a title based upon material, tone, perhaps a stray shard of dialogue, or whatever happened to strike him. But on this occasion, thanks to his son, he had already made up his mind to do it backwards. And so he touched electric fingertips to the keyboard, which gave virtual life to a brand-new Microsoft Word document, which in turn would ultimately give life to a brand new story, a story which one day might, theoretically at least, *not* be doomed to mass public indifference but rather read by thousands or even millions of strange, nameless souls who he would never meet, which he now entitled:

"A COMMUNITY OF HOLINESS"
a short-story by C. Edison Barnes

    Done. Done. He had a title, and yet he had not even started the story. This was a first. But he wasn't worried. He knew where he was going with it. In fact suddenly it seemed altogether a day for anything *but* work, this suddenly wasn't a day for writing at all, rather this was a day for savoring and celebrating the *decision* to write. Surely something far more important in the Grand Scheme. So a couple of lazy paragraphs into it he suddenly stopped. Stopped cold. Which surprised even himself. He pushed the 'save' button, turned off the computer, downed the glass of wine in one gigantic, confident, defiant swallow, locked his office door and bounded clumsily down the stairs. Soon he was roaring off in his convertible, headed for nowhere in particular. One of the greatest feelings in the world, he thought now, driving a car not just to get somewhere but rather for the joy of driving itself....like back in Iowa, he now thought further, back when Ike was king and cares were few, when the whole family would pile into the long white Rambler Station Wagon and go for a drive before dinner just to drive....so many, many times....oh so very long ago....but oh, those were the days. And so too, now, he drove just to drive. Aimlessly. With the top down. All he knew about where he was going was that eventually, maybe in a couple hours, he would wind up over in Old Town Pasadena and then head straight for the nearest bar. He didn't even bother to shut the front door. *So what* if the lure of an open door might bring forth matinee burglars from out of the woodwork? He didn't care. He didn't care if they took it all. It was all her stuff anyway....
    No, he wasn't worried. For once in his life he wasn't worried. About anything. He had a title, and he had the raw material. The story would take care of itself.

Some Misfits Misplacing Some Golden Dreams

REFLECTIONS OF A CAR WINDOW

Author's Notes

This is the first short-story yours truly ever wrote. The first draft was completed way back in November or December of 1976. I was up at Berkeley at the time, studying history, political science, and journalism (and also spending too much time at the racetrack, the local poker rooms, and various Lake Tahoe casinos), when one day I spied a teeny little advertisement in a local paper. SHORT-STORY CONTEST it said. At the time I didn't know anything about writing short-stories, had never even thought about it, amazingly, and when it came to fiction I wasn't even particularly well-read. At the time, all I wanted to be was a sportswriter.

But when I saw the hyphenated word 'short-story' in that ad something happened. Something dormant deep inside of me ignited, as if someone had lit a magic fuse. Nothing like it has happened to me before or since. It was very strange. I went to the campus library and checked out every book on fiction writing I could get my hands on. I read them all. And I started writing. By this time I was pretty much totally ignoring all my classes, and I had even stopped going to the racetrack; at least temporarily. Soon I had completely married myself to Fiction, and soon after that our first child, *Reflections,* was born.

You know how they say all babies are ugly except to their parents? That's the way it was with me. To me, *Reflections* was beautiful. It had the look and feel of a triumph, and seemed like a perfectly wonderful short-story. But it wasn't. It had a certain original pulse and some good angles, but overall it wasn't very good. I've rewritten it twice since. You get the good version.

I don't know if it's my Midwestern roots or what, but even though at my core I'm something of a happy agnostic I've always had a thing for movies about Christianity. As in Jesus-era Christianity. This story and *The Soap Opera Theory Of Existence* are both Christian allegories, and by way of homage a key line in each story is 'borrowed' from my favorite Jesus-era movie, "*The Robe*", starring Richard Burton and Victor Mature. I'll leave the detective work to you.

Oh, by the way, I lost the contest. (Like I say, circa 1976 I was just not a very good writer. But I got better.)

REFLECTIONS OF A CAR WINDOW

The smog actually woke my ass up that Friday. But L.A. summers are like that. You can be lying in bed, sound asleep, with the windows closed and everything, and somehow it'll *still* get through the windows and the walls and your eyelids and man it'll sting your goddam eyes so god-awful bad that they just pop right open. But the odd thing is that they sting just as bad open, so you right away wind up closing them again. But once a guy's awake he can't very well go around with his eyes closed so then you try opening them up again, and it still hurts, so then you try it closed again which like I said doesn't even work, so then open, then closed, open, closed, open, closed, god. Well anyway. All I'm saying is it's a vicious cycle. (Or vicious circle, whichever one it is.) And there's just no escaping it, either. Not in this stupid town. My bad luck on that particular Friday was that the worst season of the year in Los Angeles is always late spring and summer—for smog I mean—and our famous L.A. smog is definitely at its kill-yourself worst right smack in the middle of the god damn day. Like when I'm usually trying to get some sleep.

I remember the digital clock on the nightstand said exactly 3:16 p.m. Not exactly a round number, huh? Funny the things that stick in a guy's head. Even at the exact groggy moment he wakes up from a dead-ass, well-deserved, nine or ten hour nap. And I freely admit I would've likely hung out in that bed for quite awhile had I not remembered it was Friday. The poker game was always Friday. Third Friday of every month. The guys usually arrived around six, so I didn't have much time to clean the place up. Man, it was always such a hassle to fight through all the dirty clothes and empty beer cans and half-eaten bags of chips and cookies and crap that always seemed to be cluttering up my one-room flat by Friday. Like a conspiracy. It really used to bother me that the guys never volunteered to hold the game at one of their places once in awhile.

Y'know I never did like getting up in the morning, especially when there was cleaning up to do. I'm a little better about it now, but I still can't honestly say I dig it. And I remember that that particular Friday things were grungier than usual. The two college chicks next door were over the night before, and that meant that many more beer cans. In other words, a lot more. And strange clothes. Potato chips. Oreos. Y'know something, for females they sure were slobs....and good and loud about everything too.... royal pains in the ass, to tell the truth (but both worth it, thank god). A shoulder shawl somebody forgot and a matching blue-knit stocking cap (Who wears a stocking cap in the middle of June?) had also found their way into the sea of shirts and socks and worn-out jeans that I, naturally, always *meant* to get laundered by Friday, but that lay instead as usual, I admit, in a neat little semicircular ring around the bed as if I'd actually arranged it that way. It was funny. I was completely surrounded by a great filthy moat of cans, clothes, wrappers, old newspapers, lace panties, even a few dirty dishes. I guess it's just one of the great mysteries surrounding the game of poker. It's just amazing the way things always pile up on a guy right before a game.

Then, when I finally did find a flat place to stand, man I was really jolted, the old one-two, by both the icy stab of cold hardwood through my feet and a steady rhythmic pounding in my head left over from the previous night's recreation. That bastard of a landlord! I paid my thirty bucks a week (okay, okay, I made sure the government paid it), the least he could've done was provide some god damn complimentary heat, huh? Here it was ninety-five friggin' degrees outside, for Christ's sake, and I had cold feet. How is that even possible? Well, I suppose I could tell you that the circulation in my lower extremities has been poor ever since I was overseas, but why waste such a clever little lie on something that wasn't even my fault? Chalk it up to those paper-thin walls, I guess. Because as I made my way to the door (which by the way was so close to the foot of the bed that you almost couldn't even open it) I distinctly recall thinking about how drab and insubstantial those walls looked. Oh, they were always drab. My fault. I had intended to put up some mirrors or posters or something, *some* thing, but I just never seemed to find the time. Or maybe they were just the kind of empty, dead-drab walls nobody ever thinks to give a good god damn about, I sure as hell didn't.

Picking the morning paper up off the front stoop used to be just about the best god damn part of my day, now that I think about it. At least it afforded me a daily, built-in opportunity to silently curse and condemn this so-called "city of the angels" we live in. My pad was just north of Downtown, just off Silverlake Boulevard. The place was wedged right smack in the center of a bunch of similar one-roomers, which, I remember, were all crammed together on a crowded little hill facing south, overlooking The Basin. The Feds call it "low-income housing". Man. Well, at least thirty bucks a week bought a view, that's my point. But the first thing I noticed that Friday morning, the Friday we're talking about, was that for the first time in the five years I'd lived there the paperboy hadn't done his job. No paper. Yeah, that's when I figure I should've figured out that this would not be a day like other days. But at the time I was more than willing to chalk it up to not having paid my bill in, well, who knows how long. Several months, maybe. So I guess I can be forgiven for not attaching any special significance or omen to the paperboy's lack of professionalism. And I'm not by nature an 'omen' kind of a guy anyway. Besides, my head hurt too much to risk making it worse by doing a bunch of stupid unnecessary reading. So instead of standing there just looking stupid I pretended to do a little stretching, just in case somebody was watching.

Then I looked out and over the what and the where (what I could see of it, at least) of the Nowhere City. An unusually thick cloud-blanket of late-spring smog didn't actually permit me to review the endless cemetery rows of office buildings and high-rises. I mean I couldn't actually *see* all those iron tombstones of "progress" we're so goddam proud of here, littering Downtown, Wilshire, Westwood, Century City, Beverly Hills. But I didn't have to. I didn't have to actually *see* the buildings, any more than I had to actually see the mindless multitudes sitting behind their stupid desks, begging strangers for money, scratching out an "existence" eight, nine, ten, twelve hours a day every goddam day of their pitiful, insignificant, miserable little lives. The familiar nausea arriving in the pit of my stomach assured me that they were still down there. Idiots. They go to school until they're eighteen, spend the next four years busting ass through college, and then attach themselves like blood-sucking parasites to desk jobs that work away at them day-after-day, year-after-year, until they wind up in the ground before they're fifty. That's living? Any wonder it's the *women* who control most of the wealth in this country? You'd think more of us dudes would play it smart. I worked just six months last year, just long enough to qualify me for my ninety-three fat and tax free dollars, which is what I get every week from the Unemployment Office. Add that to my monthly check from the Veterans Administration, and I was set. I suppose. I mean I was, well, you know what I mean.

ii

Back inside right away the phone rang. It reminded me I hadn't paid that bill, either. Of this I made a clear mental note. That's one thing you can't get away with in this god-forsaken town, not paying the phone bill. No way, man. The phone company is like Big Brother, and everyone knows Big Brother always gets his way in the end. Anyway, it was Tom. Tom was my very best friend, years ago that is, when we all went to Hollywood High (and up until that Friday, to tell you the god's honest truth, I *still* sort of figured us for best friends). Hell, I don't mind admitting I even suffered through four months of college with the guy, over at USC, but my temper took care of that. Some so-called professor was really getting on my case one day, really jerking my pud, and so I punched his lights out. He had it coming. But they said they had to "make an example out of me", and I was expelled. And not just from the class. From the campus.

But don't feel sorry for me. I probably should've sent them a thank-you note.

Now Tom, on the other hand, his is a truly *sad* tale! During the four or five years since he graduated, all he's been able to get is a fifty-hour-a-week gig teaching junior high, with most of his weeknights wasted either at his night job at a Glendale department store or taking graduate classes in philosophy and theology over at Cal State L.A. God, what a moron. I kept telling him that he was just like the other ten million sides of beef in this crazy burg, crowding their way into the nine-to-nine slaughterhouse, but he insisted he liked it. Thinking back, I doubt if Tom has ever actually admitted making a mistake in his life.

"Hey hey hey *hey*, what's the haps, big guy?" Tom said, in his customary over-effervescence.

"Trying to get some sleep, small guy." You don't know how I hated talking to Tom on the phone sometimes.

"What time's the game? There *is* gonna be a *game* tonight...."

"Relax. Six o'clock, as usual."

"Cool! Hey listen, big man, whaddaya say to raisin' the stakes just this once—"

"No way, little man, buck limit. You insist on playin' at my place, I insist on playin' by my rules. Which reminds me, make sure you goldbricks bring enough beer." Tom was always trying to get away with stuff like that.

"I wish your food stamps could be used to buy beer, 'sure would save us *working* stiffs some dough!" Tom said with a laugh. Like I say, he was always a cheap little bastard. "By the way, Gordy's bringin' over a new babe. He told me to prep you."

I didn't think much about it at the time. We always tried to have our chicks come to the games, kinda like a bunch of thirties gangsters having their stupid molls around to make 'em feel like big shots. Besides, we always used to make them run to the store for beer, chips, Oreos, cigarettes, whatever we needed, y'know? But I was disappointed to hear Gordy was coming. I thought he'd gotten the message the previous time we'd played. I mean I really figured it being just me, Tom, and Pete; in other words, three-handed cutthroat only. Gordy and I....well, let's just say we hadn't been getting along.

"Just make god damn sure he brings enough extra beer for this so-called babe," I remember saying with authority.

"You say so, guy. Later."

"Later." It was always a relief to hang up on Tom.

Boy, the smog was really rough on me that Friday, I have to tell you. I'm not kidding. And it wasn't just my eyes. My lungs hurt like hell too. It was one of those days we have in L.A. where you can really only breathe it in half way. Which was a drag, because I knew I still had to clean up the place and a little extra oxygen would have come in handy. I remember the last thing in the goddam world I was in the mood to do was clean up anything, just so a bunch of overpaid working refugees from the colleges could sit around and pretend to be big-time gamblers at my expense, but I showed character and forced myself. I threw myself into the task. First, I managed to fit all the bottles and cans under the sink, which, except for a tiny ice-box, was the whole kitchen. I had to do all my cooking on a stupid little hot-plate I kept on the counter. Hell, at least it was convenient. Then I stuffed all the dirty smelly clothes in the shower, which was behind this cheap cardboard partition that separated the "bathroom" from the "kitchen" and which, at the time, wasn't working anyway. Which was actually a lucky break because all the plumbing was connected. I used to always imagine waking up one day, hopping in the shower, turning the dials, and being doused with scraps of stale, chewed-up food borrowed from the goddam garbage disposal. That bastard of a landlord....But I figured since the shower was temporarily out of order that made it the logical purgatory for all the dirty clothes; mine and everyone else's.

Then I jumped right over the bed to get to the other side of the room. Easier than walking all the way around it, man. The rickety thing was only about three or four feet wide, for Christ's sake, it didn't exactly take an Olympic-class leap to accomplish it. So then I just kept on working. The four collapsible wooden chairs and card table, my only other furniture, were strewn around the room as if they'd been used as projectile weapons in a barroom brawl or something. Funny, I really couldn't remember much about the night before....But those college chicks really turned into reckless bitches after a few beers, though. They must've been drunker than usual. At least they always gave you your money's worth.

So then, finally, I arranged the wooden chairs neatly around the table. Let the games begin! What a relief, I thought. I was tired. I forgot and took a deep breath and coughed, and it hurt. Y'know, it wasn't a big room to begin with, maybe fifteen by twenty. But it looked even smaller that final Friday. Smaller than ever. Maybe it was that ridiculous symmetry. I mean the way the bed bisected the room into two equal halves, kitchen and head on one side, table and chairs on the other. I really don't know. But hell, at the time it sure wasn't worth losing any sleep over. And since the game wasn't for another couple hours, I decided a little more sleep certainly couldn't do me any harm.

iii

The second time I was dislodged from my comfortable bed that goddamned day was by the pounding of Gordy's fat fist on the door. Yeah, sure I knew it was Gordy. He always had that obnoxious way of making his presence known, the fatty. I glanced at the clock on the nightstand. 6:02 p.m. And I was only going to doze off for a few minutes....

"C'mon, ace, open up!" he bellowed through the door. I could also make out the high-pitched giggling of Tom and Pete. Those three always arrived together. They sounded happy. I think they'd already had a couple on the way over.

"Alright already—gimme a minute," I said. Remembering that Gordy was bringing his hot new gash with him I threw on a pair of old gray cords that I always kept wadded up under the bed for emergencies. It was too hot for a shirt, though. I was in a bad mood. And I sure didn't feel like playing cards, but the game was sort of a sacred ritual with the guys. I opened the door, and like a goddam drunken stampede they tumbled in.

"What's the haps, man, ready for your regular plucking and cleaning?" said Tom, as he jokingly employed my stomach as a punching bag. That Tom. Always was the clown. He had to be to get any attention, though, because he was such a runt of a guy. I doubt if he ever weighed more than a buck-thirty, and even that's padding it a pound or two. So the sight of him peppering my gut with his tiny little fists always made me laugh. I admit it. We really were best friends once.

"Take yer goddam pattycake mitts off me, you worm-eaten little twerp, or I'll be forced to frag yer skinny ass," I think I said, and, "You other jerks can stick the buzz juice in the ice-box. Crack me one first, though."

Gordy and I didn't say word one to each other. I should've known.

"I brought a couple new decks along, big fella," said Pete, who was a mighty big man himself, not big and slobby like Gordy, but solid. I mean the man didn't say much, but he was built like a stone post: "Picked 'em up in Vegas last week."

"Howd'ja do?"

"Had a hot streak. Almost broke even."

"Haw, haw, haw," Gordy wheezed in that sarcastic way that only fat people do. I literally hated that cartoon-character laugh of his, no lie. "You'd better leave the comedy to Tom, 'else there's no reason left to keep him around—ha!" he said. What a brilliant, rib-crackling humorist. Christ....

"So what about this red-hot new slice of yours, Gordy? Last-minute cancellation? Temporary sanity?" I was trying the needle.

"You should know."

"Shut up, Tom."

"Ah, I was just funnin', Pete-boy" Tom said.

"Relax, ace, she'll be here in a minute. She's got the address. Said she knew right where it was, in fact."

"Yeah. Said she knew right where it was."

"I said shut up."

"Okay, okay."

"C'mon gents, let's see those rolls! Ante up, and let's play us some *pokah*!"

Gordy. There was a part of me that always detested the guy, even as far back as the old days, when he was leader of the gang and I used to follow him around like a goddam puppydog. His face was beet-red ugly, which in his case is even uglier than butt-ugly, and his beet-red cheeks always puffed up when he laughed like a couple of golf balls were inside. His reddish-orange hair, parted down almost at the top of his left ear, seemed to grow progressively thinner each time he ran his chubby hand through it. He sat down in the chair closest to the bed. Ugly rolls of flab oozed out, from under the vest of his stupid tight-fitting three-piece suit. He couldn't even button the bottom button. Gordy liked to call it his "prosperous rotundity". Actually, that was part of his overall defense mechanism. I learned a little bit about that stuff when I was hanging out at the V.A. Hospital. It was just his way of refusing to acknowledge the fact that he was, is, one of this planet's biggest, grossest, fattest fat slobs. A three-piece suit in late June? during a record heat wave? I don't have to tell you who stunk to high heaven. And based on past history, naturally I was figuring this new chick of his was probably just as disgusting as he was.

And just as I was thinking that very thought there was a delicate knock. Itching to see this stray junk-yard dog Gordy had thrown a net over I jumped up and spilled half my beer down my front and all over my pants, because I was in a hurry to answer the door myself. But when I opened the door, man. *Man*. Man, I could barely believe my own goddam eyes.

iv

"Carla James, meet yer elegant host!"

The fat pig not only didn't stand up, he didn't bother to turn around, either. But we didn't have to be introduced. Cee-Jay and I were a pretty tight pair three summers back, or at least I thought so. Her old man had the big bucks, a thriving construction business, Beverly Hills mansion, the whole picture. I never would've even *met* a society chick like that if I hadn't cracked up her Porsche on the Long Beach Freeway. Man, was she pissed.... But that was just her trouble. She was so goddam used to throwing money around and having guys fawn all over her all the time she just couldn't appreciate the fact that some people actually have hard times and no rich daddies to smooth it all over.

I'll never forget the day she dumped me. That was on a Friday too. I remember she wanted to see this movie in Westwood Village. Hell, even back then movies went for five bucks a shot in Westwood, but she pouted and whined and wouldn't be talked out of it. So we drove over there. Just as we pulled up in front of the theater I got this brilliant idea, that I should just stall her, you know, so we'd miss the opening credits of the picture. Like anybody else, she just hated coming in late to the start of a movie. (You know. It's kind of a nervous tick. Or what they call a "psychological phenomenon" over at the V.A.)

Anyway, I knew she wouldn't want to go in at all if she knew she'd miss the start. This might sound like going to a whole lot of trouble just to save a sawbuck, but it was the principle of the thing with me. Anyway, did I feed that girl some line! Get this: I told her that a person always looks better in his reflection in a car window than he or she does in real life, or something like that. She said I was a crazy, but I poured it on heavy. "See how much more muscular I am? See? It's the distortion—the curve of the glass, sweets! Look how much bigger and rounder and fuller your goddam *boobs* are," I explained. She kept saying I was nuts but I kept insisting it was all part of natural law, or maybe I said it was a scientific axiom, or maybe both, whatever, I was ad-libbing my ass off. So finally she starts to buy it, and then she started squinting right into the goddam window. "See?" I said. She kept squinting. And so there she stands, in the middle of the street, staring into a car window, squinting at her own reflection, looking like a complete fool. Finally I couldn't stand it. I just burst out laughing. It was a regular laugh riot. She looks at me all confused and I let her just stew for a little bit but then I finally point to my watch, give her a little remorseful kiss on the cheek, and I say something sugary sweet like "I'm so sorry, my love", but I still couldn't squelch the belly laughs. Naturally she blew up. "You *mock* me!" she said. Mock. That's the only time I've ever heard anybody use the word 'mock' in actual conversation. Mock....chicks got no goddam sense of humor, man. Anyway, bottom line is we got into a huge fight, she sulks off to sit on a bench, and since I wasn't about to buy into her bad mood and it was my car I just drove off and left her there, but it'd already ruined my whole goddam day. Hell, ruined my whole goddam year, who am I kiddin'. I swear to god, when you come right down to it, women are the cause of more--------

"Pleased t'meetcha....I said I'm very glad to *meet* you."

"Yeah. Yeah, right," I think I mumbled, breaking out of my transfixed state. It was apparent that she had no intention of copping to our past relationship, which was just Jake with me. "Go ahead and throw your coat on the bed, *Miss* James. Might as well sit there too, there's only the four chairs." She didn't say anything. She just threw her coat on the bed. And man, she was looking around like she really hadn't ever seen me before. What a performance.

But I was nervous. Y'see, I never expected to see her again.

Anyway, she had to cross right in front of me to get over to the bed. She brushed up against me a little, but played it like no big deal. Then she eased herself slowly and downright cautiously onto my soiled, unmade sheets, like they might crack and crumble if she wasn't careful, lazily tossing her long brown hair out of her blue eyes as she reclined on her side. Right then I realized I wasn't looking at the same Carla James that I ditched in front of a west-side movie theater three goddam years before. Not hardly. For one thing, her beautiful brown hair had always been her best feature, the fine product of a solid hour every single day holed up in the bathroom in front of a mirror. But *this* creature's hair was dull, stringy, practically *greasy*; like she'd just stepped out of an acid rain shower or something. And her face was covered with a totally embarrassing number of god knows how many red-and-white pimples. Real zits, I never would have believed it. And not just girl zits, in some cases, but she also had some big ugly scary purple man-type zits, *man*. I mean this girl didn't seem to care *what* the hell she looked like. But then, and this just killed me, when she shifted her position on the bed her skirt hiked up a few inches, high up on her right thigh, and she tried as discreetly as she could to yank it back down, and no wonder. Her once-dazzling legs had withered away into scrawny, pencil-thin stalks. I would've bet she'd dropped a good twenty pounds.... or should I say a *bad* twenty pounds....hell, you know what I mean. When a fat chick drops twenty pounds it's a triumph. But when a perfect chick drops twenty pounds it's a goddam disaster....

"C'mon, ace, you gonna play or not," Gordy whined. His stubby fingers were clumsily shuffling Pete's new Vegas deck. He dealt out five cards to each of us. We always played five-draw.

"Dime," said Pete.

"Call." Just my luck; my seat faced the bed. I could hardly take my eyes off her. Fortunately (I guess) my seat also faced Gordy. Remember I said he took the chair next to the bed so she was lying right behind him, and naturally it was hard to focus on anything in the same visual field as that fat pig. But good god, man. She was so skinny. I just hated seeing a fine chick go downhill, that's all. She just wasn't the same article. It was sad.

"Make it two bucks," Tom said. Jerk. I calmly reminded him that it was a buck limit. Said he didn't remember me ever setting such a low limit. I refreshed his memory. He just called.

"I'll give you losers a break and just call!" Gordy bellowed, tossing a dime chip into the pot. He was always saying dumb-ass things like that. That pompous superior attitude of his always irritated me. But my two *other* good pals thought it was hysterical. I guess money will always be the best barter to purchase friendship. They were laughing and nodding their heads and fawning all over him.

"Gimme three."

"Two."

"Three."

"Dealer takes one. Your bet, Pete my boy."

"Check it dark."

"I believe I'll go a quarter," I said. I figured my kings up would be more than enough. It occurred to me that Cee-Jay had never actually seen me play cards....

"I'm gone," said Tom.

"I'll hafta kick you a buck, ace!" Gordy grinned and bellowed.

"Too much for a first hand," Pete said.

"Call."

"All diamonds."

"Damn!" I remember blurting out, as I slammed my worthless two pair into the pot full of chips. Y'know he was always beating my good hands like that. Always filling straights and flushes on low-percentage draws. It was always the same, and I'm not just making that up. It's true. Hell, thinking about it still makes me mad. I bet he cheated sometimes.

"Down, boy."

"Yeah, take it easy, buddy."

"God, I hope it's not gonna be one of *those* nights...."

"Gordon, you didn't tell me your friend had such a temper," Cee-Jay said, just to tease me I guess, and I actually did wind up feeling a little embarrassed. But the fact remains that Gordy always won, it seemed, and

I....well, sometimes it seems like I always lost. Always. When it counted anyway. Close but *not* close, y'know? God damn it.

TWO

By 8:30 I was down thirty bucks, so I borrowed a ten from Tom. Some friend. I practically had to steal it from him. I don't know what he was so goddam worried about, about a little bitty loan I mean, he never expected me to pay back the small ones anyway. He even *said* he doubted I'd ever pay him back! I mean he *said* it. But don't feel sorry for him. He pulls in plenty of dough at his stupid department store and dumb-ass teaching jobs, and I'm just a poor jobless veteran trying to get by on welfare and a small disability check every month from Big Brother. Anyway, by 8:30 Tom and Pete were both hovering around even, maybe down a buck or two each. That left Gordy with all the scratch....

This is when things started to get a little weird.

"Hey Tom, why don't you be a saint and pop up'n fetch me a nice cold beer?" I inquired in my usual calm and polite manner.

"Get it yourself," Tom snapped back. Boy, did that surprise me. Hell, he was miles closer to the ice-box than I was. What ever happened to good old poker-table camaraderie? There just happen to be a few sacred, unwritten rules about conduct at the poker table, and Tom had just broken the main one. And in front of a chick, no less. But he was serious. He wasn't budging. Naturally I didn't want to make a big scene. And naturally I didn't want to have to climb over the bed like I usually did, with her lying right there and everything, so I conspicuously walked all the way around it.

"Don't be afraid of Carla, ace, she won't bite....unless you ask her in a nice way! Haw, haw, haw!"

But I couldn't keep from at least glancing at her. After that crack of Gordy's I thought she'd be anticipating my glance, but she wasn't. She was staring straight ahead, her blue eyes sort of black and glazed and practically glued to the hail of colored chips being tossed into the center of the table. Like she was hypnotized or something. She didn't even look like a girl anymore. She was just a....I don't know, a *person*. I didn't say anything.

I didn't even bother to offer her anything to drink, remembering how vulnerable she used to be to the stuff. Poor Carla....the way she looked, I remember thinking how it was no wonder an ugly slug like Gordy could have reeled her in....

"Who else wants a beer?" I said, always the perfect host, and would you believe good old Tom says, "I'll take one, big guy." Can you believe that? The big jerk. Y'know something, I felt like making him get it himself, but I had too much important stuff racing through my mind.

"Ditto," Pete piped up in that squeaky nasally voice of his that never matched his size.

When I opened the ice-box I was surprised to find that there were only two cans left.

"Sorry, dude, 'fraid Tom gets the last one." I tossed one of the cans to Tom who made a good one-hand catch, I quickly popped the other, and swigged half of it in one long gulp in order to lay claim to it rather than taking a deep breath first and taking my time and savoring that first small sip and, you know, enjoying it. I was nervous.

"Looks like we'll hafta play the booze hand early!" Gordy declared loudly.

Unless you play cards, you might not be familiar with a term like booze hand. It's simple. The winner of the booze hand had to run out and buy the beer when we ran out. It was never a problem for me. I always folded early, no matter what I was holding. If you don't stay in, 'no way can you win, right? Nobody ever caught on. Actually, I almost couldn't afford to fold the two pair Pete picked this hand to deal me. Typically, Gordy wound up winning the hand, kings full of queens. If I'd stayed in he wouldn't have even filled up, of course, because he would have drawn different cards, which is pretty irritating. That guy filled more boats on two-draws than any player I ever sat down with. But hell, at least he could afford it. Remember, he was up over thirty bucks on the night, booze hand be damned. *My* thirty bucks.

"C'mere, babe," Gordy now commanded, casually pulling a fat roll of bills from his vest pocket and peeling off a couple, and Carla obeyed. "Take this down to the store and pick up two or three six-packs for yer big daddy, hm? Don't matter what kind. It's right down the street, you can't miss it. A buncha Jewish guys run it, but they're still open practically all night on Fridays, open-minded fellows that they are!" he bellowed. He was really ordering her around, but she didn't even seem to notice. She just bent down and he kissed her on the cheek, that blotchy zitty cheek, without taking his greedy beady eyes off the table. It was sickening.

"Want anything else?"

"Naw, just hurry yer tight little ass back here with the beer. Winning's hard work, and I'm thirsty. Get goin'."

She accepted the crumpled bills from Gordy without expression, turned to leave, but paused briefly in the doorway to look back over her shoulder and directly into my eyes. You might laugh, but that was the worst moment of the whole god damn night. The way she looked at me. The light over the door, I admit, probably made her face appear even more pale than it probably was. But her eyes just had no spark left in them. They were dead. She parted her lips, and I thought for a moment she was actually going to say something, out loud I mean, but she obviously thought better of it and instead merely mouthed the words "*I forgive you, sweetie*", in my direction. Is that the living end or what? *She* forgiving *me*. Hell, I never wanted to go to that movie in Westwood in the first place, *I* should have been forgiving *her*. But if she was trying to get back at me for driving off and leaving her there, it worked. I mean there's nothing like having a big bowl of guilt poured over your head, right? Christ, that's all I needed.

"Be back before you know it," she said. No response.

Then the door swung open, revealing an uncommonly humid L.A. night, and into this thick, heavy-hot darkness she disappeared.

ii

"How many? C'mon, ace, how many?"

"….oh. Three, I guess." By 9:15 my mind wasn't even on the game anymore. It showed in my performance. I never did manage to win two hands in a row, and that's a tough thing to do in a four-man game. Instead I was cruelly subjected, again and again, to the nauseating sight of Gordy's chubby little hands reaching out into the middle of the tabletop, and greedily pulling in a pile of chips and bills and coins. Again and again and again….

"Hey look! One of those bicentennial quarters! I'll just go ahead and add it to my junk silver collection. Who bet it?"

"I did," I said.

"*You*, ace? Figures. My guess is you've got a thousand of 'em stashed away, a thousand shining, glittering symbols of your latent, hot-blooded patriotism! Am I right or not."

"Doesn't the bicentennial mean anything to you, Gordy?"

"Means he's getting rich on other people's optimism," Tom said.

"Haw, haw!"

"Means all is forgiven," Pete said.

"I'm serious," I said louder, and I was. I mean here Gordy and Pete go and beat it up north, and get fat, while I'm way the hell over there crawling on my goddam belly. It's not right. And I'm sure Tom would've gone with them if it wasn't for his studies: "Do us both a favor. You look at that quarter and tell me what it makes you think of," I said.

"I think it means Pete's right," fat Gordy finally said. "It means all our past sins are forgiven—provided my main man Jimmy the C whips Ford's ass, of course."

"Sorta like our very own lifetime get-out-of-jail-free card."

"It's in the bag."

"Unless Ford has a better idea."

"Man, you've gotta stop watching so much tee-vee."

"Haw, haw, haw!"

"But he *will* whip him, though. I say it's in the bag."

"Yeah."

"So what happened to you, ace?" Gordy said. For once he was looking right at me: "You were a die-hard pacifist once. I'm sayin' you usta be a regular peace-lovin' man, just like the rest of us. Then all the sudden it's this violence trip. I can't believe you let 'em talk you into going over there, man. Like the whole thing was *okay*."

"I was called. And so were you. It was our responsibility." Christ, hard to believe that cliché crap was comin' outa *me*....

"But what *good* did it all do you? And what did you ever get out of it, huh? Except a permanent necktie, that is."

"Ease up, Gord."

I was starting to get angry so I changed the pace. I got up and pulled a dirty white dress shirt out of the shower and put it on. It wasn't like I was cold, I just felt like wearing a shirt. I don't know why. But boy it sure did stink, though. Usually you can't tell if you stink, but it was so hot and I'd been flop-sweating throughout the day and my broken plumbing and everything and so this time I could tell. And if *my* pits stunk, you can just imagine how ripe somebody fat like fat old Gordy must have been. Just for the hell of it I left it unbuttoned, except the top button. I sat back down and glanced at my cards.

"Wish she'd get back with the beer. It's like an oven in here," Pete complained. He'd only taken two cards so I knew he was bluffing. Or at least keeping a kicker: "By the way, Gordo, I thought you said that store was owned by some rich Italian family."

"The Wops do own it, Pete, the Heebs just run it for 'em. Percentage deal. Most of the customers are Italian, though."

"All I ever see in there are Italians," I admitted. I took three.

"She shudda been back by now," Tom said. "Gimme two. Where in blazes is she?"

"Yeah, Gord, what's the deal? If I don't get a beer in me soon I'm gonna *die* in this filthy sink-hole."

"Aw, she probably got into a floating crap game with a couple of those Italians!" Gordy said. Naturally, they laughed right along with him. Brown-nosers.

"Christ almighty, does anybody here remember when the smog actually went away in this town when it got dark?"

"And it actually got *cool* at night?"

"At least it finally *is* night."

"Longest day of the year, it said in the paper."

"So what. Day or night it's still too much smog."

"It ain't smog if ya can't see it."

"Who says?"

"All I know is if it hurts my throat, it's smog."

"Have a cigarette."

"I'm just sayin' it's not like it was, that's all."

"Amen."

"Hey, we can sit around reminiscing about the fifties and the sixties and how great it was to be a kid some other time," Tom said, "But right now, all I wanna hear about is how my main man Gordon here managed to land such a luscious, sleazy babe!"

"Dealer takes one. No big deal, children. When you got what it takes...."

"Don't gimme that."

"C'mon Gordy, give. At least where'd ya meet her?"

"I wanna know too," Pete chimed in. "Maybe she's got a sister or a mother that wouldn't mind a little—"

"Wait a minute. You didn't know her? I thought you said you knew her," Tom cut in.

"No. I didn't know her," Pete said.

"I thought you said you knew her long before Gordy even met her."

"No, I didn't. I didn't know her."

"I thought you said—"

"No, man, what I said was—"

"Jesus-God, will you two magpies just *shut up*? All you guys ever talk about is chicks! Let's play cards. I'm stuck plenty, and we're not playin' fast enough to suit me—I bet a goddam dollar!" I couldn't believe I'd said all that. We *always* talked about women during poker, it was a tradition. In fact the poker table may just be the best goddam place in the whole damned world to talk about women. I guess you can tell that everybody was in sort of a bad mood....

"Hey, chill out, nut case. Yer just bitter because nowadays yer thinkin' you were a *fool* for goin' over there, and you wish you'd come north with *us*," Pete said, as if that had anything to do with anything. He shouldn't have said that. And by the way, that was bullshit, Pete sayin' he didn't know Carla. I've known the guy for years. He knew god damn well that back then Carla and I were going out, and goin' at it hot and heavy....unless he didn't recognize this version of her any better than I almost didn't.... Anyway, he had a big mouth, so he kept using it: "Besides, it's my bet. Ten cents. C'mon, Gord, you big stud. Let's hear it."

"Okay guys, it's this way. She comes into my shop about three weeks ago. Never saw her before. But right away I can see she's got me scoped out, y'know? So I say to myself, 'Gordy, this bitch is built good enough to make a bishop kick a hole in a stained-glass window, *don't blow it!*' One thing led to another and, well....well now that I think about it, I don't think yer virgin ears should suffer anymore."

"Come on!"

"Yeah, Gordo, I haven't had a woman in so long I'm starting to think I'm queer."

"You are queer."

"Shut up, goddammit!" I yelled. I guess I'd had it. "I raise Pete's puny bet a dollar."

"Puny?"

"Take it easy, guys."

"I'm out," Tom said. Now he was looking at me kind of funny. Then he smiled at Gordy and said, "C'mon, pal, with all due respect what the hell does she see in you?"

"Since when did *you* become the great moralizer, ace?" Gordy bellowed, ignoring Tom's question and glaring right at me. "I notice *you* never miss a chance to brag a little when you hook into something good. Raise a dollar."

"I'm out," Pete said. Coward....

"Raise a dollar *back*," I snarled. I was mad. But Gordy acted like he didn't even hear me. He was busy pretending to fend off all of Tom and Pete's stupid questions. But finally he gave in. Even he could be obnoxious for only so long. It was his big moment now, so he put his cards face down, leaned back as best he could being a fat guy, and told them exactly what they wanted to hear:

"Well, I gotta be honest. I just think we each got something the other wants. She's got this rich old man in Beverly Hills, see? She doesn't talk much about him, but I know he's the head of this big construction company in town. Anyway, I figure a sharp guy like me can really take off if he ever gets that kind of money under him. And what I got to offer her is, well, *me*. Hey, I mean the girl was pretty desperate for a man, if you follow. With chicks it always comes down to the old pocket salami, the old one-eyed trouser mouse, right? The guys at work tell me they see her all the time, they say all she does is drive up and down Silverlake Boulevard, looking for fresh action, and I don't mean professionally either. She just needs it. Been at it for almost three years, from what they tell me, and it sure shows. You saw her—she's pretty wasted now, even though it's obvious she was pretty hot at one time. And when a chick is past her prime neither her looks or her guy's looks matter very much. And that's where I come in. I figure she was probably on the make for the first legitimate hunk a'meat that was ever gonna come along, no matter what the rest of the package looked like. I'm it, baby. I am *it*. Okay, ace, I'll see ya. Whaddaya got?"

I never hated Gordy more than at that moment.

"Three kings," I said. I was trembling a little. I could feel this bizarre sort of rage gurgling up inside me.

"Sorry, 'G.I. Joe'. Tens over."

When I saw him lay down those three tens and two sevens, I really lost control. I just dove across the table and drove my fist solidly into that stupid red-faced grin. The table collapsed, naturally, sending poker chips and beer and cards flying in all directions, cigarettes, snack food, everything. I landed right on top of the guy. I hit him again and again. He wouldn't fight back. I hit his fat bleeding face with both fists, I didn't want to stop. It felt great.

"What are you doing! Get this psycho nut *offa* me!"

I could feel Tom and Pete's close presence behind me, and expected them to just pull us apart. Well, I was half right. Pete grabbed Gordy and dragged him away from me, over to the door. But Tom, supposedly my best friend in this whole lousy world, just went kablooey. He started pounding me but good. I didn't think he had it in him, the little terrier! I was caught way off guard, and before I knew it I was flat on the floor, getting the stuffing kicked right out of me. He hit me, choked me, kicked me, elbowed me, whatever he could think of. I don't know how long it all lasted. It must've been over in a matter of seconds, but it seemed like longer. Man, did I bleed, from my mouth, my nose, everywhere. I saw a tooth on the floor beside me. *My own tooth*! Just like in a movie fight or something.

"Get Gordy to the car, Pete," I heard Tom say. The room was cloudy. I tried to get up, but really there was no way I could have. Maybe I drank too much, maybe that's why I couldn't stand up to him. I don't know. All I know is my stomach and head hurt like hell. Finally, through the filmy, bloody swelling across my eyes, I was barely able to make out the grave, humorless figure of good old Tom standing over me.

He was talking like some kind of lunatic. "You worthless punk," he said. "You bastard. I thought you'd get it together someday, but you never did. We were your friends and we would have helped you, but you went over there anyway you stupid fool. And then when you finally got out of the tank I doubted that you were back to normal, but dammit, you were even worse! Why didn't you just stick with *us*? You could have come with *us*! You just bagged it, man. Everything we ever believed in....you just bagged the whole thing. We were your friends....we were your friends...."

Then, incredible as it may sound, he spat in my face. I mean he actually spat *on my face*. I even thought he was going to rib-kick me again, but he resisted the temptation. He just left me lying there, lying in a little puddle of poker chips, blood, and warm beer.

iii

I woke up early Saturday morning, which at the time wasn't usual, but when your whole body's just been used as a punching bag I suppose it's to be expected. I never made it to the bed. I must have passed out on the floor right where Tom left me. Out like a light. The pain was worse than a hangover, at least any hangover I can ever remember having. And my neck hurt too. I've got this old scar y'see, and since that's where Tom was choking me it was pretty damn sore for awhile.

Funny that Carla never did make it back with the beer, but I'm glad. Looks like she finally wised up and threw off that fat jerk Gordy, at least I hope so. Turns out I really cared about that girl. I sure hope I bump into her again, I mean one of these days, though I really don't see how. Hell, I still got her coat.

As for Pete and Tom....well, I still haven't been able to figure out exactly why Tom went off on me like that, that was so against his nature, but I'm working on it. I guess you can tell I'm having a little trouble sorting things out. Things just don't fit together like they used to. It's not like it was.

I do think I'm better off without those guys, though. We'll see.

You could actually see the L.A. skyline that Saturday. The town looked pretty good for a change. A little grainy, sure, but we're stuck with that here. I pulled an old brown sportcoat out of the shower and started walking south on Silverlake, towards Downtown. I knew there wouldn't be a lot of businesses open on a Saturday, but I figured it couldn't hurt to look around a little. Make a few inquiries, as they say. Whatever. Anyway, I started walking. Those first few steps were a little wobbly, but after awhile I could at least walk a straight line.

CLOSE FINISH

Author's Notes

The racetrack has been a recurrent theme in my work, most notably in my sweeping, 'modern-day epic' novel WHERE GODS GAMBLE, *a tale of American mythology,* which, as mentioned, was published in 2011. I loved the track growing up, and later on as a writer I used it often because as a literary backdrop the track has always worked well; for it is a place that abounds with symbolism, metaphor, and the many manic microcosms of the Human Condition.

    I got the idea of doing *Close Finish* in the 1st-person from a story called *Haircut* by Ring Lardner. Lardner, as an artist, successfully handles the problem of what to do about the fact that the 1st-person narrator always has the narrowest possible point-of-view. He is limited by what he sees, hears, and thinks. So are we the readers, for that matter. There is no broad omniscience to obviate that problem. Therefore, I believe the 1st-person narrator's delightfully *weak* perspective, his very *lack* of authority, must become the star of any 1st-person story. The reader has to believe there's more going on there than meets the eye, and he needs to want to dig deeper on his own to come up with a version closer to the truth. Why else would a storyist choose a method of narration so clumsy and barbarous?

    I don't have many 1st-person short-stories. A few. However, it should be mentioned that one of my four novels to date, THE BASKETBALL EXPATRIATE, published in 1999, is also a 1st-person narrative. I only employ the 1st-person technique when the tension between what the narrator *says* happened and what must have *really* happened makes for the best story. As the saying goes: "material discovers method". So true.

    *One final note: Regarding the specific horse race *Close Finish* pivots around, the 1978 Hollywood Gold Cup? Well, I still have a large, blown-up and framed photograph of it on my wall. The images of the horses are more than three-decades faded, but my memory is not; I can still point to each and every horse in that race and tell you his name....

CLOSE FINISH

My friend, I'm tellin' ya. You are not gonna believe this story.

I wouldn't a'believed it myself, 'cept that it was Robby Spangler that gave it to me. You know Robby? He gallops horses sometimes for McAnally in the mornings. Good kid. He exaggerates a might, sometimes, but e's about as likely to tell a flat-out lie as….well, as *you* are to miss a big *stakes* race! Oh here, lemme freshen that up for ya. No no no, you don't hafta grease me, Hollywood Park's got enough juice these days without it having to send in the Feds to separate you from two *more* of yer hard-earned fish. Ha! Just gimme that same deuce's worth on the three-horse in the fifth. If 'e wins we'll split the profits, how's that?

Now, what was I sayin'….oh yeah, about Carl Mellinger. Poor kid. You didn't know ol' Carl, did ya? You wudda liked him, at least before the track got to him. And did it ever get to him. I guess you could say the track was the *undoing* of poor ol' Carl. And by the time it all went down 'e was about as compulsive a'gambler as I've ever seen, and I've been here tendin' this same stinkin' bar since sixty-one.

Anyway, the way Robby tells it, it all came to a head right by that T.V. monitor over there. Yeah, the one right over there, right by the 'large transactions' room. But first lemme fill you in on what led up to it, so's you'll know what the hell I'm talkin' about.

Like I say, Carl wasn't always a gambler. Usta come out here with his old man in the mid-sixties, when 'e wasn't much more'n a punk kid. The old man was really loaded, so Carl never usta hafta to worry about money. He just liked the races for their own sake. Which of course is the best way to be. Native Diver was smokin' hot back then, everyone just loved him, and Carl would practically beg his old man to bring him out here just ta see the old guy run. *You* 'member Native Diver, right? Won three straight Gold Cups, 'member? Y'member the way his big ol' black tail'd stick straight out when 'e ran, swishin' back and forth and such? Aren't any more like *him* around, nope, not anymore, just a buncha flash-in-the-pans. Things sure do change….a stakes horse usta *be* a stakes horse, and folks usta feel *safe* walkin' the streets at night—ha! Funny thing, since the 'Diver retired I don't pay much attention to the good horses, even the so-called top class horses….anyway, I hadn't seen Carl for years until about six weeks ago, when 'e strolls right up, slaps his hand down on this very bar and says, "Howzit goin', Buck?"—Buck, that's my nickname, short for Buckingham—and I says, "Carl Mellinger, you ol' sonuvagun, where you been keepin' yerself, my boy?"

    Well, turns out e'd been off gittin' one a'those fancy Ivy League educations, Princeton or Harvard, can't remember which one to save my life. Then 'e tells me e's gone and got himself a wife and kid, and sunk most all of his dough into some screwy land development business. I even sunk fifty bucks of my own into it, an' I guess I'll never see *those* ten fins again! Heh, heh, heh. Anyhow, it seemed like things were goin' pretty good for the guy, 'e even said that's why 'e never came out to the track any more, and even the day it happened 'e said that 'e was just out here that day ta see J.O. Tobin run. Y'know, my friend, J.O. *is* a little like the 'Diver, now that I think of it….steel-gray, almost black, a free-runnin' horse that's plenty hard to catch once e's got an easy lead. That's the way Carl himself put it, sayin' 'e just had ta see if J.O. could fly early and finish late like the 'Diver. I shudda been wise to him by then, 'cuz by that time the whole dang trouble was pretty much out of hand. But I'm gittin' ahead of myself….

    Hey, looks like the fifth race just finished. Joe! Hey Joe! Where was the three-horse? Whazzat? Fourth! You sure? Damn! Serves me right for bettin' a sprinter goin' around two turns. Oh here, bud, lemme pour ya some *good* Scotch, not that labeled pisswater they make me sell. Oh no, it's on me, just send out four or five bucks for us on the favorite in the sixth—if 'e wins I'll take half, same as before, okay? Good, I just hate to see people drink imitation twelve-year Scotch to the tune of five bucks a shot. Joe doesn't like to pour it either. Yeah, that Joe's been tendin' bar around here almost as long as me. Good guy that Joe, 'cept whenever I ask him who won 'e always yells back any horse's number but mine.

    Well, after that first time when 'e showed up as an adult I didn't see Carl again 'till about four or five weeks later. I asked him how 'e was, and 'e said somethin' about his investments suddenly not doin' too well, but we didn't talk much 'cuz 'e was too busy pushin' hundred-dollar bills through the seller's window. Yeah, 'Benjies'. Lots of 'em, too. I usta glance at his losing tickets, so I know what I'm talkin' about. His business couldn't a-been doin' *that* bad! So much for comin' out to the track just ta watch the pretty horses run....

Well, naturally 'e was gettin' pounded pretty good, but 'e kept comin' back for more. It got to the point where I'd see him most every day. Oh, every now and then e'd hit it big, but the kid was always tryin' to parlay it into a bonanza, and so 'e always threw it right back. Well, you and I both know what *that* kind of tomfoolery will usually get'cha, don't we. Hm? Oh sure, go ahead, I'll save yer seat and watch yer stuff, don't worry....

Say, that's pretty darn good Scotch, ain't it? No wonder it took ya half the damn day to take a piss! Here, have another....when's that sixth race goin' off anyway, did'ja place our bet? Good, can't stand the wait. Anyway, like I says, Carl was takin' a regular beating. He even took ta drinkin', and I mean drinkin' heavy, became my best customer in fact. Ha! Aw, I guess I shouldn't laugh. I know ol' Carl didn't think it was very funny. Such a good kid, too. A *good* kid. Although he could get a little overly dramatic with you at times. "Things aren't so good, Buck," e'd say, an' then he'd gripe about his business, or sometimes somethin' else, just ta throw me off the track, but then e'd go and bet three or four hundred fish on some no-chance gluepot like it was no big deal, like he was buyin' a pack of chewin' gum or the morning paper or somethin', and of course the nag would always run way up the track and so then e'd throw up his hands and—

Whazzat Joe? The *eight* horse! Geezus, I thought *sure* that was our horse in front at the sixteenth pole! I tell ya, I can't see the T.V. screen so good anymore from this far away. Guess I need a new pair of specs. What'd 'e pay, Joe? Eighteen dollars! Joe, do me a favor—next time I ask you a question, pretend ya don't know me, will ya?

But anyway, Carl was losin' pretty regular by this time, an' I remember thinkin' to myself how sorry I was for him. Like I say, 'e was a great kid before the track got to him, you shudda known him then.

Near the end it got so bad that it was just gol'-darned pathetic. Just last week he was here at my bar, gulpin' down Jack Daniels after Jack Daniels, an' we was watchin' a race together on the T.V.—just a cheap claiming race, six and a half furlongs, slop horses. Now in the old days Carl never cudda got excited over *any* cheap claiming race, but when they hit the far turn he durn near went crazy. Carl had Pincay's horse, on the outside, an' Shoemaker's mount was in tight on the rail. By the time they hit the stretch it was strictly a two-horse affair. Pincay was really whippin' an' drivin' his mount, you know how 'e butchers the backside of a horse, an' Carl was yellin' at the top of his lungs how no jock alive can out-finish Pincay. Truth is, though, that nobody can do the things that Shoe can do at the wire, an' 'e was just hand-ridin' mostly, showin' his horse the whip an' occasionally hittin' him kinda gentle-like with the left hand. That Shoe, 'e never gets over-excited in the stretch, the old fart. That's why 'e wins.

When they hit the wire it looked like Pincay got it by a head bob, but you know how the T.V. camera is a few feet behind the wire and so the angle is off a tad, an' so when they put Shoe's number up Carl went a little nuts. "*Robbery! Highway robbery!*" 'e was yellin' at the T.V., swearin' a blue streak at the stewards and the placing judges and everyone else he could think of. Oh man, you shudda *seen* him! It was actually kinda funny, 'cuz he and I usta joke all the time about the dumb putzes who don't take the camera angle into account an' blame the track instead. And now all of a'sudden ol' Carl was one of those putzes!

The last time I saw him was the day it happened, just last weekend. It was the day of the Gold Cup. I didn't see much of him, though, 'cuz I was pretty busy with the extra crowd. But the way Robby tells it—oh, I forgot to tell ya, Robby and Carl were good friends in high school, best friends in fact, an' Robby came to work for McAnally about the same time that Carl went off to Harvard or Princeton—anyway, the way Robby tells it Carl was more keyed up than ever, bettin' a small fortune practically on every race. I don't know where 'e was gettin' the money, but 'e sure wasn't investing any in real estate, that's for sure. Robby'd ask him about it, and Carl would just say, "*I gotta have it, Rob, and I gotta have it today!*", or somethin' overly-dramatic like that. That's the way it is when the track really gets inside ya. Ya just hafta win the whole grandstand all at once. Life and death. You know how it is.

Anyway, I guess you've probably figured out by now that all that malarkey about him comin' out just to see J.O. Tobin run was just a big fat lie….

So it all came down to the seventh race, the race just before J.O.'s Gold Cup. It was just a cheap allowance race, non-winners of two races, but for ol' Carl it might as well've been the Gold Cup and the Kentucky Derby all rolled into one. Robby told me later that Carl bet more on Pincay's horse in that little allowance race than Robby makes in six months. 'Course McAnally doesn't *pay* Robby a whole helluva lot, but six months' wages is a lotta dough no matter *what* kinda job you got. Well, Pincay had the lead into the stretch but wouldn'tcha just know it'd be ol' Shoemaker again, chargin' right down the middle of the stretch to screw things up for ol'

Carl. He was right on Pincay's outside flank, and that worked to Pincay's disadvantage 'cuz 'e couldn't hit his horse with the left hand too much for fear of makin' him come out and over into Shoe's horse and then bein' disqualified, an' 'e wasn't responding to the right hand whip at all, so in the end 'e just didn't have enough horse ta hold Shoe off. They threw up the "photo" sign, but it was obvious to anyone who could see it that Shoe got there by a head.

Now this is the part I don't quite understand. Robby says that instead a-bein' wiped out by losin' the biggest bet of his life, Carl was just standin' there at the T.V. like 'e was *waitin'* for somethin'. Said his face was kinda creepy-like. Hell, they'd already called it official and put up the prices, but Robby said Carl just stood there like a statue, blank faced, like 'e didn't care about anything! Huh? Oh sure, you can have some more, all ya hafta do is open up yer yap and ask—here, how about a double….y'know, thinkin' back, I guess he cudda been just waitin' around ta see the replay….yeah, that's probably it. I shudda thought of it sooner. Gamblers have a way of thinkin' that if they watch the replay carefully enough that somehow the order of finish will just miraculously change altogether. Yeah, they really think about stuff like that. And believe me, I've seen and served enough hard-core gamblers over the years to know what I'm talkin' about.

But the thing is, 'e never got the chance ta see that replay. This is what I been leadin' up to. The race hadn't been over for five minutes when these two guys come up ta Carl and drag him away from the T.V. and over to that room where they handle the large transactions. Robby'd bet on Shoe's horse so 'e was on his way over to the regular cashier's line when it happened, bless his heart, but I know 'e saw it good enough. Anyway, it was obvious that these guys wanted somethin' from Carl but like I says 'e didn't seem ta care much about anything, and in fact 'e looked like 'e was tryin' to get back to the T.V. ta see that replay; least that's the way Robby saw it, an' I know Robby wouldn't fudge about somethin' *this* important, even if 'e *does* have quite an imagination. Incidentally, these thugs were big. Real big. An' they were wearin' sunglasses even though it's kinda dark over by the large transactions room.

Anyway, I guess these guys were talkin' to Carl real serious-like, an' pushin' him around a little bit too. But Carl didn't care—'e wasn't even lookin' at 'em, Robby says. He was tryin' to get a look at somethin' over by the walking ring, where J.O. Tobin and the others were tuning up for the big race, which was too far away ta see anyway. So these guys keep badgerin' Carl, really puttin' the heat on, an' Carl finally shrugs his shoulders an' says somethin' to 'em an' that's when it happened. One a'these guys goes and whomps Carl in the stomach, an' it looked to Robby at the time like just a good hard punch, but 'e shudda known by the way Carl doubled over that e'd been stabbed. God, it was awful. I mean it musta been. I was busy with the weekend crowd, of course, but I put a lotta stock in the way Robby tells things. Robby said 'e was still on his feet but bleedin' all over, and nobody seemed to notice, at least I didn't. I don't know how 'e made it to the walking ring. Yeah, 'e made it all the way out from under the grandstand and right up to the damn walking ring, how's that for spunk! He walked right by the T.V., too. You wudda thought 'e wudda wanted ta see that replay. Guess not. Ah heck, *who knows* what a guy is thinkin' when the Grim Reaper finally comes to get him. Anyway, that was it—'e just fell over and died. Poor kid. That's when I finally noticed all the commotion, but I didn't even know that it was Carl 'till a couple days later when Robby told me. Y'know, I wonder why Robby didn't just come up to me right away and tell me the whole story right when it happened, seein' as how he saw the whole thing and seein' as how we's such good friends and all....

Anyway, this Carl thing, I guess you can tell it's hit me pretty hard. I mean I know e's just one guy and all, and I know we've had to put up with some pretty awful crazy-guy crap in this country lately. You know, what with that guy Ted Bundy and that Son of Sam fella....oh, and that guy right here in L.A. that's got everybody so scared spitless lately, the one who chokes everybody, whadda they call him? Oh that's right, the Hillside Strangler....hey, that's not *you*, is it? Ha! Anyway, I know it seems, I dunno, seems sorta weird getting all worked up over one guy. But it's different when it's someone you know. It's different when it's a buddy.

Funny thing, though, that is if yer lookin' for funny....if e'd lasted just another half an hour Carl wudda got to see his last Gold Cup....just half a dad-blasted hour....which is just as well he didn't, considerin' how J.O. Tobin gave it up in the stretch after gittin' away to such an easy lead. I bet Carl'd agree with me, too. J.O.'s no Native Diver, that's for sure.

Hey, you takin' off? Wait a minute, c'mon, *wait* a minute—what about the seventh? You can't go yet! We *gotta* bet the seventh, I got a tip on the two-horse, I'm not kiddin', they're takin' the blinks off him, and the word along the backstretch is e's ready to ramble! I figure since I supplied the horse you can supply the cash, say four fins? Twenty bucks ain't much to risk on a sure thing, right? Ha-ha! We'll split the winnings fifty-fifty, same as before. Okay? You sure? Good, thanks a lot, pal. Yer a mensch. Here, have another drink on me....or should I say on Hollywood Park! I'll have one too, one bein' my absolute limit these days. One last drink on the house before ya go, one for luck, they won't mind. Hell, with any luck at all we'll *both* do better than ol' Carl Mellinger did. Poor kid. Poor, poor kid. Talk about bein' given every advantage in life, and then not knowin' what in blue blazes to do about it....But like I say, once the track grabs ya it never lets go.

Heckuva story though, huh? I *told'ja* you wouldn't believe it, my friend.

THE BEGGAR DRIVES A METAL HORSE

Author's Notes

My personal tribute to Thomas Wolfe, Wolfe being one of my all-time favorite writers of fiction. His sprawling triumph of novelized autobiography, YOU CAN'T GO HOME AGAIN, was probably my favorite novel growing up, and might still be. Indeed, the title of this short-story is taken (which is to say stolen) from the title of one of the chapters of that very novel, although I did switch the words around a bit to fit neatly on top of my story....

The Beggar Drives A Metal Horse is one of those stories which poured eagerly out of me during those so-productive early years. I would say it was penned in either 1980 or 1981. It is also one of those rare short-stories I wrote practically straight through, start-to-finish, in just a couple weeks, with virtually no rewrites or re-tweaks to speak of; none at all. The whole story came out fully baked, exactly the way I envisioned it in my head before I wrote it. It's not too detailed a piece, more of a sketch than a proper story. Or maybe more accurately a parable. It is what it is.

It is also pretty much the only story I have ever written without a discernable period of reference. There is no real way to determine exactly what year—or even what decade—it might have taken place in. It exists in geographical space, but not in time.

Speaking of geography, I very much like the fact that in a collection of stories about Los Angeles this one spans virtually the entire width of the city; from the super-mansions of Bel Air to the west, all the way over to Eagle Rock, which is part of (and buried somewhat anonymously within) the far humbler hamlet of East L.A.

And if you're ever in L.A., and decide to drive the same route Webster Jordan drives in *Beggar*, you'll see a wonderful L.A. landmark. Yes, there *really is* a ten-story boulder shaped like an eagle's head....

THE BEGGAR DRIVES A METAL HORSE

Webster Jordan lowered his bones onto the spongy-soft springs of his favorite easy chair, and prepared to lose himself in the comfortable prose of Thomas Wolfe. This he did in spite of the world's various criticisms of the author; his endless digressions, the endless sentences within the endless digressions, the ten-dollar words, frequent fondness for alliteration, a love of hyphens, the dearth of symbolism or any real purpose (but is that fair?), the lack of consistency in scope and skeleton and structure and, above all, the length, always the horrible length, always the total and premeditated disdain for the twin geniuses Simplicity and Brevity.

Yes, Webster Jordan knew very well the criticisms of Thomas Wolfe, yet Thomas Wolfe was the only writer he would read. He couldn't care less about other people or long-dead critics. Jordan read for entertainment, and that is Wolfe's strong suit; his talent for perception and keen grasp of life, life laid out in that marvelous narration, an always mellifluous confluence of ideas and thoughts and delightful phrases, and ultimately those perfectly painted pictures of the absurdity of existence itself—strong, fresh and original, yet strangely familiar to the feeling, thinking reader. After reading Thomas Wolfe, Jordan always had the feeling that he'd received something valuable, something as old as Man, something true.

As he was exploring the first few pages the phone rang:

During the time it took him to walk from his living room chair to the phone which hung not ten feet away on the kitchen wall, Jordan's mind pondered all possibilities as to who might be calling him. He didn't require that much time. It was a period in his life of change, of "transition", and there were less than a dozen people on planet Earth, including creditors, that were privy to his telephone number.

"Hello."

"Hello, Web?"

It was a girl's voice, coated with sugar and purring like a predator cat's, but not as powerful a purr as that of a lion or tiger. If a lynx could speak it would have a voice very much like this girl's.

"Who's this?"

"Why it's Jackie—Jackie *Enders*! Surely it hasn't been *that* long, you silly goose!"

But it had. Six long years had shown their backsides to him since Webster Jordan last cast his eyes on the girl at the other end of the line. He couldn't see her, yet even the sound of her lynx-like voice was enough to conjure up an image of Aphrodite before him. The shock had rendered him mute, a more or less wordless, mindless idiot....

"Web? Web, are you there?"

"Yeah....yeah, I'm still here," Jordan managed. "It's just kind of a surprise, that's all." So much more than merely surprise, considering their relationship was nothing more than an occasional "hello" as they passed each other on the way to their next class in high school. Not that Jordan wouldn't have appreciated a more involved relationship, but goddesses rarely involve themselves with the common mortal male.

"Well it's only that I *just* moved back to L.A. and so I just *had* to look you *up*!" the girl effused. "I thought maybe you could come over to my new place and we could have a drink and talk over old times."

"Old times?"

"Sure! It's been so long, Web, how about it?"

Jordan dumbfoundedly agreed, and she gave him her new address. They said "good-bye" and Jordan hung up the phone.

He walked over to the window and looked out and over what he could see of the modest sub-city of Eagle Rock. The town spread out before him into hills and flatlands, the simple frame houses with their shingled composition rooftops popping up in no particular pattern, humble residential dots on the land. What did she mean by "old times"? Two people who had shared barely fifty words of conversation between them didn't *have* any "old times", Jordan mused. And any old times Jordan had at all he thought he had abandoned when he moved to Eagle Rock, a member of Los Angeles that tightropes a narrow path between poverty and lower middle-class, tucked neatly between Glendale and Pasadena but belonging to neither. He knew no one here. Even the college girl who occupied the other half of his duplex he did not know. Here, he had decided two years before, he could live divorced from his unhappy past, within the simple and secure cocoon of self-induced anonymity.

But what, again, of Jackie Enders? She had called him out of the clear blue sky, and by nightfall he would see again his incarnation of unrequited love. Could this really be happening? He nervously paced the hardwood floor in anticipation. Finally he sat down, picked up the book, but even the comfortable prose of Thomas Wolfe could not quell the beating of his heart, so he carefully rested the book on the arm of the chair and retired to the bedroom for an afternoon of sleep.

Webster Jordan's Mustang convertible wheeled off Figueroa Street and onto the westbound on-ramp of the Ventura Freeway, charging quickly up the long stretch of concrete to cut a sixty-mile-an-hour hole in the dusk air. Behind him, looming up higher than a ten-story building, sat Eagle Head Rock, in stony splendor, perched solidly against a hill to the freeway's north side, the weather-worn cave of its left eye peering down at the tiny cars flitting by. Eagle Head Rock is the symbol of its community, bearing an uncanny resemblance to its namesake. Its cave-carved eyes and conspicuous beak point into a canyon to the north, and the towering single boulder that forms the rounded crown of its skull is visible for miles around. Jordan glanced back out of reflex at that giant head. It seemed to be welcoming all eastbound traffic, and with the same stoic expression on its stony face it was saying, to the fleeing-westward Web Jordan, *"you'll be back"*; and Jordan surely knew in his heart that it was right. Soon Eagle Head Rock disappeared from view, and Jordan, grateful, was left alone to contend with the twenty-five miles of real estate that separates Eagle Rock from Bel Air.

Jordan's Mustang convertible gulped up the concrete in great bites, and spat the road out intact again behind them. They were going seventy now. The sun was dull and red in his windshield, bathing the once-white clouds in the salmon-colored solution that is meant to signal the dawn of night. Jordan's thoughts were at all times of Jackie Enders. He could picture her exactly as he last saw her, that day at the beach, the day he almost told her how he felt, six years ago, early June, senior year….the long blonde hair dripping down around her shoulders, the smooth, tan skin on a fiercely athletic body, the black bikini which hid virtually none of it, and the legs….well, legs that every man pictures inexorably entwined with his own. A bikini-clad goddess could not have struck a more heavenly pose in Jordan's mind. And yet, though his entire being had longed for her for most of his young adult life, he approached the appointment with confused trepidation. Indeed, the question of just *why* she had called him, why *him*, was far from being answered. And what was she doing living in Bel Air, anyway? Nobody has that kind of money, Jordan whispered to himself.

He looked up at the green, billboard-like sign hanging above the freeway. It listed Buena Vista St., Hollywood Way, and Cahuenga Blvd. as streets upcoming. He was getting closer. And so, flinging off his inhibitions as best he could, he pushed the gas pedal even more urgently against the Mustang's floorboard and raced off to join the girl he loved and never knew.

The house was an ordinary mansion, typical of a Bel Air estate, but to Webster Jordan it was the stuff of Asgard, Olympus, or Nirvana itself. The two stories were flanked by pillars of white on either side, with smaller pillars in front supporting a second-story balcony. The roof looked to Jordan like a thousand separate pieces of driftwood. And the front yard was virtually a football field leaning on its side, a great hill of green, and it took Jordan thirty seconds to scale it to the door. Awed, out of breath, and admittedly somewhat embarrassed, he rang the bell.

"Oh hello, Web, come on in!"

She stood in the doorway as he remembered her, the hair, the face, the body, the legs; legs poured into skin-tight white pants which Jordan forced himself to look away from.

"Thanks, Jackie. Great to see you," he said. "Say, do you live with someone here?"

"Nope. It's all mine!" she giggled.

The next thing Jordan observed was two drinks standing ready on a coffee table in the living room.

"C'mon, let's have a drink," the girl said, and led him by the hand.

The next few minutes were spent in a lame effort by both to create conversation from the vague fragments of their common past. During this time Jordan was at once looking around, staring bewildered at the opulence surrounding him.

Finally, without word or provocation, and to Jordan's great surprise, she leaned over and gently kissed him.

"What was that for?" he asked.

"What's the matter?" she asked in return, applying an extra measure of the natural "cat" in her voice. He could stand it no longer. He grabbed her, and, fueled by the fury and passion of six years of false hopes and broken dreams, he kissed her, fully and savagely, making up in small part for the days and years of suppressed emotion and desire. He employed his arms as levers to crush her body against his own, pressing as much of his male flesh against her quivering female form as possible. After what seemed to him a blessed eternity they broke. Before he could speak she again took him by the hand and, without a word, led him to the stairs.

The morning light found Webster Jordan staring at the bedroom ceiling. Jackie Enders lay beside him, still asleep. A thin, translucent bed sheet was the only obstacle between her naked beauty and his naked eye.

He had been awake for two hours, thinking, searching, wondering what had gone wrong. The great quest was ended, a great fantasy of his life miraculously fulfilled, yet at the very core of his spirit there lurked an empty feeling of gloom, of betrayal, indeed of despair. It was all wrong. He should have been feeling at the top of his game, at least quietly satisfied, or at the very least not totally miserable for a change, but it wasn't like that at all. There was no "special" feeling. No feeling at all. It was all wrong, something was very, very wrong.

She began to stir, finally woke up, and regarded Jordan indifferently with one open eye. "Hello," she said dully.

"Good morning!" Jordan cooed, trying his best to pull himself up and out of the abyss, "Sleep well?"

"Oh, all right I suppose," was her dull answer. She sat up. The sheet fell away from her to reveal her unclothed body, a golden, perfect thing. Last night it was everything. Now it was nothing.

"I just can't get over this place," Jordan said. "It's awesome. Since when did you become so rich?"

"Since I divorced my last husband," the girl droned. "The trick isn't who you marry, it's what you marry into."

"What does he do?" Jordan asked. He was just making conversation now.

"Oh, he's a big real estate man up in Frisco. The divorce was final about a month ago, that's when I moved back down here. Y'know, you're about the only guy left from high school who still lives around here. It took me a long time to look somebody up."

"Somebody?"

"Well, *anybody*, that is….ever since Bill left, there hasn't *been* anybody. It's been so long."

Webster Jordan looked like a man who had just been hit in the face.

"If you don't mind I'm going to get some more sleep," she said, curling up again under the sheet. "You can let yourself out."

The sun hung low in the eastern sky and threw its light on the angry and bewildered face of Webster Jordan, as he and his Mustang convertible made the long trip back on the Ventura Freeway. Jordan had done much thinking in the last twenty hours, particularly in the last hour, but little had come of it, only a dumb and pathetic stupor, and it's a small wonder he was able to keep his Mustang between the white lines at all. But drive he did, and by the time he was halfway home the sun had climbed above the windshield, and at least he could take off his sunglasses and focus on the long road ahead.

Suddenly the whole exaggerated melodrama of his life unfolded before him! His thoughts reeled back to his early days, indeed to his very conception, and suddenly his windshield was a movie screen: Webster Jordan the youth….the bastard brat of a greasy-spoon waitress, left at home all alone while his mother chases the elusive husband, a frequent visitor to the sickbed, a maker of harmless mischief but always punished like a felon. He is uncared for, neglected, slapped and slugged, a wretched, hopeless, diseased bundle of bones, nerves, and soft muscle, the embarrassment of humankind.

Webster Jordan the adolescent….an orphan now, scrawny, void of self-respect, likes girls but cowers in their presence, hates his new parents but takes their money with a smile, watches television until ordered to bed—then watches two hours more. He hates school, it shows in his grades. He loves baseball, but cannot make the school team. His life is a parade of rejection, alienation, and inadequacy, trying and trying but always falling short, a prelude to future failures.

Webster Jordan the high school student….he falls in with the fast crowd, slips easily into booze and dope, then acid and mescaline. He slashes tires to stay popular, and steals with two hundred dollars in his pocket. Girls universally reject him and he resorts to "self abuse". He runs for class president, wins, but is thrown from office by a failing grade in algebra. Finally he is expelled from school for breaking a desk over his best friend's head.

Webster Jordan the man….out of school, his parents' money makes a job unnecessary. He hangs around the house, a proud slob, promising his folks daily he'll "do something" tomorrow, but tomorrow never comes. By day he drinks and smokes in front of the television, by night he counts the transvestites on Hollywood Boulevard. Nothing on the horizon. He robs an all-night gas station for the hell of it, is squealed on by a friend. Two years probation. His parents curse him, labeling him a common street thug. He moves out.

Webster Jordan alone….his apartment is small, his prospects smaller. He remains indoors, goes out only for food, a recipient of welfare and proud of it. He reads a little, sleeps a lot. He smokes constantly, eats merely to stay alive. He knows no one, sees no one, and slowly slips into a quicksand of depravity and cynicism: "The world's a cesspool and there's not a damn thing I can do about it!" He cries, but no one hears.

And in the end, Web Jordan….a hopeless dupe, utterly gullible, ready in a moment to believe the whole sad chronicle of his personal history is a lie. Is he merely curious or just a slave to his own juvenile appetites? No matter, the result is the same. He is reduced to a mere tool, the willing and unwitting foil for a hungry woman's passion. For the first time he is introduced face-to-face to his true self; lazy and lascivious, sorry and superficial, more pitiful than pitiable, and a generally miserable excuse for a human being. All this during the long, slow, lonely drive home.

Before him, on the left, soon appeared the stony visage of Eagle Head Rock. Its ten stories might as well have been a hundred. It loomed over the Ventura Freeway like some gigantic granite god. And the look in its eye was familiar: "*I told you so!*" it might as well have been saying. "*I said you'd come back and you did, back to resume your miserable, pathetic little life! Welcome, Webster Jordan—welcome back!*" The words, though imaginary, stung at the center of Jordan's brain. They branded him like a hot iron, and Jordan swore to himself he felt actual pain as a result. Then, at that moment, for the first time in that miserable life, a spark of defiance raced through his body like an electric current. "No!" he said aloud to the lifeless rock head, "No, I won't go on living in that lousy little apartment! You think you're so goddam smart?—I'll show you! A quick stop to get my things and I'm gone! I'll get a job, pay my bills, live like a real person for the first time! I'LL SHOW YOU!!!"

Webster Jordan meant what he said. He had never meant anything so much in his entire life. With his own words having barely purged his soul, he sped past Eagle Head Rock and down the Figueroa Street off-ramp.

Inside the apartment fatigue hit him. The lack of sleep, the hours of driving, the various exhaustions of his Bel Air adventure, the battle with Eagle Head Rock; all had taken their toll, and only now, within the darkly sedate confines of this sad little room, did he realize just how tired he was. He plopped down heavily in his chair, glancing at the book still resting on the arm.

The title looked huge.

THE GRUMP AND THE GROUND SQUIRREL

Author's Notes

I began this story in 2006 and fooled around with it for a couple of years. Then I stopped work on it altogether (for some reason), and then, finally, I finished it last year. (And then did some last-minute cosmetics and patchwork on it *this* year!)

I figure 9/11 is this generation's Pearl Harbor, and I wanted to have something in this collection that dealt with it a little bit. It's not only the enveloping action of the story, but I also think it's safe to say that the title character, the irascible 'Grump' himself, offers up a fairly fresh, albeit unpopular, perspective on this great American tragedy....

And history is nothing without fresh perspectives.

I have always believed that there are many kinds of patriotism. The American Revolution, World War Two, vigorous support of our troops, and a genuine appreciation of the truly rare and spectacular menu of personal freedoms our soldiers have fought and died for are all examples of what I call 'good' patriotism. Being an old Berkeley history major and the son of a WWII vet, I consider myself a patriot.

But patriotism absent intellect, moral discernment, and a sober evaluation of history's great lessons is a recipe for disaster; is in fact patriotism gone mad. I think the Confederate States of America, the Japanese internment camps of the 1940s, Vietnam, and 90% of our recent misadventures in the Middle East are all ample proof of that....

THE GRUMP AND THE GROUND SQUIRREL

"—so anyway, son, anyway, right when I'm lookin' out the front window—you know, my kitchen window—up pops his evil little head and I get so dad-blasted mad I mean if I had a gun I wudda—but I *don't* have a gun, and so I run out there, and the minute he sees me right back down into the ground he goes the little coward but then I grab—and I don't know why I never thoughta this before—I grab the gol' darn garden hose and I turn it on and I stuff it right smack down his cotton-pickin' little hole and then I turn the spigot 'hard as I can to full, and I mean *full throttle*, hah!—and then I run right back to the front door and hide behind one of the hedges to watch the fun."

"Dad...."

"No wait, listen."

"Dad...."

"Just *listen*."

"Dad, I—"

"—so anyway, I squat right down, all the way down to butt-resting-on-heels down, and I wait. And wait. And *wait*. And nothing. Not a thing. I would never've believed that hole was that deep. But I figure I'm about eighty-six years older than the little bastard and that means, I figure, that I'm a lot more patient than he is, so's I just leave the hose on and leave it stuck down the hole and I go inside and into the kitchen to watch the three-thirty adventure of *Andy Griffith* on the Nickelodeon Channel. It was so funny! It was the one where the goat eats the stick of dynamite and—well *you* remember, don'tcha?—when Barney figures out that the goat ate the dynamite his eyes bug out like a coupla big ol' deviled eggs? And then Barney and Andy spend the rest of the show trying to keep everyone from the mayor to Otis the drunk from kicking or grabbing or shooting or bumping into the goat for fear the goat'll blow up and blow up everyone in Mayberry along with it? Remember? I just love that episode....anyway, so that's half an hour gone by, and tell you the truth I'd plum forgot about the little shit-heel but then I remember and so I go back out there expecting to find my front yard completely soaked from the water burbling on up from the hole like the way water spurts up when something overflows, and I definitely expected him to be lying there on the wet grass like a drowned rat—and I mean definitely. But he *wasn't*! And it wasn't even wet, the grass I mean. Why? Because the water from the hose hadn't filled up the darn hole yet, even after almost forty-five minutes! Unbelievable. And that's when I remembered. I remembered reading an article a couple years back in one of my nature magazines that those little buggers can dig themselves two or three miles of tunnels in just a couple of days."

"Dad, how do you feel?"

"Whaddaya mean how do I feel, I feel fine. I'm trying to tell you about my ground squirrel, fer Pete's sake."

"It's more than one ground squirrel, Dad."

"No, I don't think so. He's the only one I've ever seen pop up."

"That doesn't mean there aren't others. And how do you know it's even the same one, popping up every time?"

"Oh, it's him all right. I recognize him."

"Oh, you recognize him."

"Sure. It's him. Trust me, it's him."

"Any more gut aches?"

"No, that's only at the beginning or the end of the cycle," he lied. "I'm fine."

"Maybe we should just lay off the juice altogether."

"Lay *off* of it? Just let me die, huh?"

"That's not what I meant and you know it...."

"I know. I'm such a card!"

"Promise me you'll call me if it flares up again?"

"Yeah yeah yeah. Don't worry about me so much. Son, I gotta go. It'll be time for the three-thirty in a coupla minutes."

"Man, how can you stand to watch the same cheesy sixties re-runs all the time? The same goddam reruns, over and over and over."

"Don't blaspheme, my boy."

"Seriously. Why don'tcha try watching something else once in awhile?"

"Leave me alone. I've earned the right to watch what I want to watch, 'earned it just by living this long, for the luvva God."

"Don't you ever watch the news?"
"No."
"No?"
"*No*! Too depressing. Make that boring. I like a good comedy at my age."
"They're still diggin' bodies out."
"Expect they will be for weeks yet."
"It's just awful."
"Only feels awful 'cuz you're on the wrong side."
"Jesus, Dad...."
"Gotta go, my boy. Call me tomorrow. Bye-bye....and don't blaspheme!"

The old man hung up and began to shuffle into the kitchen in the same urgent jumble of motion. In a hurry. Three-thirty on the dot. He switched on the T.V. (it was already on the right channel), and the ever-catchy, opening theme-song intro for *The Andy Griffith Show* started up on cue. The familiar clip where Andy and his pre-teen son Opie are walking along the river with their fishing poles to the sound of some guy snapping his fingers and whistling the theme song. The old man whistled right along. He always did. Even when there were people in the room.

He sat down at the kitchen table. Commercial....a couple free minutes to prepare....Spread out before him were various sections of his three favorite local newspapers; the *L.A. Times,* the *Pasadena Star-News,* and the *Daily News.* At his withered right hand were a half dozen carefully sharpened pencils and a yellow 'Magic Marker' pen. And one good pair of scissors. To his left were his beloved file folders. Each folder was meticulously labeled in the upper right-hand corner tab. Each folder represented exactly one category. One folder for politics. One folder for religion. One for Iran, one for Iraq. There was a folder dedicated exclusively to stories related to physical anomalies and deformities. Folders for unusual deaths, celebrity deaths, amusing celebrity sexual indiscretions, medical marvels, and interesting murders. Folders for disease, natural disasters, Katie Couric, sports milestones, George W. Bush, George H. W. Bush, George Will, Bill Clinton, Monica Lewinsky, Hilary Clinton, Stephen W. Hawking, O.J. Simpson, Dr. Gott, Ann Coulter, the naked mole rat, the dung beetle, Oprah, and Saddam Hussein. Virtually any person or topic on the world stage that interested him would merit the creation of a folder, and so he kept a handful of blank folders handy too; just in case a new folder needed to be created at a moment's notice. His workstation was a paradigm of efficiency. He was always prepared, always ready to begin his daily triage of the local newspapers whenever the mood might wash over him.

Not yet, though. The first segment of commercials was almost over. Any minute the show would be starting. Any minute.

The phone rang.

"Yeah?"

"Daddy, it's me. How—"

"Hello, kitten. Can't talk now."

"But Daddy, what are—"

"Can't talk. Show's starting. Call back at four."

He hung up.

The old man never checked the *TV Guide* in advance to see which episode would be playing. Not him. He had always told his children that it was far more fun and scads more exciting to be surprised. But that wasn't really it. He'd seen every adventure of *The Andy Griffith Show* at least five or six times, so it wasn't as if the suspense ever lasted past the first thirty seconds anyway. The not knowing in advance was just part of his personal doctrine of behavior. His way of staying in step with his own concept of an orderly, well-lived life.

The three-thirty adventure was the one where Andy kept capturing these wanted criminals, and every time he'd catch them and throw them in jail Barney would accidentally let them go. So Andy would have to go out and capture them all over again. And then Barney would get tricked into letting them out again. And again. And *again*. "That Barney Fife—now there's a government stooge who just don't learn from experience!" he said aloud to himself. The old man watched the show in a hunched-over position, sitting on a stool less than four feet from the television, holding the scissors in his right hand and the yellow Magic Marker in his left to save time. The kitchen table was to his right. The minute they went to a commercial he turned to his right and began skimming through the newspapers. Not too much in the news caught his eye on this particular occasion, though he did spy an interesting filler article about a man in New Jersey who killed three of his five small children for the insurance money, figuring that if he didn't kill them all it would look more random, meaning more likely to look like somebody else did it, but he made the mistake of bragging about this brilliance to some strangers in a bar and they called the authorities. This admitted killer, the article went on to say, was pleading *"Not Guilty by reason of insanity"*, which meant that the old man was now faced with a difficult decision. He thumbed through his files. He pulled out two of the file folders. They were the ones labeled 'interesting murders' and 'crippled legal system'. He held one in each hand, first looking at one, then the other, again and again, back and forth. The show was coming back on in a few seconds. Hurriedly he grabbed the scissors, cut out the article, highlighted in yellow the most important passages, and then neatly slid the scrap of paper into the file folder marked 'crippled legal system', just as the grainy, familiar figures of Andy Griffith and Don Knotts rematerialized in black-and-white on the tiny screen.

At the end it looked like the crooks were going to escape for good, but just as Knotts (as Barney) was letting them out for the final time the hapless Gomer Pyle happened to be up on the roof taking down some Christmas lights and a few of them broke and it sounded like gunshots to the crooks, who promptly threw up their hands and surrendered to Andy yet again, and that was it. (This was the only juncture of the entire episode during which the old man either laughed or smiled. He did both.).

The show ended at precisely 3:58 and at exactly 4:00 o'clock the phone rang again:

"What is it."

"Oh, Daddy! Is *that* how you answer your phone now?"

"No, I knew it was you. I knew you'd call right at four to resume bothering me."

"How do you feel, Daddy?"

"I wish you dad-blasted kids would stop asking me that. I'm fine."

"Daddy, I—"

"I'm fine and I'll *be* fine, right up until the day I'm not fine and then quite soon after that I'll quite happily be dead."

"Daddy, please don't talk that way. Please."

The old man grunted something and for a couple of seconds there was sort of an intermission of silence bisecting their short conversation:

"I'm sorry, kitten. I know how upset you get about everything."

"It's just—"

"It's just that I've lived a very good life, and at my age I'm already playing with the house's money. Hell, when I was born Woodrow Wilson was president, fer cryin' out loud. So don't feel so all-fired *sorry* for me. I'm already looking forward to what happens next. Yessiree-bob, I'm *looking forward* bein' able to chew the fat with God, I wanna ask him what happens now, look him in the eye, 'see if he's a good guy or not. And I wanna see if yer mother is as pretty as she ever was....That's how I look at it, and that's how you two should look at it."

"I'll try, Daddy. I'll try. It's just so—"

"Why don't you ask me about my ground squirrel? Your brother doesn't seem interested."

If the woman heard him she betrayed no notice. All the old man could hear through the receiver was the wet, muffled sound of a nose blowing snot into a Kleenex.

"Daddy, you do have grandchildren, you know."

"I know I have grandchildren, and I love them all very much. What's *that* got to do with the price of rice?"

"It's just that I don't quite know what to tell them. Ellen asks about it all the time. And little Brian, well, he's so sweet and trusting and happy, I just can't stand the idea of—"

"Tell 'em the truth, that's my advice. Life's crappy enough without feeding young whelps a bowlful of cherries, and then expecting them not to barf it all back up the first time they realize they've been conned by overprotective adults."

She laughed a little.

"Daddy, why are you so *grumpy* all the time?"

"I'm not grumpy. I'm eighty-six years old. There's a difference."

"Oh, Daddy! You are still so funny...."

"That's what you should tell your kids, sweetheart, that their grampa is eighty-six years old and has a disease that eighty-six-year-old people get as a reward for living a good life. Tell 'em the truth about the other thing, too."

"We're trying to. But it's just awful. Just a *crime*. I can still barely believe it."

"Ah, buffalo chips. Crime my old and wrinkled ass! You know what I think? I think you and your brother and everyone else in this mollycoddled country of ours needs to force down a teaspoon or two of objectivity. All this blind jingoism is why they all hate us."

"Oh, Daddy, *please*! You can't tell me you're not morally outraged about this."

"Well I'm not happy it happened, and it is outrageous, but I don't see what morality has to do with it. People shouldn't try to make war nice."

"It's *civilians*! That's the *difference*, Daddy. Wars are not strictly about military targets anymore. These people have declared war on regular people, on good, decent, *innocent people*. I mean it's *unprecedented*!"

"Unprecedented you say? Ha! I think the good and decent people of Berlin, Dresden, Leningrad, Tokyo, Hiroshima, and Nagasaki would disagree."

"No, what I meat was—"

"Not to mention the equally good and decent people of Vicksburg, Atlanta, Richmond, Lawrence Kansas, London, and Honolulu."

"Daddy, I don't want to argue with you—"

"Good. I'm busy."

"Daddy...."

"Gotta go, kitten. Bye-bye, sweetie pie."

The next morning the old man woke up early. He had a plan. Water had proven to be a colossal failure, it was time to employ a more sophisticated (albeit not yet widely accepted) brand of warfare. *Chemicals*. Poison the little devil. That was his plan, a brand new and very good plan, something innovative, something old and new at the same time. He'd seen an ad in the Sunday paper for something called "ground squirrel bait". He didn't know exactly what it was or even if it would work, but the name sounded promising. Cheap, too. He would head out to the market immediately after consuming his daily morning portions of oatmeal, walnuts, and prune juice.

Eight-thirty. Dressed and ready. The old man exited his modest one-story ranch house on Santa Anita Avenue just above Sierra Madre Boulevard to begin his oft-practiced, 1.2 mile trek down to the Ralphs Market on Foothill Boulevard. He turned around briefly to gaze at his house. Modest....that's a laugh, he thought....that's how they'd sold it to him, as a conservative, 'modest' ranch estate....'bought the dump for a piddly fifty-seven grand back in seventy-five, 'worth over a million now....a million dollars, he said to himself, fer cryin' out loud....the world's gone crazy, he said to himself, he was sure of it....hell, 'paid only eight thousand for my duplex just south of Downtown L.A., he said to himself, right after the war, right around 14th St. and San Pedro back when that was a *spiffy* little neighborhood, not some grimy industrial slum like it is now, and *that* place had even more square footage than *this* one....

He talked to himself a lot these days.

He checked the mileage 'pedometer' clipped to his belt to make sure it was turned on. Then, after pasting a smile of manufactured joy on top of the pain-grimace that invariably took over his face whenever he commenced the painful practice of walking, he began. It was a curious perambulation. Snails could grow impatient from witnessing such a painfully slow shuffling, this hunched-over substitute for walking he had devised. But it was necessary. For one thing, the right leg barely worked anymore. A shell fragment he picked up on Omaha Beach fifty-seven years earlier that was still lodged in his thigh didn't mix well with the arthritis which lately infected the rest of the leg. So he sort of dragged it. Like a mummy. He always laughed at the notion that nearly seventy years after seeing Boris Karloff in *The Mummy* for a nickel back in Elgin, Illinois, he would wind up adopting Karloff's theatrical, shuffling gait. As for the hunched-over part, that was merely his necessary response to the constant pain in his gut, the wages of cancer. But this old man was a walker. Always was, always liked it. And this was an old man who was indoctrinated right from the cradle to appreciate, and cling stubbornly, to the good things in his world. Therefore, the relative slowness of his progress during his walking, during his eighty-seventh year of life, was more or less irrelevant.

So southward down Santa Anita Avenue he went. In fact this poorly named Santa Anita Avenue really wasn't a mere avenue at all, this veritable *boulevard* of jacarandas and maples, with a wide soft strip of perfect green grass running right down the middle of this north/south thoroughfare so that wealthy joggers could glide along as comfortably as would genteel princes and princesses under the protective aegis of the jacarandas and a bored, over-stocked police force. Leave it to a town like Arcadia to lay down such soft, springy sod upon which its nobility might deign to jog, to take the pressure off those aging, soon-to-be-replaced knee and hip joints. He knew that only the wealthiest, most rustic, most 'perfect' towns in L.A. County had grass running down the middle of streets so that people could feel good about their jogging. Even the very word which lent his final home town its name, 'arcadia', means *"a place in which people are imagined or believed to enjoy a perfect life of rustic simplicity"*. He'd looked it up. Yet twenty minutes away from Arcadia were virtual ghettos, some black, some Asian, some Hispanic. Some of these virtual ghettos were as close as Pasadena, right next door, with gangs and drugs and everything. Places where there was doubtless very little jogging going on, and certainly none on grass boulevards....The old man couldn't help but think that fifty years ago he could have shown these Arcadian joggers a thing or two about jogging. At least his mind was still fit, damn it. After only a tenth of a mile he passed the Highland Oaks Elementary School and was already hunched over slightly, his right leg struggling to keep up with his left. Typical, painful, necessary. He crossed Perkins Drive, a right-turning minivan having to stop dead in the street to allow him to shuffle out of the way, then Yorkshire Drive, then Ontare Street. After Ontare was a big street, called Orange Grove; he checked the pedometer. Exactly point-three miles, as always. Then Hacienda, Woodland Lane, and Sycamore Avenue, before finally arriving at Foothill. He winced. The sudden shift from a business-free boulevard of bucolic, pastoral splendor to an intersection of noise, lights, pace, and dog-eat-dog industry—gas stations, a bank, a strip mall—had always produced mixed emotions in the pit of his disintegrating stomach. He checked the pedometer; point-seven miles. Just as it always had been. He turned left at the corner. But first he rested, for about thirty seconds. He wiped the rivulets of sweat off his slick bald pate, drying his hand on the horseshoe of snow-white hair which surrounded it. Over halfway there....

Now heading east, he knew he had only point-five miles to go to get to Ralphs. Good thing. The throb in his leg was beginning to challenge the fire in his gut, always an excruciating competition. But he was a tough old coot. He was up to it. Among the many things that bothered him about his current world, intense physical pain was fairly far down the list.

He passed the 'Century 21' real estate office and doubled his grimace. It was a name he always hated. A name which would, by itself, keep him from using that firm, should he ever decide to sell the over-priced house he was already busy putting in order. He shuffled past First Avenue, past the Kentucky Fried Chicken store, past McDonald's, past Second Avenue, and once safely across Second he was finally at Ralphs Market. He checked the pedometer; 1.2 miles in all. Just as it had always been. The journey completed nearly an hour after it was begun....

He rested for a few minutes before going inside the Ralphs. The shattering pain in his leg and gut were reasons enough, but it was actually the nearly incomprehensible level of fatigue he so often suffered through nowadays which required he not move for awhile. He was literally near death, he knew that, he just had no way of knowing how near. And so he had to rest. And once again he had to laugh. When he was a young man he could run five miles before breakfast, put in a full day's work on his father's farm laying fence and carrying eighty-pound milk canisters, or plowing the rock-scrabble fields till his hands bled, and at night he'd *still* be rarin' to go, determined and eager to go into town to chase the skirts. And now, he barely had the strength to walk a mile. He resented the fatigue cancer brought to him far more than the pain....

Once inside Ralphs it only took him a couple minutes to find it. A small package. He read the label: **"GROUND SQUIRREL BAIT", The Wilco Co., LOMPOC, Calif.** That's the ticket, he said aloud. And only fourteen bucks! He paid the cashier in one-dollar bills and small change and headed back.

Tired....so tired....he rested at Santa Anita & Foothill this time....that giant intersection was less than halfway home going this direction, but it had to be done. Besides, he always rested twice on the way back anyway. 'Only way he had any hope of pulling it off. Leaning against the stoplight at the northeast corner he squinted across the street, at the two gas stations on the other side of the intersection. An Arco 'minimarket' on the northwest corner, a Union '76 station on the southwest. He wondered why the world called them gas stations rather than oil stations, for that's what it was all about, what it was always about. Oil. Gas was just the friendlier word for it. Nearly a dollar and a half for a gallon nowadays....insane.

He wondered about the misguided men in the planes. Misguided not because of the targets and vaporized victims of their mission, that was their business and their beliefs, rather misguided that their religion of choice dictated that there was honor in dying intentionally and wholly unnecessarily in order to express those beliefs, leaving behind their widows, and their orphans, who would now have to brace themselves for the years of inevitable, fervent reprisals. Not to mention the loneliness and the pain of loss. Madness. Where was their sense of proportion? In his 9th decade of life, the old man still clung to it with the desperation of a trout struggling with a worm on a hook....

Ready to go on. Heading north, another point-seven miles to his house. The word 'north' merely meant 'uphill' these days, the ultimate insult to his 57-year-old injury. His right leg was by this time virtually dead weight, his right foot a thing to be dragged, or at best something to use to push off of in order to get his left leg started. The Mummy had nothing on him. It was the gait of an aging, white-haired balding monster. Steady as she goes....past Sycamore, Woodland, Hacienda, Orange Grove....he was out of breath by Orange Grove so he stopped. He checked the pedometer. Point-four miles past Foothill Boulevard. As always. He needed ten full minutes this time, to recover, his heart pounding like a jackhammer.

A little boy approached him, bounding out from behind a card table he had set up on his front lawn. "Are you all right, Mister?" he queried with genuine concern. "Doin' great, son," replied the old man between deep breaths. He looked at the boy. He didn't remember seeing him on his walk down to Ralphs. At around five feet tall he was just about the old man's height, now that he was so perpetually hunched over. Such a fine, tall, straight-spined lad, he thought. Skinny, freckled and pale, with spiked red-orange hair like his head might have been a just-struck match. He looked over the boy's shoulder to the card table with cardboard boxes behind it. "What'cha sellin'?" he inquired. The boy replied, "Firecrackers, sir." He smiled perfect suburban teeth. "They're *illegal*!" he added proudly. The old man smiled. "Got any cherry bombs?" The boy's eyes brightened: "You bet!" he said, "Fifty cents each. Only got about four left." Only, he says....this boy's a natural salesman. "I'll take 'em all," said the old man. The boy ran back to his boxes, found the contraband, and exchanged it for the last two one-dollar bills the old man had on him. "Thanks kid. These might be necessary," he said. He stuffed them in the other baggy pocket of his trousers, the one that didn't contain the ground squirrel bait, and continued on.

By the time he had dragged himself, literally dragged himself, all the way back to his house, he was ready to die. The pain was so great in his gut that it felt like it would soon explode. He knew hearts often exploded in cardiac patients, he'd read about it, there were articles about it in his 'unusual deaths' folder, he wondered now if the abdominal wall—or, more precisely, intestinal wall—ever suffered similar combustion. And the leg? Could he have uttered the word "amputate" aloud and magically had it be so, he would he have done it. He leaned against his car as he recovered, a Lincoln Continental. It had been seven months since he'd actually driven the car....and it had been almost three hours since he set out on his 2.4 mile, 14 dollar, make that 16 dollar, mission....ridiculous.

But he'd made it. Once again he'd made it. He had made it yet again. Almost two and a half miles on one leg and a few remaining feet of intestine. And the best thing about it was that these epic treks to Ralphs were a secret. If his two fifty-something kids knew he was in the habit of walking all the way down there and back they would kill him. 'None of their damn business anyway. Two and a half miles. He was Magellan, circumnavigating the whole of his personal, disintegrating, 21st-century world....

Even before commencing his post-voyage nap he made sure to bait some traps and lower the seductive poison into the holes.

⇒ ⇐

The ground squirrel bait didn't work. He checked the traps twice a day for three days. Nothing. 'Worse than a cockroach, he said softly to himself.

But he wasn't beaten. Americans are never beaten, he said to himself. They die, they fail, they're naïve damn fools for the most part, but they're never technically beaten when they put their minds to something, he almost said out loud. He had a plan. A back-up plan.

The old man shuffled over to the junk drawer next to the refrigerator. There was a convenient piece of thin, pliable wire. Perfect. He reached into the cavernous front pocket of his baggy blue slacks, which he had not removed for three days even to sleep (And what was the point of even *bathing* more than twice a week, at this stage?), and pulled out the four cherry bombs. Four pink, globular agents of death. He entwined the wire around the base of all four fuses, so that they made sort of a daisy chain of small explosives. With each pink ball the approximate equivalent of an eighth of a stick of dynamite. Not exactly the 20,000 tons of TNT his government had dropped on Hiroshima as a legitimate means to an end, he mused, but it would have to do.

He went outside. Showdown time. He held the chain of death above the ground squirrel's hole. With a cigarette lighter he quickly lit each of the four fuses. Instantly he dropped the whole thing down the chute. He began shuffling furiously away. Not much time....he'd read about how that B-29 pilot over Hiroshima had had to accelerate to the max while flying slightly downhill in order to achieve the highest degree of speed possible, so that they would able to fly far enough out of range to avoid the nuclear blast. The old man had no plane to help him get free, and downhill for him was literally and figuratively to the grave. So he simply worked as hard as he could. He bent over to mask the pain and he shuffled, and limped, and humped his way furiously across his front yard, straining and grimacing to put at least a little space between him and----------

WHOOOOMMM!!!

The blast, four staccato concussions overlapping into one, knocked him down. Maybe it was the force of the device, maybe it was the startling shock of noise, it didn't make any difference, he was down. Face down. But all right. Nose and chin scraped to hell, but so what. He rolled over and sat up. He stared at the hole. Smoke eddied out from below. The smell was reminiscent of the rank, sulfur-laden factories he'd worked his life away in....also reminiscent of doing a little drag racing as a teenager, about an hour west of here in the San Fernando Valley of his youth, the sweet stench of burned rubber on a Saturday night. He wiped the blood from his ruined face, wiped it off again when it returned. The question was....well, he didn't even know what the question was....

But in a few seconds he got his answer. The ground squirrel finally poked his head above the flat plane of the lawn. His eyes seemed to find the old man's eyes right away. At least that's what the old man thought. The creature was making an odd screeching sound. There was blood on its head, and its furry body—as it emerged slowly and fully from the hole—seemed covered in dust. It crawled all the way out. The old man just stared, awed, enraptured. The ground squirrel walked a few inches, hesitating as he went, and if a ground squirrel were drunk it might look very much like this squirrel. And then, quite theatrically, like a stricken soldier in an old Audie Murphy movie, it simply fell to the earth and lay there.

The old man stared in utter disbelief.

After a long time he managed to make his way into the house. Into the bedroom. Into the bed. The sun had barely gone down when he fell asleep. A sleep longer and deeper than any of its two thousand or so most-recent predecessors....

He was still sleeping at 3:15 p.m., the next afternoon, when the phone rang:

"....who 'zis?"

"It's me."

"What....uh, what time is it?"

"It's only a quarter after, Dad. You've still got fifteen minutes before *Andy Griffith* comes on, so you can talk to your only son for a few minutes."

The old man sat up in bed. His gut felt like it might burn a hole right through the dry, wrinkled skin of his belly.

"It's not that. It's...." He needed to catch his breath. It was hard.

"Dad, are you all right?"

"I would appreciate it if you'd....you'd make that the last time you *ever* ask me that question. In return for me siring you and raising you."

"....okay. I promise."

"Thank you."

"I just talked to your daughter. She was pretty upset."

"Your sister was upset about something? That's shocking news."

"She said she talked to you a few days ago, and you were saying all sorts of crazy things."

"So now I'm crazy too?"

"She said you were talking like one of the terrorists. Like last week was no better or worse than dropping the A-bombs on Japan. Like they're no better or worse than we are. She said you weren't upset at all by it. She was pretty freaked out."

"I should have sent you both to private schools. Maybe you wudda learned something."

"Pop, I studied plenty of history in school. You don't hafta give me that 'one man's terrorist is another man's freedom fighter' jazz...."

Suddenly he remembered the events of the past twenty-four hours. And instantly he became bathed in a feeling of almost indescribable happiness:

"Why don't you ever ask me about what's important to *me*?"

"What?"

"My ground squirrel. You never ask me about it."

"Oh, Christ. Are we back to that again?"

"Aren't you even curious?"

"No! No, I'm *not* curious! It's just a squirrel, *god-dammit*."

"Do not take the Lord's name in vain with me, son. We've been over this. It's *blasphemy*. That's not how I raised you. Say anything else you like, just not that."

"Sorry."

"I got him, son. I killed him. I was beginning to have doubts I'd have time. But I guess it was God's will."

"What does God have to do with it? It's a *squirrel*."

"God has *everything* to do with it! I should be dead by now, all the doctors say so. But I'm not. I've decided that God's a great guy, he's truly great to let me win this one last contest before I give up the ghost. What a guy!"

"*Dad*! I think you're finally losing your *mind*, man!"

"Oh come on, my boy. Dig a little deeper for a change, won'tcha? Don'tcha get it? I won, dad-blast it. I *won*! I couldn't drive the little bastard out using conventional methods so I nuked him, 'dropped the mother of all firecrackers right on top of his furry little head, the fink. Come into *my* yard, will ya?—take over *my* yard, like you *own* it?—not in this lifetime, you mother. Ha-ha-ha-ha-ha-ha-ha! Now that's a cause *worth* dyin' for."

"Dad—"

"Son, I love you, but don't you dare ruin this for me. Please? When yer my age it's all about feeling good about your life, about your accomplishments, about winning and losing. About *living*." There was silence at each end of the telephone line. Suddenly all the pain went away, and the old man, from head to toe, felt as good as he had felt since....well, since he couldn't remember when. And not from just the absence of pain in his gut. The constant stab in his right let was also, for the moment, gone. What a blessing, he thought. For just a moment, his mind drifted back in time, back in time 57 years to that cold damp morning crossing The Channel, when his eyes caught sight of Omaha Beach for the first time.... those few precious moments, before the shelling which would cripple him had even started....now that was a *day*, he thought. A sight to behold. A feeling to remember forever. The greatest day he ever had, because out of the roughly 31,500 days of his life it was the day when he was most thoroughly, most definitively, alive....until now: "This is a *great day*, son. Because I *won*. I won I won I won I won I *won*! Now I can die happy. Now I can die a happy man. Yessiree-bob, if I die today—and I just might, the way I've been feelin' lately—it's *still* a great day. And that's what I'll tell God when I see him. It's a great day to be alive, my son. Great day in the morning! I won...."

THE SOAP OPERA THEORY OF EXISTENCE

Author's Notes

A story started in the 80s, finished in the 90s, and then rewritten twice since 2000.

Soap is, to date, one of only two stories I have ever produced using an 'effaced' narrator (*homeless man* being the other), meaning a narrative style essentially devoid of any narrator at all. In other words, a story where there is only dialogue and a few simply stated and soberly rendered scenic details to move the story forward, without the benefit of the author's opinions and viewpoints.

And not just the author's opinions and viewpoints. In effaced narration, none of the characters' personal opinions or viewpoints are revealed to the reader either, except through what they actually say. Which makes reading such a story very much like reading a scene from a play.

During the mid 80s, late 80s, and early 90s—when I was writing, rewriting, and finalizing the first couple drafts of *Soap*—I was very slow to embrace modern technology. Never mind that I was slow to embrace cell phones or the Internet, I didn't even have a decent word processor back then. So I used to go down to my father's office in the middle of the night and use his computer. He was an optometrist in Pasadena, California. Many was the night when I would take all my handwritten notes on chapters of novels and sections of short-stories like *Soap*, drive on down to Dad's office, and enter all the data into his computer. And then do additional rewrites on the data I had just logged in.

Sometimes I'd go to a coffee shop first, write for two or three hours over five or six cups of coffee, and *then* go to Dad's office to log it all in.

Anyway, whenever I read this story or any others written, rewritten, or logged in during that time, I think of that shabby little office at the intersection of Walnut & Hill, and all those deathly-quiet nights I spent there, all alone, working away till three, four, sometimes five o'clock in the morning. If you're curious, that's pretty much what the life of an unknown, unsuccessful, yet no less dedicated writer, is like….

THE SOAP OPERA THEORY OF EXISTENCE

"When's Monday?"

"Huh?...wha' wuzzat you said?"

"Monday."

"What about it?"

"When is it? I need to be home by Monday. Monday afternoon."

"Who cares...."

"I do. I promised Billy."

"He'll understand. Someday."

"No he won't. Not Billy. He made me promise to be there. He gets so *nervous*!"

"It's not yer fault, man."

"Maybe not. But I promised."

"Meagan will take care of it. She'll explain it to Billy. In a good way."

"I promised her, too."

"Promised her what?"

"Promised her I'd be careful."

"Oh. Well then I guess it *is* yer fault, then! People shouldn't make promises beyond the limits of their competence. You always were the clumsy one."

"I already said I was sorry. What more do you want from me?"

....Two men huddled together on a rocky ledge. Below them fell several hundred feet of air, culminating in the quick, coursing hum of a river. The air was clean, with respect to both mouth and nose, and the river's only competition for their collective ear came from the wind, slapping loud and often against the far canyon wall. Night embraced them, for the second time. The green had long since disappeared from

the trees, and the rock of the far wall, once a smug, forbidding face of brown and gray blemishes, had gradually fused into black; an endless, formless countenance of black, only black. And the river, too, was without form, the sun's flight cloaking it in mystery, with only its persistent single-note song to fill the void and remind them it was there. It was cold....

"Well if it had to happen here, I'm glad at least it didn't happen down in the smog. Never could get used to it, 'all the years I lived here. Better to face the music when you can *breathe*, at least! But that's about the only good thing about this stupid mess, 'far as I'm concerned."

"What are you talking about?"

"Same thing yer thinkin' about. And don't tell me yer not thinkin' about it, shit-for-brains, 'cuz I know you are."

"You always did think you knew everything."

"Compared ta *you* I always *did*. 'Course that's not sayin' much. Y'never did much actual thinkin', 'specially when you could find some *one*, or some *book*, or some stupid goddam *thing* ta do yer thinkin' for ya."

"Would you please watch your language?"

"My what? My *language*? Oh. Oh, that's right. I forgot it was you."

"It just bothers me, okay?"

"Hey, no problem! Never mind we're stuck here on the virtual fuckin' edge of the whole goddam world, the important thing is that we mind our manners."

"I'm only asking for a little common courtesy."

"Common courtesy? Sure! Why not, and my apologies too. I'm so sorry. So deeply sorry I forgot about my fuckin' language. I'll be careful, man, no problem. No tellin' what *other* assholes I might offend up here if I don't watch my mouth."

"That's a fine way to talk at a time like this...."

"A-*ha*! Then you *admit* it!"

"I don't know what you're talking about."

....The men wore blue jeans and flannel shirts. The shirts were identical, red-and-green checks four inches square. A present from one of their wives. One of the men wore brand new hiking boots, which he paid over a hundred dollars for; his companion wore tennis shoes. They could easily have been mannequins in the window of a sporting goods store....

"God, I sure wish I had my damn backpack."

"And what good would that do you?"

"There was a helluva lotta food in there, stupid. Not to mention my nice warm sleeping bag and my goddam ski jacket."

"Relax."

"Oh sure, relax. Easy for you to say."

"Be patient. We're in God's hands now."

"It's yer fault I lost it, you know."

"No one told you to grab me. You could have just let me go, it wouldn't have mattered either way."

"It wouldn't have mattered?"

"Well, except to Billy, of course! But Meagan's a strong woman, her faith is as strong as oak. She could easily handle things alone, I know that for a fact, so even Billy would have been fine eventually."

"But as for you, you wouldn't have cared if I just *dropped* you?"

"As for me? How could I possibly complain about exchanging this wonderful world of ours for an even more Heavenly paradise? Anyway, either way you would have been doing me a favor."

"Oh, shut up."

....A white bird sat on a branch a few feet above them. The branch issued directly from the rock, like a lone dark whisker protruding from an even darker face, and the bird looked down on the two men. Even in this dearth of light, his whiteness was clear and stark against the flat dark face of the canyon. He had been observing them for some time....

"I could just kill that damn bird," said the man with the hiking boots, saying it just as passionately as he had said it four or five times already, and his companion smiled as serenely as he had smiled on each previous occasion. They moved their bodies closer together.

"It's really not that bad up here, you know it?" said the man wearing the tennis shoes. "It really isn't. I think I'm actually warmer now than when we started out."

"Hypothermia."

"Hm?"

"Hypothermia."

"I beg your pardon?"

The men looked at each other. One's expression was continually amending itself; his companion's remained serene.

"*Hypothermia*, you fool. That's when ya *think* ya feel warm, but what's really happening is that yer body temperature has dropped and yer sorta freezin' up from the inside out....don'tcha get it? We're dying of *exposure*, my Bible-beating old chum, and from all indications *yer* gonna go *first*!"

"How you clutter your mind with such meaningless nonsense."

"At least I have a mind to clutter."

"And you never choose to apply it to anything uplifting."

"I'm the goddam *king* of uplifting."

"Seriously, you *never* have. Never anything pure or simple or beautiful.... Why can't we talk anymore? We used to be like brothers. But the last few years we don't seem to have anything in common, and when I try to talk to you about anything that's even remotely—"

"Stop it. This is not the time for yer usual holier-than-thou small talk, buddyboy."

"Hm?"

"I mean it's bad enough that with all the perfectly digestible people in the world, I gotta wind up cashin' in my chips with a wild-eyed 'flamer' like you."

"I beg—"

"Don't beg. Don't beg don't preach don't pray. Just don't do anything."

"Look, exactly what is it you—"

"What I mean is, if ya got something important or genuinely relevant to say, say it. Otherwise, don't bother me. This is no damn time ta flap yer gums. I had enough of your superstitious drivel *last* night. I'm not in the mood."

There was a pause.

"I'm sorry. I was just looking to pass the time until they find us," said the man with the serene, tranquil expression.

The other man's face amended itself again, and again; and yet again: "Y'mean to tell me ya *still* don't think we've bought it?" he said through an incredulous, crooked smile.

"Everything that happens is part of God's plan."

"Oh, God's plan...."

"And I believe a small part of that plan is that I be there at Billy's recital like I promised. Monday."

"Geezuschrist, man, it's like there's a lead sheet between yer fat head and the rest of the whole goddam world! What's it take ta get through ta you? *I mean is the man human?*" he inquired loudly of the far canyon wall. His teeth chattered, but the incredulous smile remained.

> ....*The man with the serene countenance added his own smile to that expression, and calmly rolled up the flannel sleeves. Sitting with his legs stretched out in front of him, he now rolled over on his side so that most of his upper-body weight was borne by his bare left arm. The elbow of that arm, the skin, was therefore digging hard and without protection into the cold hard ground. He didn't say anything. The other man, sitting curled up with his knees against his chest, watched and shook his head. He blew on his fingers, and then, before they could cool, he thrust them down the front of his blue jeans. He took innumerable long deep breaths. Time passed....*

Finally: "Tell me something. Not that I care squat, but just outa curiosity—'ya happen ta know what *your* part in this grand plan is supposta be?"

"I don't pretend to know. All I can say is that I know it hasn't happened yet, so therefore it can't be my time to die. Is that simple enough?"

"Simple enough for a simpleton."

"Relax. It'll be fine."

"Sure. Everything's just fine. Everything's *dandy*."

"Someone will come, don't worry. I know that someone will come."

"Sure. I'm not worried. Everything's fine."

"That's better."

"I'm not worried because my idiot-savant boyhood friend intuitively knows someone is coming."

They both laughed.

"And in the meantime, don't bother handing me any of this hypowhatever business, because it's nothing but intellectual Godless gibberish and so you're not going to scare me with it so you shouldn't even bother and that's that."

"So someone's gonna just stumble upon this particular section of the ridge, any minute now, just like he was strollin' right down goddam Wilshire Fucking Boulevard, and you *know* this, of course, simply because yer teeny weenie little part in this great, gargantuan plan hasn't....I dunno, been *revealed* to you yet?—'zat it?"

"That's it."

"But *how* do you know?"

"I have faith."

"Faith? Faith in *what*?"

"In God's plan. I told you. Everybody is placed on this Earth for a purpose."

"Which is...."

"To do God's work."

"And for the record, just exactly *what is* God's work?"

"Oh! Well, uh....well, it's just, uh....um....well—"

"*Brilliant*! That's absolutely brilliant. That's what I like about you, corkbrain, 'always right there with the quick, snappy come-back."

....The man with the serene expression slowly and calmly got to his feet. He carefully brushed the dirt from his elbow, jeans, and flannel shirt. He carefully and meticulously re-tucked his flannel shirt into his jeans. He could only take two steps back before he was flush against the face of the canyon, which he did, then sat down and leaned back against the hard flat rock. His expression did not change. He was imperturbable. His good mood, inexorable....

"And I suppose you have a *better* explanation as to why we're here on this Earth?" the serene one said calmly.

"Just so happens I do," began the other man. He also shifted his position on the ledge. Sitting cross-legged now, he made pointed and sweeping hand gestures as he talked, like he might have been lecturing a class: "Try and look at things rationally, for a change. I know it's hard for you doin' this much actual thinking in one calendar day, but we've got nothing better ta do and since it's probably your *last* calendar day and it's the last time you'll ever hafta worry about it, or me, just try'n humor me, okay? Okay then, listen. Only a moron would believe that God was doin' somethin' noble when he created Man, no offense, and it's pretty obvious he hasn't exactly done us any favors by—no no no! No interruptions! Just shake yer head if ya don't understand. Okay? Anyway, he didn't do *me* any favors, I can tell ya that. And we both know there could have been no practical excuse for his actions, either. I mean what the hell for? If he's so all-seeing and all-knowing and all-powerful and all-this'n-that, he couldn't possibly have any critical use for a buncha frail, worthless, useless and insignificant creatures like us, right? Right? That's right! So I figure the answer must lie somewhere within the entertainment medium. Yeah, I said entertainment, you heard me. Even a god must get bored. The way I figure it, he must've created Man on a day when he was especially hard up for laughs, given him more or less a free will, saw to it that he would continually and compulsively multiply like so many goddam rabbits trapped in a hutch, and ever since the first one of us crawled up out of the slime and ooze he has placed us in touchy situations like this one just ta see how we'll react. Get it? It's like watching a giant soap opera, 'cept it's *better*. It's better cuz he's got the equivalent of *millions* of TV's, all over the world, and since he's God he can change the goddam channel any goddam time he wants! This isn't some half-baked idea, buddyboy. I been working on this thing for a good long time. I call it 'The Soap Opera Theory Of Existence'....whaddaya think?"

"You're crazy."

"Ah, that may be, that may very well be, but in all my thirty-five rapidly disappearing years, my tight-sphinctered old friend, I have yet to hear a more coldly logical and perfectly plausible theory to explain Man's sorry and inauspicious genesis—if you'll excuse the bad pun."

> ....*The white bird which had been observing them now spread and beat his wide wings against the air. He lifted himself powerfully, easily, effortlessly from his branch to rise high above them, ascending far up into the dark firmament, rising with a pristine, surpassing grace, and in an instant was diving into the endless black void of the gorge. With him went all remaining vestiges of light and contrast within their bleak domain. The wind was more urgently upon them now, and with its violent whisper in their ears and no light to assist them they had nothing in the way of evidence to confirm that the river was still there....*

"What makes you think God needs us for entertainment?"

"Everybody needs entertainment."

"What makes you think a case of Heavenly boredom could be cured by things as small and insignificant as Human Beings?"

"Are you kidding? With our track record? Why, we're the greatest show on Earth!"

"And how's that? I thought your opinion of the species was pretty low."

"It is. And that's why. If we were predictable or virtuous, it wouldn't be entertaining."

"I can't believe I'm even listening to this...."

"Y'see the great thing about the Human Race, about humans, is that God—assuming there really is one—can count on us to make plenty of poor choices. Heaven knows we don't always make the right decision, especially if we're under a little pressure. Even if the right choice is patently obvious. I mean yer a lawyer, but you still dig history, right? I'm bettin' you still gobble up the history books, like you did when we were young."

"So?"

"So let's look at history. Napoleon and Hitler should both have attacked Russia in April, you usta tell me that all the time, right? Yet both of those cute little imps waited all the way until late July to invade, and before they knew it they were losing their respective wars, not to beatable enemy troops, but to the invincible Russian winter. Take Bobby Lee. He *had* to know that doing an end run around Meade's main army and then dashing off for Washington was the play. To save the nation's capital, Lincoln would have sued for peace in a heartbeat! But what does Lee do instead? He panics, completely loses his patience, in effect he goes temporarily insane some historians would say, he attacks the impregnable, heavily fortified Union center at Cemetery Ridge, and a couple hours later Gettysburg, and by extension the war, is lost. And finally, there's simply no reason in the world Baker should have lifted Ortiz as early as one out in the 7th when he was still workin' on a shut-out, that was *crazy*, and even if he *was* gonna bring in Rodriguez they both shudda known that throwin' Spiezio all fastballs, *only* fastballs, *eight straight* fastballs, was suicide!!!"

"What in the blessed name of Jehovah are you talking about?"

"Not Jehovah—*Spiezio*."

"Who?"

"The guy who hit the three-run homer that ruined the oh-two World Series, 'member?"

"What the—"

"My point is that Dusty Baker, under pressure, made a clearly, patently, and absolutely wrong-headed decision. A ridiculously bad decision that even an eighth-grade schoolgirl wouldn't have made. So the Giants lose a game they had in the bag, God gets his daily dose of side-splitting entertainment, and the whole damn Series is shot to hell."

"Not for me. I rooted for the Angels in that Series!"

"Oh, of course. Angels. That figures."

"That's got nothing to do with it."

"Sure. Like you'd ever root against God's team."

"Remember, I *live* in Orange County. Just east of the stadium in fact."

"Dumb-ass."

"—and I was at that game, too. My firm has season tickets. My gosh, it's so *exciting* when everyone starts cheering at once for a common cause! I should have invited you. It was delightful."

"Yer an idiot."

> ....*There was a short break in the conversation for personal housekeeping. An undeclared truce, a necessary respite. Time passed. Time to use to rub cold flesh, gulp thin air, and gather fraying emotions. It was the man with the tennis shoes who spoke first....*

"Seriously. This is another joke, correct? Tell me this whole thing is a little game you cooked up just to pass the time, hm?"

"I never joke about religion, bud. Never could find the funny in it," said the other man. He squinted at the watch that hung loosely around his left wrist. He pushed the little button on the side, and a tiny sprout of light was generated within the crystal face. It read 4:11 a.m. The digital seconds ticked away, 55, 56, 57-----

His tranquil companion tightened the laces of his tennis shoes and yawned. "Okay, so it's not a joke," he said. "Then tell me this. If we're all part of a giant soap opera, as you say, what about you and me?"

"What *about* you and me."

"I'm asking about you and me specifically. I'm asking why should we, of all people, be so conveniently placed here to fret and shiver and suffer on this ledge?"

"Why not?"

"Well, for one thing, we haven't seen each other in what, a year? We haven't really been close since high school. And why did we land *here*, virtually uninjured, and not fall all the way to the river like our equipment and sleeping bags? It's not like we had all the room in the world, you know. If we don't happen to land just right, we go over the edge for sure. And what about the distance of the fall? What about it? Any more of a drop and we might not survive it, any less of a drop and one of us could probably stand on the other's shoulders and pull himself back up to the trail. Isn't all that just a little too coincidental? I should think a fine logical mind such as yours would be offended!"

He laughed, but the other man—unflinching—adopted and maintained an indifferent, stoical expression.

"I told ya, it's for God's entertainment."

"Too coincidental."

"*No!* The more coincidental it is, the more it proves my point, 'see? Don't you get it? *Of course* we landed just right and didn't fall all the way to the river! He did it *on purpose*! The whole thing's *artificial*! It's just *theater*! He just wants ta see what we'll do, what we'll say, how we'll *react*!"

"Oh, I see. How we'll react."

"You got it. And I bet he's getting' stomach cramps from laughin' at you, my wild-eyed, idiotic friend."

"Fascinating. I suppose that explains why it was I who slipped and not you."

"Whaddaya mean?"

"You know. To see if you'd risk your own life just to try and catch *me*."

The other man paused. His eyes widened and narrowed. He took a breath.

"Why wouldn't I try and catch you?" he said finally.

"That's just it—why *wouldn't* you? Was it a conscious decision or just a reflex? Guilt or nobility? And of course had you known about this convenient ledge, you might never have had to leave the trail in the first place, correct? You might have simply let me go. You might simply have watched me plop safely to Earth, scurried off for help, or maybe *not* for help, who knows, and either way you'd be relaxing right now in your delightfully well-furnished, west-side apartment, sipping on one of your beloved Irish coffees. But still you lunged. And you caught me. And down we went. Do you suppose God found your performance....entertaining?"

The other man waited a long time before answering. His brow flinched and furrowed, and when he spoke it was through his clenched front teeth:

"Ya don't hafta be so goddam sarcastic about it," the other man said soberly.

The reply did not come right away.

"You're right. That wasn't very Christian of me. I'm sorry."

....More time passed. An hour or two. The two men did not converse. Not a word passed between them. Darkness weighed on them like a great blanket, quiet enveloped them like a shroud. And then the wind was suddenly at its busiest, hissing its way through the canyon crease, consistently flush against their cold and squinting faces, pushing back their hair, periodically forcing shut their eyes. To be heard at all, their voices required extra passion....

"I gotta tell you something!" shouted the other man. His teeth continued to gnash, his face drew tight with anxiety. The words came slowly, and he fought the wind's howl to be heard: "It's something that's been bothering me for a long time, goddammit! Remember back in eleventh grade....when you were....were too damn shy ta ask Mary Beth DeLoach if she'd go with....go with you? To homecoming?...so you asked me if I'd go'n tell her that you—"

"You never told her," his serene companion said. The voice was calm, but more than sharp enough to be heard through the wind: "You never told her so you could....be with her....yourself."

"Wha—How come you....when did you find out?" wailed the other.

"I've always known," his composed companion said. He looked across the gorge to the far canyon wall, still a wall no human eye could see. "I forgot about that a long time ago."

"And you....forgave me?"

"His son forgave you from the Cross!" he cried into the wind's wild howl. "Could I do less?"

....The other man did not look at his companion. Nor did he attempt to speak and say his peace. His old friend was content to lean back against the rock with his eyes closed. He, too, had no new words worth challenging the wind. But when the serene one leaned over to tighten his shoelaces, and then tightened them again, it compelled the other man—pausing only to wait for a brief respite from the wind's angry snarl—to speak....

"By the way, buddy, ya shouldn't tie yer shoes so tight."
"But my feet are cold."
"That's why. Stops the circulation."
"Ridiculous."

The other, as if guilt and anger were fighting for control of his chapped brow, tried to hold back but could not: "Y'see, that's exactly what I'm talkin' about!" he screamed.

"Take it easy."

"Why won't you listen to me!"

"I'm listening. It's not like I have any—"

"Then *listen*! Lookit....God sticks us up here on this ledge and makes sure we're goners. One guy knows the score, makes perfect scientific sense, the other guy won't buy any of it cuz he's a wild-eyed, flamin' religious zealot who can't think for himself. Won't even listen to a....to an old buddy. In fact, the second guy persists in doin' everything in his power to *speed it up*! See? That's what I mean by seein' how people react, it's hilarious! I tell ya, he must be goin' *nuts* up there!"

"The Soap Opera Theory Of Existence...."

"You got it!"

"I told you, I am not going to die."

....The other man belched forth a laugh that demanded to be heard, but the rejuvenated wind would not allow it and so he stopped. That wind, which had begun as a sigh and grown to a hiss, had now graduated into a shrill wild whistle, so swiftly did it race through the narrow canyon. It was colder now. Colder than it had been at any point during the entire forty hours of their ordeal. The white bird which had been watching them and then left was now back, finally, suddenly, perched again in his usual spot, standing whiter than ever against the dark face of the canyon, and the twin triple-spears of his talons tightened their grip on that solitary branch above their ledge....

After a while the wind died down a bit, and they could talk in normal voices:

"I wonder if it was daytime if we could see anything down there," the other man said.

The tranquil one said nothing.

"Y'know when the sun comes up," the other man went on, "I bet the only building we'll be able to actually see from up here is the Library Tower."

"The what?"

"You know. With the smog."

"What does smog have to do with anything?"
"I've just always thought it was weird, that's all."
"You think everything's weird."
"I mean the way smog looks from high altitude, or from an airplane. It's like a goddam ceiling."
"So?"
"I'm just saying."
"You've always been hung up on silly things like that."
"I'm tryin' ta talk to ya."
"You need to keep trying."
"It's like a brownish-white ceiling of clouds. But the Library Tower is so tall it would probably poke right up through it. Y'think?"
"If you say so. Try and get some rest."

He looked at his serene companion, now resting his upper body against the flat rock like it was a high-backed chair. He studied the left side of his face. The left eye was closed. Then it would open, however slightly. But usually it was closed. The other man opened his mouth to speak several times, but he remained silent, struggling, searching. He grimaced in a manner that could have suggested any number of emotions. No hurry. He stared at his old friend's peaceful, tranquil face for a very long time before trying to continue:

"Y'know I....I really cared about her, man. I mean I really did."
"I know you did."
"I guess maybe I even....kinda loved her. I mean a little bit."
"I know."
"I mean she was the first time I ever—"
"She was meant for you."

There was a pause:

"Yeah, sure. 'Guess someone shudda told *her* that," the other man said finally. The continual transmogrification of his face could have been perceived as running the gamut from guilt to warmth to mirth to anger and finally to despair, and everything in between. He criss-crossed his forearms against his chest, digging each hand into its opposite armpit. He sucked clean deep breaths through his mouth and nose. He squinted in all directions. There still was no new light.

"Sure wish I had my damn sleeping bag. I can't believe my stupid jacket's rolled up in it," he said.

"Me too," said the serene one. "I'm awfully tired."

"Really? Y'mean *really* tired?"

"You bet. I can barely keep my eyes open. I'm still not very cold, though. I just know I'd be a lot more comfortable in a bag."

"Whaddaya doin'?"

"I'm going to take a nap." He curled up in an embryonic ball against the cold, dark face of the canyon.

"You can't!"

"Sure I can. I'm really not that cold, except my fingers and toes. But I just can't....keep my....darn *eyes* open! It's weird....I didn't really think I was that....tired, but I....but I suppose it's as good a way as any to pass the time until they come for us. I can't imagine why....I didn't think of it before." He yawned, and lowered the side of his head to the dirt floor of the ledge. He closed his eyes.

"How can you be so goddam dumb? Don't you know that going to sleep is the *last* thing you should do? Yer *numb*, not warm, stupid! You can't just lie there and *wait* for it, man, ya just can't, it doesn't make *sense*!"

"Billy's expecting me on Monday. Someone will come along."

"Billy's got nothing to do with it!"

"I told you, I'm not going to die."

"But you gotta stay awake!" the other said urgently. "If we hold on, yer *right*—there's still an outside chance somebody might come by!"

The serene one said nothing.

"You don't *know* what's gonna happen, god damn you!"

"If I were going to die," the serene one finally, calmly said, "I would have already done something important by now. And you would have saved the backpack, not me....and of course there's Billy, he still needs me....so cheer up! You should be *happy*! According to you, the Lord should get a big fat kick out of me taking a snooze against the side of one of His majestic purple mountains, even as you concurrently yell your various stock insults at me. That's good theater, if you've got nothing else to do....isn't that how your soap opera theory works?"

"What if he *wants* you to die? What if his *plan* for you is for you to die? What about *that*?"

"That would be fine. It's His decision."

"Geezus Fucking Christ, what does it take ta get *through* to you!"

The serene man smiled. The eyes remained closed. "You know what?" he said. "The trouble with you non-believers is that you wind up worrying about everything."

Then he went to sleep.

The other man shook him gently by the shoulders, then did nothing for a minute or two. Then he slapped a cold hand, twice, against the cold left side of his old friend's face. The smile remained. Then the right side. Nothing. He squinted long and tight-jawed at his old friend and unlikely companion's body. The body could be seen more clearly, now, the first glimmer of light in several hours having just arrived to help him. Soon he whispered, "Hey....hey man," and then a little louder, "Hey, bud? C'mon, buddy....c'mon, get up. Get up! Please *get up!*" and finally, "Oh god, oh god, oh geezusgod! Oh, man...." He tried to massage the cold hands and face, but only for a few moments.

....Dawn. The wind slapped softly against gray canyon walls, and the river, silver-blue, played a maudlin tune below. The sun climbed slowly over the ridge. Its light warmed the air, and split the trees, and made them green again. The other man, sitting, his arms curled tightly around his knees, lifted his chapped and grimacing face toward the white bird but the bird wasn't there. Then he looked at the body beside him. The face was white. The lips were blue. The smile remained. Fixed, imperturbable, inexorable. Serene....

"It's just not fair," the other man said.

TWO THOUSAND FIVE

Author's Notes

A recent story. Wrote it about four years ago.

    I got the idea for the story by driving by this old burned-down mansion in Pasadena, which had been used as Stately Wayne Manor in the old *Batman* TV show in the 60s. I had a job at the time where I had to drive right by the charred ruins, every day, right around the time it burned down in 2005 and for a year or two thereafter. At some point it finally struck me as odd that a year or two could go by and a huge, beautiful home like this one could be allowed to just sit there, burned out, totally neglected, without being rebuilt. For some reason, it got me to thinking about some of the weird, dead-end jobs I've had over the years, while patiently waiting for my turn as a 'name' writer. My subconscious mind told me that all of these things were connected somehow. Symbolically, at least.

    If there's one thing I know something about it's working at dead-end jobs for bosses who like being bosses. It was a pretty easy story for me to write.

    This kind of wistful, nostalgic, retrospective piece is a perfect vehicle for a 1st-person narrative. The unexpressed angst tells its own story.

    Stately Wayne Manor is no more. They finally cleared everything away and built something else. But at the end of this story I have added a picture of it for you, taken right after it burned down….

TWO THOUSAND FIVE

Two thousand and five will always be a memorable year for me, at least compared to the rest of my rather unmemorable life. It's the year Stately Wayne Manor burned down.

Maybe you're not old enough for that to mean anything. You'd have to be at least fifty, or at the very least in your late-forties. It was the big house in the old *Batman* T.V. series. Way back in the nineteen-sixties. Remember? Batman's 'secret identity' was millionaire Bruce Wayne, *de facto* prince of the fictional metropolis of Gotham City, and he lived right above the 'Bat Cave' in this big brick-and-wood Tudor mansion. And so whenever they wanted to show where Bruce Wayne lived they'd flash a wide-angle shot of this mansion. In the T.V. world it's what's called the 'establishing' shot. And it was always referred to—by the show's deep-voiced narrator—as "Stately Wayne Manor", never just Bruce Wayne's house or millionaire Bruce Wayne's estate or Batman's house, and never just "Wayne Manor"; it was always *Stately* Wayne Manor. And so that's exactly the way any grown-up sixties kid would refer to it too. Like me.

Anyway, that's the house that burned down. Stately Wayne Manor. Happened on Wednesday, October 5th, 2005. I remember the exact date and day, well, exactly, because my job at the time had these stupid staff meetings on the first Thursday of every month, and last October the 6th was a Thursday, and I remember I was driving to work when I heard about it. I also remember it was right around a quarter till nine when I actually heard the news, on the radio, because those stupid staff meetings were always scheduled for 9:00 o'clock sharp, and I could tell by the way traffic was backing up on the westbound 210 Freeway that there was no way I was going to make it all the way to Sherman Oaks by nine. As usual.

So like I say, right around a quarter till nine I clicked on the car radio to check on the traffic, turned it to 980 AM, Station KFWB, just for a minute, just to see if there was some sort of a traffic tie-up somewhere along the seventeen miles of beat-up, weatherworn asphalt between Pasadena and Sherman Oaks. When you're giving a sob story to your boss, I think it always comes off a little better if it's the truth. Or at least based on the truth. Otherwise I would never have even turned on the radio, and I might have missed everything, because I never listened to the car radio in the mornings on the way to work. Too depressing just having *to go* to work, no point in adding to the misery. But that day, as fate would have it, I guess I figured I needed to see about the traffic, seeing as how I was going to be late, again. Sometimes the transition lanes of the 134 Freeway between Glendale and Burbank would really clog up during rush hour, and I figured such was probably the case this time too, which meant that I was doomed to arrive even later than usual for that stupid 9:00 o'clock meeting. In other words I knew I was about to get in trouble for being later than usual to a meeting no sane person would ever even willingly attend....

But the traffic report wasn't due for another few minutes yet. They were still doing the news. This is how they spun it: *"...one of Pasadena's most famous local landmarks burned down last night...a huge, sixteen-thousand-square-foot Tudor style mansion that served as the home of Bruce Wayne, a.k.a. Batman, in the nineteen-sixties television series of the same name, was gutted by fire Wednesday night in Pasadena's fashionable Arroyo District...flames could be seen leaping high into the Pasadena sky for miles around...more than seventy firefighters comprised of fire crews from Pasadena, Glendale, and Burbank were on the scene, to no avail...Stately Wayne Manor is no more... cause of the blaze was not immediately known..."*

Y'see? Even the radio guy referred to it as stately.

And so wouldn'tcha just know that at that very moment, that precise, *exact moment*, I'd just left the 210 and was creeping along that particular section of the 134 Freeway which spans the Arroyo District, and sure enough, as I looked to my left just south of the freeway, right where it had always been, there it was. Or rather there it wasn't. Smack up against the west face of the Arroyo. Stately Wayne Manor, burned to death.

I just couldn't believe it.

I mean I'd just heard the guy on the radio tell the whole story, but actually *seeing* it, seeing it all bare and blackened and blown-up looking, nothing left but a brick facade and three or four brick chimneys, well, you know what they say. Seeing *is* believing.

I didn't get to work till around 9:25, which of course meant that I was twenty-five minutes late. (Actually *fifty*-five minutes late, seeing as how I was supposed to be in the office and at my desk by 8:30 every day, as in 8:30 sharp, meeting or no meeting.) The staff meeting was just about over. I slipped into the conference room just as they were going over 'sales goals'. The sales goals part was always at the end, the last act of the charade....

So as the meeting broke up my boss sees me, points his finger at me like some stupid cop in a cheesy old 'B' movie, and says, "I want to see you. In my office. Now." Well, you can imagine how *that* sounded. I mean with me being so late and he being—like most managers—so terminally anal about such things. I knew he wasn't going to ask me to split a cup of coffee with him, put it that way.

"What's up, boss?" I said sweetly.

"I need you to start working full time," he said.

"What do you mean? I'm already full time."

"Coming in at nine-thirty and taking a two-hour lunch and leaving at five is not my idea of full time."

Oh. Sarcasm. I'd forgotten what a brilliant comedic genius that guy was....

"Is there something wrong with my production?" I asked.

"You're production is fine. You're one of my best salesmen. I just need you to get to the office by eight-thirty and work full time."

"Why is that eight-thirty thing so important to you?"

"Fundamentals and punctuality are always important in business."

"What difference does cliché stuff like *that* make, as long as the sales are there?"

"It makes a difference to me."

No need to go on and on about it. You get the idea.

So I promised him to be more diligent about my hours and attendance and whatnot, because when you get right down to the nuts of it that's really all he wanted to hear. So I promised him, just to get him off my back. Sad. It's been like that in virtually every 'sales organization' I've ever worked for. I'm not going to bore you with what we actually sold or what kind of a 'sales organization' it was, because not only is it boring as hell but it doesn't have anything to do with anything. I do think it's kind of strange, though, that I would get into this big argument with my boss on the very same day I learned that Stately Wayne Manor burned down. I mean I'd never gotten into an argument with anyone I've ever worked for in sales in my entire life, there's no percentage in it, I don't need it, I've *avoided* it, and I've worked in sales for....well, for a long time, let's just leave it at that.

Driving home that night from work (I didn't leave the office until 6:30) I couldn't stop thinking about Stately Wayne Manor. It still didn't seem real that it was gone. And a *fire*? What started it? Was anybody home? Why didn't they put it out right away? Are the owners even aware that they're living above the Bat Cave? These are the questions that were rattling around in my head. (Actually, to be precise, the Bat Cave was somewhere else. What I mean is, the Stately Wayne Manor house was just the 'establishing' shot, the Bat Cave was below the main house, I mean in the show, I mean that was the inference, the illusion, but the actual Bat Cave set was just that, a *set*, a movie set or T.V. set or whatever. Just to be clear. Doesn't matter.)

So I was looking forward to seeing the burned-out wreckage on the way home, but that didn't happen. I didn't think it through. Y'see, coming home—heading east—the house isn't visible from a moving car. It's situated smack up against the west wall of the Arroyo, which is a big bowl-like valley running north-and-south along the western boundary of Pasadena, so by the time an eastbound car passes by the western edge of the Arroyo that car is *already past* the house, which means that at that point the house is behind you, high up, and off to your right. Which means you can't even find it in your rearview mirror. It's in your blind spot.

So I knew I'd have to wait until I was driving to work the next morning to see it again.

You might not believe this about a grown man sneaking up on middle age, but I practically didn't sleep at all that night. That's right; because of Stately Wayne Manor. Don't exactly know why. Maybe it had something to do with *Batman* being my favorite show when I was a little kid. I liked the cool villains, like the Penguin and the Joker, and the Riddler, Catwoman, Mr. Freeze, and I liked how the stories were always told in two parts, part one on Tuesday and then part two on Thursday ("*same Bat-time!, same Bat-channel!*"), and of course I liked how Batman always went about his business with integrity and always triumphed in the end. He always made me feel so good inside. But why should that have anything to do with me being in a *bad* mood forty years *later*? See what I mean? Crazy.

The next morning, that Friday, I made sure to drive as slowly as I could on the westbound 210 Freeway where it turns into the 134. I'm talking like forty miles per hour. And in the far left-hand 'fast' lane too.

I know that must have pissed a lot of people off! I myself just hate it when I wind up behind some slowpoke in the fast lane. So if you were behind me on the 134 that morning I apologize. But I wanted to make sure

I got a real good look at it this time. Since the house sits—or rather *sat*—in the section of the Arroyo just south of where the westbound 210 Freeway sort of turns into the westbound 134—to my left—I knew I needed to be in the far-left lane to get the best view. Sure enough, there it was again. Stately Wayne Manor, vaporized into history, burned to a veritable crisp. It still didn't seem possible. All that was left was the brickwork; a couple of brick facades and a few brick chimneys sticking up like so many sunburned fingers. That's it. That's all that was left of a sixteen-thousand-square-foot house. I slowed down even more, down to about thirty-five mph. People were honking, but I didn't care. I mean what were they going to do? Shoot me? (Actually, in *this* crazy town, that isn't exactly such a far-fetched notion.). I guess I was willing to risk it, though. Man, what a sight….y'know, it occurred to me, glancing to my left at the wreckage and then back to the road and then back to the naked burned brickwork and back again, that the strangest thing about how the house looked was that there was no roof. Now I know it's hardly surprising that a house that had just suffered several hours of fatal fire would wind up without a roof, but it still looked weird. Reminded me for some reason of pictures I'd studied in college. World War Two pictures. Bombed-out houses where the explosions went through and gutted the roofs but still left portions of the rest of the house standing. Pictures of London, Dresden, Hiroshima. That's back when I was studying to be a history teacher. Never actually wound up getting a teaching job, though. (Of course that's also right about the time I was engaged to be married, and that didn't exactly pan out either.). I always liked history. At first I wasn't too keen on teaching, at least not right away, no money in it, I just liked history for its own sake. I liked the actual studying. But then later on, as I got older, I just figured I might get a kick out of passing on what I'd learned of history and what its relevance to day-to-day living was to a classroom of kids, since I never had any kids of my own. But every time I started to look into it I got sidetracked somehow. Man, I hadn't thought about any of that stuff in years….I mean that was another *lifetime* ago….don't know why I hadn't thought about it lately, though….I guess a man's memory can get sidetracked just as easily as his hopes and dreams. Funny how time gets away from a guy.

    I kept my word and got to work 'on time'. Yep, 8:30 sharp. Kept my word and kept the boss-man happy. Boy, was *he* all smiles! Smiled all day long. Like he'd actually accomplished something *himself*, the old duff. Well, truth be told, all he 'accomplished' was to put me in a bad mood. Sucked all the enthusiasm right out of me. I don't think I made a single damn phone call all day. I absolutely hated having to get to the office early, hated it at every job I ever had, fighting through gridlock traffic just to make some burned-out idiot dinosaur of a manager happy. Y'know something, not only did I not make any money for him that day, not a red cent, but I bet I could have pinched his wallet right out of his hip pocket and removed all the money right there in front of him and then hocked up and spat out a big slimy loogie right smack into the middle of that now-empty wallet and then folded it closed and squeezed it and handed it back to him all wet and gross and goopy and then burned down the whole damned office for good measure and it all would have been perfectly okay with him because I got to the office at 8:30 in the morning. Pathetic.

Actually, my boss wasn't much older than me. Late-fifties, but looked late-sixties. You know the type....stooped over, sort of Hunchback-of-Notre-Dame-ish, with a bowlegged stooped-over walk and pasty-white skin and hair growing out of the ears, huge eyebrows, all the telltale signs of someone all-too-happy to grow old before their time. Like a lot of people who work in offices their whole life, I guess. People who work in 'sales organizations'. You know.

Anyway, the minute he sees me he says,
"Good morning!"
and then later in the morning,
"Good to see you at your desk so early today!"
and later,
"Good job!"
and after lunch,
"Good show!"
and finally,
"Good night, see you bright and early on Monday!"
Good good good good good. Everything was good. Good grief.

I had a lousy weekend that weekend. I felt terrible. Couldn't eat, couldn't sleep, couldn't anything. Now I'm no fool. I knew something was happening to me, that I had reached some sort of crossroads in my life. Maybe having to get to the office so early that Friday triggered something. I don't know. Otherwise, I have no idea why this was happening, or why that weekend, but I'm not sure that's even important. The point is that it *was* happening, for whatever reason. I sure was depressed about it.

Genuinely, legitimately, thoroughly depressed. Truth is I always get a little down when I start thinking about everything. And since I couldn't sleep or eat or anything else, I certainly had enough time on my hands to think. I bet I thought about everything that had ever happened to me—or *hadn't* happened to me—in my entire life. Seriously. I told you that two thousand and five was 'memorable'. But the previous twenty-five years suddenly seemed, I don't know, somehow totally *un*memorable, as if they never even happened. On the other hand, I was able to recall the events of my *first* twenty-five years with elephant-like clarity. The best years. The best years, I think, in any man's life.

You want to know why the early years are the best years? It's simple: *nothing has happened yet*! When he's a boy, or a young man, a guy thinks anything and everything is possible. Of course in the real world everything *isn't* possible, but he doesn't *know* that yet. And that's the genius of youth. Ignorance. Ignorance is what makes being young great; the not knowing what's going to happen, and not knowing that if there's something you dearly want and have dreamed of that in sad fact it *might not ever* happen, and in fact *probably won't* happen, because, after all, when you don't know one way or the other if anything's possible because not enough time has gone by and you haven't lived long enough, and when you're still young and so blessedly ignorant, well, you think you have all the time in the world. That's why the early years are the best. The ignorance. At least that's the way it was with me....anyway, it was a lousy weekend.

I woke up very late on Monday, my alarm didn't go off for some reason, and so I took it as a sign.

I took a long shower. I took my time getting dressed. I dressed in worn-out, faded bluejeans and a T-shirt, more like I was going to the beach than heading for the office. And I drove as slowly as I could in the fast lane without driving the drivers behind me into a collective state of Road Rage. By the time my car passed Orange Grove Boulevard— even before I reached the Arroyo—I knew what I had to do.

But first, fording the Arroyo afforded me a rather pleasant nostalgic diversion. Sort of a solo, solitary road trip back through time. For just north of the freeway, to my right, lay the Rose Bowl; while just below the freeway, to my left, stood the ruins of Stately Wayne Manor. A virtual one hundred and eighty degree panorama of my childhood. Y'know, since I happened to go to high school right here in Pasadena I actually graduated from high school in the Rose Bowl itself, the ceremony taking place right smack in the middle of that hallowed green ground. The same stadium where a few years before I sat with my father, right on the fifty-yard line, and watched O.J. Simpson run eighty yards for a touchdown against Ohio State in the 1969 Rose Bowl game. And so what happens to 'The Juice' a quarter century later? The poor sap actually goes on trial for murder. Twice. And as for the *Batman* show, well, when I was a kid he was the one guy in the world I knew I could count on, every Tuesday and Thursday night at seven o'clock. And so what happens to *him*? Forty years later a bunch of saps let his house burn down. Go figure.

I loved Batman. I loved him the way only a little kid can love something. He stood for things, and he never gave up. He was cool and he cared. They didn't call him 'The Caped Crusader' for nothing. He taught me that anything was attainable. He proved it to me, again and again, every single time I tuned in to watch the show. And Batman wasn't a freak. He wasn't otherworldly, like Superman was. He was a super hero without any actual super powers, more proof that an ordinary man can do extraordinary things. So then what the hell happened? When, at what point exactly, did a young man's dreams dissolve into an old man's idle daydreams? I don't know. I guess I just woke up one day and, well, woke up....

Anyway, I got to the office around 10:30. Perfect. Not at all early, but not too late for me to be able to make my point. I didn't *sneak* in, either. Strolled in like I owned the place. I literally sauntered right by my boss's office (he was sitting nervously and hunched over his desk), and when he looked up and saw me I tell you his face went red as a ripe tomato. A gray-haired tomato. A gray-haired tomato with glasses, dandruff, strange spidery eyebrows, and gray hair growing out of its ears. Perfect.

It didn't hurt that in addition to the bluejeans and green T-shirt I'd selected as that day's garb, I was also clad in bright green, high-top tennis shoes with no socks. Call it *my* superhero uniform....

"Hey! I want to see you!" he said.

"Sure thing," I replied very casually, without slowing down. "Just let me know when."

"When? *Now* is when! Get the hell in here!"

It's not that he didn't have a sense of humor. It's just that he wasn't too bright.

"What's up?" I said sweetly. I closed the door behind me and sat down, facing him. His desk was like a big dark-brown island between us. An island of miscommunication maybe? (If I knew anything about symbolism I'd try to paint some kind of relevant analogy or metaphor for you, but alas I'm only a broken-down old salesman....)

He just sat there for a long time staring at me, without saying anything. I just smiled.

"Do you have any idea what time it is?" he finally began.

I made a big show of looking at my wristwatch.

"Is this a trick question?" I re-queried.

"Don't be glib with me—and another thing, do you for one moment honestly think that *that* is how a professional man dresses for *work*?!?"

"No, I honestly don't," I replied with unimpeachable honesty.

"Okay. Fine. Everybody's a comedian. That's just fine. I'm all for my salesmen having a good time. But bottom line, our well-documented dress code aside, you just can't work here if you come in at ten-thirty. You just can't."

"I understand."

"What I'm saying is you can't do both. That's just the reality of the situation."

"I know. And I couldn't agree with you more."

"You couldn't?—I mean you do? That's great! Terrific! That's a good boy."

"Thank you."

"I'm serious. I mean I really appreciate your being so understanding about it. I really do."

"You're welcome."

"I mean I've always considered you an integral part of my team here."

"I'm deeply touched."

"So then tomorrow I can count on you to be at your desk at eight-thirty *sharp*, right?"

"Right. But only if right means wrong."

His face fell totally slack, just like he was doing another scene from a bad 'B' movie. What a boob.

"Uh, what do you mean exactly, by that crack?" he said.

"I mean I *agree* with you," I said softly and slowly. "I agree I can't work here. You yourself have illustrated why this is so, and quite eloquently. And I appreciate *your* being so understanding about it."

He paused for a few seconds, at first no doubt just trying to regroup and gather himself, but then it was as if he was steeling himself for battle:

"Come-come, man. Come on. There's no need to be overly dramatic about this."

"Again, I wholeheartedly agree."

"I mean a manager asking his employee to report to work on time is certainly a perfectly reasonable request, right?"

"Perfectly reasonable."

"So then can we *please* just make sure to be here by eight-thirty? From now on?"

"I don't know what 'we' means."

"We means *you*!"

"Then no. We can't."

By this time the old gray guy was actually beginning to squirm in his seat. Like a little kid who has to pee.

"Look, what is this all about? Another job? You've gone and got yourself a better job, right? Is that it?"

"That's too many questions. You're making my head hurt."

"What?"

"Hey wait a minute, are you saying there are better jobs out there than this one?"

"What in Sam Hill are you—"

"Relax, boss. No job."

"No job?"

"No. I haven't accepted another job."

"You haven't accepted another job...."

"That's correct."

"That's correct?"

"Your regurgitation skills are extraordinary!"

"My what?"

"Relax. There is no other job. Period. I swear to you I'd never accept another crummy, dead-end job over this one. Word of honor."

"You're one of my best damned salesmen. You wouldn't just up and quit without having another job to go to. Without cause? For no good reason? You just *wouldn't*. I mean *no one* would do that! So then what's this all about?"

"Well, I'm guessing it's not about me being one of your best damned salesmen."

"Oh, I get it. This is a joke, right? This is one of your stupid childish jokes, and you've decided to have some fun at my expense. That's why the funny clothes, that's why the late arrival. Right? You had me worried!"

"I sincerely apologize for causing you to worry."

I started to get up from my chair to leave.

"Hey. Where are you going?"

"How should I know? I'm not used to having nothing to do at eleven o'clock in the morning on a work day. Got any suggestions?" I walked over to the door. He stood up. He started making wild gestures with his hands.

"*Hey*! Come on, let's *talk* about this!"

"No offense, but I'm suddenly way too busy to talk to you."

"*But you're one of my best salesmen!*"

"So you say."

I opened the door.

"Wait. Seriously, man, just wait a second. Just wait."

I waited a few seconds while he composed himself. I would be lying if I told you I didn't get a kick out of the whole thing.

"Well?"

He took a deep breath. His eyes were closed. Then he started blinking like he had a nervous twitch or something. Suddenly I almost felt sorry for him.

"So you don't have another job....and it can't be about money....you do good work, for which you're compensated fairly, downright handsomely.... and it can't be about coming in at a reasonable hour....so then *what*? There has to be a reason. That's all I'm asking for. A reason. You owe me that."

"I don't owe you a damn thing," I said.

"Okay, fine. You don't owe me a thing. Then how about a little common courtesy? You quit a job, you give a reason. That's what a *man* does, anyway. Come on."

I paused within the doorway's waiting jaws and considered his point. Fact is, I really didn't know why I was quitting. Or why then. At least not entirely, not precisely. I'm *still* not sure of everything that went into it. But he wanted an answer and maybe he did deserve something, some sort of closure to make him feel better about his pathetic existence. Or at least something he could jot down in my 'file' to make him feel like a 'manager'. Problem was, I really couldn't think of anything. All I could think about, oddly enough, was the chronological history of my life. Funny time to stroll down Memory Lane, huh? But that's what I did. I thought about my childhood, growing up, high school, college, almost getting married a couple times but never quite getting there, always getting sidetracked from doing all the things I'd always wanted to do, all my failed hopes and dreams piling up like dirty dishes in the sink, as the giddy optimism of youth faded and metastasized into middle age....then I caught myself. I shook my head a little, needing to snap out of it. I had to get out of there. I was worried that if I didn't leave right then that maybe I'd lose my momentum, and that I'd never find the guts to go again. So I looked right into my boss's eyes, and what I finally said was....

"Did you hear about Stately Wayne Manor burning down last week?"

"What???"

"Stately Wayne Manor. From the old *Batman* T.V. show."

"So?"

"Big fire. It was all over the news. Burned right to the ground."

"So what? What's that got to do with anything?"

"Well, you wanted a reason."

And I started to walk out yet again.

"Hey....Hey *wait*! This is *crazy*!"

"Life *is* weird, isn't it?" I said by way of agreement.

"But you're talking pure gibberish—you're not making any *sense*!"

"Again, I apologize."

"Come on, I don't deserve this. You can't tell me you're leaving a perfectly good job where you're well paid and treated fairly because some dumb *house* burned down. Certainly you can do better than that."

"Sorry," I said, a phony hangdog expression no doubt taking complete control of my face: "That's all I got."

And I left.

You know something? I could still hear him screaming even after I was out in the lobby, right up until the moment the elevator doors squeezed shut.

Postscript:
Well, enough of two thousand and five. Ancient history. Truthfully, two thousand and six hasn't been a bad year, but certainly nothing to write home about, as the silly old saying goes. Still haven't gotten another job. Still don't feel a bit bad about it.

You want to know what the weirdest thing is? They *still* haven't done anything with Stately Wayne Manor! It's still just sitting there, an empty, burned-out shell, no walls no roof no nothing, with its burned brick chimneys pointing up to the sky no different than the day after the fire. That was over a year ago, folks. Pretty soon it'll be two thousand and seven; are they just going to leave it like that forever? Is that the way things work in this world nowadays? Doesn't anything ever happen the way it's *supposed* to happen anymore?

You tell me.

homeless man

Author's Notes

The plight of the homeless is something no writer can do justice to, but we should all try anyway.

I think other than *The Black Bee*, this is not only the shortest short-story in the collection but also one of the shortest short-stories I have ever written *or* read! But a very short short-story can be just as powerful as a very long one. I got the idea from the Hemingway story *Old Man At The Bridge*, which is also very short. But it is one of my favorite Hemingway tales because it hits the reader like a sledgehammer. If anything, the very shortness of the story makes it a better story, much in the manner that in boxing often a short crisp punch can be more effective than an elongated, drawn-out one. With *Bridge*, Hemingway succeeds at delivering that short compact punch. I hope I have accomplished that feat as well.

We don't get to read what either protagonist thinks in *homeless man*, or even what I think. It is almost completely effaced narration. In other words, you the reader have to do most of the work.

homeless man and *A Community Of Holiness* are the two most-recently-completed stories in "L. A. JOURNAL". Each was completed just this last summer. Right around August/September of 2012. Right before this book went to the printer. Just in time.

homeless man

Downtown L.A. A typical October morning. Rush hour.

A man in a Toyota Camry took the 3rd-Street exit of the northbound Harbor Freeway. As he pulled far over and high up on the shoulder, safely clear of traffic, he glanced at an old man standing to the left of the 3rd-Street off-ramp and holding a small cardboard sign.

The man got out of the Camry and locked it. The Camry cost $26,995 new, five years ago. It was now fully paid off, and still worth about twelve thousand. On his way to work, he was dressed in his usual freshly laundered and perfectly pressed white dress shirt, gray suit with maroon pinstripes, and a matching maroon silk tie. He smoothed out the wrinkles of the sleeves and pants while getting his bearings. It was only 8:30, and the 3rd-Street off-ramp was only about five blocks from his office in the Library Tower (which had been renamed the U.S. Bank Tower a few years ago but being the tallest building west of the Mississippi most people in L.A. still referred to it by its more familiar, socially-accepted handle), and he was not required to be seated at his desk until 9:00 o'clock sharp, so he had time. He looked at his distorted reflection in the Camry's driver's-side window before going over. He frowned back at the falsely fattened face in it frowning at him. He loosened his tie and turned up the collar of the gray jacket, even though at seventy-three degrees outside it was neither hot enough to justify the former action nor cold enough to provoke the latter. He walked back and crossed over to where the older man was standing in his little patch of concrete between the off-ramp and the freeway, taking care to pick the right moment to weave his way between the steady stream of early-morning commuters exiting at Third. But before he approached his quarry he reached into his wallet, removed two crisp, brand-new, ten-dollar bills, and carefully returned the wallet (which only last week he had paid 119 dollars for) to its usual locality, tucked safely in his back left pants pocket with the button buttoned.

"Hey! How's it going?"

The older man said nothing.

"Listen, I don't want to bother you....but I've been meaning to talk to you."

The older man said nothing. He let the cardboard sign drop casually to the ground. The ink-scribbled word "homeless"—in quotes—glared back up into a gray, indifferent sky. One hand scratched nonchalantly along the groin of his severely faded bluejeans. (He also reached out and put his other hand on a shopping cart filled with blankets and old clothes and left it there, as if worried the younger man might seek to appropriate it from him.)

"Okay?"

The older man still said nothing. Instead he widened his eyes and quizzically cocked his head, and now scratched himself enthusiastically. All over. But said nothing.

"I mean I don't want to interview you or anything like that....I just want to ask you a few questions."

"Isn't that what an interview is?"

The younger man smiled. At the same time he reached into his jacket pocket and produced the two bills. He held one in each hand, and reached both hands out toward the older man.

"I mean I'll give you twenty dollars. For your time. For just a few minutes."

"So now it's a *paid* interview."

"I mean it, twenty bucks. I mean that's more than you'd make working this exit all morning, right?"

"Do you always start every single sentence with 'I mean'?"

The younger man paused a few seconds before responding:

"Isn't using 'always' and 'every single' in the same sentence a bit redundant?"

At this the older man betrayed an ability to smile for the first time. There was suddenly a twinkle in his tired blue eyes, and the golden spark of Humanity behind them. The bearded, leathery face, framed left right and above by thick tangled mats of dusty unwashed hair, could have almost been classified as happy. But at almost the very moment the smile began to metastasize into full-blown laughter the whole face tightened into a grimace, a grimace accompanied by a rather urgent rash of wholesale scratching. A more urgent variety of scratching than before. His right hand dug vigorously into the left armpit of his faded red T-shirt, while his left hand busied itself even more urgently, again, between his legs....

"I don't know why you'd wanna talk to a guy like me," said the older man.

"Come on. Twenty bucks. Ten now, ten after. And you don't have to answer any question you don't want to answer. Come on."

The older man looked directly at the younger man's face for the first time. He continued to scratch himself with vigor. Not scratching the faded red T-shirt this time, but instead the chalk-white skin beneath it.

And I don't hafta talk about anything I don't wanna talk about?"

"No."

He snatched one of the ten-dollar bills for a reply and immediately began to walk down the off-ramp, under the underpass and around behind one of its concrete pillars, out of sight, very much in a manner suggesting he was embarrassed to be seen in close company with his gray-suited benefactor. He glanced back once, not at that younger, gray-suited man, but rather at the shopping cart bloated of blankets and old clothes, as if to make sure it wasn't going anywhere. The younger man followed.

"I just wanted to find out what happens to people, what happened to *you*," the younger man began. "First of all, you look to be in your late sixties, so I'm assuming you were in Vietnam....*were* you in Vietnam?"

The older, dusty-haired man lowered his eyes. Then lowered his head.

"I mean—uh, that is to say maybe you had some sort of a post-traumatic stress problem? Lots of vets do. It's no disgrace."

The older man gazed up to the sky and grimaced for a reply. After a while he lowered his head. He did not look at the younger man. He began to scratch himself again.

"Okay okay, we'll skip that," the younger man said finally. "But that was over forty years ago. What about lately? Did you lose a good job?"

The older man said nothing.

"Did you ever *have* a job?"

The older man raised his head and glared fire into the younger man's eyes, then modified his expression as if to indicate not that he was angry, but rather as if he'd just decided that the younger man was kind of crazy....

"Okay, so it's not a job thing," the younger man said, beginning to fidget, wringing his hands together, demonstrating all the time-honored symptoms of frustration. He left the other ten-dollar bill visibly protruding from the fingers of his left hand, obviously making sure that the older man could see it at all times. "Maybe it's a woman thing. Do your problems stem from that? A divorce maybe? Or your wife could have died suddenly, or prematurely....that kind of thing could ruin anybody."

The older man continued to stare directly into the younger man's eyes. But this time his expression was blank.

"So it wasn't a woman?"

The older man did not reply, but instead immediately reached down the front of his bluejeans in order to obtain a more direct and efficient benefit from his scratching. Perhaps as if that act alone was sufficient response to the previous question.

"Alright, forget about that. I guess it's the economy then, right? It always comes down to the economy in this country. They say it's the worst economy since how awful your father and my grandfather had it, my friend—like back during The Depression!"

The old man glanced back at his shopping cart. It had not gone anywhere.

"But I just don't understand how that affects you. I mean affects you specifically. Don't you get a Social Security check every month?"

The older man said nothing.

"And isn't there anyone who cares about you who you can stay with so you don't have to sleep next to the freeway?"

The older man just stared.

"Are you ever going to say anything?"

The older man opened his mouth as if to speak and then closed it.

"Well then what about the election?"

The older man shrugged as if to betray he didn't understand:

"The *election*. Does it come down to that? And are you even going to vote? I mean Romney says one thing and Obama says another. Romney has one set of ideas he says will help the economy, Obama says the other guys started it so you need to give me four more years to *fix* it. What do you think? Do you think the election of one of these guys over the other will make the difference? I mean make the difference as far as *you're* concerned? One guy's for more and more government programs, the other guy preaches 'tough love'. But they both talk about strengthening the middle class a lot more than they talk about poor people like you. I guess it comes down to either pulling yourself *up* or waiting for the trickle *down*. Right? Is that how you see it? I mean is it really possible you're just waiting around for the results of the election to see which way the wind blows?"

The older man now looked directly and urgently into the eyes of the younger man. His mouth fell slightly open, his eyes narrowed into slits. The expression on his face would not have been more startled and confused if the younger man had just landed there from Mars. Several silent seconds went by. Finally the older man held out his hands—palms up—and shrugged his shoulders, while uttering the only three words he had uttered since he accepted the first ten-dollar bill:

"I'm homeless, man."

Before the younger man could say a word in reply the older man reached down, snatched the other ten-dollar bill still protruding from the fingers of the younger man's left hand, turned on his heel, and walked briskly back to his shopping cart. After a few seconds the younger man darted across the off-ramp and quickly got into his Camry. Before driving away he glanced in his rearview mirror. Once. The homeless man was holding the cardboard sign with one hand, and scratching himself with the other.